A catalogue record for this book is available at *Library and Archives Canada*:
395 Wellington St,
Ottawa, ON
K1A 0N4

*Cataloguing in Publication Data available upon request.*

Crown, Bruce, 1989—
*Forlorn Passions* / Bruce Crown
FICTION / Thrillers/Suspense
FICTION / Literary
Toronto : AP Publications, 2014.

Printed in Canada and the United States of America.

978-0-9918883-2-0 (Softcover)
978-0-9958492-3-5 (Hardback)
978-0-9918883-3-7 (eBook)

Cover Art: *Lovers XVI* by Mahmoud Meraji

BRUCE CROWN

# FORLORN PASSIONS

I call my distant self, when you I see,
To speed it home to heaven, which you are;
And as a fish to its bait in the sea,
I rush to your beauty that beacons, a star.
But since a heart, if cut in two, lives not,
Mine gives itself to you, entire and free:
So, you know well how little is left to me.
And since a soul, between two goals, cannot
But choose the better, with you I must be
If to live, not to die, is my desire:
For I am simply wood, but you are fire.

Michelangelo, §19

I did believe, the day I suddenly
Beheld so many wonders become one,
My eyes had reached, as eagle in the sun,
The least of beauties I still long to see.
But soon I knew how wrong man's mind can be:
Who, wingless, like an angel hopes to run,
He casts a seed on stones, his words are none
But wind, his thoughts of God, mortality.
Since, then, your dazzling beauty does not let
My heart come near, and even from afar
Seems to deny me hope, what shall I do?
What help, what guidance can I find, to get
Closer at last to this immortal star
That burns me, near, and kills me if I go?

     Michelangelo, §89

TO JELA

Whose sunlit hair and sky coloured eyes appears to me in misty dreams for only a second but lasts eternally for as long as I glide over the mystifying fog of this so-called life.

# PRELUDE

Idiots write prefaces and fools read them; I guess that makes us two of a kind.

*BC. March 2013*

BRUCE CROWN
FORLORN PASSIONS

# NIHIL

FIRST, OUR ENEMIES were the natives, then they were the Nazis, then after a while it was the communists. Finally, at the pinnacle of what we're calling civilization, our enemies are the Islamic terrorists. Our enemies seem to change over the course of history, along with our ways of fighting them. But what hasn't changed is government profit; politicians and leaders seem to always be getting richer by the blood of our soldiers. Makes you wonder who the *real* enemy has been all this time.

\* \* \*

I'm not some pseudo-metaphysical self-labeled philosopher searching for existentialism, God, *Science*, or some measure of indoctrinated truth through mists of cigar smoke and marijuana haze—like 99% of your youth happily labeled 'our future'—stuffing white garbage up their noses during bi-sexual orgies like some misguided hipster or sad idealist. It's simple to nitpick bad writing, mediocre character-development, shallow themes, and an idiotic meshing of letters to form words that might match what you want to hear (or in consequence, read) and stamp as *Best-Seller* with some shiny gold star. The pursuit of truth... *real* truth has been murdered by your ravish consumerism, your misguided sense of righteousness, and your undeserving pride that you live in the greatest country on the planet simply because that's where *you* live.

You're told what to wear (*GQ, Cosmo*), what to eat (*Quasi-healthy delis, McDonalds, Subway*). How to speak (*like a politician, always pass the buck and never take responsibility for your actions*). What to watch (*horrendously corrupt Hollywood garbage made to look like 'art' or doctored truth*). What to think (*who the enemy is [the terrorists] and who your allies are [your government]*), and despite considering yourself an educated person, an intellectual, or a critical thinker, (or whatever self-proclaimed title of grandeur you've bestowed upon yourself), you've never really given this any thought have you? You give $200 to the animal shelter every year (and *may*be adopt a pet) and write a paper on corruption in the nonexistent Middle East (it is not a continent, the 'Middle East' is in Asia—a region you've decided to label because it is easier to create disunity, to separate one populous from another—better to just refer to them as the *terrorists*), and you think you're ready to change the world? The world has changed *you*.

* * *

The problem lies with false inception, name three creative and intelligent men or women.

Go on. I have nothing but time at the present moment.

You're probably thinking (1) Philippe Mellier, (2) James Dimon, (3) Donald Trump, (4) Oprah Winfrey, or *God* forbid (5) Barack Obama. The really clever ones among you might also think of (a) Carlos Slim, (b) Brian T. Moynihan, and/or (c) Warren Buffet, or maybe a handful of other reckless leeches that walk the earth pretending to be our equals.

You don't know why you thought of them. You think you know (and you probably have some quantified half-assed rationalization as to why *those* particular names popped in your head), but you can't really pinpoint the *real* reason can you? You're much more *developed* and intelligent for it to *only* be about money, aren't you?

Don't make me laugh. You've been conditioned to equate success with affluence, it's the nature of the beast, but I will not be unfair, maybe less than 0.1% of you thought of Tesla, Da Vinci, Picasso, MacAlistair Ritchie, Norman Borlaug, Adorno, or Jose Mujica. Men or women who fought for their principles or beliefs despite those beliefs running contrary to the status quo or *only* to their own benefit. They are the selfless, sacrificial lambs that we never hear about; the 20-year old marine with a pregnant girlfriend ordered to slay an entire village because some warlord is *fudging* the price of opium, weapons, oil, or simply because he's bored; the 32-year old single mother working three jobs to buy food for her son while your venture capitalists ask for trillion-dollar bailouts from your *democratically* elected government.

Some people don't alter their moralities, beliefs, or principles for a few extra votes, they didn't lobby their shareholders, embezzle pension funds from the same guys they pay minimum wage... but we never hear about the first group doing these things do we?

Your earbuds continuously blast some top-of-the-charts auto-tuned teenager to drown out the clanking of the train wheel on the tracks so you don't have to talk to that blue-collar worker sitting next to you. Yeah... that guy, the one who's snoozing and might miss his stop because he's working three minimum-wage jobs to put food on the table for his family while his divorce attorney bills $650/hour and a *retired* president makes $400, 000 per year plus a $50, 000 expense account off your tax dollars (up from $200, 000 when George Bush became president. Yes, that same guy who caused your *recession* and said Iraq had *weapons of mass destruction*). Don't take my word for it... whip out your smartphone and search it. I'll make it easy: *"Compensation of the President,"* Title 3, Section 102, of the US Code.

Life isn't all that funny once you think about it *honestly* is it? The world isn't all sunshine, lollipops, and rainbows when you step out of the bubble of consumerist self-delusion. Yet we persist, eat our cheeseburgers, line up for iPhones, read surreal garbage that furthers gender and race stereotypes and causes more segregation than we can afford, listen to crap on those same iPhones we lined up for and drink watered-down coffee at thrice the price because it makes us feel good about ourselves. We have *freedom*; most places in the world do not, but who's *really* free? The eagle in the sky, the Brazilian kid with a soccer ball running around all day, or us because we can print whatever we want, and say whatever we want as long it is within the confines of the rigid rules set in place? We use our freedoms in the precise way we're permitted to.

What do we have to feel so prideful of, so good about ... our *flawless* justice system? Our measures of societal *equality*? Could it be our *tolerance*? We're so tolerant of other systems and governments that we force them to adopt our tolerance, most of the time under threat of nuclear war, trade sanctions or some obscure embargoes.

We've... simply failed ourselves. We've failed each other, and either we heal... now, together, as a whole, or we'll all die as individuals.

\* \* \*

For those who claim they knew all this, I applaud you graciously.

Can't you hear it? It's the sound of one hand clapping.

# Ricercar
## The Warehouse
### Now

*Who am I* is the question that races through my mind as her temple vein tries to pounce the gun away. It wouldn't matter; a .44 magnum at that range would blow her away like an exploding watermelon. I can't hold back the two or three tears that sprint down my cheek as I surrender my piece.

"It's down," I'm cautious when I put the gun down on the floor. I don't expect him to be a man of his word. "Now let her go."

"Kick it to me…"

I slide the gun towards him. Hope *always* leads to disappointment.

An African philosopher said when you die, time stops, and you relive your life over and over and over again in a sort of *ad infintum* rending of your soul. I know now what he was talking about.

# TOCCATA
## 9 YEARS AGO

YOU ONLY TURN 21 once was the repeating thought glimpsing in my head like a bad song on repeat as I dropped my bag at my grandfather's. Ethan was an affluent man who lived in this... castle outside of town. Life was simple the day I set that first box down in his atrium and moved into his estate. I went to school, came home, played video games, talked to friends, and rinsed and repeated. My mom always said that a man's 21st birthday was a big deal, that we'd do something special, that she had something important to tell me on that day.

Fate has never been without a sense of dramatic irony. Your *God* gave me a most peculiar present a week before my 21st birthday. He thought murdering my mom was an utter riot of an idea, and all you religious fanatics nod your head and chalk it up to *His plan*. I'm nothing if not a simple man, screw your *God* and his plan, I want my mother back. I don't want *God's* help. I don't want his *presents*, and least of all, anything to do with him. Nearly everyone learns about the universal last stop on our train ride of a life with the death of their German shepherd or their goldfish. I learned about death through the murder of my parents; and no, I didn't become a comic-book hero with a misguided sense of justice or morality trying to eradicate crime from a rabid metropolis, although I do deal with clowns on a regular basis.

There I was, at my grandfather's estate, a place that also housed the uncanny knack to creep me out as a child. It was old yore Scandinavian gothic architecture with a dark air and a rather ominous smell and feel.

I had just graduated Oxford or Yale or Harvard, whichever you like, since I spent a year at each. They thought I was something of a genius; that I was *destined* for great things... that success was a part of who I was.... What a load of crap.

I had my degree in aerodynamics and aeronautical engineering and half a Masters degree completed (from a Harvard Fellowship of course) when Good ol' God decided to step in and put his *plan* into motion.

Ethan was an amazing man, he did what he could to get me to move on, to help me get *back* on my feet, psychiatrists at $400 per second, psychologists at $350 per minute, but none of those idiots could ever understand. Their books, education and infinite *wisdom* could never quite grasp that this wasn't like some athletic slump you'll get over as long as you put your mind to it, which made it ten times worse when they kept nodding "Mmhmm," or whispering "I understand." Some of the really clever ones try identifying with you, and worst of all, sympathizing. None of it mattered anyway, eventually, everyone wants the anger in your soul to dissipate, for you to bury the rage if you can't overcome it, it's what's expected. It's what society wants, but I knew it'd never dissipate. Such things are... never overcome.

## Cantabile

BECOMING AN AIR Force pilot was one of the best ideas I'd ever had. It was a childhood dream that was reinforced when my mom's friend said something to me. I didn't even know the guy that well — hell, I can barely remember his name — but he's always had my implicit gratitude for subtly letting me know that there is always a choice in doing what you want, a freedom to keep fighting, a nobility in moving forward. To become an eagle rather than a pigeon.

\* \* \*

I never knew my father, it'd always been my mom and I and I was fine with it, it was what my mom wanted and I respected her decision. She never let me speak ill of him—and boy did I try when I got a little older—but she always said not to question what you don't understand, "To stop barking like an ignorant dog."

It was obvious he didn't run out on her or anything. She never even went on a date as far as I remember. It wasn't because of me either, I kept bugging her to go out and meet somebody. She *never*, not once, took on a lover.

## Basic Training

THE PSYCH TEST for the army was a joke. They're always looking for lost or maladjusted young outlaws with problems with authority, and my problems with authority weren't big enough to give them cause for alarm... at least not yet. Besides, an orphan angry at the world with an '*us against them*' mentality? The army is practically home to idiots like me.

Some washed-up-has-been with stars-for-murder on his chest looked at me through the desk and said they've never seen scores this high on an aptitude test. What'd he say? ... "It's actually designed so people don't score this high." Lucky me... I was right on track to becoming Tom Cruise from Top Gun. Yeah... I threw up in my mouth. They fast tracked me to an *elite* squad after Basic.

I walked into the hangar like a goon ready to get yelled at and called Nancy by some old-guy who was too stupid to retire. There, was where it all began.

Apparently two other schmucks also scored *the impossible.*

"Hey, I'm Mackey. Everyone calls me Mack," he looked like a wanna-be Justin Bieber. A swag or post-modern yolo *bro* that was only doing this so he could flash the ID to a naïve babe knee-deep in squalor at an uptown dive and say, "Yeah... I'm a pilot."

He was a vapid man with a buzz-cut who looked more like he used a bowl to cut his hair rather than over-gelling it like the less-than-average people who shared his demeanor. Nothing even remotely valuable ever came out of his big mouth other than his numerous conquests of women. Naturally he probably exaggerated these *"conquests"* in desperate attempts to make himself seem more desirable than he really was. Not only that, but this overcompensation made him appear less experienced with women than he let on, for the way he described them was cruel and misogynistic; it simply made no sense to me. Then again, he'd yet to have met an angel like I had. He'd never learned what it meant to have loved *and* lost because he'd never truly loved anything. He'd never lost something he'd really treasured, something he'd *really* cared about because he couldn't treasure anything other than his haircut.

I wondered how he scored so high, watching him swipe his fingers like an idiot on his Pear or Grape product… whatever the hell those things are called.

The other guy was a slim-build-tough-guy leaning against the F-15 in the hangar with a little cigarillo on his lip. It looked like a Partagas Black Label Clásico — my mom somehow knew a lot about cigars even though she never smoked in her life. He didn't look like an extrovert, him I could understand being handpicked, they don't pick us for these teams for our charming personalities or bedside manners.

I didn't want to start on a bad note. Besides, most people love the 'brothers-in-arms' crap they feed you at basic.

I walked up to him and extended my hand but he beat me to first words,

"This is it huh? Ocean's 3? The Acemen? The Harbingers of *Justiceeeee?*" he extended the e, "No, no no, I got a good one… Rainbow 3…" he roared with laughter, "You know, that Clansky-or-whatever-the-hell with his mediocre army books…"

I gave him a puzzling stare. The man had *just* died; he wasn't a terrible novelist…

"Never mind."

"Vi, or Vick," he didn't shake my hand so I withdrew it. What a grade-A prick. I walked back towards Mack, his spikey hair was moussed or gelled so much it looked as hard as a rock.

Crunch, the prick crushed his cigar under his Tod's driving loafer, not bad for an army pawn.

"Nice hat," he approached me.

I always wear this white homburg with a black leather strap my mom gave me on my 19<sup>th</sup> birthday. She never told me where she got it.

I tapped the brim of my hat with my index finger, the outlaw's greeting. He extended his hand, "I didn't mean anything by it. I just like time to myself, especially when I'm enjoying a cigar... I'm Virgil."

"Pleased to meet you," Mack shook his hand, eventually so did I.

It didn't take long for Mack to get settled in, start boasting about his *seductive* charm somehow irresistible to *hot broads*—his words. I'm sure you know the type.

"So last night, I'm off-base, and this broad just walks right to me—"

"Atten....TION!" the lieutenant colonel entered dressed in his military blues.

We fell in formation instantly.

"Here we are," the glare reflecting off the F-15 blinded us as it hit the medals covering the entirety of his front torso.

"Why are you 3 here? *That* is the question. The 55, 000 dollar question, that's how much you'll make each year. So it's not about the money, you can't score a decent babe with *that*! Why are you standing there? Maybe, in a good generation, *maybe*... twenty people get this chance every twenty years—what you guys have scored... and each of you has his reasons. You guys... can be any-thing—"

"But we *want* to die for country. To be all we can be!" Virgil's one-liner amused me greatly; we snickered like schoolgirls at a slumber party. I started to like him.

"... And all twenty," he slowly turned to face Virgil and his eyes widened with a thin smile, "Are, and always will be clowns: the outlaws, the drifters, the men or women unfit for society, the ass-holes we hated in high school but secretly wanted to be. Still, the question remains... what do you believe? Do you believe that events in our world start as small as a flap of a butterfly's wings? And if you do, do you believe that the same events can grow and multiply and become what you never imagined? Do you believe in chaos gentlemen? That the world is chaotic, random?"

...

We looked at each other. Was he done, or did he want an answer?

"Well? ... DO YA?" his scream echoed in the hangar and shook the 25,000-pound F-15 parked right beside us.

"SIR YES SIR," we screamed in unison. Virgil was partly laughing in such a way that it sounded sardonic.

"GOOD! But—there's always a but isn't there? Believing in chaos doesn't mean we will be its prison bitch. Oh no, that's where you 3 come in. You will find those threats," he walked back and forth in front of us, "Those... delicate butterflies before they flap their little wings and eliminate them. You will be quick. You will be quiet. You will be... weapons," he walked up and tapped the F-15 a couple of times and then walked back towards us.

"So... *Why* are you here?" he rubbed one of the medals on his chest.

We all looked at each other. Mack finally said, "SIR TO OVERCOME CHAOS SIR!"

"I am Lieutenant Colonel W.B Milton. Welcome to the Air Force gentlemen. You are the little piece of honey on top of the cream. You are one level above those *cream of the crop* idiots, they are monkeys compared to you thre... SON WHAT THE HELL ARE YOU DOING?"

Mack and I broke formation and peered to the left to see Virgil lighting a cigar.

"Oh... you weren't done Lue?" this guy interested me.

"Army men never smoke son."

"Lue, I respect you. We all do. But give that army men crap a rest. There are only three of us, and we're here. We'll do what needs to be done so others don't have to. We'll kill, dismember, and torture whoever you want so the ignorant buffoons back in the cities can drink their soy-bean-vanilla-latte-with-cream and a pump of caramel and surf the net on their smartphones. We'll... what did the suck-up say? 'OVERCOME CHAOS SIR!'" he mocked Mack's salute to the Lt-Col from earlier, "Overcome chaos? Pffffttt, yeah. We'll do that," he lit the cigar, "As long as you respect us Lue. We're rare breeds; twenty in twenty remember?"

The lieutenant colonel sighed, "Why's it always the biggest pricks that score this high?"

We all laughed.

"All right gentlemen. Tomorrow at 0430. Hell Month."

'Hell Month.' 31 days of training. Weight-lifting and cardio: 6 hours a day, reading on military history and procedure: 4 hours a day, psych tests and *mind* training like how to withstand torture and beat a polygraph: 3 hours a day... the usual crap.

# A Month in Dante's Inferno

THE LUE TRAINS with us in the seventh circle. 30 km run. 3 hours of weight lifting. An hour in the jungle with a 55 pound bag on your back... not bad for an old man. He periodically asks us why we're here, to which after much discussion with Mack and Virg in our quarters, we unanimously agreed on "To overcome chaos sir." Mainly because we thought it was hilarious. You can't overcome chaos. Chaos is a constant. It's like saying you can have nine babies in one month by sleeping with nine different women. Constants can't be changed, that's what makes them constants; you can't change the speed of light any more than you can change how you feel. The guys always looked to me for orders and guidance; we were all the same rank so it didn't make much sense but I figured better to follow your own bad advice than someone else's.

Two or three weeks in, the four of us are having steak in the Lue's quarters. It's big, empty, and rather minimalist except for a picture of him with his unit at what looks like Korea, Vietnam, or some other war-ridden hellhole, one of the guys off to the right had flexed his muscle with a pipe on his lip rightly nicknamed *Popeye*. The place is nice, well-kept, and the Lue wasn't a textbook jerkwad like those exaggerated boot camp sergeants in those abysmal army movies.

"Why are you here guys?"

"Sir?" I looked up from my steak, playing with the spices on top of it.

Virgil glanced over to me with his eyes darting everywhere as if to tell me he had no idea what the hell is going on, "To overcome ch —"

"Oh save it Virg... I'm serious."

Mack inhaled a huge piece of steak and looked back down at

his plate, trying to chew it amicably but failing miserably.

"You three... *you* graduated Harvard at 17," he pointed at Virg with his eyes, "*You* went to Oxford and Yale and were on track to a PhD in Aerodynamic Engineering at the ripe age of 21... and Mack, you had three athletic scholarships ready to go from three top-tier schools. Seriously guys, why this?" he looked at the picture of his unit. "Here... our failures are known to every Tom Dick and Harry while our successes fall only on deaf ears. It's death, hostile civilians, greedy politicians, and more death, and forget about love, you could be here now and across the world in 11 minutes. If you're lucky you'll be blown to the next world in much less than 11 seconds."

"You trying to get us to quit Lue?" Virg took a sip of his water. Water and apple juice are all we're allowed during Hell Month.

"I've been doing this for so long I can't for the life of me remember what I believed when I started. Last time we had a team like this was 7 years ago, and you mouth off like you did with your cigar stunt—we're smoking some, all of us, after we trudge through Dante's Inferno with *Virgil*—and you get popped in the face. We don't operate on the same rules as the rest of the army. Either that or we throw you in the stockade, hell we can do whatever we want to ya! Controlling macho orphans and psychos is our job, and we're good at it."

"Well, why didn't you? Slap me around I mean," Virg was the most curious out of the 3 of us.

"Would it have worked?"

Virg shook his head, "No. But you should've tried. Earned the respect. Established order. Without order, only *chaos* remains," he was also the clever one.

"Very good, maybe this is a three in thirty group... and because you asked, I'll tell you. No one has ever asked *me* why," the Lue took a sip of his drink and cleared his throat. He seemed vulnerable, human. "November 30th, my old unit and I," he looked at the picture again, "Meet at the this bar on the edge of town. You know, it's a tradition, no matter where we are or what we're doing we never miss it. We plan *for* this thing. As the seasons passed and years fell off the calendar, our numbers progressively decreased. Anyway, the last time, this November 30th that just passed, I went to the bar as usual, ordered my Guinness and waited at our table, and waited, and waited," he sniffed and wiped his nose with his handkerchief, "I waited all night, thinking some of the guys were late, like in those old quaint stories where a character waits at the candlelit table for the others. It was about 0430 when I realized that they were all dead. I was the last one alive, and all for what? So some dictator could or could not steal oil from another dictator halfway around the world?" he took a big bite out of his steak, his teeth tearing apart the meat like a hungry lion on a wounded gazelle. The silence was awkward until Virg said,

"We won't let you down Lue."

We were walking back to our quarters after lunch, the LT— pronounced eltee, my little nickname for the Lieutenant Colonel; I was a little jealous of Virg's *Lue*—gave us the day off.

"November 30th. That's the Gulf War right?" I'd read it during our military history research but wasn't one hundred percent.

"Yeah," Virg nodded while raising an eyebrow and flaring his nostrils in contempt at Mack, who was wearing those flashy white earbuds listening to techno, *dumbstep* or some other garbage on his Kumquat MP3 player.

He turned back to me, "Speaking of... you know what Major General's John Sedwick's last words were?"

Mack tugged on the wire at his chest and yanked his buds off, "WHAT?"

"Major General's Sedwick's last words... they were trapped from enemy fire—a lone sniper in the horizon—at Spotsylvania, and his men were huddling and hiding in a trench near a tree line, he stood up and said 'Hiding? Fidgeting? I'm ashamed of you men! He couldn't hit an elephant at this distan—' and he was shot mid-sentence."

"What's it mean?" Mack slowed down his gait as we approached the door.

"It's something isn't it? That's something in the universe… has to be, giving you a glimmer of the truth…"

I interrupted Virg, "Even if it takes you to the wrong end of a shallow grave," I opened the door and we entered, Mack, Virg, then me. We all collapsed on our beds, tired from the last two weeks. The rest was much obliged.

"Some truths… aren't worth knowing," Virg opened a book and read it on his bed as I dazed in-and-out of consciousness. I couldn't sleep properly, periodically awakening to the sound of Mack's snoring or Virgil turning the page of his book, which in a dreamlike-knives-in-my-eyes-half-open-kind-of-glance seemed to be '*Complete Works of Plato.*'

# THE WAREHOUSE
## NOW

THE SOUND OF the sliding gun set my teeth on edge. My last hope of success slipped into an imaginary fun house like a court of *law* or heaven's pearly gates.

He touches her hair, "Look at her, she's so beautiful," he twirls a finger on one of her curls, "I like your hair."

"He's going to kill you you know," her voice is a sweet paradise of things to come, if we ever make it out of here alive of course.

"Wow! Feisty. That's how I like them," he licks her cheek and looks straight at me as he does it. She wouldn't be in this place if I didn't give a damn about her, if I treated her like I've treated everything else in this desolate wasteland. She whimpers like a lone leaf hanging on a dead tree during a cold winter night.

"Big man. Talking smack holding a big gun. You know what they say about guys with big guns don't ya?" Virgil wakes up with little birds flying around his forehead like a cartoon character. He sits up and shakes his head back into his skull.

I've lost too many things in my life to lose something here. I mouth 'I'll get you out of here' to her. I know she's scared, even if she's doing her best not to show it. I *will* get her out, even if it's the last thing I do, the truth that takes me straight to the graveyard.

"You alright Virg?"

"Yeah… in-a-not-at-all-okay-terrible-kind-of-way," his witty one-liners leave little to be desired, that's why I respect him, that's why I like him, he is who he is, he is what you see, nothing more, nothing less. What you see here, that's Virgil, there's no deep layer of panache, no obscure slyness, no manipulation games. He's an endangered species and slowly dying out among all these hipster goons and snapback-wearing-mama's-boys who think they've had it tough up in their uptown apartments.

Everyone has ups and downs but I feel like my entire life has been one low point followed by another. I'm tired of coming to a crossroads and finding one road to be redemption and the other damnation and being unable to walk on either until I'm deemed ready or dead. I was consumed by the pursuit of myself; the best travels are thought to be inward but they're easy to get lost in. You might catch yourself unwilling to change. I have to dredge open past wounds I can no longer keep buried. In this embrace, the blinding light reminds me of the outside world. A world I'd forgotten about and didn't want to contemplate. It's time to move on and forget about who I *was* and start venturing towards who I *am*. "Tu se' colei che l'umana natura nobilitasti sì, che 'l suo fattore non disdegnò di farsi sua fattura," I know Virgil will understand.

He scoffs weakly, "E io, che mai per mio veder non arsi più ch'i' fo per lo suo, tutti miei prieghi ti porgo, e priego che non sieno scarsi."

It was on. I had no choice but to *hope* we'd get out alive, and I hated it.

"Nice to see the benefits of a classical education. It's cute, this whole brothers-in-arms-act," the malefactor waves the gun at both of us, then presses her closer to his chest, "Here's what *I* think!" he raises the magnum and the muzzle flash blinds me.

Silence.

# THREE CONCERTOS

"YOU ARE NOW Air Force Captains. Pilots. You are birds of prey, the alpha and omega of the sky. You will attack swiftly and defend vigorously. You *will* gather as much intel on enemy forces as *in*humanly possible. You will not only overcome chaos, you will become it, adapt to it, and predict its next move. You will succeed— Virg you owe me a cigar."

"SIR YES SIR," three rebels screamed in unison. His superiors should've known the LT was a good man. The kind of man who regrets having only one life to give for his country. The kind of man that detests the necessity of his vocation, and yet, here he was, acting as a mentor to three maladjusted young men lost in misunderstanding, his way of atoning for all the men's lives he'd taken in his youth I guess.

Half an hour later. The bar. Slumped back losers, women, booze, and stories of loss and failure. The four of us felt right at home.

"You know what Da Vinci's last words were?" Virgil had this perverse fascination with last words, people who struggled to sum up their lives in but a few words. How could you possibly sum up endless years of torture and despair with a few mere words? Then you die, and none of it mattered. Lives rarely matter, but the words... the words become immortal. Wittgenstein would turn in his grave.

"Really Virg?" Mack was already tapping the screen of his Grape smartphone like a jitterbug, walking towards some women at the end of the bar. I watched him approach them; he breathed into his palm to check his breath, put his phone in his pocket and slowly poked his hair, well if you can call what he had hair. He separated a couple of spikes trying to make them look natural; his attempts were feeble.

I felt Virg turn to me but my face was completely hidden by my hat. My fingertips played with the glass full of bourbon, I looked at his nose, then his wild-mannered eyes through the brim of my trusty friend, "Today is not a good day for me Virg," I catch Mack cozying up to a dame at some table and they get up to leave not too long after.

"Oh?" like I said, Virg was the most curious out of the three of us.

"My mom was murdered today."

"What happened?" he wasn't going to let it go.

"Some thug trying to teach some other guy a lesson in respect," I sipped the bourbon; it burned more than it should have. "She simply existed no more, and nothing she did mattered anymore," I knew he wanted to ask me what her last words were, but I hadn't been there... I wouldn't know.

"Is this how you kids party nowadays? We partied harder during Desert Storm!" the LT gulped down his straight gin, "Jesus, you're bumming *me* out! Hawk has the right idea," he pointed his cup at Mack as the latter pecked some bimbo on the cheek and helped her put on her jacket before walking out with her. He hastened out first, neglecting to hold the door open for his *date*. She fumbled with her jacket sleeves and stumbled after him.

"Lue... any women in your life?" it was around this time I started finding Virgil's inquisitiveness strikingly irksome.

"Me? Look at me son, I'm sitting in a bar, medals shined, drinking with my progenies miles away from home, you don't want lady advice from me."

"Oh come on Lue... Air Force Pilot? Desert Storm? Some babes dig that stuff."

Yeah... the psychos, I thought.

"Well..." another sip of his gin, his wise eyes dashed around the room scanning for possible situations. You never *really* forget your training, "Three did. Two I chased off. And the third... or the first if we're going chronologically, died."

The comment he made during that lunch about loss and death finally made sense. The music, and I used that term *very* loosely, was absolutely dreadful—there's a special place in Dante's Inferno for beings who don't respect bourbon—I couldn't handle it, I chugged the rest of my drink and walked away, "I'm gonna go."

I had to leave, walk around, do some thinking. What little remained of me I held on perilously. I opened the bar door and heavy thunder nearly forced me back in. *Just perfect*, my luck at its finest. The bourbon I liked to think of as the imaginary nepenthes from *The Odyssey* didn't really help anymore. I popped the collar on my long-coat—I wasn't wearing the personalized Air Force wind-breaker they gave us with Captain whatever-your-name-is etched on the sleeves, and neither was Virg—and walked out.

"Give me that cigar," I heard LT say to Virg over the sound of the *music* as it meshed with the pitter-patter of raindrops falling on the pavement. The door closed behind me but my thoughts re-mained.

I found myself lying against the wheel of that same F-15 from the first day after Basic, taking swigs of bourbon from a glass and bottle I'd hidden in our quarters and weeping for a reason unknown even to me.

Virg stumbled into the hangar drunk like a frat boy on Christ-mas with a cigar half-lit but burning on his lip. He sat down next to me.

"What *were* Da Vinci's last words?" he hadn't noticed my... *depressive episode,* the therapists called it. I was curious, that man was the closest thing to God in the history of our pathetic planet.

"You sure you wanna know? It's really morbid... and ya know, you're sen-*sa*-tive."

I looked up from beneath my hat just enough to let him know how serious I was but not enough for him to see my eyes.

"Oh you're serious: 'I have offended God and mankind because my work did not reach the quality it should have.' Much better than the other one, this one *really* makes you think."

"More than I'd like," a cold breeze ran up my back, and it wasn't the howling wind outside.

* * *

I zig-zagged back onto our quarters; when you're a drunk, you learn how to navigate your surroundings so you don't topple over. I was still lost in my fool's paradise, thinking about my mom, about my love back at Oxford, wondering how much of my trust fund I hadn't drank away like everything else of any real value in my life with a mind facilely rejecting most crap others tried to shove down my throat.

Mack and Virg were playing cards.

"She was *soooooooo* fine Virg. Her legs spread wide open, I thrust inside her evenly, that's the trick you know, smooth, rhythmic thrusts from your pelvis. ... You have to put your hips into it," Virg didn't look like he was listening to Mack's epic from the fabled bro-universe of uselessness, "She's got her legs around my back, screaming my name, and finally... bliss, her abs contract and relax, that's how you can tell you know, when they're faking it—raise 3," he put 3 chips on the table, "The abs don't contract, and as I rolled off of her, she let out this satisfied moan," he leaned back into his chair and adjusted his belt.

I sat beside Mack holding the King of Spades, "What's the game?"

"Basic high card," Mack loved to hear his own voice when it mattered least, like everyone else with a flair for the dramatic.

"My favorite book is *The Picture of Dorian Gray*. Oscar Wilde. You idiots know it?"

I don't know about Mack, but I *had* read it. Mack rapidly tapped on his uTablet before loading up a page of the summary and skimmed through it.

"Haven't read it, but it sounds good," Mack cracked us up.

"Well… Oscar Wilde was very witty; his humor was generally unappreciated—"

"Save it Virg, tell us what his last words were!" I didn't need him to ease us into it. I wanted to know the mere words that summed up this grand life.

"Well, what's in record is actually debatable and not his last words, but rather something he said a couple of weeks before his death—'My wallpaper and I are fighting a duel to the death. One or the other of us has to go'—anyway, later on, he had a bottle of his hotel's most expensive champagne sent up to his room, when asked later how he was going to pay for it, he quipped, 'I am dying beyond my means.' It was like he knew he was gonna die. I wonder, would we know if we were about to die? Would some augury symbol somehow let you know? I mean sure you would know if you're sick, if you're mortal—we're all mortal… but if you're not, would you know? Would you live that day like any other? Or would some part of you, deep inside, know what's to become of you, would *God*… give you some sign?"

Virg was clever but not always running on a full charge, *God?* God gets his jollies watching people suffer. You'd think an orphan like Virg would know that. God, the only prayers *He* answers are about his beard, otherwise he prays for pain and despair. A regular sociopath.

Virg raised another 4 after Mack called his previous raise, "It's that time champ. You gonna fold? Look at me, can you tell if I'm bluffing? Oooooooo," he flicked the card like a magician and caught it with his other hand. Neither of us saw what it was but it looked like a low heart, though low could also mean ace.

Mack threw his card face down.

"Like a cheap suit… Air Force captain winning with an ace… how fitting."

"What'd you have?"

"You... will never know," Virg played meaningless mind games on matters that had little to no importance, the facetious nature of an intelligent man with little to live for, and he was well aware of this fact. He put the card in his pocket and packed up the rest. "That's enough foreplay for one evening," raking his winnings towards his side of the table and lighting a cigar. Mack got up and slowly walked towards the door. I adjusted my hat to scratch my hair, wondering about our mission at 0700 tomorrow. The files were right there in front of me. I looked through them, an enemy weapons cache somewhere secluded with anti-aircraft missiles, nothing we hadn't done before.

The door swung open. LT's neck craned in, "0645 boys."

I flicked the brim of my hat. Virg nodded and then looked at me, "*God*damn cowboy."

LT's eyes darted around our humble quarters, "Where's Mack?" It was already 1245, and LT didn't want us to be hungover come kick-off time like that mission three weeks ago, Mack almost got himself killed.

"Probably went to the bar boss. He took his Air Force windbreaker," Virg deescalated the situation, "Don't worry Lue, he'll be here when the time comes."

# ARIA

I YAWNED AWAKE ready to blow stuff up like a 90s action-star. I'd become what I despised, a *misguided* schmuck following the status-quo for the sole purpose of fitting in. Whatever… gunrunners, terrorists, bankers, dictators, *goons*; we all have it coming.

I opened my locker and hung my hat inside, the short little curls slightly snuck onto my forehead when I wasn't wearing it. Jesus, I looked like a middle-school wanna-be rock star. I used one of those thin sport sweatbands to tame it back, and the helmet did the rest.

Virg came out puffing a cigar; I inadvertently went to flick the brim of my hat but my index finger hit empty air since it was hanging in my locker. He knew what I meant, his mumbling nod, '*God-*damn cowboy,' preceded his strapping of his overalls tighter.

Our mission uniforms were generic pilot grays. We all looked alike. *How unique.* Virg broke the silence,

"Mehr licht."

I sighed, "*Who?*"

"Goethe. Translates to 'more light,' doesn't that just… clench your jaw? *More light.*"

"Maybe he meant it literally, they used candles back then," for someone who spent most of his time reading, I always wondered why *I* had to point these things out to a genius like Virg.

"May*be*… but still, the man wrote *Faust*, he'd certainly seen darkness, he was — oh my Lord…" Virg looked across the hangar at someone approaching from behind it.

It was Mack wearing a pair of pilot's aviators and hair styled to appear natural with his earbuds hanging around his ears. Way to be an outlaw Mack, he looked like every pilot *ever*.

"You look like Tom Cruise," Virg scowled.

"Thanks," he had this stupid grin on his face as if to say *'I know what I'm doing'* but unfortunately all it did is make him look like an ignorant buffoon.

"It wasn't a compliment."

I laughed, "You know your hair goes *under* the helmet right? And the helmets have sun-visors... it's not the 80s."

"Yeah yeah yeah... I know, I—"

Virg interrupted him, "Walk back behind the hangar and then walk through again, towards us, in slow-motion this time..."

LT approached, "Gentlemen we're ready to..." he looked at Mack, "Jesus son, you look like that fairy from *Top Gun*. A regular *ace*. What was wrong with the way you looked before?"

We all laughed, except Mack of course.

"Come on... this isn't your first rodeo hoss... you *know* your hair goes *in* the helmet?"

Virg and I howled with laughter.

"Yeah yeah yeah, don't hate the playa, hate the game."

"Hate the idiot playing," I was starting to like Virg's snappy remarks.

"Here we are gentlemen, you've been Captains for months now. You know what you're doing and you know what to do. There is nothing more I can teach you. You've made me proud gentlemen, given this old ticker," he tapped his heart under those obscene amount of medals, "Some hope that the future is in good hands." He looked off into the distance while playing with his freshly polished medals. The moment was fleeting. The disciplinarian in him immediately raged out, his stoic face uttered, "You're attacking a weapons cache: 120 enemy combatants, 0 civilians," his voice dropped to a whisper, "If you spot civilians about, say your weapons suffered catastrophic damage and come back... 37 missions without a single civilian casualty and I'd love it if we could keep it that way."

Those who've left their bootprints in the trenches are those who value human life most. They get unwanted glimpses into the savage nature we really have underneath all the expensive clothes and moisturized skin. This of course, rules out the politicians, feminists, and liberals who are far too cozy hiding behind their daddies' wallets and sophomoric mentalities as those who feign having tasted the true consequence of a single blood-drop darkening the sand.

"SIR YES SIR!"

"Overcome chaos gentlemen," LT nodded and walked away, the sun progressively rose behind him and gave him this *really* cool ambiance.

The purr of the F-15 engine was sweet music to my ears— Beethoven's *Für Elise* (well, actually that's the common name, it's *really* the Bagatelle No. 25 in A minor), forced my eyes closed, to contemplate its genius and wonder who we really are… and what we think we know about our weaknesses or strengths. It always took me a moment to really bask in the beauty of the engine's humming. The plane vibrated me to paradise and that high up in the sky, you're probably not far from it either, if you believe in paradise of course. Unfortunately I've never had the luxury of faith. The only thing you can *really* enjoy is the unadulterated freedom. It's pure. You go wherever you please and do whatever you want all faster than the speed of sound… insofar as anyone *could* be free. In the end we're still bound by the laws of life, or death, and the universe. If you're dumb enough to ignore the small fact that no one is *really* free from the hands of tyranny and the shadowed soul.

Yet, most people think *they're* free drinking Cosmicloots every morning and checking emails on their Blackberry or Google devices. Such indolence impressed me to the point of humor.

"Eagle One, com-check."

"This is Eagle One. That's a 10-4," my code-name.

"Hawk Wing, com-check."

"Go for Hawk Wing," Mack's last name was Hawkins, so we all got a *real* good kick out of his assigned codename.

"Raven Nest, com-check."

"This is Raven Nest... let's play *Who Wants to be a Dead Gunrunner?*" Virg hates gunrunners; some gangsta-looking rich white-boy trying to prove something to his buddies shot his dad. A meaningless death. The worst part was that Virgil wasn't there to hear his father's last words.

We all laughed. Mack because he thought Virg was *really* funny, but I laughed at the irony. Virgil worked for the biggest gunrunner on the planet, the largest in the history of mankind in fact, and every gun he sells now breaks the all-time record. The president of the US of A moves more weapons in 32 hours than any gunrunner does in 6 months. I couldn't fathom how he always mustered the nerve to sit at the head of the Human Rights panel in spite of this fact. Maybe he just ignored it, hid from it, just like Virg was. Under it all, we're all the same.

"Nice," Mack snickered.

"Mission parameters only please," the prick on the com had a stick up his ass, sitting behind some radio safe and sound while we were out there scrambling the jets to enemy territory, ready to die for Queen, country, oil, or whatever the bureaucrats demanded...

"Raven Nest to control, come in control!" Virg sounded a little panicked, probably about to make a wisecrack.

"This is control, go ahead Raven Nest."

"Shut the hell up down there will ya?"

We laughed again. This time it *was* funny.

"Damn special ops teams," control muttered, "Eagle One, you're leading this mission. Raven, you're advanced recon. Hawk, you're support *only*."

Hawk piloted an XB-70, made in 50s for the sole purpose of

avoiding interceptors and other jet fighters, reaching top speeds of over 1, 890 miles per hour (or Mach 3.05).

That's why he always got the support roles. The plane works as a strategic bomber, designed to prepare the B-70, a nuclear-armed bomber for the US, and America adores its nuclear bombs more than its citizens. It's an excruciatingly difficult plane to maneuver and pilot... for politicians and average-minded buffoons of course, and not the birds of prey LT trained us to be.

"Thanks for telling us how to do our job control, where *would* we be without you?" I hate pencil-pushers slightly less than politicians and hipsters.

"Eagle One, I can call off your entire mission from right here!" control was going through another power trip, reminded me of my driver licensing exam.

"Raven to control... shut... up," we were too far from base for control to have any real power. Virg and I flew parallel beside each other in F-15E Strike Eagles, and Hawk's XB-70 acted as our tail in sort of a makeshift reverse triangle.

"Nice," I said to Virg.

"Desk-*jokey* sitting comfortably at home with a babe on his arm..."

"I'm still here T3." T3. *Our* codename. There were three of us, and the randomly assigned letter happened to be T. The LT said we're the Terrific Trio to our allies, mostly because we're an elite squad with 100% mission completion rate, and Terrible Trio to our enemies, because our name is often the last breath exhaled on their dead. Perspective at its finest.

We laughed again; Virgil sped ahead and did a barrel roll in front of us, "Look ma! No hands!"

"That's a 31 million dollar plane my friend, you break it, you buy it," I read about it in our research. It costs anywhere from 28 to 35 million dollars for a single F-15 (dependent on whether it's model A, B, C, D, E, K, J, or S). The K is the most advanced, running up a taxpayer bill of 100 million dollars per plane, supplied to the Koreans, whom we've bombed before.

I had to get to know my baby; she was my life. The plane was all I had. I took care of her and she took care of me.

"T3. Status report."

"Is this guy serious? Switch to private coms boys!" Mack was an overcompensating gigolo, but *damn* did he know computers, part of the reason he joined was because his father wanted him to go into football, hockey or some other jock-infected athletic program where the guys are physically talented but can barely read and write. Mack himself wanted to study computers. He signed on to become a programmer but scored high enough to be on this team. He set up this private com system by hacking into the communications mainframe and giving us own our encrypted band while simultaneously receiving from the default military channel at the touch of a button. Control couldn't hear us unless we pushed that button (and we could hear each other while having the option to lock control out), but we could always hear control perfectly, this was way against procedure, way against protocol, there was actually prison time involved in messing with military communication systems—light treason or whatever trumped up charges jealous idiots could throw out, but who was gonna tell?

I pushed ahead of Virg, "Eagle One approaching enemy base, I wager we're right over Uzbekistan or Azerbaijan right about... ... now."

"Oooo, Eagle Oneeeee, you shouldn't have... such a romantic..." Virg's voice cracked me up.

"That's a roger Eagle One. You are to proceed, authorization of Strike Eagle 1-3-9-1-2-1-2-9-5, strike code Mike, India, Lima, Lima, Sierra, November, Juliet, Echo, Lima, Alpha. Over."

"... Here... we... go," I swooped down from the cloud like an eagle spotting a little snake well within range of their anti-aircraft defenses, 'Look ma... ' it was nothing I couldn't handle, even though I secretly wanted one of them to hit me and blow me to smithereens. There was no point in living, in loving. We bomb places, lie to dames to get in their pants, brood, and bomb more places, all because politicians need to line their pockets with more gold… what's the point… *really?* I didn't like what I'd become, nor was I fond of what I seemed to be becoming. The thought had frightened me in the past so I'd gotten good at hiding from myself whenever I did something I didn't like.

My thumb shook over the big red button as I tightened my grip on the throttle, the magic button released four AGM-65 Maverick air-to-surface missiles and the ashes left behind were a glimmer of hope for the world that chaos could be beaten and evil could be eradicated, and the world was safe and sound for sheeple. *Democracy* coupled with venture capitalism was winning. I sounded like an idealistic philosopher with nothing better to do than brood over people's classless demeanours and unattractive attitudes.

Virgil laughed maniacally over the com as he fired (up to a possible) 510 rounds of M-56 20 mm bullets out of the 6-barreled gatling cannons on either side of our wings, destroying their air defences and turning their turrets and enemy foot-soldiers to mush. We whistled back towards base.

"Hey… idiot? You there?"

"Raven, this is control."

"That's a mission complete. Accomplished. Zero civilian causalities. Enemies drinking tea with Allah and banging loads of virgins."

"That's a 10-4."

"Get the goulash out, we'll be home soon *Can't-troll.*"

Control didn't catch Virgil's quip, "Well done T3. Come on home.           Champagne's on ice for ya," as if we needed some desk-jockey's validation.

Beethoven's Für Elise nibbled in my ear on the way back, "That's a 10-4. Eagle One over and out." The barrel rolls and stunts had become a tradition after a completed mission, our own little way of rebelling in a strict institution formed with too many overzealous rules and contrived order.

LT approached us as the music of our engines dimmed down. Virgil was already puffing on a cigar and Mack was swiping his little fingers on his tablet with his eyes still hidden behind those ridiculous mirrored aviators.

"I'm proud of you gentlemen, 38 missions accomplished without a single hiccup."

"SIR THANK YOU SIR!" our respect for the LT was ineffable, you have to respect those who search for truth, but never those who tell you they have found it. LT was the former.

"Take the day off boys."

Virgil exhaled smoke, "Much obliged Lue," and he handed a cigar to the LT.

\* \* \*

Virgil screamed down the bar, "Drink to me, drink to my health, you know I can't drink anymore."

"Hear hear," a bozo shouted out across the place.

The bourbon burned my throat again, "Who said that?" the idiot sitting at the end of the bar might've thought Virgil was toasting to good health, but I knew about his morbid fascination. He was too emphatic about this obsession to ignore the seemingly *random* quips he abruptly screamed out.

The bourbon tinged my cheek this time, "Who?" I asked again.

"Pablo Picasso."

"That's a good one," he was wearing me down. I was getting used to it, a little curious myself as to what great minds equated to truth; your last words after all, should be the most important, you're not going to breathe anymore, to feel anymore, so you might as well let the next guy know what you've discovered, try to show that your life wasn't meaningless, that it meant something, that *you*, found something.

Mack was already with a girl, and the second bartender at the opposite end of the counter eyed me viciously, licking her lips while looking straight at my body. She kept trying to switch posts with the other bartender and tried to catch my eyes from underneath my hat. Coming over more than she needed to so she could ask how the bourbon is. Bourbon, Kentucky bourbon especially, is like Dante's *Inferno* in a glass, fire walks down your throat, lungs, and heart and everything in between with an unpleasant after-taste. We got along just fine.

She was nearly perfect, scarlet hair that reminded me of *our* orbiting Mars that she constantly flipped back in my direction, forcing me to smell her peachy shampoo. Her eyes were a radiating gorgeous green above a petite nose and luscious lips that matched her hair. Her body wouldn't quit if you paid it. I'd seen her before; she's always here, and this place was like my second home. One night she gave Mack a hard time when she refused to serve him because he was already plastered and had started hitting on her. I kind of liked her.

"I'm gonna go," Virgil turned to me.

"That's perfect timing... who was it?" ...

Seconds passed, "Virg? Who said th..." oh... he actually meant he was leaving. I turned back to my glass, suddenly full while the dame behind the counter stared right at me, "Thanks angel," more and more I felt like Humphrey Bogart in a rainy noir, and like him, more and more I believed in less and less.

"I've seen you around... you never say much. Nothing like your friends," and she guided my glance to Mack leaving with some bimbo.

"They like the sound of their own voices," there was no reason to lie to her. We saw her every day, it wasn't anything she hadn't already figured out.

She batted her lashes at me; it brought sweet tears to my mind's eye, "And you don't?"

"Not particularly. I grieve about it on lonely winter nights staring out a window with one of *these*," I lifted my cup, "In my hand," it was very difficult and agonizingly painful but I managed to smile at her.

"Mmmmm… intense," her seductive lips beamed with a calling of things to come.

I looked up through the brim of my hat, meeting her eyes and locking in a long stare. It was easy to get lost in her eyes if you were some hopeless romantic or some Disney prince, "You like working here?"

"Sometimes," she gave me the once-over from top to bottom.

I lifted my hat up with my index finger and held her gaze into my eyes. They grew deeper.

"You have nice eyes. Why do you hide them behind that hat?"

"Every man has his reasons for what he does, no matter how benign."

"I'm serious, they're a narrowing light-blue. I've never seen anything like them before," she moved closer in an attempt to examine my irises in the dimly lit bar.

I pushed my hat back down and smiled a little.

"Say… last call is in 12 minutes, what'd 'a say you wait for me and we kill the rest of this bottle…." She put a bottle of top-shelf bourbon on the counter, "… Back at my place?"

I looked at her through my hat, "Deal," a sip of the inferno. It didn't burn as much.

I helped her close up, putting up the bar stools and chairs. I walked around the counter to help her with the bottles when she backed up into me; her hair and neck smelled fantastic. I put my hand on her waist. She reached around and eventually turned around. Kissing her, I thought of the absurd idea of trying to change your fate, to change who you are and who you're meant to be. We didn't make it back to her place. I took her on the counter, on the table, pretty much everywhere in the bar. She was wild, gnawing on my fingertips as I penetrated her, moaning heavily and panting uncontrollably each time I thrust deeper into her until her eyes rolled to the back of her head and her satisfaction was guaranteed.

I loathed myself, hated what I'd been, what I was, and what I was sure to become.

## The Warehouse
## Now

THE SOUND OF the gunshot makes my ears ring. I try to rush to her but he stops me by pointing the gun directly at my chest, "Uh uh uh!" he sneers.

I look down at my chest. I'm not hit. I look to my right and see Virgil cradling Mack as he stoops to the floor and blood squirts out of his stomach.

Virgil turns back, "You're a coward! Shooting an unarmed man," he puts his palm under Mack's struggling head.

"It's too dark," Mack barely gets out, a sort of half-whisper in between the gargles of blood sloshing out of his mouth, "Hit the lights will ya?"

"I got you buddy," Virgil says.

"Stupid, you think you can sneak up on *me?* Come on!" his pride forces me to look him right in the eye. He turns to her, rubbing the muzzle of his magnum on her temple, "Look at his eyes, look into them, those big pretty eyes, he's thinking he's going to kill me. If you weren't here, and I didn't have this gun, he'd kill me. ... YOU KNOW WHY?" he screams the last three words, "Because he's an animal, *that's* what he *is*, a *bastard*."

Mack convulses and writhes for a couple of seconds before suddenly stopping, Virgil tightens his grip on his hand until Mack lets go slowly, exhaling one final time.

# Canzonetta I

Entry No. 12, 178.

Time: 4:19 A.M.

Disposition at time of entry: sullen, introverted, enraged.

I slept for 3 hours and 20 minutes last night having at last found some closure regarding my relationship with Cressida. Ahriman informed me that the root of her behavior was not hatred, disdain, or a lack of affection, but rather, that she was simply being unfaithful. I blame this betrayal on myself for permitting emotion into my thought process. I vowed such things away after Elsa.

Nonetheless, this could not have been the sole reason for my much-coveted rest since I learned during my last meeting with Dr. Ariadne that sleep deprivation is equivalent to temporary psychosis. Discovered by American soldiers during the Korean or Vietnam War; I am hard pressed to remember which, but *whichever* useless war it was, I am sure it was irrelevant.

Lara has been most satisfactory, the unusual rattling noise ceased after picking her up from service and she has been nothing but courteous to my needs since.

I chanced upon the latest issue of *Ducati* magazine while I was waiting in the lounge of the dealership and took a particular liking to their *Streetfighter* model, but was afraid that such a purchase would upset Lara.

Sebastian is being most intransigent. He has still yet to tell me why he bought such absurd sounding license plates for Lara and his own car. *Da King*; it makes me sound less than a man, like an over-compensating buffoon or a politician.

He was also surprisingly tame when we visited *Stupenda*, but that was mostly due to the owner's 19-year-old daughter working the counter that day. She *is* beautiful, so I understood and humoured him. It turned out, business *was* slow the prior week (we are not barbarians or government officials) and the owner, Oppriméret, paid his balance in full as soon as he was able. This pleased me greatly; I behaved as a gentleman ought to.

I saw Calvano's granddaughter, Helen today at Cosmicloots café, ordering her usual double espresso with a shot of honey. She's sweet, and although we nodded at each other and she smiled; I couldn't return the kindness. I hadn't practiced my casual 'hey' smile in too long and feared that I would either look too friendly or too creepy.

I have always liked or perhaps even loved her—for what is more worth pursing than forbidden love? Furthermore, I house a sneaking suspicion that she also likes *me*... however, I've always refrained from acting on these feelings because they are most illogical, and quite candidly, rather cliché, for it would be too Shakespearean, too... *Romeo and Juliet* if I pursued her romantically.

When it came my turn to order, I was so wrapped up in thinking about Helen that I hesitated and stuttered as I ordered the Chilean coffee with ginger extract, and adding to my dismay about my earlier faux pas, I was charged 4.35€ for the ostentatiously labeled 'small' size. On that point, it is worthwhile to note that the name of the sizes in this *thing* resembling a café are nothing more than feeble and ignorant attempts to demonstrate a unity of culture and multi-language, but make no sense for those who actually speak the languages. Small means twenty, medium means biggest, and large means moderate. None of them are even from the same language, furthering the confusion for those unfamiliar with the concept of this neo-post-modern garbage swill they pass off as coffee.

It hurt me physically to hand the barista, Susan, my 5€ bill and I immediately began perspiring. The coffee itself is as always, much too watered down and not fresh enough but I could not bring myself to throw it out, and knew that I'd be right back here tomorrow morning since I have always been desperate in my guise to appear typical, average, and normal to peering onlookers.

I saw the target today with his girlfriend looking rather out-of-place at the shelter. He watched as she handed the homeless soup and other necessities. He didn't even help, standing there and watching like her bodyguard, no doubt thinking very highly of himself as his Hermès phone case proved.

I have devised a most genius plan to capture them both and will keep my eye on him until the proper moment, at which time I will inform Sebastian's cousin to move in for the extraction. I must ask him questions of dire importance, especially regarding the origin of his hat; the female I require for business.

I will now attend to my home-gym for my shoulder and chest exercise, following which I will drink a glass of milk, chew some painkillers, and make further entries in this ridiculous journal.

# REQUIEM

## 6 YEARS AGO

IT WAS A fortnight before my birthday, which I awaited with much anticipation… yes I'm being sarcastic you bozo. I despised my birthday; it was a day like any other day but worse, reminding me of events no amount of bourbon would ever drown, and I was slowly learning this fact.

It was a basic mission, an asset and his henchmen shacked up in some house in an obscure abandoned village outside of this little town in Uganda.

Für Elise played in my head as we took off, 2600 miles/hour and we reached the target in a matter of minutes. I swooped down, business as usual and approached the target. My eyes shifted to an old woman carrying a little child. I looked around; the village was anything but abandoned. Our intel was wrong.

"Uhh, control this is Eagle One. Come in. Over."

"Go ahead Eagle One."

"I spot civilians down there control, our intel said the place was deserted except for the target. Please advise. Over."

"What the hell is going on boss?" Virgil asked me.

"I don't know… I bet control does though."

"Come in T3."

I didn't like his tone, "Control. We're aborting, we're coming home."

"That's a negative T3. Proceed as advised. Mission is still a go. Confirm when you're over the target for strike authorization codes."

"What the actual hell?" Mack's voice whistled over the main com.

"Control, repeat transmission, it sounded like you said we're still a go right after I confirmed the presence of a civilization greater than ours," it *must've* been my hearing.

"Looks to be about 400 people control," Virgil chimed in with a quick count of the ants treading their dreams beneath our feet.

"T3, you are a go for mission *Go Free*."

"Think he means Go Oil," Virgil raged.

Screw it. "Control. That's a negative on the op, our weapons system has suffered catastrophic failure, we are unable to proceed."

Mack pulled out a little screwdriver and started messing with his cockpit, unscrewing things so the onboard computer told control we were unable to proceed.

"T3, I'm not reading any malfunctions here from the digital onboard computers we've installed on your jets. This is a priority mission for the *interest* of national security. You *will* be held for insubordination if you do not proceed."

I looked down the horizon with the African sun rising ahead of me. I was never supposed to fly low but I didn't care, my *life* was about to end so I slowed down and flew as low as I could to the red sands. One of the ants took the shape of a man and limped towards the engulfing engine of my F-15 with a piece of wood he was using as a walking stick. His poncho flapped in the wind, his face, serene and relaxed. Something about him sparked something in me. I couldn't do it. I wasn't strong enough, or weak enough. I had scruples about levelling an *entire* city. There is a fine line between delivering what *we* deem *true* justice and having to follow *every* order given by some idiot in a conference room with a lot of undeserved medals because oil prices are too low or too high for the companies they're running in the Oval Office, or the companies running the Oval Office; perspective is everything.

The button throbbed on my thumb...

"*Vi...* come on brother, the mission is the mission. They'll hang you for this!"

I wanted to fly away, to turn around and go home, swallow a

bullet and be silently free inside the shadow of my being. It almost seemed like a tear escaped through my helmet and gave my thumb the extra weight to push the button for the blood money the president was going to use to bail out some Wall Street firm. It seemed like a dream until I heard the clanking sound of the bomb being released. Everything fell silent.

I couldn't hear Für Elise anymore. I flew completely inverted, eventually hearing the soft thump of the detonation, the throttle vibrated my entire body as I mustered the courage to contemplate 400 lives lost for a *single* asset we couldn't even confirm was there in the first place. At least oil or diamond prices were exactly where Obama wanted them. I flew back to base upside down. My brain felt heavier than it actually was, wanting to tear through my skull. I'd become a killer, a mercenary on a salary blowing away *bad* guys, a rent-a-clown with missiles with no identity, no mind or soul. A *thing* that turned other things to dust at the whim of the world's largest gunrunner.

"You're a dead man control," I was going to take it all out on the idiot behind the mic. It was irrational but I needed something, *someone* to blame other than myself.

"Repeat that Eagle One."

"*You*. Are. A. Dead. Man."

My head weighed more with each passing second, my brain pulsated with a gripping ache that made me want to throw up, to eject while flying inverted and become Aunt Jemima pancake batter. To at least cost these bastards 30 million bucks for the plane that's supposed to represent freedom rather than oppression. It was petty, childish, and I still couldn't do it.

I landed the plane harshly, nearly exploding to bits when the wheels touched the ground. The sound of the engine dying down was what calmed me now. I never wanted to soar the skies again. I couldn't hear Beethoven or Chopin in the back of my mind anymore. Only that stupid tune by that even stupider Korean kid.

My helmet bounced off the pavement and the visor cracked, much like my psyche.

\* \* \*

First things first. I punched Mack square in the face and my fist landed cleanly on his cheek. *The mission is the mission?* Virg stepped between us. I went for control next. *Bros* are all the same, they can lift 2 million pounds and *act* like Arnold, but when push comes to shove, when the going gets tough, most of their chest puffing is nothing but empty air. They run away with their tail tucked between their pants. Some of them have the training, none of them have the will, and ask any warrior, will is everything.

More radio controllers jumped in and tried to take me away. They were no match. A general came in and they fell into formation. I stood up, heaving like an old politician with a hooker, ready to pounce and tear him to pieces with my mitts. I took a step forward and Virgil held me back, apologizing like an imbecile,

"Sir, we're very sorry SIR! He suffers from Young Man's Disease SIR!"

That's a new one, a brand-new label some psychologist probably thought up because it'd have been too low for her to say that the person was *normal*. No one is normal, and therapists love to label you almost as much as they love to analyze your decisions and tell you why you're always wrong.

"Very well soldiers. At ease," boys will be boys. He didn't ask, and no one told.

Five or six pressed and dressed sheeple baa-ed behind him and took me away for disobeying orders and threatening control, destroying some comrades' jaws, jeopardizing the mission and the *national security* of our nation. I laughed when they put me in the stockade and awaited my court martial. They appointed some young, flair-for-the-dramatic hipster as my attorney, and he wanted my take on things, trying to get me to weasel out of my decision, get me to say I wasn't myself. Emotionally distressed or something. He had the

audacity to offer his take on the mission being so close to the anniversary of my mother's death as the justification for this emotional
upheaval. The damn *sophist* ought to be a politician. I fired him, but
not before I threatened to rip his tongue out and enjoy it with a nice
Merlot. I take responsibility for my actions. I never learned to weasel
my way out of consequences like a dirty rat, an investment banker,
or some flashy day-trader.

I asked the guard outside my cell for some Kentucky Bourbon
and he laughed, I said 'fine' and told him I'd settle for *Hudson Baby
Bourbon*. He laughed again. I had to live with it... for now.

* * *

For some reason I'd zoned out, couldn't stop thinking about
Jack Nicholson from *A Few Good Men* screaming '*You can't handle
the truth!*' I suddenly realized not many people could, that's why I
was in this courtroom. No one could understand what I was ordered
to do, the depth of the decision I made that wasn't even mine. To
level an entire city, kill children, women, men, *a lot of good men*. All
for what? Some absurd veil of national security? A misguided idea of
justice?

The gavel snapped me out of this obscure contemplation,

"Order!" *God* shrieked in response to Virgil's protests to this
farce. He yelled something about a guy named Thrasymachus;
might, right, truth, calling him a lover of sights and sounds or
something. I didn't understand it. It was probably from Plato.

I couldn't quite hear what he was saying, my ears made this
dreadful whistling sound. I felt deaf. Truth was Elise... I mean Für
Elise. To hear its notes nimbly echoing from a somber piano somewhere in seclusion.

The judge ordered him out and Virgil exited begrudgingly,
calling everyone a sheep and everything a sensible before catching
my eye and making a crack about Edward Abbey's last words: '*I did
what I could*'—I looked it up later—The LT stood up beside me. He
wanted to help, probably try to take all the blame, but I wasn't going

to let him.

"Your honour, if I may," he cleared his throat, "Ahem, we should not be hasty. The T3 initiative has had a 100% mission completion rate and zero civilian casualties up until *Operation Go Free*, it is prejudicial and unjust to punish one man for not following an order that he believed was a violation of our constitutional right to protect the constitution itself, namely freedom to life, to free speech, to liberty and the pursuit of happiness. Laws that he believes we are obligated to abide by if we are to serve on the panel of Human Rights in the United Nations. For how can we ascribe ourselves the most civilized, most advanced country in the world if we do not hold ourselves to the same standards we hold other countries?"

The LT should've been a lawyer, even I almost bought it.

"Such things apply to *our* citizens only," the judge steepled his fingers, "The suspected terrorists, or *victims* as the media calls them, were not native to us so your first point is moot. Furthermore, the number one rule of military personnel is to follow the orders given lieutenant colonel, by your superiors. You ought to know that. Needless to say this is a convoluted and complicated case, even with the blatant insubordination by Captain —", he flipped the pages in front of him to read out my name. "The mission was complete, the parameters met, *however*... we cannot have an initiative which pours tax-payers' money into a team obeying orders when they see fit with their own personal ideal of justice at the helm. We cannot have rogue soldiers living and being paid by the military. It is simply against what we believe in as a nation, and as individuals.

Therefore I hereby disband initiative T3 and sentence the captain to 36 months in military prison, to be served immediately." Bang. The Hammer of Thor came down quicker than lightning.

There are people who do things to other people, sick people doing sick things, things I wish I could unsee. I believe such people should die. But the problem is, even if these people exist—the pathologically sadistic sociopaths with a horrifying childhood—who's to decide which of these assholes deserve death? The army? *You? Me?*

Even if I were some sage—I'm not—my wails fall on empty air. No one ever asked me or wanted my input. The *justice* system decides who lives and dies: that's cops, DA's, judges, defense attorneys, stenographers, or therapists; they're all human beings, all capable of being wrong, careless, or just lazy. None of it matters, mistakes will always be made, and the wrong people will die. The kicker is, some of those people *will* be innocent... and those cops, DA's, judges, defense attorneys... those in the system, all sleep soundly on their comfortable mattresses in their expensive mansions or apartments.

There it was, *truth* as the *justice* system would have it. The Honorable Judge Wotan's speech was eloquent. In fact it was so bombast that it nearly persuaded *me* to how deserving I was of the fate he attributed me. He should run for mayor or something.

## Dark Matter

### 5 years ago

I CAUGHT A glimpse of my reflection handcuffed and being escorted to my cell; it wasn't the same man staring back anymore.

A prison cell is a black hole. A room with no windows and a perpetual darkness that seems to squeeze you and close in on you during moments of singular thoughts. No thoughts are clear in this dungeon. The smell of crap, sweat, and year-old meat-and-potatoes make it hard to breathe. Here I was, 11 minutes from anywhere in the world wanting to be anywhere else. Well, I really wanted to blow my brains out but men like me rarely get what they want from inside this miserable oubliette in some little town a million miles from civilization.

The sound of the prison cell closing sealed my fate every *damn* time I sat down on that gristly mattress, ... what the government thinks passes for a mattress. I barely slept 3 hours a night. Sometimes I hallucinated things like my mom coming to visit me through the bars, wearing my homburg in the cell, the taste of bourbon burning my tongue. When my mom died one of the psychiatrists told me hallucinations were *normal* when you're suffering from insomnia, fifty grand worth of therapy and at least I learned *one* thing. When I slept longer than 3 hours I had nightmares, faces I'd never seen with their eyes missing reaching out to me, asking for help. One of them, a little girl missing her lips looks right at me, trying to say something but can't because her tongue is in her palm. She looks very similar to the denomination of people in that city *I* bombed. An old man with voids as eyes mumbles I'm an animal, pointing his wooden stick at me. I forced myself to stay awake. I didn't need these thoughts.

\* \* \*

Dear Captain Virgil van Leeghiéri,

Military prison is… I could try describing to you what it's like, but I wouldn't do it even a little bit of *justice*. I'm in here, so what I write might be biased. I can try showing you. Remember that movie we saw? *The Last Castle* with Robert Redford, about military prison? It's sort of like that, in-a-gross-understatement-not-at-all-like-that-kind-of-way. I mean… what do you think happens when you stick men too psycho for the *army* in closed spaces with millions of arbitrary rules trying to govern their behavior? Yeah… chaos. Half the time I just pop some wannabe infantry or macho navy schmuck just to get thrown into solitary. A 4' by 5' cell with nothing but darkness, it's like floating in space, including the no oxygen, and no room for faith in anything but the darkness. I don't know why I enjoy it so much, why I'm drawn to the void, the same thing that attracts a moth to a flame I guess, masochism. My chevrons meant nothing in there. And I finally realized they meant nothing anywhere.

Your old friend,

V.

Solitary confinement meant I wore the orange jumpsuit, the one you always see on TV. The blue jumpsuit is for *saner* inmates, a more gen pop (general population) vibe. Last but not least are the yellow and green jumpsuits: they do work around the prison. Yellows are janitors, renovators, and mailmen while greens make license plates.

\* \* \*

I liked the guard on the late shift on weekdays and he liked me I guess, as much as a prisoner and a guard could like each other.

Rickard Marlowe. He was adamant in me calling him Rick. I wagered he was about 20 years older than me, married with a 23-year-old daughter. He was still in top physical condition, and he had to be to control these animals, but there was a certain poise to the way he walked and stood.

Some young marine in the cafeteria one day bragged about this woman and daughter he'd raped in Afghanistan or Iraq (I tuned in after he'd already said where he served), and I found myself in confinement a couple of minutes later, nearly killing him before a couple of guys flung me off his bloody cheeks. I might be a self-righteous prick with an exaggerated sense of morality, but I'm not against rearranging a guy's jaw because he thinks the horror he's committed is in reality a comedy.

As the guard closed the confinement door I wondered how alike that marine and I really were. We'd both killed innocents. Maybe I lost my temper because he showed me a part of myself I didn't know existed or had repressed. Is that who I am? A psycho killer? Am I the sum of the things I've done or is the *soul* something more? Can I live with the things I've done? Maybe I couldn't find who I was, find my identity because I was afraid of what I might find and perhaps this was best. I didn't know who I was, whether or not I felt things, or could feel ever again.

The old man with no eyes called me an animal and evaporated into ash, his jaw still whispering 'animal' as it poofed into rising dust from the ground. I gasped awake to Rick's voice,

"You alright boss?"

"Yeah…"

"Nightmare?"

"Every damn time."

"Still, better there than here I figure huh?"

The little light coming from the tray slot blinded me. I had no sense of time or direction. I couldn't even know how long I'd slept, it had to be longer than 3 hours but less than four and a half. I could see Rick looking around outside the room. The door cringed open.

"Come," he whispered. This was highly unorthodox; he could've lost his job. I stepped outside and he'd set up a table with two chairs.

I noticed all the others doors were open and unoccupied in the confinement area. I guess no one was dumber than I to do something idiotic enough to get thrown in here. In a castle full of morons, I stood alone as the stupidest. A gold star for me, or one of those smiley stickers.

I sat down on one of the chairs and Rick and I talked about life, family, and the world. He's a good guy. He showed me a picture of his wife. She was Balkan, which I found comforting since he's black. It gave me a slither of light I guess, that he'd overcome the chaotic systematic disunity governments create with segregation and counter-intuitive affirmative-action laws. Equality can never exist if governments are constantly separating obscure qualities that hold no foundation for anything other than simple aesthetics.

The old man tore me apart this time as he screamed 'a beast!'

Awake.

It was my 29th birthday. I found myself wondering about my father. Who he was, what he did for a living, whether he knew I existed and whether he cared. I don't know why but that's where my mind went, you can't choose your thoughts any more than you can choose who you are.

I was in solitary again, this time for talking back to a guard because he called me a convict. I threatened to take his baton and shove it down his throat and listen to him choke on it. In hindsight, it was a bad idea, but nothing in this place could inspire a good idea so I ran with it.

I hated this place. To my delight, I found Rick covering for a friend. He opened the door and guided me to the chair again. Two cupcakes, mine with a burning question mark candle on it. He could go to jail for this, letting me out without an unrestrained escort.

"I know you're not like them," he said in a soft mannered tone as he pulled my chair back.

I sat down and he sung *Happy Birthday*, his voice was even and sonorous. My faith in humanity couldn't have gotten any worse until that moment, launching me into a hopeful state about hope. He sat across from me. I was still in awe, how'd he know it was today?

"I looked up your b-day from your file. Come on... eat! It's good," he took a bite of his cupcake.

"You don't have to do this Rick. You could get in trouble, you have a family—" I didn't want anyone to go through something they don't have to on my account.

"I don't want to hear it Vi," he fumbled inside his pockets and handed me a photograph of his daughter, "Amelia. 22. Graduating in two years."

"She's beautiful."

"Hey! Don't get any ideas...."

"I didn't mean—"

"Vi, I'm joking with you."

I stared at him. He was a funny guy. She *was* beautiful, not pale enough to be Balkan or dark enough to be black. She had her mom's scorching hazel irises and curly hair, but Rick's big, inquisitive eyes and athletic shoulders.

"She has your eyes."

"Don't insult my daughter Vi," he chuckled and slammed down a bottle of Pappy Van Winkles on the table. 90 proof, about $100 a bottle. He was also a man of fine taste.

He made the time... bearable.

# Canzonetta II

Entry No. 12, 166.

Time: 4:37 A.M.

Disposition at time of entry: slightly displeased with a hint of fury, but the Bach somehow manages to calm the inner rage in me.

I couldn't sleep again last night—that's 69 hours without any rest—my body seems to have grown a tolerance to Dr. Ariadne's pills, and I am weary to up my dosage personally without consulting her first, it might not mix well with the Oxycodone or the Clonazepam I seem woefully addicted to.

I am quite distraught by Lara's behavior, last night there was a weird clinging noise as I turned her ignition over, and it bothered me so profusely that I was forced to call the service centre and make an appointment for later in the day. I asked them why there was only one Aston Martin mechanic in our fair city, and although my question was utterly serious, the starved-for-attention hussy thought I was being sarcastic and laughed. I hung up immediately, in hopes that she'd confirmed my appointment when I show up there at 1:15 P.M.

Some weird sounding man working for the *Veritas Daily* left me a message yearning for a comment on my grandfather's indictment, and even had the audacity to ask me where he could find my mother.

In a thriller, I must note that last week was the closest call hitherto, as the target was practically eye-to-eye with me as he charged across the street—he could've been killed by traffic! He would've identified me had it not been for Lara's tinted windows, and he is not the type to believe that it would've been a mere coincidence, especially after two already *seemingly* random incidents at the bar and hotel. I must be more vigilant and keep my distance in the future. Perhaps I will ask the boys to follow him instead, he is not hard to spot in a crowd with that ridiculous hat.

Later today I will deal with the owner of *Stupenda* with Ahriman and Sebastian since this is the third time he has shorted Sofus on his visit. I will not threaten his wife or daughter, but I cannot say the same for Sebastian; he has been on edge as of late, and no measures have been taken to rectify his mood.

I read about Bushido yesterday, the code of samurai honour and loyalty from the olden days of their history; the entertainment propaganda machines in efforts to maximize profits have radically romanticized their way of life. This however, does not change the central tenet of Bushido, something they refer to as *giri*. A word that implies 'loyalty,' or a strong sense of duty to oneself and their peers, although in all my dealings with the Japanese and my travels to Japan I have yet to see such a concept actualized in our varying societies. Anyway, their way of life is supposed to revolve around seven virtues: integrity, respect, heroic courage, honour, compassion, honesty and sincerity, and duty and loyalty. It's theoretical anyway, not meant to be taken literally. No longer does our planet host honour, respect, or courage. No longer do we value sincerity, duty, or dignity. This is not surprising; archaic philosophies and beliefs are almost immediately abandoned when they cannot be ascribed to the arbitrary moral codes society suddenly chooses to accept. Our steal, plunder, consume, and deceive mentality has no room for honour and bravery.

I'm hallucinating a little bit. It must be the insomnia. It's like I'm awake but asleep at the same time. I see the man staring at the flower through the pavement. He stares me right in the eye and blows smoke in my face. Just then, a cigar appears in his hand that wasn't there before. He hands it to me and I examine it; it's a Monte Cristo. He smiles and fades away.

I dozed off, thought I saw Elsa, and immediately sobbed awake. I am now certain that I am hallucinating, for I could not have seen her. It must've been a dream. Where do dreams come from?

I fail to see how this is supposed to be helping me, but Dr. Ariadne continues to insist that I make these entries, after which I plan to practice smiling in the mirror so I don't look like a sociopath should an opportunity present itself for one.

## CHORALE FANTASIA

THE LITTLE GIRL broke out into tears when she tried to talk but then realized her lips had been burned off. She grabbed my collar and froze me solid; an aching pain tore me to pieces from inside. It felt like a rat nibbling harder and harder on my intestines before I finally exploded.

Awake.

"5030857! You've got a visitor," some guard clanged his baton on the bars down the hall.

I looked up from Rick's copy of Dostoyevsky's *The Idiot* and approached the round table and circular seats with Virg placed across me. I don't have to talk to him through glass with a wire telephone since I'm not in here for murder, though I should be.

Seeing him, I couldn't get the picture of that old man out of my head, 400 people were dead. I told myself it wasn't my fault, that I didn't have a choice, that I was following *orders*. I try to tell myself a lot of things, all of it nonsense.

"I know you're not a fan of birthdays but I came to see you anyway, kill two birds with one stone sort of thing."

"Much obliged old friend."

"Listen," Virgil was straight to business, "Mack and I got this great gig, bodyguards for this judge and his family. There have been threats against him. I told him about you, told him we need a third. He has a son *and* a daughter."

"This is my problem how?"

"Don't get sassy with me Vi. You'll watch the daughter. You're getting out next week, we'll pick you up..."

"No thanks," I had prior engagements with a bottle of bourbon and a bullet.

"Don't be a sophist," he scoffed.

I pretended to agree, "I'll need a couple of days. And a piece. Oh, and a single armour-piercing bullet," usually people in my line of work—dishonourably discharged Air Force Captains with a paramount respect for human life—become commercial pilots for passenger planes, but they don't let suicidal alcoholics apply anymore... another notch in the government's national security/anti-terrorism belt.

"A *single* bullet?"

"I don't intend on missing," when would this dreadful day end?

"*Hard-core* bullets are hard to come by Vi."

"Come by it. Get it done. Don't tell me what we can't do."

"I take it you're on board then."

"Yeah... whatever, I'll protect the slave of justice perpetuating what he openly despises without batting an eye."

"That's the spirit! ... Pay's amazing, plus the bourbon's free."

"Great," now I was *really* excited. A drunk never passes up an opportunity to drink.

"When you're free Vi, it'll be great, the T3 reunited at last."

"*If* I get out of this labyrinth you mean..."

"None of us get out, don't you know what Simon Bolivar's last words were?"

"I get the impression you're about to tell me."

"Yes I am! 'Damn it! How will I ever get out of this labyrinth?'"

"He also said, 'The United States appears to be destined by providence to plague its people with misery in the name of liberty.'" Enslaved to freedom, naught but sheep to national security laws like Providing Appropriate Tools Required to Intercept and Obstruct Terrorism Act of 2001 a.k.a. the Patriot Act, corporations... all of it in the name of *freedom*, a concept invented by some young British land-owner. Anyone who ever recounts the concept of freedom as attainable or believes themselves to be free obviously hasn't read Kant's critiques on Pure and Practical reason.

A bodyguard for a pretty socialite, I was moving up in the world. Like all idiots I naturally assumed she was pretty because she was rich. You can buy anything with money, even people, even... beauty.

"Oh," he nodded to the guard standing near us, "Nearly forgot. Happy birthday," and he slid a book across the table.

I caught it at the edge: *Appointment in Samarra* by John O'Hara.

## CHORALE SETTING
## ONE WEEK LATER

RICK REQUESTED THE day for some reason. I was signing out my personal effects as the doors behind me slid open, sounding a little like Für Elise but not quite. It was faint, practically inaudible. There was a moment of panic when I looked into the box and couldn't find my hat until Rick appeared and handed it to me.

"I asked if I could give it back. I know how much it means to you, and I know what you did… and I thank you man."

It seemed to me that he'd mourn my departure not because I belonged in this place, because we were friends now, and I didn't understand. I put the hat on and flicked its brim. *Hello old friend*, and said goodbye to my new friend of old.

The other guard behind the fence practically screamed, "Vero K. Bergljót, you are hereby dishonourably discharged from the Air Force having completed your sentence for insubordination and assault of a fellow comrade. May God have mercy on your poor soul."

God, what a joke *that* concept is.

I untangled and latched my bracelet to my wrist as the prison fence opened to a desert road, but a *free* desert road—as much as we can be free in this *Big Brother* of a void.

Mack and Virg were leaning against a Mercedes ML 63 AMG on the other side towards the scorching horizon. Mack's mirrored aviators reflected the sun into my eyes and blinded me momentarily. They were both wearing suits, Mack navy, Virg black with thin grey stripes. Mack always grew out his beard a little, giving him more of a homeless vibe than the action-hero panache he hoped to convey. He thought it made him look older and more mature, but his incredibly counterintuitive gangsta SnapBack resting lightly on his empty head above those pilot shades in front of his unseeing eyes depicted a whole other personality altogether. Nevertheless, and like always, I had his back. Maybe it was a misguided sense of friendship or loyalty, but it was *my* misguided sense.

"Nice suits, you look like bankers," they looked like goombahs or wise-guys, but I wasn't going to start *another* day with negativity.

The familiar smell of Virgil's Partagas filled my nostrils, "Never thought I'd miss that smell," which only meant he still hadn't found a woman to change that filthy habit of his.

"Vi!" Mack gave me one of those awkward *bro*mance hugs, you know the one, with the one hand in mine and elbow reaching around my back, his way of affection I guess.

"Now I can cross the Shifting Sands," Virgil's first words to me in freedom looking down the empty fields beside us. The Shifting Sands were from *The Wizard of Oz*, that guess was as good as any,

"Frank Baum," everything was empty. Words began to lose their meaning.

His mouth gaped in awe. The cigar on his lip rolled off and a little spark reflected from the sun for a moment before landing on the boiling pavement.

"How'd you know?" the panic in his eyes escalated to the point of alarm.

I had him right where I wanted him, his trivial and useless tidbits of information were what made him useful. They were how he differentiated himself from others. It made him unique. Without the things that make people unique, we're all the same. I'd taken that away. He was *not* happy about it.

"Lucky guess."

His hand shook as he opened the door, the three of us got in. Mack sat in the driver's seat while Virg and I slipped into the backseat. Virg whipped out a bottle of Blanton's Original Single Barrel; smoother than poet's prose but just as abstract.

"Still like your bourbon the same way?"

"Yeah... floating in front of me."

We drove into town. They set me up in a two-bedroom apartment near the judge's estate. It's nothing like my grandfather's place but it'll do. Blue wallpaper with thick black stripes surrounded the entire place while venetian blinds idled in front of the window, and a king-sized bed tucked into Egyptian cotton sought to give me the rest I hadn't had since I fought for *freedom* for my country. A dark brown leather couch and a rectangular mahogany coffee table covered the corner opposite the door. Virg wasn't kidding when he said the pay was good.

I wanted to move on, to drown my sorrows, preferably in bourbon. Why *had* I taken this job? What was the reason, and why did I have this crippling feeling that something rotten was about to happen?

Virg handed me a .38 magnum and a box of regular ammo.

"The hardcore I asked for?" I knew what I was going to use it for at the opportune time.

"Whoop! Nearly forgot," he put the armour piercing shell in my palm, "Still haven't told me why you need it."

"Better to have it and not need it..."

"Say no more. Be at the place in 48 hours, 8 A.M. sharp. Address is on the fridge."

"Yeah."

"I'm serious Vi, don't be late. You're guarding the girl you lucky duck. She's pretty. The prettiest girl in Sweden," he yapped while I looked around at the freedom the oil companies had bought with the blood and tears of innocent souls.

"The judge is paid off by some mob family to sentence a rival wiseguy to prison for life, so naturally, they're pissed and out for blood, but the former *really* wants that particular guy in jail, so they're paying us to protect him, *and* the judge is paying us more. Only he thinks our loyalty can be bought," you have to appreciate the wondrous the irony in that... a judge seeking to *buy* a higher ideal like loyalty with mere cash?"

"And why isn't it?"

"Because they're a good family. Give them a chance."

... The silence had become uncomfortable so I left it there.

"Great... we'll be caught in the middle of a mob war if things go south." I wanted to know who I'd have to deal with *when* things went south, "Which families?"

"I don't know man. The Calvanos and the Torrinos? The Corrinos and the Talvanos? Who cares who they are, some *eye*talians bent on anarchy."

"Get out now, *I want to sleep,*" I lied through my teeth. I wanted bourbon followed by that armour-piercing round.

"That's funny, did you do some reading in prison?"

"Some Dante. Dostoyevsky. Adam Smith. Camus. Hemingway."

"Oh, I thought... never mind."

"What?"

"*I want to sleep* were Mór Jókai's last words, and you also knew Baum's so I thought you researched last words or something."

"That's *your* thing." He walked towards the door, "Hey Virgil..."

He turned back, "Yeah?"

"What's Young Man's Disease?"

"Huh?"

"Young Man's Disease. You told General Dragineski I had *Young Man's Disease* the day I *got free.*"

"Oh..." he chuckled, "Love. Young women need a young man to save them. The damsel in distress. You know... King Arthur's knights. *All* men need the damsel in distress, and if they can save that *one* girl, they can redeem themselves, solidify their identity, overcome doubt, become the person they'd hoped they'd be," a little dimple crept from the left side of his face.

"Virg that doesn't make sense. It wasn't about a woman."

"No it wasn't, not yet."

Is there a cure for this? I wondered. A cure other than death?

The door closed behind him. I didn't bother locking it in hopes that some guy would barge in and put me out of morbid misery and make a few bucks selling my couch and sheets while he was at it.

Does nobody understand? Does no one realize how futile our actions are? How feeble *we* are? I stood outside the terrace until dark. I craved the shadows, the darkness in the dead of night, that's what I believed in, the starving homeless guy pacing down the road beneath my balcony drinking what looked to be vodka out of a brown paper bag, the sound of a rolling can of Pepsi mixed with the smell of sewage and garbage. My veins were tired of pumping poison through my body. It was hardly worth it.

There was a black Aston Martin parked across my building. An elegant car for any overcompensating buffoon with too much money to care about anything or anyone other than a hunk of metal. It was a little dark but I thought I saw the driver cleaning a bloody hunting knife, but it'd also been a while since I slept so I probably hallucinated the whole thing.

The fridge was filled with my favorite stuff: eggs, steaks, ground beef, some chicken, and a bowl of iceberg with croutons. I searched the place thoroughly, not a drop of bourbon… that damn Virg, smarter than he lets on.

I cracked open the book he'd bought me. The first page was a short story by William Somerset with the same title as the book written in 1933.

'The speaker is Death.

There was a merchant in Baghdad who sent his servant to the market to buy provisions and in a little while the servant came back, white, and trembling, and said, 'Master, just now when I was in the marketplace I was jostled by a woman in the crowd and when I turned I saw that it was Death that jostled me. She looked at me and made a threatening gesture; now, lend me your horse, and I will ride away from this city and avoid my fate. I will go to Samarra and there Death will not find me.' The merchant lent him his horse and the servant mounted it, and he dug his spurs in its flanks and as fast as the horse could gallop he went. Then the merchant went down to the marketplace and he saw me standing in the crowd and he came to me and said, 'Why did you make a threatening gesture to my servant when you saw him this morning?' 'That was not a threatening gesture,' I replied, 'It was only a start of surprise. I was astonished to see him in Baghdad, for I had an appointment with him tonight in Samarra."

Death is a woman. Accurate considering the Latin noun for Death is *mors*, from the genitive *mortis* of feminine gender. I didn't *always* ogle the brunette. Sometimes I listened.

It was enough reading for one night.

## ANACRUSIS

I GRABBED THE keys next to the cell phone Virg left on the counter and locked the door behind me. The Aston Martin was still there when I came out of the lobby. There *was* a guy cleaning a knife inside and even though the windows were tinted, I could definitely see what he was doing. I don't know why but I approached him. He saw me suddenly, dropped the knife and peeled out, kicking up old newspapers and garbage like some bad guy in a mystery thriller... his plate was *Da King*. What a loser.

Ring a ding ding my leg vibrated. What the hell was this? *Kumquat uPhone*. Did *I* feel like an idiot... this whole time I thought it was *Grape*. Tom–*a*–to, Tom–*aā*–to, some truths aren't really worth pursuing, the trick is to distinguish which *are*.

The word VIRGIL and a picture of him acting like a mime with his tongue sticking out from beside the cigar resting on his lip stared back at me through the screen and a green rectangle told me to *slide to answer.*

"Go for V."

"Where are you? Stay away from the bars. I need you to stay sharp..."

I looked around, "You drive a black Aston Martin?"

"What? No! I wish!"

"I'm at home," a car whooshed by me and I hoped Virgil didn't hear it over the horrendous connection of this mediocre device, maybe it was the trillion dollar network; he wasn't able to hear me even now.

"Good. See you tomorrow at eight."

"Thought you said in 48 hours."

"Sharp as *eva*! Seriously though, schedule's moved up..."

"I'll be there."

A red rectangle now told me to *end*. I tapped it, hoping I would.

The wind crowed something I couldn't make out. I needed to sleep but I hated going to bed. I hated getting up even more. I preferred the hallucinations to the nightmares.

Like all things, the midtown of a big metropolis is most pleasant just before dawn, a little after optimal darkness, depending on how you define 'pleasant' of course. The lessened hue of stale pizza and mediocre-at-best Cosmicloots coffee is not as prevalent and most importantly, there are no hipsters with red Zara skinny jeans and Ray-Ban wayfarers (some of them still on long after the sun has set), or trust fund white-boys with snapbacks and XXXL t-shirts and loose Rocawear jeans.

A dead cigar crunched under my loafer. I thought of Virgil. I tried opening the door to *Yore Amici*—the local dive. Clank. A door-wedge nearly stopped me from entering, some literary symbolism? Maybe I shouldn't go in, drinking is a vice, a vice in excess, maybe I should take Virgil's advice… the worst vice is *ad*vice.

I forced the door open. It was no mystery, no plot-twist, my weakness was the firewater Machiavellians use to manipulate dames, and if I was lucky, it'd be the end of me, and I'd *leave Las Vegas*.

"Sit anywhere you like sir," the bartender and I were already getting along.

"Kentucky bourbon," it was one of those nights.

"We're about 20 minutes to last-call."

"Lucky me…."

There was another loser wearing an over-the-shelf Harry Rosen or Fifth Ave. sport coat and yellow polo with an absurd Mohawk eyeing the only other customer in the place, an attractive honey sitting alone at the end of the bar. I didn't look over but my peripheral vision was more than enough to see that she was worth knowing in different circumstances.

The coaster danced like a figure skater before Nicole—the bartender's name, etched on a silver chain hanging around her neck —put the glass on it.

"Last call," she looked at the banana.

"One Appletini for me, and a ..." he looked over to the dame at the end of the bar, "Whatever she's drinking for her."

Last call. It was about that time. He'd probably been drinking liquid courage all night, waiting for his chance to hit on her. I had little choice in assuming he was a three-time loser with a wad-of-cash to wave around and a bozo smile to boot. About to prate his many accomplishments as a man of the world and his travels among the world's top markets.

I couldn't see her from where I was sitting, his pudgy demeanour blocked her slim build; I thought I felt her glance over to him, "Not..." she sniffled, "Tonight," I saw her through the mirror of the bar, her face was buried in her chest, staring at her chalice and playing with the pick that held the lime in her glass. She sucked on the lime for a bit and ate its skin.

"You okay sweetie?" Nicole seemed like the best kind of bartender: pretty, funny, young, and compassionate.

"Yes... I think," the angel replied in a silvery voice as she rubbed one of her puffing eyes with her index finger, "I couldn't sleep."

Join the club, I thought, followed by an intense chill down my back that her voice sounded eerily familiar.

"*Come*... oooon," the chump desperately turned to her, "You said you were okay just a second ago."

Jesus, give it up you pathetic excuse for a human being. I looked up from the brim of my hat for the first time and spotted Nicole's discomfort. Who was this guy? Some *yolo* or *swag* wanna-be *Justin Bieber* or some resident clown that escaped the circus minus the funny jokes?

"I know what'll cheer you up," his hoarse voice *was* the funny joke.

I inadvertently growled, his shoulders propped back and he caught my glance. I stared right back at his eyes; they were shallow and shuttered, having never housed any real depth, "What does a man have to do to get a quiet drink in this city?"

"Mind your business cowboy," he was my favourite kind of puss-cake, the kind that thought of himself as a tough-guy, some 80s macho mix of Arnold or Stallone.

"Don't make a display bigshot, displays aren't becoming of everyone," my voice was calmer than I would've liked. I didn't want to come off as a psychopath and scare the babes.

"What's it to you tiger?" the little nicknames he thought were making him sound hardened were really getting on my nerves.

"She's not interested. Drink your Cosmo. Pay Nicole. Then get the hell out of here," another sip of the Inferno, it went down smoother than I anticipated.

"You can't talk to '*me*' like that!?!?! I'm a day-trader," actually I took back what I said, he *was* kind of funny, he thought that meant something to me, as if he was supposed to be allotted some respect because he did what society had deemed appropriately respectable.

"Then tip Nicole handsomely," the rest of the Inferno burned through my heart all the way down to my pathetic soul.

"Hey! Look at me when I'm talking to you!" he hissed.

He seemed quite keen on spending the night in the ICU.

I signalled Nicole for a refill and slowly turned to him, "I heard you, you're bragging about being a legal thief. What was it... commodities trader? ... Pfffft, you enervate your victims as you pounce from one deal to the next with your dick tucked between your legs with all the people supposed to be watching the planet in your pocket. You stuff the air, pollute the water, and eventually bees' honey will taste like metal from the toxic onslaught you assholes pump into the air. You move faster and faster. You don't want anyone to think, to prepare, you negotiate with futures, buy, sell, trade, short, exchange collars... when really... there isn't a future for any of us."

The staredown went longer than he wanted; he reached inside his boasted sport coat and paid. Cash. 20s.

"Schmuck..." Okay okay, I'll give you that one, I was having fun.

He slipped off the tall leather chair and I saw the angel for the first time, only it wasn't the first time I'd seen her. She looked familiar to me.

"Thanks," Nicole said for the both of them.

"Don't thank me. I just wanted some quiet."

She put a half-filled glass of the bourbon on the table and filled the beaut's drink up as well, "On the house."

I looked at the end of the bar through the mirror; her eyes were bloodshot with the kind of fierce cherried foreshadow that I imagined resembled a burning heart. I didn't know angels could cry. You learn something new every day, even if it's the kind of thing you'd rather never know for eternity. The kind of thing you'd sell your soul to forget.

"He's probably some addict looking for one-night of fun. Men like that are addicted to control, to power," she looked at Nicole, "And the only... interesting men are interested in other things," she looked at me through the mirror for a second, or was it a hallucination?

Addiction is an interesting concept. We say someone is addicted to alcohol, addicted to sex, or addicted to drugs, but all of them are outlets for the most addictive human impulse: love, the master addiction, and she fed *my* master addiction with every glance into my eyes.

Virgil's 'Young Man's Disease' echoed in my mind.

I was trying to do the right thing, if the right thing could ever be deduced and done in this world.

She quivered as she took a sip of her drink: a dry martini with three olives, shaken with lime I presumed. The red lipstick left on its brim made my heart pounce.

"I couldn't sleep," she moved a seat closer. There was only one empty seat between us now. I needed a sip of the fourth circle of hell to think clearly.

"Join the club," gulp.

"It was weird. I took a walk in a cemetery. I don't even know why, something drew me there," she closed her eyes and exhaled, no doubt thinking about the graves she'd walked by.

Who the hell walks through a cemetery in misty, drizzling weather at three in the morning?

It was only a matter of time before Nicole would come and tell us to leave, closing time was around the corner.

"A cemetery? That's not foreboding at all," I think I walked through a cemetery once. It was a Wednesday.

"Thanks by the way, for getting that idiot out of here. He was staring all night. He hit on the bartender first. I just wanted—"

"A quiet drink?"

"Yeah!"

"It was no trouble. At the time, all I wanted from this world was silence."

"At the time? And now?"

"I never think that far ahead," I wanted her. She crawled into every bit of me and had her way with my thoughts, my being, and my very existence.

I moved into the empty seat and turned her chin towards me with my thumb, her eyes were a little swelled from the tears she'd let flow at whatever caused the pain I'd believed was impossible for such a beautiful woman. Her sleeveless dress brought out her snowy shoulders and her neck had the enigma of a desert, a mirage deluding you into thinking you *can* win the Cartesian duel.

I tried to spot a single flaw, just *one,* and I couldn't, which only made me feel worse. I wanted an excuse to walk away. I *needed* an excuse to walk away. Charlie Sheen may be an overcompensating gigolo cokehead, but that doesn't make what he said about hearts untrue.

But really, deep inside the far recesses of my subconscious, I knew why I wanted to find a flaw with her. I was afraid, and the feeling was entirely new to me. I was afraid that *Paradiso* was a lie, a forsaken veil like justice, happiness, or faith.

The rest of the bourbon went down like water and my thoughts became clear. We can't fight who we are, go to war with ourselves, we'd only end up losing ourselves.

"Why were you crying?" was I being sadistic? Or masochistic?

"Many reasons," her nostrils flared momentarily as if she caught the catalyst of reasons deep within herself. If tears could build stairs, I'd be up in that imaginary *Paradiso* with her.... Such hope is for children.

"Whatever they were, they aren't worth it. It's never worth it. Angels like you shouldn't cry and deprive us of your liquid irises. I know it's difficult, you have no idea how much I know, but you shouldn't corrupt your halo because the world is miserable and greedy," the water tasted like bourbon again. 'Young Man's Disease,' Virgil's chuckled in my head again.

"I seem to be only attracted to men that are bad for me."

Masochistic, it was definitely a masochistic move.

The best idea was to walk away. Slap a 50 on the counter for Nicole and walk out the door; men like me never get back the things they've lost.

But since when was I a-best-idea-kind-of-guy?

Her lips tasted as sweet as warm morning honey. I whispered in her ear that I was hoping this feeling would go away, that she'd forget about me. Her hand tapped against my leg and she left it there. I backed away, locked in a stare with her. All I could think about was my final walk in the cemetery.

Hope is life's great big lie. There is no light at the end of the tunnel; the light only shows you how great the darkness can be before surrounding it like a void, how meaningless and insignificant your actions and life have been. The numbers at the end of your bank statements mean nothing. Your Kumquat phones are no longer of use; they don't have wifi in Hell.

I closed the door behind me. The sound of the igniting match flickered my thoughts in the darkness. She lit a cigarette, its orange ember in sync with my breathing reminded me of the fire I saw from my F-15 on that day; the men, women, and children turning to dust. I took the cigarette and inhaled harshly, blackening my lungs. The universe and I stood together in still darkness.

She zipped up her tight wine-coloured leather jacket. It suited her athletic body, but hell, not many things, with the exception of XXXL t-shirts, loose pants, Ray-Ban wayfarers at night, and Zara skinny jeans would make me look at her with anything less than absolute astonishment, and even then, it wouldn't be for a lack of aesthetic reasons.

She was an African sunrise over a secluded European lake. "What's your name?"

"Lauren, but it's spelled L-O-R-Y-N-E."

When I was young I imagined life was like a movie that you could stop and rewind whenever you wanted, and start over from wherever you pleased. I soon realized it's more like a live-play. A tragic comedy that ends when we're waved off stage when that red light goes off, signalling that inevitable stroll in the cemetery.

"Yours?"

"My friends call me Vi," it was *that* kind of city; *Kristine* was Christeen and *Cindy* was Sindee.

"Like the movie?"

"I guess so."

Her pupils dilated. She bit her bottom lip. Every part of me wanted every part of her, and I wagered she wasn't feeling any different.

A migraine arrived like a Caribbean plane coming back from vacation, gift wrapped with pink ribbons and a hangover that'd arrive right on cue in the morning, or now, depending on the perspective.

If they gave out degrees for stupidity, I'd have multiple PhDs by now.

I kissed her again. The breeze lifted her into my arms. I ran my pinky finger down her cheek where I felt one of those abysmal tears that'd been loitering on her Olympian face. My heart sank like a submarine. We could probably see a shooting star over the Milky Way if we were standing over that secluded lake in Scandinavia, but we weren't. We were standing in a land of urine, consumption, and greed.

The burden with holding dream girls in your arms is that they eventually become real. For some reason I thought about *Faust* when our lips locked. Like having made some deal with the devil: unadulterated passion in exchange for my soul. I'd sign that contract in blood gladly. I don't know why I thought it but that's where my mind went. You don't choose how you feel.

"What are you thinking about?" her golden eyebrow arched perfectly in reflection of her curious heart.

There was no reason to lie, "Faust."

"Goethe?"

"Yes."

"I've been meaning to read it… in German though. How is it?"

"Complicated."

"You seem like the kind of man who'd read Faust in—"

The wind howled something in my ear I couldn't quite make out. Metropolitan cities feel the same everywhere: stale pizza and bad coffee meshed with a riveting coldness crawling up your bones and never dissipating no matter where you are or what time of year it is. Construction noises sledge on your head like a drill piercing your brain, or cops try to guide traffic but instead make things worse. I looked back into her eyes unable to pinpoint the colour. They looked as expansive as the universe, constantly increasing in depth. That shooting star over the lake was sounding better and better, perhaps this *was* the opportune moment. I'd never been that lucky.

# CANZONETTA III

ENTRY NO. 12, 193.

Time: 11:47 P.M.

Disposition at time of entry: restless, fatigued, desolate.


I did some research and finally learned where dreams come from. I had to make a note while I was talking to Elise (who looked fantastic) and her *boyfriend*, bodyguard, or whoever he is. I've now met him face to face and cannot *bump* into him again to avoid suspicion.

Dreams come from neurons firing high-voltage impulses into the forebrain. I can't really pronounce or spell it properly but I will make the attempt: acetylcholine neurons?

Moving on, these impulses become what we perceive as pictures. The real mystery is, *scientists* don't know why specific pictures are selected, perhaps they should request more funding for other, useless studies, they hypothesize that they must be randomized, for what deranged mind would *choose* to have nightmares? Finally, our sensations of these pictures become our dreams.

At the same time, I looked out to the party and noticed all the other people there, each faker than a starlet's chest. I couldn't detect a single iota of sincerity in anything anyone was saying, other than Elise, who repelled everyone's desperate advances like a warrior princess. She would've been a great friend to Elsa, and could've also formed a perfect social circle with Helen. The three of them are very similar.

# Empfindung
## Two months ago

FIRST DAY ON the job. Virg and I drove to the estate together. He told me he's met some pretty girl, thinks she might be the one,

"You have no feelings Virg. Don't lie to the poor dame because you want to get in her pants," I snapped at him. I abhor liars.

He took a big drag of his cigarillo, smoke filled the air as each word left his mouth, "Au contraire mon frère, I've fallen in love thrice: once in Toronto, once in Stockholm, and once in Aruba... with the same girl."

"This dame?"

"Yeah," he took another drag of his cigarillo, the Partagas smell overrode the new-car smell and made the Benz smell weird.

"The clients don't mind the smell?"

"Yours does, that's why you're getting the girl. She can't stand smoke—she's the prettiest girl in Sweden—and you're the only one who doesn't smoke. Don't worry, she has her own car."

"You've already said that," the prettiest girl in Sweden? Anytime I've heard anyone described like that it's been some gross exaggeration or some Hollywood bimbo who's pumped so full of silicon she was in danger of becoming a self-aware AI.

"Have I? I forgot," he laughed, "I just want you to know how beautiful she is."

"Whatever," since when does Virgil care about the women I deem attractive? Does he see me as someone superficial, some who only pursues beautiful women? If he was right, was it wrong? Doesn't everyone pursue the people they've deemed 'beautiful?'

"Since when does Mack smoke?"

"Cigarettes. Winstons."

I'd asked *when,* not *what.* He wasn't listening, seemed nervy. We exited the car and walked towards one of the houses on the estate —there were a total of three, the big one in the centre I assumed belonged to the judge. My gait exuded reluctance. Virgil grabbed my bicep and pushed me to the left of the path while he continued straight ahead towards the centre manor.

I noticed cameras all around the house, except the wire that went around the corner and didn't connect to anything.

"The cameras don't work. Get some new ones... good ones."

"How did you... never mind," he pointed me forward with his stare.

I walked up the front steps and looked at the antique 15th or 14th century Venetian door and the words 'justice is blind' scribbled above the top frame. I looked it at and then back at Virgil, who hadn't moved from the part of the path that split into three and instead just stood there and watched me. He waved me forward, trying to whisper but really screaming,

"Go on, she's expecting you."

I don't think she's expecting *me*... how would she know what to expect? I don't know what to expect of myself, of my being, and she's expecting *me*? *You're really reading too much into a simple idiom. Get a hold of yourself.*

I read the mantra as 'abandon all hope, all those who enter in.' There was no doubt about it being the gateway to Hell.

I pulled the doors open like an Italian knight about to proclaim his love. The doors separated down the centre and the sun sizzled my nape, making me look like a dark mystery man about to save some damsel in distress... '*Young Man's Disease.*'

I thought how *'justice is blind'* had a wonderfully executed deceptive double meaning, the meaning *they* want to pass on, that justice is blind to circumstance. That is, it's objective. It doesn't care where you're from or how much money you have in the bank. You break its rules and you're going to pay, simple, effective, easy on the ears, but that's hardly what truth is. The second meaning is much more convoluted and dense, justice is blind means that justice can't see what's right in front of it, corrupt judges and politicians hold it up and it smugly holds up the scales. Only an idiot would think the amount of money in your checking account or your popularity in the 'society' page is irrelevant if you broke one of Madame Justice's arbitrarily rules.

The place looked bigger from inside. I looked around, a hardwood floor underneath Persian rugs. A spiral staircase that I assumed had gold-plated rails. A marble kitchen, a handmade coffee table in the den and an antique violin sitting in a display case in the corner of the room. I slowed down as I approached a small wooden round table with a shelf sitting in the opposite corner of the violin. The folded newspaper on it caught my attention. It was turned to the astrology and crossword page, most of the answers were filled in —with a green pen and in the quintessential penmanship of a woman who has too much time on her hands—except for 25 across: "Zero," 3 letters, and 64 down: "Idea," 7 letters. Near the crease of the fold were the day's horoscopes, and for some masochistic reason, I glanced under *Leo*.

*'You love the spotlight and this confidence means you're popular with the opposite sex. You're happy and successful, although at times you feel quite introverted. Be wary of femme fatales. Do not trust easily.'*

It was general enough to be specific. I chuckled throatily and let out this desperate yelp that I didn't know I was capable of. This proved the myth of astrology as nothing more than a pseudo-supernatural fallacy with little to say other than over-generalized assumptions that the stars' positions at the time of your birth affects your destiny. Another method of social control, misinformation and delusions fed to the sheeple as tall tales of coveted insider-knowledge.

I detected movement outside. Someone shuffled something in the swimming pool area past the den. I approached to the sounds of ice cubes falling in the bottom of a big glass.

A dame. Tanning in the winter sun sporting aviators like Mack's, her nipples so hard they could cut diamonds.

"Nice hat," were her first words to me as she adjusted herself on the beach chair. The wind caught her hair and it sent a wave of euphoria up my nose, ablaze with a crimson foreboding of things to come. A natural and alluring blood-red straightened to perfection and parted to one-side—my right, her left, perspective is important. Her eyes were a sort-of mix between aqua-blue and hazel-yellow that I couldn't quite identify. Her body was toned and hued behind an overtone of a peaches-and-cream complexion; she was the perfect depiction of what underwear models define as 'attractive.'

She flexed her flat and defined abs as she got up. Her legs reflected her dedication to fitness and her shoulders were at worst enigmatic, athletically built but still ladylike; it ached to look away.

I watched her walk over to a small glass table 3 or 4 steps from the beach chair, she picked—

"You're the strong, silent type aren't you? ... Grrrrreeat," she mimicked Tony the Tiger voice from those God-awful cereal commercials.

She took a sip of the steaming hot chocolate she picked up from the table, leaning closer to me to catch my eyes from beneath the brim of my hat, "Not bad looking though, *if* you didn't hide those pretty eyes behind that stupid hat. This *ain't* the wild west *pardner*. No *YEE-HAW* here," she mocked me, and I kinda liked it. I would've cracked a smile, if I could remember how to do it without looking awkward and insincere.

She sighed the chilly air, shivering suddenly when she took another gulp of her hot chocolate, which probably burned her tongue. Her teeth clattered together.

I put the towel and robe around her and guided her in.

"... *And* a gentleman, my my. My very own cowboy knight. No. Knight cowboy? Rebel knight? Hmmm, we *have* to think up a name for you."

"My name's Vero Madame, everyone calls me Vi."

"… And it talks… Can I keep it daddy?" she clapped her hands together coyly and bounced up and down, her rounded C-sized breasts imitating a young man's dream.

"Funny," I pushed the brim of my hat up a little with my index finger and followed her into the minimalist marble kitchen.

"Drink?" she went on her tippy-toes to reach into the cabinet and grab two glasses from the top.

I thought I hallucinated it, whispered it, or just flat out didn't say it, but I actually said,

"Bourbon."

A slip. I can't remember the name… with that overeager and sexually repressed psychoanalyst. Besides, a drunk never passes up an opportunity to quench the thirsts of the conscience, not when you could get some Dante's Inferno in a glass. Hell, I was past the gate anyway, already four or five circles in, might as well had made it official.

"Vero, it's 7:45 in the morning, I'm not giving you alcohol."

"My mom called me Vero. Call me Vi Madame," a rage crept up and started welling up inside me.

"Well *Vero*, my name's Elise."

Did she just say *Elise?* No. She didn't. You hallucinated it.

Say something you goon.

… SAY SOMETHING!

"… Like the sonata?"

"There's a *song* named *Elise*? What was the guy … deaf?" she must've misheard me.

Coy. Dry. Witty. Beautiful. Perfect. I couldn't remember why I took this assignment. I felt lost. Alone. Isolated. I wonder if there's anything like a pretty dame to elevate you from the drowning sorrows imprisoning you in the twilight zone.

"Actually Madame, a *sonata* doesn't have lyrics. The name of the piece wouldn't matter."

"I know," maybe she heard me perfectly; maybe she was just teasing.

Dames... let the mind games begin.

I stood in the kitchen as she walked through the house. Her bare feet softly touching the hardwood floor in the main room. I followed the sound upstairs before she reappeared back in the kitchen. Her legs went on for light years. She bent down into the fridge. I *had* to look away. Her body. Her face. She looked... I couldn't even conjure up a comparison to describe who, or *what* she looked like.

"There we are!" she jumped up abruptly, "Apple juice. Breakfast of champions," she said while flexing her bicep.

"The breakfast of champions is the opposition Madame Phoenix," I snickered.

"Hmmm. Clever," her voice lowered my heartbeat to a whisper, but she was a corrupt judge's daughter. What the hell was happening? I seemed to be lusting after her because on the surface she was beautiful. Come on! I'm smarter than that.... Aren't I?

I took the cup from her hand. Our fingers touched for a second and hers lingered there. I slightly remembered why I didn't want to push the button, but couldn't remember if pushing it was worth it in hindsight.

"Thank you Madame."

"Call me Elise."

I can't. I couldn't. There was no way I was *ever* calling her... Elise.

"So no bourbon?" I needed to take the edge off. Old familiar feelings were creeping around in the back of my head, and I didn't like them one bit.

The old man's whisper, 'You're an animal,' repeated in my ear continuously like a techno beat.

"Still only 7:49 Vero."

And I take it she wasn't going to settle for calling *me* Vi. We'd get along just fine.

"I lost track of time. I don't sleep much."

"Who *can* these days?" She ate a multivitamin and washed it down with Perrier before disappearing up the stairs again.

I gulped down the apple juice and took my hat off, my fingers tingled as I ran them through my hair.

Moments later she reappeared in the staircase adjusting an earring wearing a long elegant black dress and a black overcoat matched with a small leather belt. Her earrings were small diamond studs resting on her ravishing ears.

She saw me distracted and quickly threw a laser-cut key at me. I caught it with my left hand, catching a glimpse of the Land Rover logo etched on the big black piece as it flew threw the air.

"Nice reflexes," she smiled, "You're driving."

That *was* part of the job description. I looked at the key for the one feature that matters in all vehicles: the remote starter. She picked up the paper and we walked to the garage.

"Step behind me Madame," I pressed the ignition button on the key. Actually, to *press* the ignition button is to hold down both the *lock* and *unlock* buttons. The car hummed to a start.

She scoffed, "It's *my* garage Vero," pushing past me to get in. I walked faster than I wanted so I could catch up to her and get her door. That wasn't part of the job description but it *was* part of my identity.

"Such a gentleman," she got in.

A Land Rover Evoque is comfortable. A powerful engine with enough luxuries on the inside to barely justify the ridiculous MSRP for a hunk of metal those thieves charge at car dealerships. We were barely past the estate when I caught her in the rearview staring at the crossword.

"Idea… Idea… I've got an —. … Damn it!"

"It's *concept* Madame."

"What's that Vero?"

"The answer. Seven letters. Idea. The answer is 'concept.'"

"Concept…" her hand scribbled in the answer, "You're right!" she sounded surprised.

"Let's see how smart you *really* are," great, she was the competitive type. Everything was a game. What had I gotten myself into?

"Zero, three letters cowboy."

I sighed, "Nil."

"Who *are* you Vero?"

If you could answer that for me, I'd be infinitely grateful, "Just a guy." What I should've said was, 'I'm just a drunk,' but hey, you can't fault a man for a making a mistake, that's your God's job.

"We're going to Don's funeral. I forgot to give you the address," there was only one way in and one way out of the place anyway. You had to drive for 25 minutes before anything even remotely resembling a choice was presented. Makes you think about life doesn't it? Minus the pretty girl in the back seat of course, and you being the driver.

"I have it Madame," Virg texted it to me last night. If I could get this damn black brick to work, this awful contraption everyone idolizes, I'd know where the hell we were going. I tapped Virgil's name, "Calling Virgil," a computerized woman told me, "No no no you idiot!"

"Don't talk to me like that Ve-ro," the computer responded.

"What the…" did a computer just give me an order?

I caught Elise simper in the rearview. Actually, simper is a loose term to use, it was more like she was laughing so hard it wasn't even a laugh anymore, but more like an old man's silent cackle.

"Here, give it to me. What are you trying to do?" she took her hands off her stomach and reached towards me. The moments we were having always seemed to end too soon.

I took my eye off the road for a second and reached behind me, our fingers touched for the second time and a surge of electricity warmed my body, "Messages Madame, Virg… Virgil said he *texted* me the address."

"You tap 'messages,' then the name of the person who messaged you. You only have one message anyway, from 'Virg.' … And one contact! I'll add my number too, just so you have it," her manicured fingers tapped on the sweatshop-assembled glass before I felt her reach ahead and I grabbed the fancy paperweight.

"Thank you Madame," I read the screen and whispered the address to myself, "1666 Indevitatus Rd. Off of route 47."

"Sounds right," her eyes were still buried in the paper.

The *extrovert* in me wanted to know whose funeral we were going to, not that I minded going to funerals. They're pleasant for those who look for salvation in death or those who are constantly surrounded by it. You don't have to smile or pretend to laugh at some clown's jokes. You don't have to make small talk with any idiot overflowing with self-proclaimed vanity. Funerals were, sadly enough, the only place I actually felt like I belonged.

I escorted Elise into the place. A picture of a young man wearing a red polo was propped up on a tripod as we entered and it greeted us with its surrounding white flowers. He was *too* young to be dead, but that's life.

I spotted Virgil standing beside what I presumed to be the judge if his posture could be a reflection of his occupation, or if I were granted the luxury of *judging* a book by its cover. Virg gave me one of those *manly* silent nods. I spotted Mack standing shamefully in the corner as if he'd been crying.

I was alone. I looked around and couldn't find Elise. Great. Couldn't even keep my eye on a spoiled socialite. I looked around thoughtlessly before I noticed her approaching the podium, her elegance only fabled in stories of maidens, knights, dames, and queens.

"Don was my brother...."

Her brother? First day on the job and I drove the princess to her brother's funeral? I shot Virg a leering glance that he pretended not to see. Boy did I need a sip of Dante's Inferno. Don's probably enjoying it up there, or down there, wherever he is. Something about Elise's voice compelled me to listen,

"...We all know he was not a nice man. Everyone he knew probably hated him. I know him and I never got along, too many differentiating ideals, but that's the beauty of family. Even if you're on the opposite poles of the planet, you find a way to endure. You fight against the odds. You battle against unrelenting enemies who are not family... and that's why he was taken from us," she took a moment to collect herself, reciting the whole thing from memory or coming up with it as she went along,

"... After having said all this, I realize that although an infinite distance separated us as brother and sister, we were closer than both of us really thought. I've spent many nights thinking why things have been this way, and the best answer I could come up with is simply that the importance of family is paramount. We had many differences, but no matter what happened, who said what, who did what, Don never sacrificed the ideal of fidelity and loyalty. An ideal that extends beyond our mere physical embodiment and he always looked out for me as his baby sister. I hope that he will be the same loyal brother I always knew, even if he is no longer with us. I can only *hope* that wherever he is, he is drawn to protect some other, weaker soul."

Now I understood why Virgil pushed so hard for *this* to be my first day. Why he wanted me to start right away. He thought he was a master puppeteer, but all he was getting at was a cheesy matchmaker from a Hollywood romantic comedy. What was he trying to show? That she was also going through despair? She's also experienced death? He was slowly but surely getting on my nerves.

* * *

I saw her talking to some people during the wake afterwards and she handled things quite well. ... Better than I would have. Virg, the judge, and Mack all hovered around her inspired radiance.

I slipped away into one of the other rooms of this vast funeral home. The place was just morbid enough to qualify as a funeral parlour, something out of an episode of *Six Feet Under*, plain colours: either beige, tan, or a gloomy blue on every wall. Carpets with a sort of dead mushy hue, a very dark purple, blue, or just flat out black... even the hardwood parquet in the main room was dark brown bordering on midnight black. I slipped in and the door closed behind me. A solitary white piano sat in the corner, which was a nice change of pace from all the darkness in here. I wheeled the bench out and sat down, playing with the fall-board and with the thought of my dirge, for my mom, for Ethan, for Don. Death was everywhere. It was in every place, at every turn, when would it be mine? Living rendered me restless.

I put my hat on top of the piano, finally pushing the fall-board back. My fingers stained the newly polished keys as I touched them, stripping them of their purity. I tried playing Für Elise but couldn't get past the fourth note. I wasn't in the mood to do anything, apart from blowing my own brains out after a nice bottle of bourbon.

I found myself staring out the window in a nameless pain, forgetting what I was thinking about, especially as the door squeaked open.

"Vero?" Elise called.

I fumbled to put my hat on and rubbed my eyes. I turned around and faced her, "Yes Madame?"

"I'd like to go now. I'm tired of the people."

Aren't we all? "Yes Madame."

She locked her hand and elbow with mine as I escorted her out. I stepped in front of her and held the buttons together; the car vibrated to a start. The cure for Young Man's Disease was a thunderous needle that needed to be stabbed directly into the heart.

On the drive back I thought about the .38 and the flask of bourbon I was going to hide in the glove box when opportunity permitted. Each time I looked through the brim of my hat at the rearview, I caught her staring at me looking visibly distraught, her eyes the colour of her brother's polo in that picture at the door.

Finally she said, "Who *are* you Vero?"

"Madame. Please call me Vi," she wasn't going to let this question go, and I didn't have an answer. I never had an answer. How could I describe to her in *her* terms who I was when I didn't even know on *my* own terms?

"No one's ever called me Madame before."

"I'm not no one Madame," nice, what a goon thing to say. We're all nobodies you fool, but that means we're somebody right? And if we're all somebodies, then it means we're nobodies again. I hated thinking about this stuff.

"Vero, did you know an F15-E fighter-jet is 65 feet in length?"

Why was she talking about F-15s? Had Virgil said something? The coincidence would be too convenient if I simply attributed it to chaos.

"Yes."

"You did not know that! Don't lie to me."

"I hate to correct you Madame, but it's actually 63.8 feet long, with a wingspan of 42.8 feet and it stands tall at 18.5 feet."

I heard her tapping her phone, muttering, "No way you're right. No way you know. There's just no way," before she stopped in silence and flat out stared at me through the mirror, "How in the.... How did you know that?"

"Madame, I know you wish to make mundane conversation so you don't have to deal with the reality of what, of *where* we're coming from, but that's not... talking about planes with me will not make the pain any less bearable."

"You know about this sort of pain?"

"Someone dying of natural causes is fully understandable. You shrug it off and move on. Death is a part of life. But murder... someone taking your loved one's life is like this unrelenting rage that attaches itself to your spine and follows you everywhere. It's an overwhelming grief and unfortunately it doesn't get easier. Eventually you'll start wishing the person that died never existed in the first place just so you wouldn't feel this melancholy."

"..." it took a moment for it to sink in.

"Thank you Vero."

I flicked my hat to her gaze in the rearview, "Have you read Somerset's *Appointment in Samarra?*"

She shook her head.

# CANZONETTA IV

ENTRY NO. 11, 427.

Time: 7:38 A.M.

Disposition at time of entry: rather content, dare I write 'happy?' and vexingly overjoyed.

~

I've yet to go to bed even though the clock approaches 7:40 in the A.M., but this is not because of the insomnia, or the fear of the nightmares that bring me eye-to-eye with the victims' inquisitive gazes. In fact, it's been a while since my mind has seduced Elsa's lamenting cries echoing through the hospital walls.

I've felt it unnecessary to make any further entries until now, and I make this entry only because my journal continues to resemble the ramblings of an aberrantly withdrawn man with no chance of hope. This entry, along with the preceding entry will attempt to change that.

~

I took Cressida to *Raffinato* last night. She is quite sophisticated and a very smooth conversationalist. While it is true that her beauty is unmatched (many men turned their heads as we walked from the bar to the club, and one lobotomy victim even lifted his palm out in some social game butterflies call 'high-fiving,' expecting me to touch his hand as some denotation of respect or ecstasy). What makes her physical beauty even further striking is her intelligence, which shockingly, even gave *me* a run for my money. She argued that Mill's utilitarianism, although seemingly accepted by practically every powerful government, is completely unfounded and rather archaic. I wanted to feel her lips whenever they touched, making a sort of pouting motion each time she pronounced 'Mill.'

Our conversation took a turn for the better when the couple

behind us started talking about metaphysics, truth, and *science*. Suddenly, Cressida's supple ears perked up so she could listen. I will try my best to recite the conversation accurately.

"He has the right ideas. He's an utter genius!" the man said to his date.

"Genius is an understatement for a man like Hitchens," she nodded.

Cressida burst out laughing and turned around in her refined and smooth manner, "I'm sorry to interrupt your meal," she whispered eloquently as the *man* ogled her chest and midriff, "But did you say *Hitchens*?"

"Yes!" the woman practically screamed, her voice a startling contrast to Cressida, "He's changed my life, Hitchens' Razor is simply the most genius, original thought I've ever come across! He's a man of *truth*!"

"That's great," Cressida smiled, "I'm sorry to have bothered you," and she turned around and rolled her eyes at me, "What idiots."

"How so?" I asked, testing to see if she *actually* knew what she was talking about.

"Hitchens is easily one of the top-10 dumbest bozos to have walked on our planet, and that's saying a lot in this day and age. It's an insult to philosophers and intellectuals that he considers himself one."

"You mean he's *not* a man of truth?" I gasped. *Nil nisi bonum* crowded my thoughts.

"He's not, look at his *dull* razor," she looked around with her chin held high, "What is asserted without evidence can be dismissed without it."

"Go on," she had me at "Top-10 bozo," but I wasn't going to interrupt her.

"What's he's essentially saying is that he needs proof to believe some aura of truth. *Needs!* Like some narcissist, he needs it! Who is *he* to demand evidence!? Say I tell you 'I have my phone in my purse right here,'" she lifted her purse from underneath our table, "But there is no viable evidence that it's there, you have to take my word for it... it's idiocy; nothing more than a mere caricature of truth.

Such audacity in disregarding the pursuit of truth itself; valuing *evidence* has no bearing for fact. By his account, you have no choice but to dismiss my claim, that my phone isn't in there, since I've shown you no proof! But!" she pulled out her phone from her purse, "Tada! If my phone *is* there, that is, it is in fact a truth, then you've gone and disregarded this so-called truth. Your process is sophistical and arrogant rather than deductive."

"Seems like they haven't read Gettier's *Is Justified True Belief Knowledge*? And that's from 1963! These *questions* that they consider original have already been answered, and *dismissed*," I wasn't quite as dumb as I was making myself out to be. That's just what I was telling myself, I *was* a simple idiot.

"Oh... you understand," her serene voice was music to my ears; her eyes were a painting of the planet, lit up by the candlelight that eased my heartbeat still. Could I have won the lottery? Or was I dead? And this was simply an angel to guide me out of Purgatory?

The couple behind us heard enough to keep their fat-mouths closed until we'd left. Cressida wanted to dance and although I was reluctant, I took her to FACE. It didn't hurt my case that everyone there knows me and we bypassed the line like rap-stars in chest-puffed-full-of-hot-air mediocre music videos. I watched her mingle with the crowd and reject the coop of *men* that surrounded her, watching from a distance. I was exerting myself to the point of fatigue in order to keep up appearances, to appear average and common. Eventually she came up to me and asked over the deafening music if I was ever going to dance. I told her I didn't dance but I loved watching her, and she quipped that I'm trouble or something, that she should watch out for me, although I can't really be sure since I could hardly hear her over the blaring garbage through the speakers in the walls and ceilings. My dad would turn in his grave.

We hung out in the VIP room for a while until she wanted me to escort her back to my place and we watched the sunrise from my penthouse balcony. I was not particularly after a one-night-stand or meaningless sex and this frightened me. Perhaps I'm evolving... or devolving depending on which idiot you ask.

She finally fell asleep on my bed in her pretty purple dress after much conversation, and she breathes not three feet from me like some sort of perfect being cast upon our fragile psyches so she could push us over the edge: to illustrate some measure of truth or elucidate a true belief. I feel as though the ghost of Elsa, unable to descend down to this realm herself, has sent her loyal companion to try to make me feel as I once did for her. I thought about that razor theory again, wondering about Plato's theory of knowledge and Gettier's response to such theories. It works against this new quasi-philosopher as well. Could people be that dumb, not to know the history and chronology of various ideas and thoughts? Could they be that ignorant? In this world, it's a lock.

~

To business. Sebastian and Ahriman gave me last week's progress report.

They've been following the target. Well, target*s* now... and searching for a potential weakness. They have since confirmed that her *boyfriend* is in *fact* her bodyguard, and he is good; he never leaves her side and always maintains a viable distance from a safe exit and a potential flank position. They say he is quite vigilant and always alert. Ahriman suspects that he used to be in the army or has had specialized training. He reports perfect posture and even better coordination skills and reflexes. However, they vow that he will not be a problem, that he is a functioning alcoholic at best and a de-ranged philanderer, a regular at a bar near his Midtown apartment. We must first incapacitate the bodyguard by any means necessary before we can move on the target. And perhaps then, for the first time not through some acrylic glass window and old phone, I will feel the embrace of my grandfather.

Regardless of the reports, I will make calls to our inside men in the army, police, and other enforcement agencies to check for this mystery bodyguard's files. It is most favourable that the world is this crooked, otherwise my grandfather's organization could never have been able to infiltrate *all* levels of our fair city's infrastructure; if people acted with honour, respect, courage, and bravery, dire events would hardly occur. Even if at the root, the most crooked are the lawyers, politicians, and *non*-profits.

I have ranted enough. I will not lie, the description and talk of the target's bodyguard has piqued my curiosity. I must meet him, especially since he always wears that damn hat!

# TRADE SECRETS

'YOU'RE AN ANIMAL.'

Awake.

The thunder uprooted the lethargic brood I was dreaming of. I found myself in some dull hotel room and couldn't remember how I got there. I looked around, nothing in the drawers but the Gideon's bible. This was great, I felt like that morally inverted thug from Nolan's neo-noir, only I could remember why I had this constant weight anchoring on my conscience. A honey moaned and slowly rolled over next to me. Her hair covered half her face; she was pretty. I felt like Mack and wanted to throw up. I stealthily crawled out of bed and put my clothes on, missing a button on my shirt. This wasn't who I was, I approached the beauty and pecked her on the cheek. She inhaled deeply, whispering "Call me," before leaving on the Orient Express to the land of dreams and nightmares.

The half-open bottle of bourbon called me over and told me everything I needed to know. I didn't even bother checking the time and drank straight out of the bottle. There was no need for pleasantries. A party drunk drinks at night or a pre-party, a real drunk drinks when he wakes up.

Breakfast of *champions*. I asked myself where Samarra was and how I was to get there.

After I'd left I stopped for a moment in the hallway of the hotel. Room 814. I reached into my pocket for the silly contraption that proclaimed to have all the answers, a phone number also came out of my pocket. Her name was Trish.

I pressed the only button on the phone,

"Good morning Ve-ro, how can I help you today?" the computer said in a loud voice.

I unwrapped her gift: a splintering hangover, "Not so loud you inconsiderate piece of—" great, now I was talking to machines.

After about 16 or 17 tries, I finally got to the *messages* area Elise told me about and saw a message from her, '*I need you today Vero. Come to my place ASAP please.*'

She'd been in isolation for months. The judge wouldn't let her go out for fear of her safety but she didn't need me. I'd been doing just fine since I was still on the payroll, technically *on-call* 24 hours a day, drinking my paychecks at *Yore Amici*. Everyone grieves differently.

I stopped at home first, picked up my flask, my piece, and a nice cold shower. I didn't get enough sleep, I was still hallucinating. The girl with no lips laid on my couch, mashing the buttons on the remote control and throwing it at the plasma screen Virgil had delivered. It shattered, the pieces of the parquet mirroring the remains of my soul.

First things first, I emptied the .38 and slid the armour piercing bullet in. I spun the cylinder and cocked the gun, pushing the muzzle so hard against my temple it nearly left a mark.

I squeezed the trigger with purpose.

Click.

This changed nothing. Luck and I still despised each other.

\* \* \*

I entered Elise's house feeling like crap. The day's newspaper in the same old place, this time 38 across: "Rule, Restriction," 10 letters, and 65 across:     "Burned," 6 letters, were the empty cubes.

I needed a laugh. I glanced under *Leo*, '*You will find love,*' it didn't disappoint.

Elise came down the stairs looking at the end of a NASA telescope, shining and radiating an unspoken optimism despite everything that'd happened. How I longed to be blessed with *faith*.

"We're going shopping today. Is that okay Vero?"

"Madame, you don't have to ask me. You tell me what you need me to do and I'll get it done."

"I know, you just strike me as the type who doesn't take orders well. I'm always open to hear your input."

Yeah, Virgil definitely told her something. I'll pop him in the face when I see him. What didn't he understand? What was so overwhelmingly difficult that his thick skull couldn't penetrate, that this was just a job. I didn't care about the judge, about him, even about her, at least not yet.

She understood the routine now. The remote starter turned the ignition and I opened the door for her before I got into the driver's seat. The flask and .38 safely tucked away in the glove box. I actually bought a belt holster for the piece too, just in case she wanted to get out somewhere and I thought I'd need it. Sartre's *Being & Nothingness* and Camus' *The Myth of Sisyphus* were delicately placed under the gun and flask and *Simulacres et Simulation* by Baudrillard sat on the leather beside me for silent reading or recess.

I spotted the black Aston Martin coming out of the grounds and turned around to check its plate. It was the same guy. The driver's window was a little cracked and cigar smoke wearily puffed out. It was definitely Virgil playing some game. Maybe he was checking up on me, who knows what goes on in his morbid head?

"Gucci first, then Prada Vero."

"Yes Madame."

"Stop calling me *Madame*. It makes me feel old."

"Old, young, it's all the same," there is no time in life, no real lineal sequence of events that you abstract as memories and move in a straight line. Most people think time is akin to a river that flows surely in one direction, but they are wrong. All things occur in the same time, at once, but our minds are feeble. We are so stupid that we can't process everything at once, so we perceive it as best we can: linearly.

"Hm. That's definitely something to think about," she looked down at the crossword and sighed angrily.

"Limitation."

"What's that?" she unbuckled her seatbelt and leaned forward.

"38 across. Limitation."

I heard the pen against the paper.

"You're smarter than you look. There's always one, two, or three I can't get.        That's why I have *you*. ... Burned, 6 letters."

"Singed."

"S-I-N-G-E-D," she spelt it out loud, "Yes it is. Thanks Vero."

"You're welcome," I suddenly felt naked. I heard her shuffling behind me before I'd realized she'd reached to the front and grabbed my hat.

"Madame, please don't touch that."

She played with it, examining its wear-and-tear and numerous blemishes before eventually putting it on. She hid her eyes behind its brim, suddenly looking up at me through the rearview and then hiding them under the brim again, mocking me and voguing with her lips, "Looks better on me, no?"

It most certainly did. There was absolutely no doubt in my mind that it looked better on her, but that didn't mean anything. I'm not going to get attached to her and then lose her. The king's horses and king's men were off-duty inside me.

It's just a job. It's just a job. It's *just* a job. Just keep her safe between the hours you're with her. Go home. Drink yourself to sleep. Use the armor piercing shell, and if fate grants you another day, keep her alive. Simple. Easy to remember.

"Miss, maybe this isn't going to work out. You should hire someone a little more social, enthusiastic, or talkative."

She caressed the curls on my hair and put the homburg back on my head,        "You're probably right," staring at me through the rearview.

"But?" I could always sense an oncoming 'but'.

"I don't do well with orders either — wait! Stop here."

I stopped the car and she got out before I could walk around, secure the place, and open the door for her. She marched straight into Hermès.

Look up spoiled brat in the dictionary and I'd wager you'd probably find a picture of Elise. Daddy's credit card and the prices in here were absolute bargains: bookmarks starting at $315, card cases at $295, and the single greatest invention known to man: a singular pencil at the affordable price of $105. Yeah, a pencil for a hundred bucks. I stood at the door while Elise browsed and chatted up the cute employee about 'hot' fashion trends, new arrivals, and their 'coming soon' collection.

The entire store was glass. I looked outside and spotted an idling midnight blue Lexus behind Elise's Land Rover. I watched the driver and passenger from inside the store as I heard Elise's ambient conversation with the saleswoman. She was picking out a dress and some other stuff.

I pushed the brim of my hat up with my index finger to get a better look at these clowns.

Slide to unlock. Tap camera. Hit the picture of the camera. Snap. Now I had a picture of them, the quality wasn't that great but it was enough to remind me what they looked like.

Grand total before taxes: $5, 100. The figure was deceptive, because the *Les Cannes* dress Elise picked out was $4, 200 by itself, and on top of that she bought something called an *Amiral Thalassa* bikini for $530.

There was a doorman who did my job and opened the door for her. I stopped out in front of her and hit the remote ignition buttons while carefully watching the Lexus.

"You know those guys?" I nodded towards them, pointing to the car with the edge of my hat. The .38 itched my chest. I was waiting for them to make a move. I'd have dropped the shopping bags and drew faster than a post-modern *artist* who sells empty canvases.

"No… should I?"

The Land Rover started safely. I opened the back passenger door for her and took the shopping bags to the trunk, memorizing the Lexus' license plate through a reflection on the trunk window.

*H0M0MRTU5.*

My Latin wasn't nearly good enough to see what clever novelty or truth bomb this plate was trying to illuminate, but that's what you get when you sleep through your classes, periodically eyeing the gorgeous brunette in front of you in the rare minute you're awake. *Homo* is man, but what was he trying to say? … Whatever. I had no time for such trivialities. I got into the car and drove away.    H    e didn't follow.

Next stop was Gucci. She restrained herself and only spent $2, 300.

"We need to stop at home Vero."

"Right away Madame."

* * *

"Don't leave! I'm going to shower and get changed, then we're going out again."

"I'll be here."

Her feet thumped up the stairs. I followed her movement through the house by the sound of her footsteps, staring at the ceiling like some idiot in a Saturday morning cartoon.

Slide to unlock. Phone. Contacts. Virgil. Jesus, it's a damn *phone* and I could barely make a call. What happened to flipping your phone open and dialling the number?

"Más totopos," it sounded like he was talking to someone else in the background.

"Virg, it's me."

"Vi! How's everything with the broad?"

"Don't talk about her like that. What's wrong with you?"

"I… nothing, what's the matter?"

"What are we doing Virg?"

"Huh?" I don't think he was expecting this sort of intense conversation. Not now.

"She practically spent ten grand at these high end boutiques. 10 grand Virg."

"So?"

"Are you serious? Did you hear me say it was ten *grand*? That place we bombed, the death we caused. Those people were only trying to build a dam to get natural water, our government wanted them to keep buying our bottled garbage, so we were ordered to level the village… there was no terrorist there. *We* were the terrorists brother. We… were the terro—"

"Vi, I know… it takes some time, adjusting. Stay with it old friend. It's worth it. Trust me."

"All they wanted was water Virg. Water. Now we're protecting those who perpetuate the *in*justices on the planet. They're the ones causing this," I didn't plan to get so emotional but I was on the verge of tears. "Those people starve to death, famished for a slice of bread or parched for a sip of their own goddamn water just so some debutante can spend 10 grand at a European designer boutique? How is that justice?"

"Look Vi, I know it's hard, but we *have* to do it, or else *we'll* be parched, starved."

"Better them than us, huh Virg?"

"It seems that way. Listen, we'll talk after the party tomorrow, the judge'll be home so I'll be helping you keep an eye on the broa— client."

Idiot. *End*. The sound of the running water coming from upstairs somewhat relaxed me, as much as a man like me could feel relaxed at the sound of *water*. The dust on the antique violin in the corner meant it wasn't respected enough. What could these apathetic androids know about art or music? Draw a single line through a canvas and these post-modern goombahs call it *art*. The armour-piercing bullet felt tighter in my left jacket pocket, harshly pressed against my undeservingly beating heart. I used my handkerchief to wipe the dust off the violin. There was a little cube of resin slightly beside the stand. The bow was beautiful oriental equine.

It wasn't even in tune, it look me a second to tune it. Für Elise sounded sublime on it. This time, I got to the seventh not—

"That's beautiful Vero," Elise appeared behind me, squeezing water from the curls of her auburn hair onto a designer blue towel.

I crawled inside myself, hadn't realized the sound of running water had stopped until I consciously thought about it. She caught me off guard,    "Madame!" I put the violin back on the stand and caressed the bow sneakily before putting it in its rightful place.

"Please go on Vero. I wanna hear more."

"My apologies Madame," I adjusted my hat.

"The violin *and* the piano? What dreams were you forced to abandon by walking through my door?"

"Do you play?" I *had* to ignore her question.

"Me? No, some guy owed Don money. Gave him that violin, it'd been in his family for generations. I wanted to give it back to them but he never told me who they were."

Looks better collecting dust in the corner instead of some little five-year-old playing it in hopes of one day using that ability as a solace to claw out of the projects anyway.

"Are you ready to go Madame?" I went ahead and started the car. Elise had the shopping bags with her and put them back in the trunk.

My pocket vibrated. That stupid picture of Virgil lit up the little screen.

"Go for Vi."

"Vi. Don't trust anyone. Even cops." He was out of breath, "Actually, *especially* cops. This judge might be caught in the middle of a mob war. They got cops on both sides, *ON BOTH sides*, so on and so forth. Don't trust anyone."

"I never do," *end*.

"The floral shop Vero," she fastened her seatbelt.

"Where is that Madame?"

"Just drive. I'll direct you. ... Girlfriend?"

"Huh?"

"The phone call."

"No Madame. Virgil."

"What did he want? Anything important?"

"Just pointing out the obvious."

Who am I? I had to consider that maybe I was meant to be directed by a pretty dame. Meant to take orders, maybe all I am is a second-rate over-the-hill henchman for a spoiled rich girl.

I breathed deeply. Keep them in check. Keep your emotions in check. She's a job... nothing more.

"Halloween's coming up Vero. What are you going as?" I started getting the impression she didn't respect silence as much as I did.

"I never participate in such things."

"You never went trick or treating when you were a kid?"

"Never wanted to. It's a stupid tradition."

"Valentine's day?"

"Even stupider."

"Well elaborate... don't leave a lady curious."

I chuckled... weird, I never chuckle..." Very well, it's only *one* day when men and woman bask in respecting each other. The one day where men woo their women and court them, treat them like princesses or queens."

"What's wrong with that?"

"What about the other 364 days Madame? Why don't we live

each day as if it were *Valentine's Day*, or our *birthdays*, or Halloween. Why? Because we've been told to do these things on these certain days, if I try to woo you on Halloween, it wouldn't be allowed, if I wanted to trick or treat on Valentine's day or Easter, not allowed. Rigid rules for rigid social control."

"I never thought of it like that."

"I wouldn't expect you to," after all, you are a spoiled little brat who wouldn't know a coherent and rational thought if it was meant to protect your life.

Silence plagued the rest of the drive. I snuck a couple of glances at her through the rearview; she was good at pretending to contemplate things. I had to look past her physical perfection, to see her for what she really was, see *who*, she really was. A part of me wondered if she was actually thinking about what I'd said, about whether she could make a difference, but the thought was instantly hunted down and tortured by the little logic machine that roamed my thoughts constantly in search-and-destroy mode, repeating "No hope. No light," like a Soviet boot camp sergeant from the early 70s. Appallingly, that little guy was right most of the time. No matter how bad I wanted to have faith in a higher power, how obsessive I'd become in trying to find justice, truth, or something good on this planet, I couldn't, and I was forced to listen to the reason that little guy inside me spewed continuously.

"Here it is," Elise batted her eyelashes at the floral shop to our right. *Anjcent Floral*, the dot in the J *had* to be a flower and the Ls were rose stems, such things were expected. Marketing and advertising ploys by overgrown three-year-olds in expensive suits.

A black 750 Li with the plate "Byg Fish" was parked in front of us. We've become a pat-yourself-on-the-back, nationalist-butter-eating pansy country. Only in the corrupted thought process of a soft-as-a-feathered-pillow affluent businessman would the idea to put *Byg Fish* on your car come from. Let alone the actuality of the claim. He *really* might be a big fish merely because he makes more than a certain threshold of money in a given year. The big fish couldn't *possibly* be that coal miner in China or Chile, shaking hands with the devil inches from hell where any rumble might force your life to come crashing down upon you. No, that guy can't be the big fish, the big shots are the guys with the expensive designer suits smoking cigars in boardrooms. He was right, he was a big fish, but what his infantile brain didn't realize was that coal miners, bricklayers, or waitresses were the real sharks. They've been tamed, but you can't change who you are or your biology, even if it takes years to realize who, or what you are. May the money they idolize have mercy on their souls when these 'suckers' realize just how wolfish they really are. I pray their *God* takes American Express and frequent flyer miles.

I assessed the place, looking for threats and held the door open for her.

"Thank you," the elegance in her gait sent a jolt through my body as the metal hinges on the door shocked me when I let go of them.

The door chime juxtaposed the realization that I'd forgotten my piece and flask in the glove box.

At least the place smelled nice, a quick change compared to the sickening aroma of metropolitan sewage, fried processed cheese, and mediocre coffee that attaches itself to your being.

"Whadaya think?" she held a bouquet—fuchsia roses amongst red matsumoto asters, pink mini carnations, and lush greens in a little vase—up to my nose, my hat suddenly tilted back.

I wanted to ask her how she could ignore the things not 10 blocks from us if we'd kept driving, the grungy government houses with little kids playing basketball with ripped sneakers on some makeshift rim. How could she be indifferent to the slumlords using these kids as drug-runners?

"It's nice," is what my lips went with.

That was life. That moment, frozen in time with a bouquet of flowers in my nose and a pretty girl asking my opinion. Maybe there was something wrong with *me*; there probably was, but I couldn't pinpoint *what* it was. We live one day at a time, everything comes down to the present, to the now, to today, and even if it feels like hell, perhaps it might be possible to climb out, to force a slither of hope through its blinding fires. I looked at people's faces as they sipped coffee, as they brushed past me, as they smiled at me, and I wondered about my own life. I'd made every potential mistake. I've drank all my money, abandoned anyone that'd ever loved me, and I couldn't find a single positive thing about anything I perceived or thought about. I couldn't even stand what I saw in the mirror, I'd detached from myself, not knowing who I really was or what I was supposed to be doing. I'd just only realized that as I aged, life took everything from me piece-by-piece, bit-by-bit, and I'd only learned this after I started losing things. It was a game of seconds with no margin for error, half a second too late and the opportunity passed, half a second too early and the opportunity moved on. Seconds ticked away everywhere. I fought for each second, the things from my life—no matter how trivial—*sometimes* made me want the next second more than this one, I battled for that next second because I'd also realized that adding them up in Samarra *is* what a life is, no matter how tortured.

... "It's really a blushing display of kindness. It boasts pink and red perfection to convey your warmest wishes and," the saleswoman chattered at Elise. I had no idea I'd dozed off this heavily, any henchman could've marched right in and cut her throat and I would have been none the wiser. I wasn't losing it. I'd lost it.

70 bones for 19 stems. I remote started the car, putting the flowers in the back because I could no longer endure their smell. They served to remind me of Elise, and I didn't like what was happening to me. Before I pulled out of the parking spot though, I spotted the black Aston Martin across the street. It was doubtful that it was a different one, the smoke filling the air through a lightly cracked driver's side window nicked it as the one that'd been follow-

ing me. I reached into the glove box and spun the cylinder, sliding the single bullet behind the muzzle and cocking the gun.

"What's wrong?" Elise curled behind her newspaper.

"The… come sit here when I leave, if something happens, drive away."

"Vero, what…?"

I didn't hear what she said. I'd already gotten out of the car while she was still talking. I put my hand out to the honking cars as I crossed the street, the sun reflecting the cannon in my hand. A lit cigar slipped out through the window as the Aston's engine screeched away.

*Da King* who flees.

Who was this guy and what did he want from me? I saw Elise staring at me wide-eyed in the driver's seat. I nodded and walked back, holstering the gun, beating myself up about how dumb I was. He could've been the distraction, *da goon*, while anyone could ramble in and take Elise the second I left her. She was exposed for close to 50 seconds.

"What was that about?"

"Do you know anyone that drives one of those?"

"Maybe. I don't think so. Who was he?"

"I don't know. I think he's following us, but I'm probably being paranoid," I knew I wasn't *just* being paranoid. I'd seen that car too many times for it to be sheer coincidence, but there was no point in instilling fear into the heart of a socialite who's just looking to have a good time each and every day. The reality of the big bad world *should* be known to all, but since that's impossible, I might as well protect this one soul from corruption while I can. *That's* my job.

Funny isn't it? Good intentions … I've been told the worst roads are paved with it. There is no good or bad. Men aren't black and white like a film-noir, a good man doing a bad thing when no one's around is wicked, and an evil man performing a benevolent act at a critical time will be considered good. The rest is ignorance. In our monotone world idiots see everything as bivalent. Geniuses know nothing is bivalent.

## Canzonetta V

Entry No. 16.

Time: 1:27 A.M.

Disposition at time of entry: Amped, energetic, and too jolted to sleep. Fatigue is sure to follow this morning, but I can't abide.

A warrior always falls with a sword in his hand standing on the battlefield when the smoke clears, or slowly disintegrating into the dust that we are as the battleground hazes his path to Elysium.

I wanted to tell her the truth, but I knew deep down, knew somewhere submerged behind my progressively idling heart that the truth wasn't good enough. I'd understood that sometimes hope must be rewarded at the expense of truth, even if it means playing fast and loose with the thing I hold most dear.

I was not going to expose her to this life, condemn her to forlorn passions of hope and light when no such things exist. I wasn't going to let her observe the outlaw psyche. There's nothing for people like me but pain and despair, and if you're really lucky: holding pocket aces or the inevitable checkmate against the universe, death only appears as a relief to this infinite suffering.

This was not some chivalrous crusade like Michael Corleone trying saving his family at the end of *Godfather*. I hid the truth from her not because I considered my business above her but because I didn't want her to judge me by my business. We are *not* what we repeatedly do. I wanted her to judge me by the quality of my *soul*.

Downpour is soon upon me, and the blackened sky foreboding no tomorrow would arrive at the least opportune moment.

"You have that look in your eye again… what are you thinking about?" her seductive whisper brightened my thoughts for but a second.

"That flower across the road there, look... it grew through the concrete, and it lays there... alone, swinging wherever the wind takes it."

"It has to. If it stands tall, pretends to be rigid, the wind would break it, and it'd die. Adaptation is necessary."

"But what if it was meant to break? To test itself against all consuming forces and obstacles? To see how long it could last?"

"Funny..."

"I wasn't trying to be."

"I know, I meant it's funny because we seem to be pretty much talking about everything but the flower we *seem* to be talking about."

"No, *I'm* talking about the flower," I was lying, obviously.

"You never talk about one thing... especially something so mundane and average. Things can't ever be simple," and she saw right through me.

"You know Oscar Wilde was in jail once..."

"For what?"

"I don't know, being different I suppose, and George Bernard Shaw went to see him."

"That's... odd," she leaned in, hanging on my every word. I could smell her lip-balm: green tea extract with a vanilla scent.

"Anyway, Shaw went up to Wilde, reached through the bars with a kind of shrugged-shoulders-expression, curling his eyebrows, and queried,

'Why Oscar, what are you doing in *there?*'

Wilde sat up from his cot and turned to Shaw, staring at his visitor in disdain. After about 20 seconds of silence, he whispered,

'Why George, what are *you* doing out *there?*'"

"Wow... that's..."

"Yeah."

"I wonder how that story would be told from their varying perspectives."

"Oh?"

"Of course, each was placating the other for his impertinent aphorism. The circumstance of which, seems rather indignant," she used a lot of ostentatious words but that's hardly a fault.

"It's always better to observe from the inevitable, albeit flawed human perspective rather than try to gaze down on others from all-seeing ivory towers we create for ourselves."

Never. That was the answer. The truth was never good enough. It was never complete. It was never as comprehensive, lucid, or straightforward as we, books, or philosophies give it credit for. People like her deserve to have that fleeting hope rewarded. They deserve the ensuing tranquility that arises when they imagine that light at the end of their skies even if they are fatally mistaken. *Angels* should never be exposed to the dire darkness of despair in a tunnel of cosmic nothingness, and although I never believed such maddening thoughts; I couldn't help but feel spiritual in her presence.

"*Aave*," she flinched back abruptly.

"Is that some Finnish expression?" I asked reflexively before noticing her hand shaking inside my palm and turning colder than my heart, "You okay?"

"Ghost."

I would've burst out laughing if I was the sort of man that laughed. "Where?" I was going to humour her. Like I said, some people need protection from truth.

"Over there. Looking at your flower," she seemed to crawl behind me on the bench as if to hide from the apparition.

There was a peculiar looking, almost drunk noir-P.I. from the 40s gazing contemplatively at the flower we were talking about. It was clichéd; he was wearing an exemplary black suit, designer tie and belt matching his shoes. In fact, everything was black except his hat, which was a white homburg, and from afar, it looked like he was smoking a thin cigar. I didn't know what to make of it, he looked mystical with all that black, and the contrasted white hat made it even more eerie, as if it symbolized some halo above his head.

"Babe... the private eye from a 40s noir? Standing right over the flower with the hysterical fedora?"

"You see him too? Okay... that scared the life out of me," the sunrise returned to her palm.

The *real* question was, what if he *wasn't* real, and we both merely perceived what seemed to be a bending of space-time in the physical and spiritual realm? There truly is no basis for the categorical dismissal of parapsychological phenomenon, yet it persists, the question is not why, but how. The feeble ranting of seemingly educated madmen with little power, less brains, and even less potential? Besides, who was *I* to deny this truth should it turn out to be affirmed as fact in a distant future; even perhaps, a truth that *has been* affirmed in the minds of a few hitherto. Especially if she was the one to be ascribed such an ability, perhaps she was capable of handling the misery of truth after all, of being extracted from the jaws of this deceitful system. It seemed more likely however, that she was the one to extract *me*. After all, isn't that what angels, agents of fate, or women do? Redeem lost souls from the river of Hades as we paddle through our minds with oars of agony? What a crock... there is no redemption for some people. Elsa was wasting her time.

## LEGATO

HOME SWEET HOME. I found myself lying on the couch in shame, guilt, and self-loathing. I reached for the .38, checking to see if the single bullet was still in it. I spun the cylinder and cocked the gun. The cold metal tingled my jaw. I squeezed the trigger slowly. Click, no such luck.

It was Ladies Night at *Yore Amici*. Great, lots of boozed up women followed by the losers that spend their entire youth chasing them. I sat alone in the corner; fate might not want me to kill myself, but it can't do anything about me killing this bottle of Hudson Baby Bourbon.

Some dame in a pretty pink dress sat beside me, crossing her legs and rubbing her left ankle with her right calf seductively and her index and forefinger ran up and down her temple in her attempts to get some read on me.

"Long day?"

Long century. I lifted the bottle and asked the barkeep for a glass for my new drink-mate, "Bourbon?"

"Yes! Thank you!"

She was attractive enough to hit on after a couple of drinks and just seductive enough to be charming, now I wouldn't go as far as to call her some slut who's after some meaningless sex in this very moral society... but any woman who comes onto a guy slumped over a barstool drunk on self-loathing really needs to reevaluate her life.

She leaned in closer after a sip of the Bourbon while somehow pretending it was smoother than it actually was, "I'm Eloise."

"Of course..." I could smell her face cream and perfume: Chanel No. 5. She smelled great. She looked great. A carnal affair never hurt anyone.

We brushed past some *bros* on the way out; the resident air-heads of this fine establishment and I nearly threw up, not from the bourbon. I wondered about reality and I realized that each random clown, goon, dame, or honey that I came across lived a life as vivid and complex as my own. Each person was full of their own ambitions even if they're probably misplaced. Each has friends even if they're most likely fake. All have routines even if they might be irrational, and they all worry even if they're not things an intelligent person would worry about.      These stories are continuing invisibly around me like an eagle nest too high on a mountain peak or tree branch to see, with millions of other miles of skyline and passageways connecting to other lives that I would never know even existed.      A story I might've appeared only once as a random guy sipping bourbon in the corner, bumping into them on the street and nearly causing them to drop their coffee; as a random driver that might've triggered an epiphany in the blur of traffic, or a silhouette at dusk through an apartment window frame as they contemplatively walked by my place.

* * *

"Why did you do it Vero?" the little girl finally said as the old man cried in what seemed like the corner of this black abyss.

Awake. My irises dilated in some lavish apartment. A sunlit window make-shifted as a wall and the king-sized bed with light pink bed linens warmed my body enough to move. A naked Eloise with her back to me breathed as dames do: lightly and with importance, instilling the protector's instinct or wanting to prolong their breaths, their lives, and enrich them with every second of yours.

I'd just noticed that she had a gorgeous tattoo on her right shoulder blade. It was a tiger walking out of her body only it wasn't your run-of-the-mill *I'm-a-rebellious-teenager* tattoo, half of it—the right—was grey and monotone while the left was in full color: stripes and orange fur. She was smarter than she let on. I sledged up, hobbling to a chair and sitting down and looking outside through the huge window with the city beneath my feet. On the other end of the apartment was a black piano with Chopin and Liszt sheet music open on the accompanying easel. I tried Für Elise but it wouldn't come out right, maybe I was just a bad piano player. I found my phone on the floor in one of the other rooms along with our clothes, some weird-looking toys, and a... rubber duck? It looked like we had a lot of fun.

*Missed call: Virgil. Missed call: Elise. Missed call: Mack. Missed call: Virgil. Missed call: Elise.*

Looks like I missed out. *Slide to unlock. Phone. Contacts. Virg.*

"VI!" he screamed.

"What?"

"Mother of... are you alright?"

"Why wouldn't I be?"

"We've been calling you all day. We need you tonight. Big party at some hotel uptown. Charity function."

"Give me the address and time."

"I'll text it to you."

"Tell it to me. I don't like getting my information from a computer."

Virg was giving me directions and the name of the place, but I'd stopped listening, dozed off thinking about Elise, Eloise, and Trish and every other honey I'd come across. Meeting any of them always seemed to precede a downward spiral in my life. Perhaps it was best to stay away from dames, but without women, men are nothing. I, would be nothing.

"Text it to me."

"You just said—"

*End.*

A couple of seconds later the thing vibrated in my hand. The address and time of the party flashed back at me through the screen.

*'Harriet Hotel @ 9378 Moongrove rd. 9:00. DON'T B LATE!'*

Not bad at all. A charity function for starving kids in Africa at the number one rated hotel in the country. $350 chicken dinner and champagne so the ignorant buffoons at the place can feel good about themselves making a difference while the African kids they're supposed to be helping get less than 1% of the donations, living on grains of rice that could fit on your pinky finger. I was in for a great night.

* * *

My apartment had progressively started to disgust me. I didn't need the fancy couch, the huge bed, or the comfortable linens. I'd slept in the African sun behind enemy lines. I'd slept on a metal rectangle in jail, that's what *I* deserved... that's what *we* deserve. I had more than I needed. The Kumquat directed me to a *webpage* that allotted me the comfort of listing my crap to give away to some misunderstood idealist.

The buzzing of the spinning cylinder and the sound of bourbon being poured into a glass were the only things that gave me any real relief. I pulled the hammer back and put the gun to my temple. I pulled the trigger abruptly this time.

Click.

Maybe it was time to up the ante, to put another bullet in; it was definitely something to think about. The cold showers helped; the Hermès body wash, aftershave, and lotion agreed with my body, cooling down my thoughts and feelings about humanity. They call that an oxymoron.

The concierge knocked and brought up my tuxedo. Designer. Tailored. I felt like a hypocrite putting it on, like some clichéd amoral British knight, an exile from the island of Dr. Moreau, or a self-proclaimed tragic anti-hero from an obscure Lord Byron poem. I could've used a drink, but the first eight notes of Für Elise suddenly popped into my head and I suppressed the temptation as I tightened my bow tie.

I decided to take the train. The family had a car service on retainer but I liked the train, the rhythmic cackling and sound of little train wheels on the track were soothing. Sure I was out of place on the grungy subway with a designer tuxedo, but the average person understands the need to fit in, to want to belong, to have some sense of unity in a world of chaos. The average person also has no morals or principles. They'd give anything and anyone to have their fifteen minutes of fame and fit in like an oiled up jigsaw piece onto the big picture that is our fallen society. Seeing someone that seems to have become an out of place puzzle piece is rather pleasant, even if those same people would enviously step out of their jobs and offices to protest the lavish lifestyles of their bosses.

I was breathing in the toxic air walking towards the hotel lobby and had subconsciously been making notes of the cars parked near the curb. Everything changed once I passed a certain street: the stores, the cafés, the bars, and even the cars. I realized what I was doing and recalled a Bentley, a Ferrari, a Maserati, and a high end Lincoln before I got to an old Honda Accord. It was probably one of the *help*, the waiter or custodian in one of the many five-star places in the area. It wasn't the car that caught my eye but the bumper sticker: a light blue background emulating the sky with the earth cartoonishly drawn in the foreground, the words "Save the planet," scribbled in kids' writing beside it.

Pfffttt. *Save the planet?* What a joke. Save the planet from what? From ourselves? And save it for what? For ourselves? It was a kind of perpetual stupidity in a tug-of-war battle over trivial matters. Only imbeciles see things in black and white: liberal or conservative, yes or no, this or that, and those in power laugh at those people in their morally inverted shades of grey, basking in the labels they've created so the people are easier to control. It's easier to control a 20-year-old liberal or a 32-year-old conservative than it is to control Daniel Barnes of Toronto, or Lida King of Helsinki. Things are made simpler, less dense, and although to the average eye simplification is *always* a good idea, it's often the abstract and convoluted details that reveal truth.

The hotel elevator doors dinged to the party. I didn't wear my hat out of respect for Elise. I didn't want to seem *too* out of place, especially since I had to keep a sharp eye out and follow her everywhere, and the hat would only serve to *draw* attention to the two of us.

Light pop music played in the dimmed penthouse ballroom. Waiters offered finger foods to the undeserving chumps chewing them with their mouths open, tapping their designer wingtips on the hardwood in sync with the tune.

"Vero!" Elise marched up wearing a killer mid-length silk black dress and hardly any make-up—she sure didn't need it. She hugged me affectionately and pecked me on the cheek four times: twice on the right cheek, once on the left cheek, and once on the lips.

What the fu… "Madame, don't do that."

"SHHH!" she whispered in my ear, "I told them you're my boyfriend. We're going steady. That way I don't have to constantly fend off the advances of these pigs. Oh! And you were late because you had a business meeting or something. Make something up," and she smiled into the crowd at one of the *pigs* trailing behind her.

"Ahhh. Is this is the man of the hour?" some goon walked up to me and extended his hand. I squeezed it as hard as I could.

"Taking care of our Elise I hope," he was wearing a tailored dress shirt with the letters H.C.T monogrammed near his designer cufflinks.

I stared back at him, listening to the sound of his designer straps tapping the floor lightly, waiting for an answer that never came.

"I thought you were joking when you said he was the strong silent type," it smelled like he'd bathed with one of those expensive colognes. The weakness in the air vexed me; *these were the high and mighty of our society?*

Elise laughed nervously; an impeccably dressed waiter walked beside us with a tray of champagne glasses and she swiped three.

She handed me one, and the *man of the world* another, taking microscopic sips from her own.

"I'm Henrik," he looked and sounded like Goofy: the lanky Disney character with droopy eyes, flabby ears, and a slow-mannered voice that always sounded like he just shot up some Grade-A Afghan heroin.

It was well past the socially acceptable gap in which a budding conversationalist ought to have replied, but a part of me did it on purpose to keep this loony-tune on his toes, to know that I wasn't like the rest of them. I was in no hurry to boast up my wealth and conquests.

"Pleasure," I lied.

"So…" he slurped some of what tasted like Hiedsieck Diamant Bleu cuvée, 1907. And if I was as well versed in military history as I thought I was, its 2000 bottles were lost during the First World War on route from Sweden to Russia. Given as a gift to Tsar Nicholas II. "How'd you catch this unicorn?" they average around \$3, 700 a bottle. I may not know much but I'll be damned if I didn't know alcohol.

…

Wait, has he been talking to *me* this whole time?

"Well," Elise's fingers fiddled with the neck of the glass.

"Skydiving," I interrupted before she could answer.

"Sky… diving?" Elise raised an eyebrow.

"Skydiving?" Henreek was it? lifted his chin to match mine.

"Yeah…" I put my glass back on the tray of a roaming waiter, "I was skydiving once, the chute wouldn't open. I was screwed. I pulled the reserve… nothing, and I was falling to my demise. Elise suddenly came down from the sky like the angel she is and saved me."

"Wow," Elise laughed.

"I thought you were serious for a second there!" he took

another sip of the champagne, sucking and smacking his tongue like the classless pleb he probably was.

"I was," I wanted to catch the attention of a waiter so I could tip him and ask him for some bourbon.

"Seriously…" he had this innocent looking smile on his face. I didn't buy it for a second.

Elise wiped her forehead in hopes that I had a plan.

I scoffed, "Fine, you know those Norwegian Epic cruises? Oslo to Barcelona, to Florida? A bunch of countries and a bunch of cities with those big cruise liners?"

"Yeah…" he was too curious for me to take him seriously.

"I was on one of those a while back. I had a bit too much, stumbling up and down the deck. I found myself practically about to fall over the side of the ship. And eventually I did, just fell straight over with this 76 thousand ton ship tiptoeing away from me. It was a miracle I even survived. Anyway, wet, drowning, and drunk, I peddled for a couple of seconds hoping someone would notice. Then Elise appeared as a mermaid swimming up from under the sea, and she rescued me like the princess she is."

"You oughta' be a comedian… really."

After a few awkward moments of meaningless small talk about the weather, his degrees, and other trivial crap—I wasn't really listening—Elise took my hand and we started to drift away.

"I'm no good with people," I whispered loud enough to not be *officially* whispering, but low enough so no one could hear us.

"Yeah no kidding," she joked, but she didn't have to. I knew I wasn't sociable, likeable, or extroverted. It was the only part of myself I was comfortable with. Who'd want to be close to these schmucks anyway?

He was a little odd, after two or three glances towards the other guests, he reached into his jacket pocket and came out with a custom-made artist's journal, his initials: *H.C.T.* etched in what looked liked pure white gold. Rich fools love their names on things.

As he reached for it, I thought I heard the sound of a pill bottle rattling little pieces of euphoria into my eardrum, confirming my rather *goofy* suspicion that he was in fact on drugs.

"I've got to make an entry. Excuse me babe," he turned to Elise and then nodded to me. I watched him carefully. He walked over to the corner, whipped out a Mont Blanc fountain pen, and jotted something in the little notebook, occasionally glancing around him at the other guests. I have to admit, I was curious to know what he was writing, and maybe even what he was thinking.

Later, I found myself outside on the balcony leaning against the glass railing looking into the party, watching Elise mingle with the endless sea of potential suitors, all disguised as equity investors, lawyers, bankers, or doctors. It was a regular clown gathering, a bunch of monkeys juggling their balls. I threw the rest of my wine over the railing, carefully eyeing it pour down like rain. There was a homeless guy walking into an alley and he stopped and talked with another sleeping on a flattened box. I looked back at the party. The suitors, or goons depending on the perspective, tried to squeeze Elise into one of those erotic dances you see at local scumbag hangouts. The two homeless guys were splitting a sandwich one of them found in the garbage as I turned around for a second time.

An eagle cawed, or maybe I imagined it. It sounded nothing like that ridiculous "eagle's call" Americans have claimed as their own.

A happy clown inside spat out a pig-in-a-blanket and yelled at the cute waitress holding the tray. Nothing like seeing obscene poverty contrasted with prolific excess to make a five-star party on a rooftop seem *really* deserving. I had to throw up, but other than the banker's suit forcing its way onto Elise's face there really wasn't an appropriate place for it.

Elise came onto the balcony, every single *man*—if we can call them that—closely watched her departure.

"The pervs are watching aren't they?"

"Like hungry rats."

She laughed, "Hey! Don't insult rats. They're nice animals," she handed me a glass of….

Sip, "Apple juice?"

"Yeah… I get the impression your demons love to swim," she looked into the distance at the inky night sky. Her hair got caught in the chilling breeze and forced me to smell it. "Nice view huh? … Well…" she saw what I was looking at, "Except for *that*," she pointed to the homeless guys. Another eagle caw deafened me. I definitely imagined *that* one. She sighed and looked at me right in the eye, "I don't know how to deal with it Vero," and then she looked over the railing at the pavement.

"With what Madame?"

"With *all of it*. With *them*," she pointed to the party with her eyes, "With *myself*. With *everything*. I mean… they just want to screw me and then screw me over. Another notch in the ol' belt, have the *broad* and then throw her aside. I was trying to tell Patrick Johnson about African water shortages, how our government uses its military power to perpetuate poverty. They *have* water but they're forced to buy our bottled junk. We sell their own property back to them and won't let them build filters or dams without the threat of sanctions and embargoes…"

I wanted to take her hand and fly away like the eagle I imagined. I ached to free her.

"… And he laughed. Laughed Vero, like he was some Bret Ellis character."

I smiled at her, she needed it, "Most of those characters are satires, parodies. Ellis agrees with you," I never thought a woman like her would really be this vulnerable. Dames like her usually spend years building armours around their hearts so they don't have to *really* deal with anything, until one day, they forget there's something behind the armour at all.

"Wanna know the truth?"

"Yeah," she looked at the skyline as the clouds cleared the sky and it lit up with a delicate purple tint rushing through like a straight line.

"The world and the people in it don't want honesty. People *need* bullshitters: politicians, bankers, mafias, and magicians. They *want* to be subjugated and deceived. They're sheep," I followed the thin purple line across the sky, "They want to be told they're thin, that they can *all* attain the American Dream because they're a *little* bit better than their neighbour. They *want* to be told they're making a difference and doing something worthwhile even though they're not. Sheep need manipulators to pull their strings. They wouldn't move otherwise. People couldn't decide if they want their coffee black or creamed if we didn't lead them by asking 'cream or black?' They couldn't find their nose with both hands if we didn't lead them to their lips first and pointed upwards. They need people like us... just as we need them to actualize our superiority. Titans walk the earth only when there are ants for comparison's sake. Perspective is, at its finest, the baseline for all interaction."

"You make them... make *us* sound like villains."

"Make no mistake. We are the villains, the bad guys, the ones who'll pay... but we are necessary."

"The problem is, these peopl—*we*, are very adroit at fulfilling our responsibilities."

"Which is?"

"Guiding the average minds. We'd rather oppress them and work them to death and profit from them because... because that's human nature," I lost the purple line in the blackness of the sky and looked at Elise.

"*They're* despicable then... the ones with the power."

It was a little funny to me. She was trying to distance herself from the hypocritical life she led. Instilling a sort of *them and us* mentality, but she certainly was one of *us*, even if she couldn't see it. I only needed to remind her of our Hermès bill but I didn't intend to. She was exposed, naked. I'm not a *Mad Man* or *bro*. She took a step towards me and I realized then how easy it was to take a life: the mere press of a button. The true gift, the pure gift of a man is rested in his ability to keep someone alive. It would've been child's play for me to kill her soul right there, but that... would've been worse than pressing the red button.

* * *

Elise wanted to skip the after party. *Thank the Paradiso*. We were all back at her place, all being Virg, Elise, and her best friend Amelia: a cute little brunette with too much heart and legs for her own good. I had a feeling I'd see more of her, and it had nothing to do with the feeling that there was something going on between Virg and her. Their exchanges were too 'soulful'—if I believed such things—to be platonic. I should say that, the platonic thing, he'd appreciate it.    Instead I took a sip of the bourbon and turned to him while watching Elise and Amelia passed out on the couch from alcohol or fatigue, or probably both.

"You think about my question?"

"Which?" he responded fearfully, "You're always asking questions," he knew I didn't like it when people heard, but didn't listen.

"What we're doing here. We're useless here. Our actions have no meaning, so what if some socialite is safe, or isn't safe? That doesn't help the big picture... that doesn't..." help me figure out who I am or what the hell I'm supposed to do.

"Let's just do this job. Get paid, and in a year of two, we'll be sitting on a beach, sipping bourbon until you die of liver failure."

If only life were that easy. "You know Virg, in prison, I thought a lot about whether I did the right thing, and I wondered, those people would've died anyway, if not us—"

"People die regardless."

"Alone in that cell with a copy of Divine Comedy, I started to think that redemption *was* possible. I wanted it to be possible. I created for myself some kind of false hope so I didn't immediately blow my own brains out the second I got the chance."

"Vi—"

"I don't believe in God, I couldn't. I did wonder for a while whether we'll be forgiven for the things we've done, then I thought what a crappy God She'd be if She forgave killers like us. I couldn't shake this feeling that there was something more powerful than us. You have to believe in *something*, a sort of master puppeteer, you can call it *God, no-God, Science, Clint Eastwood, the stupid flag,* or *the national anthem*, whatever the hell you want to believe," I gulped the fiery bourbon. It tasted like *water*.

"… And I asked *science, god, whatever*, for a very specific symbol, just as a token of acknowledgement, that maybe, just maybe, there's a petite chance I can be forgiven, and I won't be doomed to the Inferno if I decide to believe in heaven and hell later down the road. I wanted to know if there *really* was something out there."

"What was the symbol?"

"A red eagle, or an eagle with red wings."

"You can't trick the universe Vi. Red eagles don't exist."

"But… She's God."

"Yeah…" he blew smoke in my face. It was enough of the rekindling brothers-in-arms bonding moment. I immediately regretted telling him. He could never understand.

He looked at Amelia, then his cigar, then put it out. Her name intrigued me. The Germanic variation of some other pretty name I read about once, but no matter how hard I tried, I couldn't remember.

"You remind me of Hans Andersen," he said while staring at his sleeping beauty.

"The guy who wrote *The Ugly Duckling?*" maybe he was onto something. A jigsaw fell into place perfectly.

"Yeah… his last words were 'Don't ask me how I am! I understand nothing more!' Reminds me of your mentality."

*Who am I* and *what am I doing here* raced through my head before Virg broke the silence again.

"Nothing's going on between you and her right?" he beat me to the question, pointing to Elise with his practically nonexistent eyelashes.

"I'm her bodyguard."

"Yeah, you're a real Kevin Costner, all the tangoing with wolves."

"What are you saying?"

"You don't have to be a monk Vi, an invented skeptical Zen master. We're not cops. The only rule is to keep her safe. If that's done most effectively with you at her side, go for it."

"Skeptic comes from Greek you ignorant oaf. From *skeptikos*, it means 'inquirer.' An *inversion* of skeptical makes no sense, it would mean unquestioning. Besides, I *am* at her side," he was starting to irk me.

"I know, I meant—"

"Don't tell me what to do Virg."

"Stop punishing yourself man. The bourbon. The detachment. It doesn't hurt to feel," he didn't take his eyes off Amelia.

"Don't tell me how to feel."

"I didn't mean—"

"I know what you meant," I took another sip of the bourbon. The taste burned my tongue. I had no doubt that there was something going on between him and Amelia. He was using me as justification for his own decision. I guess in some twisted way, it'd take some of the pressure off of him if I were sleeping with Elise.

I picked Elise up and carried her to her room. She dozed in and out, mumbling that I smelt good and moved her face closer to mine. I put her down on her king-sized bed and took off her shoes, socks, and earrings and tucked her in. I moved towards the jewelry box with the earrings in my hand and opened it, a twirling ballerina spun clockwise to the sound of Moonlight Sonata. For some reason, and I don't know why, I lingered in the doorway and watched her sleep for a moment before welcoming the darkness to her room. How strange I felt; we have but one world, and yet how many of us live in vastly different ones.

\* \* \*

It was 0418 by the time my key unlocked my apartment door. I couldn't sleep, the sheer fear of seeing the old man's face coupled with the little girl's now newfound voice rattled me to the point of insomnia. I sat on the couch and spun the cylinder on my .38, this time putting it just under my eye. I started crying for the same people I was afraid of seeing in my nightmares. The trigger resisted a little at first. I wondered what Virgil's last words would be, or even my own. After contemplation, 'Forgive us,' was simple and to the point.

Click. I bellowed a scream that probably woke the neighbourhood up. Still alive, and still not too thrilled.

# CANZONETTA VI

ENTRY NO. 11, 692.

Time: 5:36 A.M.

Disposition at time of entry: Curious.

Last night was a most exquisite day. I had been planning to meet this *man on fire* for quite some time, and to my dread, it took more time than I had anticipated to devise a plan in which I could meet this gentleman without alerting him to my identity. I purchased many crappy 'style' magazines (well what passes for 'style' currently) and visited two or three fashion websites on my uPhone to see what I should look like when I visit the bar. I want him (or any potential babes that would be there) to remember me while I am there, but forget me the second I take my exit. I want to be pompous but leave no memorable impression as *that chump I once met at this bar* days or weeks following the incident.

One of the these exceptionally stupid magazines even had a *How to Date More Women* section, no doubt tailored almost exclusively for those same idiots with more air-muscles than brains that I'd have to pretend I was that night. The article *actually* argued that it is ideal and in fact okay to date more than one woman at a time since it is safe to assume that she is also dating more than one man at a time. It was a cheap and classless attempt to redefine the word 'dating,' rending it synonymous with 'casual friends who sleep with each other.' I am quite new to this mentality so I had to look out for satire or parodies, but this particular article seemed to house none, asserting with an iron fist that infidelity was okay since everyone else was doing it... but I digress.

The magazine suggested many places where I could go and 'look snazzy,' and *much* to my surprise, all of the recommended stores were in America, where the magazine was published… what a shocker. I stopped by one of those high-end luxury department stores. Excesstrom I think it was called, and purchased a rather lavish classic navy sport coat, supposedly from the Ralph Lauren *Black Label* Collection. I think the petite babe said it was called the something-cashmere sport coat… (a Tony Sport Coat?) I can't remember. What I do remember is swiping my Visa card to the charge of $2,600 American dollars, which hurt more than I care to admit. I also heartbreakingly indulged in a yellow Lacoste polo even though I only wear the black, and grey; I bought the yellow because it made me look like the golden-boy of macho-poseurs.

My costume for this play was almost complete. The feeling of excess happiness mixed with irrevocable greed and a hunger for violence washed over me like a tidal wave when I flew back home and dropped another 1,500€ for Prada shoes and a belt. However, the cherry on top, the icing on this chocolate-mousse cheesecake was at *Especiale* hair studio, where the *hair-stylist* (yes, that's an actual position, they even put it on their *business* cards) gelled, moussed, and did other nasty things to my hair to make it into a mohawk. I looked like a rooster cock-a-doodle-dooing north over the rising sun in the horizon. In *this* society, I'd fit right in.

I memorized the *how to pick up drunk girls and swiftly take advantage of them as they're passing out* (okay, I added that last part in) so I know what I'm doing when I enter: generally talking loudly with my hands and acting like a scumbag degenerate with no purpose or foresight, to become a misread, misunderstood Machiavellian. The number one thing the article stressed was to never back down or take no for an answer. I guess these guys just have to pray they don't get charged with rape.

Another important thing this cosmic joke of an article emphasized was the use of nicknames. If a guy is getting on your nerves or you want to get him to back off from protecting his beloved's honour, call him a disrespectful pet name to 'establish dominance.' I am not joking, this kind of behavior is real and proudly condoned. (I really can't wait to show this to Dr. Ariadne during our next session whenever *she* accentuates hope for humanity, for love, and for people.) For example, it says if the guy has a scar to call him 'Scarface,' if not, call him 'tiger,' or 'cowboy,' or even 'Mufasa.' Call the women 'toots,' 'cutie,' or 'broad.'

Just when I thought civilization was at the pinnacle of stupidity, my eye caught the *subscription* section, and I thought about the people that actually subscribed to magazines like this. I wanted to go skydiving and have the chute not open.

~

I knew he'd show up sooner or later, so I went to *Yore Amici* to get the lay of the land, and as soon as I walked in, I knew what I was going to do. It was as if fate smiled upon me on this moonless night.

The bartender, Nicole (her name was engraved on a cute little necklace she wore) told me I could sit where I like, so I sat at the bar and drank scotch. When it was getting late and my gut told me he'd arrive any moment, I started ordering sissy drinks like Appletinis or any other stupid cocktail my eye glimpsed across in that magazine. I started talking to the babe sitting at the bar; she looked very upset, and it was very distressing that I had to do this tonight, that this lovely woman would have to pay a most vicious price for my curiosity in wanting to know my enemy. It was the kind of place that hosted alcoholic locals with nothing to lose and confused tourists with not much to give.

I was in a full court press to take this broad home with me... and then he showed, strutting in like some modern outlaw, hat and all like he owned the place. He had that desperado aura about him as he slumped over the bar and ordered Kentucky bourbon. I will admit, I liked his style; we'd probably get along over scotch (or bourbon), operas, and classic music under the different circumstances that a parallel universe permits.

I elevated the tone in my voice to make sure he could hear me, ordering myself an Appletini and "Whatever she's drinking for her," for the lady at the bar.

She suddenly appeared to break out in tears and I despised myself. Was it my aggression that broke her, or the tightening noose of societal pressures?

Nicole asked if she was all right and I could tell she was uncomfortable with me in that place. She said she couldn't sleep. Join the club I thought, but I couldn't say that, so I just said "Come on." I felt like garbage.

I tried making a cheesy innuendo to see if I could get her to calm down, and he growled... *actually* growled like some animal and made a quip about there being no quiet place in this city.

I used *cowboy* to test his response and see if I could get under his skin. He told me not to act like a bigshot or something, then I used *tiger* and he really exploded!

I told him I was a stockbroker, it sounded like something he'd really hate and he said I should tip well and tried turning away from me.

I stood my ground just like the magazine said. He also stood his ground and made some informative speech about day-traders being the plight of society as he stared me down *the whole time*, which probably went on longer than he would've liked, but I didn't do anything; I'm not a barbarian. Plus, his gaze was quite unsettling.

I slipped off the big leather stool and made my exit. I have acquired the information I needed.

He is an intensely powerful man with a patient will. He will be hard to break, but once he does he will stay broken. His kind doesn't recover well from tragedy. I am contemplating killing the target now. Reading from Sebastian and Ahriman's reports suggests, he is attached to his subject. In this way, I can kill two birds with one stone, *and* get the judge to cooperate as well. Three birds then... 3 *little* canaries.

## SCÈNE PATHÉTIQUE

### AN HOUR AGO

"SLOW DOWN VI!!" Mack screamed, holding onto the passenger handlebar with his right hand while trying to still his trembling left palm gripping nothing on the dashboard.

"Get this through your thick skull Mack, I'm not letting either of them die."

*Bros.* They spend every waking second in the gym or at some *How to Get Laid or Die Tryin'* workshop, but when it's time to cash the checks their jaws have been writing since their little balls dropped, they can't wait to piss themselves in fear. They're like little babies minus the adorable cheeks.

Virgil was trying to light the cigar in the bouncing Land Rover. I stared at him in the rearview,

"What?" he stared back with the lit match in his hand, "Might be my last," he was calmer now. The determined look in his eye meant he was prepared to go all the way if need-be.

'Reduce speed' the computer voice in the GPS system said. I tore it off the dash and threw it out the window. It was hardly a time for distractions or games played by computerized voices doing what they were programmed to do by some skinny guy with glasses in some dark office.

"What's the plan?" Mack's shaky voice blurted out.

Virgil puffed smoke and laughed, "We never plan. We improvise."

"So… we're going to die today?" Mack choked on his words.

"Everyone dies. Rarely does anyone live," I veered through two sedans and a station wagon with one of those *Baby on Board* signs.

It was kind of amusing. We were right-on-track in becoming

three underdeveloped characters in some gritty-mediocre noir novel by some boring second-rate writer straight out of grad school.

"I feel like I do want to live Vi. Whoa... imagine those as my last words..." Virg exuded smoke through his nostrils this time.

"Please Virg," I screeched between a Citroën and a Volvo and evaded two bikers on the oncoming lane, "You have no feelings."

"Au contraire mon frère..."

"Yeah yeah yeah," I was hardly in the mood to do anything, other than put holes in the thumb-sucking nancies trying to hurt *her*.

Sunlight suddenly disappeared. Mack and I looked up through the windshield quick enough to see an ominous cloud block out the sun.

"I don't feel too confident here Captain. ... It's a sign," Mack looked further in the distance.

"Shut u—" I'd hadn't even finished saying 'shut' when this booming sound of thunder veered the car to the right shoulder as if it wanted me to pull over. Even Virgil's cigar laid limp on his lip. I exhaled all the air in my lungs and pressed on...

The sky cackled again, laughing at us like a movie-goer in some moment filled with dramatic irony, only this time it was even more frightening than the first, and it produced this terrible frisson of silence in the car, like a misty cloud or a bad fog was actually *in* the car with us.

## ALL HALLOWS' EVENING

MY APARTMENT. I was so tired I could hardly move. I stumbled onto the couch and I noticed someone crouched behind the TV. Everything blurred. I walked over to the figure, its outline in the complete dark looked like a little girl's. She turned around suddenly and grabbed my hand. Her touch burned me, sizzling my fingers and boiling my forearm. I couldn't break free, her stare was as cold as Scandinavian winter, the floor started shaking, everything fell and shattered, my ears bled. I tried pushing her but I started melting and she was like a marble statue. I tried looking through the darkness closer at her face and into her eyes. Her lips were missing. I finally broke free, not because of my strength but because she let go. My arm had been burned straight down to the bone. I could see my ulna and radius. I clenched and unclenched my hand, watching the bone carefully and desperately trying to ignore her glimmering stare in the background before the pain in my hand made it unbearable to maintain my balance. I fell to my knees at eye level with her and she spit out her tongue into my skeletal palm. I must be dreami—

Awake.

My ears enjoyed the whistling that drove me insane. I could hardly keep my eyes open, and I had to, I didn't want to fall asleep again. I hated sleeping. I reached into the nightstand for the .38 hoping to start my day with a bang.

The shrilling stopped, "Coffee?" a voice asked from one of the other rooms. The whistling must've been a kettle, the voice, a hallucination.

"Yeah," I hid the piece under the bed when I reached for my pants.

"How do you take it?" her voice was sexy, seductive, and real. I could see why I broke my own rule and brought her back to my place.

'With bourbon' I wanted to say,

"Blacker than a cold Scandinavian night in the heart of winter."

"Of course," she rolled her eyes and handed me the mug, her curvy waist right in my eye line. One of my Air Force sweaters hid a riveting set of abs. I was always a sucker for a flat stomach.

She sat beside me on the bed, half her face sunlit from a crack through the venetian blinds. Her small-flat diamond nose stud on her right nostril reflected the sunlight into my unseeing eyes, and judging from her Coach purse on my arm-chair, her Deborah Marquit French lace underwire bra hanging off my bedpost, and her black Prada flats, it was probably a real diamond, blood and all. I couldn't remember where I'd met her nor what we'd talked about, but I was never known for remembering things past 1400 hours.

Her free hand unfolded a newspaper and she flipped right to the horoscopes, what is it with honeys and supernatural advice?

"You're doing well," she looked at me up and down and arched one of her eyebrows slightly, "You don't say? Hmmm. Try something new but be careful, it could backfire!"

"Like an eighties Oldsmobile," I took a sip of the coffee. It tasted better than when I made it, which always had too much bourbon.

"What are you?" she nodded to the paper.

"Aquarius," they're lunatics, utter lunatics if they think there's a shred of truth in such things.

"That's the first lie you've told me yet. There's no way you're an Aquarius. No... way. You're either an Aries or a relapsed Leo. You despise attention and yet exude the natural-born-leader type. You feel isolated. Alone, but that's the price of leading others. A king separates himself from his subjects."

Maybe I talked more than I usually do, told her things I normally wouldn—

My eye caught something in the *Local* section and I instantly grabbed the paper from her hand and flipped to the article. The picture was familiar, a woman I was sure I knew.

'*Murderer Leaves No Clue in Bar Slaying:*

*A 29-year-old woman was found murdered yesterday near a bar after a night on the town. Eloise Doxatësson was brutally and viciously slaughtered in the uptown district near...* '

"What is it?" I'd forgotten the dame was still here.

"Huh? Nothing..."

'*No witnesses have come forward but Detective Stuart Mill has commented that the victim bore a tattoo on her right shoulder blade. Police have withheld the actual description of the tattoo. Detective Mill has also said that the killer will be brought to justice and urges anyone with related information or anyone who's been in contact with the victim in recent days to contact their local police department.*'

The picture of Eloise lying in some ditch with her hands bound and her legs spread open was vastly different from the picture of her lying beside me in bed stroking her gorgeous tiger tattoo. How could they print that picture? Are journalists that insensitive? That callous? *This* is what passes for truth nowadays? A hare racing to the printing press with some measured quantity of shock-value through an article or picture with no regard to friends, family, or even loved ones? I crumbled the paper,

"You're right."

"About what?" she took another sip of the coffee, squinting the side of her face being hit by the sun, now in full swing behind the blinds.

"Leo," I sipped my coffee, it tasted like someone had put ice in it. It was so cold my throat could barely handle it and almost closed on me.

I had to meet Elise at 0700 hours at her place.

I kissed ... I couldn't remember her name and if it weren't for her monogrammed black Gucci dress wrinkled on my floor I would've never remembered it: Helen, stitched delicately where the small of her back would reap the benefits of pure hand-crafted silk.

"I knew it!" her turquoise eyes spoke more than her mouth. It relaxed me more than I liked staring into them, and her lips... her lips were like a small piece of Eden. I always had a thing for luscious lips.

I toyed with the idea; whether to turn myself in and admit sleeping with her, Eloise I mean. Maybe I'd wait and see if the cops found out about me, if their investigation led to me—but who was I kidding, cops couldn't find syphilis in an Albanian brothel—and even if by some godless miracle they came to me, I could say I had no idea she was missing. Yeah, that's what I'd do. They'd probably focus their investigation on me anyway and waste everyone's time. An orphaned man dishonourably discharged from the Air Force with nothing to show for humanity but resentment? Usual suspect was practically invented to describe me. Plus, I stood by my actions, if I had killed her, I'd turn myself in within a heartbeat, women like that deserve better... I didn't kill her though... did I?

"Where are you babe?" Helen asked, her eyes fixated on my chest-line behind the grey sleeveless shirt I was wearing—I'm not a fan of its common name.

"I wish I knew," I wanted to lie and say something else but I wasn't fast enough. I was quicker on the .38, and what a prideful skill *that* was.

She walked to the kitchen and I heard the sink run for about 20 seconds then saw her smiling lips again, "I'm off. Call me okay?"

I got up and reeled her in while firmly holding her waist, first kissing the dimple on her left cheek before my lips met hers, "Hm-mmm."

"Oh... you really know how to make a woman swoon," she moaned, slowly backing away. I loosened my grip on her waist and she progressively slipped from my touch. The door shut behind her and a headache followed as if it had an appointment.

I walked over to the kitchen sink with my coffee and piece. She'd washed her mug, I'd only read about this kind of elegance, and there was plenty of room to misjudge her, with all her clothes, her... panache.

She'd inspired me. I washed my cup, well wash is a strong word. I rinsed it with some water after two shots of bourbon and shoved it into the sink. I picked up the piece from beside my kettle and checked the cylinder, still the one round... I spun it, the buzzing sound calmed my headache a little. I cocked the hammer, my headache faded. I swallowed the muzzle and my teeth nearly dented the cold metal. Für Elise rang in my ear. What the —

I felt the vibrating from the bedroom. It was my phone.

*Please hold.*

It got louder and only angered me further. I held my breath and squeezed the trigger.

Click. Great. Another day in this cesspool.

A picture of Elise holding up some obscure hand symbol: her ring and pinky fingers pressed against her cheek, her mouth parted open, and her eyebrows arched up like some adorable ballerina greeted me good morning.

I was wondering how they were doing this, Virgil, Elise, Mack, even Helen. I seemed to never let the phone out of my sight and yet these pictures kept changing. I wanted to know what others saw when I called them, but then I realized I never call anyone and preferred to keep it that way.

*Slide to answer.* "Hello."

"Vero. Did I wake you?"

"No Madame. Are you all right?"

"Yes. I was wondering if you could pick up a paper on your way. Ours didn't get delivered today. I know you're not my butler but it would save us a stop... you're not on your way already are you?"

I looked at the crumbled paper next to my bed, "It's not a problem Madame. I'll be there on time, perhaps a little earlier. ETA 34 minutes."

"So exact... what would I do without you?"

Exactly what you're doing now but to some other poor schmuck. I don't know why but I suddenly thought of Helen and her pouted lips as she left my *humble* abode, "See you soon Madame."

*End.*

I asked Blake where I could get a paper in the neighbourhood. I'd never wandered around sober, well... soberer than I currently was, and I only knew where the bars were. *Yore Amici* was still my favourite especially after my encounter with that boorish stockbroker —maybe they'll have one there. Thankfully Blake was kind enough to give me his copy with the crossword virtually untouched. The country has plenty of worthwhile leaders, too bad they're all stuck in dead-end jobs cutting hair, connecting calls, driving cabs, and buzzing undeserving *higher-ups* into penthouses.

I arrived 4 minutes early. Elise was squeezing water out of her hair and smiling graciously at the paper folded in my hand.

"Morning Madame."

"Elise, it's Elise. EEH-LEEZZZ," she rolled her eyes. It was going to be a long day.

She took the paper and handed me a small piece of stationary with numbered addresses on them, some itinerary for the day ahead.

I glanced at it to the sound of her hasting through the paper backwards, "Do what you've been doing. Be cautious. Some danger might suddenly walk through your door... mmmm... really?" she curled her eyebrow at me. I caught it in my peripheral. She looked and sounded dangerously like Helen.

I studied the slip more carefully:

*1) 1022 Dé Assis St: Golden Years Residence.*

A high-end retirement home. My grandpa's friends lived there. It's awesome, an endless vacation, well… endless is an ineloquent word to use but the idea is there. Something you'd find in five-star Caribbean resorts, it had to be though, it was a subsidiary of the Harriet Hotel.

*2) 1994 Center Blvd. Office of the Supreme Court.*

Her father's office: the honourable René Phoenix.

*3) Sun Rays Covenant Home.*

A homeless shelter? Maybe. What would someone like Elise want at a homeless shelter? Does she need to make herself feel like she's making a difference? Tell herself she's doing all she can?

*4) FACE nightclub. Out of town, we'll follow the signs. I don't know the exact address. It's near the woods/forest area some miles out. There's a Halloween party, I hope you have a costume :).*

This was more like the Elise I knew.

A costume party… great… a chance for the bimbos to whore themselves out with no penalty of conscience. I found myself excruciatingly curious as to what she was going as, a sailor? No. A pilot. *That* would be something.

"I'll start the car," I asked myself why these girls don't just go as whores for Halloween. Seriously, just dress like a streetwalker and approach the *bros* at the party. Why cover it up with expensive designer costumes, brand-name make up, or other things that only serve to get in the way? It was actually the one day in the year where these girls, I refuse to honour them the title of 'women', could ironically be themselves. The one day they wouldn't have to hide behind a cultivated mask of empathy, compassion, or whatever else they're supposed to have or however else they're supposed to have it.

I held the door open for her as she got into the car. She wore a plain-fitted shirt with black jeans, and a fall jacket tight against her obliques. Her athletic prowess was Olympian. Really, she could've competed in the Olympics, a gold medal for spoiled entitled brat with more money than humanity.

The first place was all dressed up but it was really a home for the legendary, a place for those with no home and no one left to care for them enough. Who Elise knew here was only one of the questions circling in my head as I pulled up to the parki—

The black Aston Martin was parked in one of the spots about five spaces away from us. I let Elise out and followed her to the door. She'd gotten the Hermès shopping bag from the trunk, the one with the $4, 000 dress in it. I wasn't smart enough to know what was going on. I looked at the plate as we walked past.

*Da King.* He was here. I'd find him.

Elise's continuous "Vero... you... have... to... sign... in..." was the only thing I could hear when I snapped out of my progressively deepened reverie at the thought of the Aston Martin and the people here... at life in general.

I signed in. The receptionist handed me an orange pen and I wished that was all but no, there were Jack-O-Lanterns, Halloween decorations, and orange and red ribbons hanging off the ceilings everywhere. I wouldn't leave it to fate if I lived here, I'd load the cylinder with 6 shells. Some of the staff were even wearing witch hats, clown noses, or those creepy prescription-glasses-and-perv-mustache things.

"Elise! Great to see you again!" the receptionist made like she knew her although I couldn't see how, I'd never been here before... have I?

"Thanks Nadia, get me a blank receipt slip thing would ya?"

"Sure El."

For an odd reason I couldn't pinpoint, Nadia calling Elise "Elle" triggered a childhood memory in me. I remembered watching my mom's fiancé or close friend helping me beat a segment of Prince of Persia Warrior Within on the PlayStation in my room, teaching me to evade the monster of darkness in the game: the personified shadow of fate. I couldn't remember its name, or *his* name either...

Stark?

"Is Mrs. Oûiså awake?" Elise pronounced the name *'Oo-zi-yah.'* It didn't really roll off the tongue when I imagined myself saying it but I'm one to talk about obscure and hard-to-pronounce names.

"Yes, you know where she is."

"Vero, hand me the pen."

I was still thinking about the Elle thing. I'm sure it was 'Stark,' it was one of those things you couldn't remember but would instantly click and come flooding back if someone else said it. What *was* his name? This was going to keep me up at night... as if I needed more things to keep me awake.

"Vero!"

"Yes Madame?"

"The pen!"

"Oh! Sorry Madame," I handed it to her.

Nadia and Elise exchanged a schoolgirls' glance at each other and snickered amongst themselves. Elise scribbled something on the little slip and handed the pen back to Nadia.

Nadia growled at me as we walked away, doing this sort of tiger's paw thing with her fingers before holding up her pinky and thumb to her ear and mouthing *call me* as Elise and I turned at the end of a weirdly designed circular corner.

"A way with the ladies Vero. I *never* would've guessed."

I almost bumped into a little end table with a Jack-O-Lantern on it, its pyscho-killer smile lit up by two tea candles inside.

Elise stopped in front of room 611B-2, looked back and said, "Follow my lead," before turning the knob and walking in.

Even a recluse would've had trouble focusing in a place like this. The room was too small for a little kid, let alone two men or women of the world who'd probably seen war, famine, prosperity, and a handful of other useful things with no one to share it with other than a lone plant and the howling wind outside their single window. A twin bed laid near the window while another was closer to the door. The window was approximately 10 by 11; my cell seemed more hospitable—at least I had Rick.

The two tenants shared one dresser. Pictures of both their families sat on top of it in an obvious power struggle for whose would be front and centre. A little plant heaved for air on the windowsill and the place smelled rather peculiar. A woman with curled snowy hair, thinner than death sat in a wheelchair facing the window with her back to Elise and I. Regardless of the horror she was living, her back was arched as straight as possible and her head was held high. I wondered why she didn't have her own room before I stopped the thought and *knew* it was probably because she couldn't afford it, or her family couldn't, or the dreadful third possibility that they'd abandoned her; their *mother...* and the thought fuelled a rage in me that forced me to compose myself and calm down. She seemed to be watching the dancing tree branches outside the window, having yet to hear our intrusion.

"Felicia!" Elise called out. That was her mother's name wasn't it? Was this her mother? I thought her mother had passed away. It was about the only thing we had in common. If this was her mother... and the rage returned.

The woman turned around in pain; her neck mobility struggled to rotate to meet Elise's eyes.

"Lisa?" was she talking to Elise?

"Yes! How are you mom?" Elise hugged her as the woman barely lifted herself off of her chair. Age begets frailty, another dour truth: as we get *wiser* we also get weaker. What does that say about truth?

The woman's eyes filled with tears almost immediately but she didn't give into her emotions—the kind of reaction you have when eating too much wasabi at a sushi bar—and she tightly embraced Elise. During this long embrace, I realized I'd yet again forgotten my flask in the glove-box and positioned myself near the door in self-loathing at the thought of my failing memory. I didn't know whether this could be considered ironic, since most of the time it's alcohol that's responsible for short-term memory loss.

The woman's eyes were the colour of Elise's hair when she opened them and caught my gaze, suddenly giving into her emotions and sobbing happily as I looked behind me—at the beige coloured wall—just to confirm that it was because of me. Great... now I was making lovely old ladies weep.

"Vito?" she called to me. Elise looked at me with frozen deer eyes and a subtle smirk darted across her lips, mouthing 'play along' and then pouting her lips and dropping her eyebrows like a puppy wanting more food.

"How... are... you? ... It's... been too long," I had no idea what was going on or what I was playing, but it felt like Russian roulette.

She looked at me quizzically as she approached, "What are you talking about? I saw you last night. Where'd you get the hat?" she hugged me tighter than I'm used to. I looked at Elise in the middle of her awkward grip on my back and she'd turned as white as the western God, slowly shaking her head, guiding me. Click.

I kissed the old lady on the cheek. "Don't get cocky Vi," she said.

"Vi?" she knew my real name? Had I been here before?

"..." she paused, "When have I ever called you *Vito*?" she satirically lifted her hands when she said it, "I thought we went over this."

A wave of relief danced through me. It wasn't anything super-natural, anything existential. There was an explanation, *Vi* also fits with *Vito*. I wouldn't have to alter my belief system, rethink every decision I'd ever made because the foundations of all my beliefs were false. I had no connection to this woman. Still, I couldn't help but think of the odds of walking into a random person's room, in all the rooms here, in this city, in this country, only to be 'mistaken' with someone else also nicknamed 'Vi.'

"Licia, I brought you your dress. I found it in the attic."

"Oh, thank you Lisa."

Lisa—I mean Elise, handed the woman the Hermès bag with the dress inside.

The woman seemed to forget about us and only served her mind in admiring the dress Lis—Elise bought her. Elise walked out and I followed. Suddenly the woman grabbed my ass and laughed mischievously. I looked back and she immediately removed her hand, winking, "Nice... you never disappoint."

Elise roared with the sort of villainous maniacal cackle you hear from the guy sitting in the big leather chair and a white cat on his lap and beckoned me over. Click.

We were walking back towards reception when I spotted someone I thought I recognized from somewhere in one of the other rooms talking to another old lady right when Elise squeezed my ass and wouldn't let go, nearly causing me to flinch. I turned to her. She shrugged sophomorically, "Wanted to see what all the fuss was about."

"Did you buy the dress for her?" I didn't really consider myself curious until I started associating myself with jungle cats, a belief that permitted me nine lives, but horrendous retentiveness meant I'd also forgotten how many I had left.

"Yeah... she has Alzheimer's and dementia, thinks I'm her daughter and asked me to bring her Hermès dress from the attic, so I asked around, looked at some old photos and found which one she was looking for. I couldn't find her family to get the actual dress, but I figured in her state she wouldn't know the real thing from a brand new one, so I bought one for her."

"Who is she to you?"

"No one in particular, I used to volunteer here and she just thought I was her daughter, and I'm guessing she thought you were... Vi? An old flame maybe," she seemed to dilate her pupils on demand. "I wasn't going to say anything to her, no point in breaking an old woman's heart like that. The things she's seen, she's practically a sage."

It wasn't until that moment that I really started basking in Elise's beauty, and immediately I hated myself. For all my high-powered perception, my eye for detail, I had myself wondering whether I'd missed this attraction, this elegance she seemed to carry with herself contrary to all other socialites on those crappy magazine covers. Click.

Nadia growled at me again on the way out. I kept my eye out for *Da King* but he was nowhere to be seen. Elise chuckled, "I think she likes you."

That makes one of us.

The first stop was crossed off the list. To the land of the blind we went, in hopes of finding a one-eyed man, to pursue *true* justice.

I turned and parked a couple of steps in front of the court-house offices. I thought I saw the Lexus that'd been following Elise parked across the street, but they must've seen me looking because after a prolonged stare—trying to deduce if it was in fact the same car—they peeled out. I was getting really paranoid.

"Let's go Madame," I was guiding her to the offices when my eye caught the front page of one of the newspapers at a newsstand.

*Another slain. Is our city home to a serial killer?* A big picture of Trish in almost identical manner to Eloise from the other paper covered the upper fold. The picture of Eloise slightly smaller was imposed near the bottom right of the fold. What the hell was going on? This was a different paper than the one Elise normally read. That's two victims I've had a connection with. I looked at my watch, we were running late. I made a mental note to pick one of these papers up: the *Everyday Sannhet* from *Yore Amici* later tonight.

The big *information* sign in the office building had Judge René Phoenix's corner office on the top floor.

Elise hummed along with the *Sonata Pathétique* playing in the elevator. Click. I was no longer playing the odds.

The doors opened and I can't remember how I got down the hallway but Elise frolicked down and walked in. I took my time and knocked... four times.

"Come in captain. You don't have to knock."

Elise tilted her head at her dad in puzzlement, "He's an Air Force captain pumpkin."

"Not anymore your honour."

"The more you know," Elise chimed in before she turned back to her dad. I left the judge's immediate office and wandered his waiting area. There was a painting of an unknown judge—it wasn't Phoenix—drawn as 20 feet tall, pointing to a small black defendant. The podium was about a thousand times the size of the man under the judge's gavel. *Justice* was about to descend upon the wooden plaque to hand out his sentence. The law is equally *just*. Both the starved and the jelly-bellies are forbidden to steal food.

But it was the photo near his office door that *really* caught my immediate belief system in a paradox. An army picture of the judge with his unit. The judge boasted a big red pipe on his lip and flexed his muscles. They all looked familiar to me; I removed it from the wall and took the photo out of its old frame, the blackened red ink on the back: '*Desert Storm, Operation Equal Measures*' hit me in the face like raindrops during a storm. The world couldn't be this small. The synapses in my brain were firing so fast I thought I was going to pass out. Judge Phoenix was 'Popeye,' he served with the Lue in Desert Storm.

"Desert Storm. Boy was that hell!" he was suddenly behind me and I hadn't heard him. *You never forget your training*.

I put the picture back in the frame and handed it to him, "Sorry your honour," I pointed to the Lue, "But this man was my training officer in the Air Force, and it was hard to believe that you two know each other."

"Lieutenant Colonel W.B Milton. The man was a legend, risked his life to save all of us or each of us without a second thought on multiple occasions. He was a machine. I guess the world *is* as small as they say huh?"

I looked around, "I have trouble believing you were part of one of those guerrilla rogue teams."

"Because I caved right? Sold out? Conformed? I had to... what was it? Overcome chaos. And over there... that's all there was."

"Why? What made you conform?"

He took a deep breath and looked at the picture of Lue again, "I had a kid on the way. I couldn't risk anything happening to me. I couldn't abandon my family. You can't hate the world forever captain. You'll end up hating yourself. You think you're running to freedom but you're really running to your fate... like that Iraqi servant. Do you know the tale?"

"Yes I do."

"People who hold contradictory beliefs are doomed to ignorance and happiness."

I wanted to keep him on point, "The Lue thinks you're all dead. Your tradition. No one else showed up one year."

"I *did* die."

Elise popped up behind me and pushed me back, "Let's go Vero."

"Thank you your honour," I said before Elise forced me out and closed her father's office door, taking my hand and hurrying towards the elevators, "We're late."

My hat nearly dropped from the idling wind on our way back and I slowed down before I remote started the car and stared at the newspaper stand. Redemption, it seemed, was becoming more and more Sisyphean.

# CANZONETTA VII

ENTRY NO. 11, 426.

Time: 3:46 A.M.

Mood at time of entry: Perplexed, self-conscious, and doubtful. Specks of melancholy, fear.

Dr. Ariadne continues to insist that I change my drink if I obdurately refuse to quit alcohol altogether. (I don't see how people can be sober in such a world and not be suicidal; alcohol keeps me sane.) It is a good thing she does not know about the pills. However, her position is hardly difficult to fathom; I detest scotch but choose to consume it regardless of this important detail. I believe I have no choice in the matter whereas the doctor feels otherwise. This was after I told her that my mother used to always say that only scotch touched my father's lips. And aside from the watch I got on my 21st birthday, scotch is one of only two relics that remain of him. I am afraid of severing this connection will mean I've lost him forever and have betrayed his memory.

Since the entries in this journal have been becoming quite gloomy and morbid, I will now express some rather pleasant news; I met someone at the bar of the Traven hotel, and although I know any hussy you meet at a bar is probably not as elegant as your ideal woman, this particular gal seems different.

Her name is Cressida, which is an odd and exotic name. I must find its meaning and origin. She is beautiful beyond any half-assed description my ailing mind would conjure up. She talked Liszt and Opera for hours, with a particular affinity to Schubert's *Die Winterreise*: the Dietrich Fischer-Dieskau and Gerald Moore version. I could scarcely believe it. In fact, I had an unexpected epiphany and finally understood Descartes' *Meditations*, unable to tell if I was awake or dreaming. She simply seems too good to be true. Delight has been washing over the waves of blood inside me, dancing with the specks of sand in the hourglass of *my* own temporal time. Elsa may perhaps finally become a distant memory of a forlorn flame; the operative word being *may*.

# HIÉRODRAME

"QUIETLY GENTS," I whispered as we got out of the car and approached the side door of the locale marked on the map. Mack and Virg cocked their guns. Mack boasted the classic .45, Virg preferred to pick his shots with the raw power of a sawed-off shotgun, and I carried a trusty .38 that looked identical to the one I'd lost. I checked the cylinder: 6 rounds. No more games. I thumbed back the hammer as Mack picked the lock. The bullet slipped into place.

The door unlatched, he pointed to his eyes and signalled Virg. We went in to clear. Everything fell silent. It was so quiet I could hear myself breathe. Virg was the point-man; I watched him ahead of Mack, and I cleared the corners while he watched my left. The door creaked closed behind us... *lasciate ogne speranza, voi ch'entrate.*

Virg looked back at me and pointed to the left when the hall split into two paths. I nodded and tapped Mack on the shoulder, pointing to Virg with my index and middle finger. He followed Virg. I went right and glanced left, suddenly seeing Virg put up his fist. We stopped and I took cover behind them on their flank. A guy scratching his thigh walked out and Virg quickly went for his knife. Quick. Efficient. Quiet. There was a sigh of relief before I moved forward as silently as I could. The path split into two again. I went right again in hopes that a simple pun would change my fate but instead I found a closed room. I snuck in hoping to find the dames rather than a chill down my spine and a knot twist in my stomach.

It was some sort of dungeon, a kill room for a very disturbed mind. The centre of the room housed a torture table with sharp scalpels I couldn't even describe, pulleys and the like were held up by chains and ropes from the ceiling. Very bright lights illuminated an operating bed and scattered little surgical tools even a med student would have a hard time identifying. But it was the blood-stains on the rusted tools that gave me this unsettling feeling of—the door slammed shut and I immediately heard gunshots. I tried to open it but couldn't. I looked around for a vantage point or another exit, to no avail.

The door burst open and I opened fire 4 times, hitting two guys before the third clipped me in the shoulder. He was not happy with how it went down so he hit me with the butt of his machine gun and my eyelids suddenly weighed a ton. I collapsed on the ground and tried to lift my piece towards him but he knocked it away, pointing the muzzle of his AK at my nose.

The moment arrived at last. I'd probably never see Elise again. I flashed to her tanning beside her pool with a pitcher of cold lemon-ade in her hand telling me it's too early for bourbon. It took her coming into my life to see who I really was and what I could become. Everything blurred, even the thoughts of that vindictive old man.

I'm *not* dying here. It would be a wasteful death.

# CANTATA

WE ARRIVED AT Sun Rays shelter in better time than I anticipated.

Elise told me to stand by the door and watch her from there. *'Gladly'* was my response and I suspected *she* thought I was being sarcastic. She disappeared behind some room and came out wearing an apron with her hair tied in a ponytail resting on the left side of her torso. She was serving soup to the homeless. The 45 minutes of watching Elise make repetitive small talk with the people she was serving along with her eloquent acceptance of 17, 18, 19 proposals from the wise gentlemen passing through seemed more like 4.5 seconds.

Imagine her as someone you know, or knew: the archetype for everything you stand for, your better half—if such a thing exists—or the one that got away and left a burning hole in your heart. I couldn't stop thinking about her. She was inside my soul, churning the ooze that kept me intact, messing with the *stuff* that made me *me*. She was changing me, creating a new version of me. I hadn't had a drink in days and I wasn't sure if I welcomed the changes. I'd lost enough women in my life, and I knew myself well enough to know that losing another would render me shattered, that the ooze would spill and evaporate so fast I'd never be able to put myself back together again like any regular humpty dumpty.

The guy who looked to be running things walked towards me. I wasn't really looking at him, I had to protect Elise—although nothing would happen to her here. The *homeless*, poor, and impoverished have more honour, class, and respect than all the politicians, leaders, and bankers of the world combined—but I caught him in my peripheral nonetheless.

"You have a very thick energy about you son," the voice of a tranquil old man presented an opportunity for pleasant conversation.

The black shirt and small clerical collar told me all I needed to know. The .38 quivered in my belt and the ticking sound of the empty barrels turning got progressively louder.

"Move along father, God left me long ago."

"Redemption is given to those who seek it my son. If you can find it in your heart to confess. I can absolve you."

"That'd take all week father."

"Redemption most heeded is least granted."

"Says something about your God doesn't it?" I couldn't help but hide my scorn. My eyes widened under the brim of my hat.

"Perhaps, but perhaps those most seeking redemption have forgotten God because they believe they are irredeemable. Perhaps they think they aren't worthy. Perhaps they have a crisis of faith because they've seen things they believe God shouldn't... no, *wouldn't* allow."

A philosophical priest? What kind of game was this? It sounded like Russian roulette with a loaded gun, "What I've seen father... faith is an illusion. No God would inflict such pain. If He or She forgives a man like me, He's a horrible God. If He doesn't, he's a contradictory God."

"Sometimes it takes pain to actualize happiness. How can we have one without the other?"

I thought about a section in Plato's *Phaedo* I read from Virg's stack of books during Basic, specifically his argument of opposites, how large wouldn't exist without small, tall without short... does that mean there is no truth without deceit? That everything is relative? That *man is the measure of all things* like Protagoras says? That we need pain to understand painlessness?

That's why you shouldn't read things in sections or take them out of context. I couldn't remember how that argument was dealt with, "Happiness? You oughta be a stand-up comedian father. You're *really* making me laugh."

The uranic smell that could only belong to Elise froze me, even in this place, "Let's go Vero.... Oh, I see you've met Father Antonini."

I flicked my hat, "Father," and escorted Elise out. I noticed the bouquet she bought spread among the people eating, each one of the flowers that came with the bouquet separated and sitting idly on the trays being used by these souls abandoned by Antonini's *God*.

The father felt necessary to quip, "My door's always open," as I walked out and this filled me with a sort of indescribable dread. He was just doing his job, and his job was to believe some abstracted bullshit about redeeming lost souls. Hell, it's what the church thrives and prints money on. Men like him could never grasp truth or understand themselves. They'd never understand their place in this universe as insignificant, their decisions as meaningless, they mustn't believe the truth: that some of us are beyond saving. They can't accept that *because* they believe in *God*, for that would mean that their *loving* and all-powerful God has doomed some of us from the start. God is supposed to punish the faithless, the wicked, the liars, and the cheaters, but if you believe this, you must believe that it was *God* who made them that way. How could I, how could anyone adulate such an obvious contradiction?

"You don't have faith Vero?" Elise's eyes were hard to ignore.

"What I've seen, heard, felt, and learned Madame, has forever made me question *God's* existence," I started the car and we got in.

A little while later she unbuckled her seatbelt and climbed onto the front seat. I kept glancing over at her but I had to keep my eye on the road. She seemed to be watching me in reticence until she said, "You're a captain? Why didn't you tell me?"

"I... uh... was, Madame," I cleared my throat.

She mockingly saluted me and giggled, "That explains how you know so much about planes."

"Can I ask you something Madame?"

"Of course Vero."

I was getting used to her calling me Vero. I kind of liked it, "Was there anything special about the woman in that retirement home, or this particular shelter?"

"No. I told you. The woman was random, and I chanced across this place. Why?"

"How did you pick them? *Why* did you pick them? Are you trying to make a difference?"

"I'm not an idiot Vero. I can't change anything. People are still going to line up for computer gadgets while others starve. They'll throw rice at weddings while others bend to pick it up. I'm only one person. One person can only do so much. But I try to do what I can. The woman in the retirement home, Felicia, she's one person, and if I can make a positive effect on her life, to make it better, or any *one* of the people that come to the shelter, at least I've done what I can, and others don't even do *that*. I like it up here. I'm going to sit here from now on," she turned on the radio and a teenage pop song shook the car, "Oh hell no!" she changed the station until some classical music played. "Here we are. This is what you like right?"

"It's your car Madame. Please listen to whatever your heart desires," how I wondered whether a murdering loser like me could ever be what her heart desired.

"I like this stuff too."

Mozart played through the car as I beat myself up over my stupidity. I'd misjudged her, rushed to self-ascertained truth too quickly without a second thought like those dogmatic atheist-movement *quasi-intellectuals* that hide behind the messianic mask of the scientific method. I was as wrong as an ignorant blue-collar bonehead who voted for the venture capitalist lawyer who went to Harvard *hoping* that he *could* change things, waiting for the American Dream that'll turn into a nightmare. Hell, the last time I was right about something was when I ordered that fifth double bourbon with Eloise, and she ended up dead. What did I know? A walking cliché looking for redemption with some heiress in all the wrong places.

"You can drop me off at home and take the car Vero. I'll come to the club with Amelia and Virg since my dad won't need him tonight. You can meet us there."

"Are you positive Madame?"

"Yes."

I thought about that ridiculous '*Save the Planet*' bumper sticker I saw a while back and I must've whispered or said something because I heard Elise sigh solemnly and whisper, "I'm trying Vero."

"It's not your responsibility Madame."

"I have to do it Vero. No one else would. If I don't, people will *die* and *suffer*."

She thought she'd tasted sorrow.

The little girl with no lips somehow yelled "LOOK OUT" just before I realized I was about to hit a deer near the estate and I veered out of the way to avoid the collision.

"Nice reflexes," Elise barely flinched.

# Bacchanale

I COULD REST for 2 hours before having to meet Elise and the gang at FACE for the Halloween party. My costume was either a suicidal bodyguard drunk on self-revulsion in a dark navy suit, or a suicidal bodyguard drunk on self-revulsion in a black suit. I asked the computerized voice for the address to FACE and it asked me whether I wanted it sent to Elise's GPS system via something called an *app*. I said yes and the directions were sent to the navigation system of Elise's Land Rover. Life was becoming dangerously convenient.

I asked it for the newspaper article I saw earlier today and read about the murders. Eloise and Trish were dead. I fumbled around my phone and pockets looking for Helen's number before I thought it through. What was I going to say? 'Uh, hey, we had one night of scorching sex, just wanted to let you know that two other girls I did that with have ended up dead... yeah, some serial killer... oh you know the one... yes the one in the paper... anyway, you free tonight?'

\* \* \*

FACE was among the palisades out of town and word on the street was that it was a mob front owned by the Torrino family, which I found odd because I thought they were all killed or caught around the time I was 18 or 19 with the capture of their don. I couldn't drink that night. I had to stay sharp. I don't know why Elise picked that club, especially since the Torrinos and Calvanos were at war with each other. One of them was bold enough to threaten a judge and his family, which meant Elise, but that wasn't her concern, it was mine. I'd keep her safe.

I got out of the car and approached the door. The smell of petrichor and oak trees was preferred to the aroma of musky marijuana, cheap cigarettes, tasteless booze, and vomit drifting back-and-forth in your nostrils in the downtown club district. The line to enter was practically a kilometre long, reaching near a footpath in the middle of the surrounding woods. Everyone was in costume, men wisely dressed as mobsters, gangsters, or inmates, and women elegantly going as street walkers, escorts, dominatrices, or strippers. I skipped past all that and some roided up rent-a-thug posing as security tried to stop me.

"I'm Madame Phoenix's personal bodyguard. Get your hand off me."

He was looking through his list before a guy in a flashy purple suit walked up and whispered something in his ear. He pointed with his neck—well, what he thought was a neck—towards the entrance and I regrettably entered the smoky club. Obnoxiously loud second-rate music blared into my brain. People stumbled all over the place from the excess alcohol and rampant idiocy. Their outrageous costumes and alter egos pained my chest like a bad case of acid reflux, and on top of all that, the place was so dark I could barely see where I was going. The *perfect* scumbag hangout.

The two costumed girls dropped a wine glass in front of me. Although the music in the club had trigged a migraine, I somehow heard the chalice fly through the air.

The sound of shattering glass was more soothing than I thought. It sounded like one of Chopin's Nocturnes.

I looked around for Elise, noting the very... tasteful dance floor. Around it, tall tables and various VIP rooms glittered in my peripheral before I thought I saw a white light radiating from one of the rooms. I pushed through the crowd on the dance floor and mounted the steps to get a better vantage point. I spotted Elise walking into one of the VIP rooms, eventually sitting beside Amelia and Virg.

I entered the room and the music died out. This room was playing slightly different music in a lowered volume. It was tolerable, ambient. Virgil nodded to me and Elise looked where he was nodding and spotted me.

"Vero!" she screamed and jumped to hug me. I caught her as she wrapped her legs around me. She was wearing a long white dress laced near her waistline with a handmade tiara made from white roses, "My favourite bodyguard."

She was an angel. I was a second-rate bodyguard drunk on self-revulsion in a black suit. It was fitting. "Madame, you're drunk."

"Nuh... uh," she was practically nibbling on my ear lobe with her legs still wrapped around me. I saw Virg burst out laughing and point Elise out to Amelia, who nodded, pointed at me and said something to Virg. He nodded his head as if to say *that makes sense* and then came to a philosophical realization. Elise finally pecked me on the cheek and got off me. I looked at Amelia again, and couldn't help but think she was familiar to me, as if I'd seen her but I hadn't because I would've remembered.

"I'm an angel! Do you like my costume?" Elise inquired, stroking her index finger down my nose.

*'You have no idea'*, is what I wanted to say but I opted for, "It isn't much of a costume to me Madame," wanting it to mean of course, that 'For you Elise, it's not a costume since you're always an angel in my eyes,' but she took it to mean 'Your costume is horrible' and I seemed to displease more than charm. She left the room and I wanted to follow but I caught myself looking at Amelia again, trying to remember where I'd seen her befor—she looked right at me and I caught an all too familiar inquisitive gaze—Rick's daughter. The picture he'd shown me on my birthday while I was inside was probably older, her hair had grown out a little but the eyes were the same eyes I'd complimented. The world shrunk by the second.

I ran after Elise, finding a trillion bros crowding her as she tried to come back from the ladies room. They played their *best* moves in reeling her in and attempting to kiss her, or feel her up, or any number of rapey things they'd been taught at the *Bang* workshops. A Batman even tried to smother her with his cape, it was very... she saw me staring down the platform and turned away in anger, humouring inmate number 37927 by *pretending* to peck him on the cheek like she did to me moments ago and whispering things in his ear.

Maybe it was her costume. The place was loud, sleazy, and quite moronic despite appearing high-end. Nonetheless, there seemed to be a perpetual light shining upon her. It followed her wherever she went and anyone in close proximity to her could feed off this positive aura and better themselves. It was as if she carried the glow Olay advertises with airbrushed actresses. It *must've* been the costume, it must've been, or maybe it was yet another nonsensical thing I was telling myself to stay detached. I couldn't pinpoint what it was about her that kept devouring my thoughts of her beauty. Was it *just* her looks? I knew I was never that shallow, it had to be her eyes since they had depth, her mouth since it spoke wisdom, her ears that perked for truth, or perhaps it was her arms that seemed to spread wings towards the sky. I just described pretty much everything, what the hell was I thinking?

I saw a hooker grinding on a guy that I only guessed was going *as a* bro: he had the over-gelled spikey rooster haircut with a symbol carved above his left ear, the tight t-shirt bulging his beer belly and tight jeans above basketball sneakers. A bro getting action in the history of the *bro-code* or dames, I laughed hysterically before *God* set the universe in balance and fury filled my chest, pushing the acid back down. Elise was trying to push inmate 37927 away but he wouldn't let her, still trying to cop a feel and lock her in a bear hug on the corner of the dance floor. I don't know how I made my way over there but I was there in the blink of an eye and pushed him off her. He slipped on spilled beer and fell back. Security saw it happen from above the platform and tried to make their way down but they wouldn't make it here in time. I put my shoe on his neck and leaned in closer so he could hear me above the sound of the electronic music.

"I see you near her again *convict*, you'll choke on the teeth I kick down your throat."

She pointed to the door and gripped my fingers tightly in her palm as we left the club, "Thanks," were the first words out of her mouth when we neared the car.

"It's my job Madame," the car hummed to a start.

She squeezed my hand tighter, "No, let's go for a walk."

She didn't quite walk through the path in the woods; she sauntered her own path in the white-covered forest as each of her steps left an imprint in the snow. We came to a fallen tree after walking for some time and she sat down on the log, breathless. I slipped my hand under hers and guided her to her feet so I could put my jacket under her. There was a secluded lake in the distance. We just sat there and watched the rippling lake weave with the dancing trees.

"Your costume is flawless... just like you."

She rubbed her cheek against my bicep like a lioness and cuddled with me, wrapping her arm around my neck. I didn't mind. Obviously.

The sun rose some hours later and I noticed she was shuddering. I had only the thin jacket to put around her shoulders, it's what a gentleman should do, and then I immediately hated my dad for never being there to teach me these things, dreading that I had to learn most of it myself.

The street was empty now save for her car parked right where I left it. She sat up front with me, dozing in and out. I dropped her off at her place at 0640 and she pecked me with her eyes half open,

"Get some rest and come back Vero," she yawned, "I want to go up to the lake house with you."

"I don't need rest Madame. We can go now if you want. You can pack your stuff. I'll go home and pack mine. I'll come back and we'll drive up immediately. You can sleep in the car."

"Don't you sleep?"

"Sometimes, when I have the time," I'm terrible at making jokes. Besides, it'd been a solid night. I didn't want the nightmares to ruin that.

She shook her head rapidly to wake herself up, "Was that a joke Vero? You're the perfect Sam Spade to my Vivian Rutledge."

"Philip Marlowe Madame,"

"Huh?"

"It's Philip Marlowe and Vivian Rutledge, Sam Spade's flame was Brigid O'Shaughnessy."

"Oh… well… either way," she sashayed up the steps and went inside.

I was being paralleled to some film-noir detective or anti-hero…. Does everyone live in Fantasyland? A world where we can't escape our labels? Doomed to listen to crap music by teenage pop stars and spend money we don't have on things we don't need because we've been indoctrinated to believe it'll being us some unquantifiable measure of happiness for unlimited time?

I couldn't stop smiling on the drive home and was in a hurry to get back to Elise. She'd stirred something in me, tamed that prowling tiger that's always wanted to eat my heart.

On my way back to the estate I drove by the florist and screeched the car to a halt. I was determined, no compelled to go in and buy her a single red rose. I couldn't pinpoint why… ask a $750/hour psychiatrist and they'll talk your ear off on why you're right or what the flower means—wanting to know how you *feel* like a bunch of circus clowns—but really, it was something I wanted to do, something I had to do. The cars behind me honked and the drivers screamed insults at my mother. The chimes dinged me inside. I inhaled deeply, it smelled better than last time. I tried selecting the perfect rose with even and symmetrical petals, just like her, but I realized that none of them were perfect like her. I finally eenymeeny-miny-moe'd and picked from a selection I'd put aside.

Elise put her bag beside mine in the trunk and rode in the passenger seat again. The drive was quiet but soothing. I was comfortable with the silence and I knew she was too. Her lake house was 4 hours away, the kind of house you read about in a Stephen King novella or film. It was a captivating wooden cabin resting on a lake in one direction and surrounded by forest in the other. A nightmare to defend against anyone looking to advance on it. Most of the windows inside were huge and looked right into the den or living room. There were too many exposed areas, too many things to cover with her in case of an emergency, but maybe I was being paranoid, no one knew about this place, at least I hoped, and no one would come up here, at least I prayed.

The drive was shorter than I had anticipated but I was thirstier than a man of *God* crossing the desert. I don't know why. It wasn't my house, my fridge, or my pineapple juice but it tasted sweeter than unpasteurized honey straight from a farmer's market.

Elise quipped, "No bourbon this time?" as I gracelessly slurped the residual juice left on the brim. I thought she was elsewhere and she covered her massive tigress's yawn with her elbow.

I looked at her through the brim of my hat and was going to make a witty retort, something along the lines of, 'There's some in it,' as I shook the cup at her, but I heard footsteps flattening the snow outside the house,

"Shhhh…" my ears perked.

They approached the door. I pulled out the .38 and cocked it. Elise's petrified face forever etched itself into my memory bank next to the eyeless old man and the lipless little girl.

"Madame! Hide!" I positioned myself with my back beside the door and watched Elise frozen in fear. "GO!" I whispered at her and she disappeared somewhere to my left. The door was locked. The knob slowly turned. The footsteps retreated to elsewhere on the porch through the wall behind me until they creaked behind the door again. A key rattled the little cogs in the knob. I looked up and saw the unlatched deadbolt.... Damn it.

The door either opened cautiously or time slowed, I didn't know which as I gripped the gun tighter.

"Elise?" the voice called out. The subtle feeling of the trigger resting against my index finger twitched it, "You there pumpkin?" and the voice was suddenly familiar.

A sigh of relief. "Your honour!" I stood up and opened the door quickly, and his gaze immediately shifted to my piece.

"Captain," he glanced at my eyes, then back at the .38, "The right man for the right job. I knew she'd be safe with you," his voice progressively broke as he completed the sentence, no doubt thinking about Mack's momentary lapse of judgment, a lapse that cost his son his life.

"I'll do *everything* I can your honour."

"Daddy!" Elise appeared and hugged him from my right. I looked around to see how it was possible, mulling over the architecture of the place. "What are you doing here?"

"I had to pick up some files," he opened his hands and hugged her again. I noticed a colossal folder held together by three elastic bands on the little bench on the porch behind him,

"I'm across the lake," he looked at me and pointed to a house over the wooden dock nearly identical to this one, "Saw the light on and thought I'd drop in and say hi!"

"Stay for a bit," Elise pleaded.

"I can't. I have to do some research for the election next week. Look over the Calvano file," he looked at me again, almost smirking, "You a political man captain?"

"Not nearly as I should be."

"Ahhhhuuuhhh," a slight realization, "Say... you're a smart guy. Give me an opinion, who do you think you'll vote for in this election? ... That is... if it's not personal."

"I never vote *for* any two-bit politician who makes mythical assertions to change the world. I vote *against* your honour."

The judge chuckled wholeheartedly and Elise cracked that smile she cracked when things were going her way.

"Like I said, a smart man. ... Say... do you fish? The river isn't completely frozen."

"No."

"That's too bad, I'm meeting George Stuart Locke later. He's the head of the subcommittee of Anti Organized Crime and Anti-Narcotics from our City Council."

"Good luck," I tilted my head back so I could see his eyes clearly.

"Won't need it. It's a catch and release river."

I looked deeper into his eyes, "You're fishing with the head of the subcommittee of the *Anti Mafia* council in a catch and release river?" the irony... was indelibly seared into my brain. How I loved the *justice* system.

"He's like a stoic sage isn't he dad?" Elise talked about me as if I weren't there, "He never lets on what he's thinking."

"Don't label a man pumpkin. Assumptions are the Gods of error," did the judge just make a *Steven Seagal* reference?

"You should see the books he keeps in the glove box. Really makes the car... smarter."

"Wait! I'm good at this. Sartre? Camus? Dostoyevsky?" the judge queried.

"Among others," I was surprised. He was a smart man, but he was a *judge* after all.

He took out the familiar red pipe and shoved some tobacco in it from his jacket and lit with a strike-anywhere match he kept in his pants pocket. The smell was not dissimilar to Virgil's Partagas black label, "A brilliant man indeed... illuminating the flaws in our system captain?"

"You're not running are you your honour? I might vote *for* for the first time in my life."

He laughed bitterly for a second, then nervously, then looked at Elise for a second and looked back to me, exhaling tobacco smoke, "No. I'm not suicidal. No doubt a man of your caliber has already figured out the flaw with our system... Harvard, Oxford, Yale... only rich idiots and poor geniuses go to *those* places."

I flicked my hat. Beethoven's *Sonata al Chiaro di Luna* played from the judge's jacket, but he took one glance at his phone and shoved the thing back into his pocket, ignoring everything but us.

Elise put one hand on my shoulder and the other on her dad's, "Don't stop now men..." she scoffed, "Explain it for the mortals."

The judge extended his hand, signalling me to begin, "No your honour, I insist."

He nodded, "The number one flaw with *democracy* pumpkin, with unadulterated *freedom* is the propaganda myth continuously perpetuated by the media. A fable of old that somehow *volume equals truth*; that if a certain threshold of people—say 50% for example—agree that 2+3=7, then it equals 7. That's how idiotic we are as a species. Truth is bivalent, what you're reading, thinking, feeling, or hearing, is either right or wrong regardless of anything else, anything external to that fact.

If 70 million people say something stupid like 2+3=7, it's still stupid isn't it? Still untrue? Then why do we think when that same logic is extended to all facets of the realm like economics, politics, or morality, we can abandon this bivalence and opt for volume?" he chuckled, "Worst of all we're taught to think only what's acceptable to think. To question things within a box, a vacuum placed by governments and years of conditioning by society. Most of all, you've been led to believe you shouldn't change things, that change is bad, that you should accept things as they are... as truth," he almost made it seem as if he were not one of the government puppets he was ranting against.

"Or else they'd constantly overwhelm and bombard you with absurd questions like: 'Why can't you understand how things work?' or 'Why are you such an outsider?' but *that* is what truth is," I chimed in.

Elise leaned back as if she'd just learned something she couldn't ignore, something she hadn't thought about, like a seed was planted in her mind as a devouring idea and couldn't be left docile any longer.

"It's worked historically, history tells us—"

The judge interrupted his pumpkin, "You take this one captain," he grabbed his files off the porch and descended the steps to the driveway, "Ta!" and he drove away in his Chrysler 300 SRT, I think, all cars look alike nowadays.

I closed the door and latched the deadbolt.

# Capriccio
## Now

I CAME TO on the table I was looking at. The light blinded me. I saw double, triple, quadruple, the world spun in circular motions, everything faded away.

"Hey... Vero... wake... up," a man sung as he slapped on both of my cheeks repeatedly. My vision slid into focus. I'd seen him before.

"Who are you?" he asked me before I realized I'd been tied down to the table, unable to move. He took the knives and tried to wipe the dried blood with a stained towel, "Blood is to hard to get off isn't it? Some things just don't wash out!"

I noticed he also had blood on his hands. Something we had in common.

"So... who are you?" he spun the table up and around so I was facing him.

Idiots only understand idiocy. Diamond with a diamond. Fire with fire. I knew I couldn't win with silence, I had to change tactics.

"If you could answer that for me, I'd forever be in your debt!" I was getting better at this one-liner thing.

"This guy..." he pointed at my face with the knife to one of the other goons standing behind me, "He's hilarious ain't he?" He stabbed me in the shoulder exactly where I'd been shot and I let out this yelp, his other hand came up and forced salt in the wound. I shook the table with my body in a feeble attempt to break free, but they had me down too tight to flinch.

"I love this guy!" he turned to a third guy to my left. Judging from his vintage Breitling, the big-mouth was probably the boss and the others were his henchmen, especially when I noticed the fashionable beard and belly of one of the guys I thought I'd seen in that blue Lexus.

He stared at the bloodstained knife again, carefully examining its blade and sliding his finger on it either to test its sharpness or look scary, "So? Who are your friends... really?"

"Okay..." some blood dripped off my lips, "You win."

He looked at his goon and nodded contently, thinking he'd broken me with a flesh wound and some parlour theatrics. What a grade-A goombah, I'll use that to my advantage. My intelligence ought to get under his skin, he aimed to please: himself, his goons, even me.

"I'm Larry," I struggled to look up to meet his gaze—my shoulder stung and trembled with pain, I could barely begin to describe it, "And I can only assume you've already got Moe and Curly by the short and curlies."

He laughed a weird laugh, where you don't really hear anything, like the movement where only our stomachs heave back and forth and you're *really* annoyed to the point of sadism.

This time the goon touched me with some metal pipe. It'd been in a furnace or heated somewhere and he burned me where I'd been stabbed and shot, cauterizing the wound. Surprisingly I didn't make a sound nor did I struggle. It didn't hurt as much as they thought it would. I'd detached myself and started thinking about how I was going to get the women out. Women... they'll be the death of me.

"Clever one-liner? That really isn't you Vero," he stabbed me again in the same place. This time it hurt more than the nightmares but I had to stay awake. I had to save Elise, to do my job, but my body had other ideas and I saw double again, then triple. Everything spun. My lashes wanted a reunion. I abided to the sound of his annoying voice, disappearing to meet the old man and the little girl.

# Tranquillitas

"So?" Elise tapped her toe on the floor.

"Huh?" where was I again?

"History tells us everything. All other alternatives have failed... you're not saying it's all a fiction are you?"

"Madame... history is simply a spoil of war like women, slaves, land, and resources. Written by those who have murdered heroes. Always unequivocally fabricated by the victors—simply search any ancient civilization or modern [1900-1999] war, and you'll see that *justice, God, truth*, whatever, was *always* on the side of the victors, on the side of fabricated justice and sanctimonious morality. Very coincidental, and also very unlikely. We've equated the words of renowned historians to truth. The right to create history and record the past—no matter how illusionary, dramatic, exaggerated, or simply false—are mere tall tales of nobility, ideal principles, and chivalrous accounts of romanticism. These are unfortunately ubiquitous in our ever declining planet. How often have we heard of the barbaric black, Asian, Indian, or West Asian man, and the altruistic white man who comes to rescue them from their evil ways and teach them of freedom and truth?

Our children's children for example, will have no choice—no matter how critical they may be, for the research and facts would not yield the result of truth, but the result of feigned and planted articles—but to accept that America *really* did want *democracy* in Iraq, Afghanistan, Iran, Egypt, Libya, Jordan, Soudan, Zaire, Sierra Leone, or a handful of other countries they've bombed. They'll never learn that each of these countries disagreed with the ideals of the U.S. and also happened to have an abundance of a natural resource that the *just* Americans felt they had a right to. Is the existence of rampant resources in each of those places a coincidence?

Of course not, since all of it has started to magically disappear into America's pockets—their elite mind you, they don't even have the vestige of civility to distribute their thefts equally among their citizens—or if they were in a really good mood, bought from those countries at 1/10th the market price. The hosts' losses chalked up to the price of bringing democracy to that particular land. It is with these thoughts that we may tackle the various problems at hand. Where history fudges the truth to tell lies, fiction *can* aspire to truth when used correctly."

"Wow, you've given this quite some thought," she listened to every word. I got the impression she wasn't listening to learn something about the world. She listened to learn something about *me*.

## BAGATELLE

THE DINNER TABLE faced the forest that doubled as a garden. I sat in the middle chair reading Camus. He's an intelligent man seeking truth, which is really all we can ask of a man. Occasionally I put my left index finger on the inner spine and closed the book to contemplate a passage I'd read by gazing on the little flower bed Elise kept near the first tree. On one of these instances I noticed Elise in the kitchen with the sound of simmering meat. The smell of spices and barbecue sauce was a pleasant addition to the aroma of classic wood, the sound of the cackling fireplace, and her inebriating shampoo—peach I think.

I suddenly heard Für Elise playing in the background throughout the house's sound system. Immediately I asked myself why it had to be *that* song. Out of all the composers hitherto, why had I seen a serene reflection of life in Beethoven, and out of the thousands of nocturnes, études, compositions, and concertos, why I was *ordained* for a certain appreciation for the one labeled 'Für Elise' while guarding a woman named Elise who also *happened* to behave like a sonata. I was three when I first heard it. I vaguely remember the moment like a misty dream I might have had, of a man putting a phone next to my ear with it playing in the background while saying my mom's name in a sing-song voice.

Was it simply fate, or hardly coincidence? A part of me fought to make me believe that it was a sheer coincidence. It *had* to be circumstantial or incidental, but in this logic there was equal probability that it wasn't. We really *could* be stooges for some master puppeteer pulling the strings or controlling the turtles under us.

"What are you looking for?" she looked over from the kitchen and watched me look around the ceiling and corners of the room, licking some sauce from her fingertips gracefully.

I closed the book, "Where is the music coming from?" I was trying to spot the speakers emitting *Für Elise*.

"What music? Ohh," she looked back and spun the pan, "Come Vero. We'll eat."

I walked over and she handed me a plate: steak—rare, steamed carrots, sliced potatoes, and diced tomatoes forming a circle around the whole thing.

"How'd you know I like my steak rare?"

She had this triumphant gaze behind her easy smile, "One of those lucky guesses you bet all your chips on," she pointed to the chair around the kitchen island and made up her own plate.

"You... want me to eat with you?" I asked. I was so used to eating alone, to *being* alo—

She furrowed her brows, "Of course. You're not my butler Vero."

I took off my hat.

"You're more like a house guest that protects me from the evil out there," she pointed outside with the steak knife in her hand before spinning it and handing it to me.

Our hands touched as I grabbed it and suddenly her cheeks turned rosy—at least I think. It was dull and cliché except I couldn't describe it any other way.

It was comfortable silence during the meal. She had astonishingly elegant table manners, then again, maybe I was too used to Virg and Mack's barbaric eating habits or the drunk bimbos at *Yore Amici* to know any better. Whichever it was, I welcomed the change.

I hadn't noticed but I caught her gaze in the middle of shoving a carrot into my mouth with her elbow resting on the desk holding up her chin and her index finger lightly brushing her lower lip.

I wiped *my* lower lip with the napkin I had on my thighs instinctively, "Do I have something?" and rubbed my mouth harder.

"Do you have a girlfriend Vero?" her eloquence transcended

mere charm.

I gulped the carrot down. It nearly got lodged in my throat, "No one I'd consider a *girlfriend*," I wiped my brow with the napkin and caught some perspiration. Why was I so nervous?

"I find that hard to believe."

I put the knife and fork down, "There *was* one person at Oxford."

"What was her name?" she leaned closer. A thin strand of her hair slid to the front and dangled under her cheek.

"Elsa."

"How'd you meet her?"

I wiped my mouth with the napkin again.

* * *

"Give me a constant…" the silence was deafening, "Come on! And I don't want to hear *gravity, electromagnetism, strong force* or *weak force* either. We know all that already!"

Oxford. Quantum Mechanics. *What* was I thinking?

"One of you! Come on! … Someone give me one constant in the universe!"

My professor was quick to distinguish between *every*one and *every one* who deserved a seat in the much coveted lecture hall.

"And don't anyone say *'time'* either. We're not idiots here."

"Uhhh," an idiot with a beanie above his ears and Oliver People's prescription glasses in front of his eyes was quick to look up from the Foolgle search idling on his uPad.

"General Relativity Professor Floria. The speed of light is the only constant—"

The *only* constant? The mainstream bozo had all the answers.

I faded away. I wasn't objective or subjective, cold or emotional, an infidel or a believer. I was simply not there, "Death," I whispered to myself.

"That's really the only constant isn't it?" the girl beside me heard what I said. A *woman*, an *attractive* woman in an advanced physics class? Truly a rare specimen. I was surprised the Science-as-God lovers hadn't flocked to her already, but then again, snakes can often tell when an eagle's talons are about to descend upon them.

"Isn't that a little dark though?" her whisper was a sweet symphony to my ears.

"Death?" I had to make sure we were on the same page.

"Well, the idea in general, everyone you know will die someday," she was quite morbid. She interested me. I could tell we'd get along.

"Not unless you die first."

"But you can never be sure…"

Oh there was a way to be sure. The only way to be sure. Those that proclaim to have considered questions of truth must've pondered whether to commit suicide.

I was battling a headache that loved to hang around like a prowling bro during last-call at those hipster bars downtown but wouldn't do anything other than nag at how awful everything is.

My temple vein throbbed some of those obscure thoughts of loves found and lost into a pool of marsh. My head felt three sizes too small for my brain. It was funny, when a storm is about to rain hellfire down upon you, you think you can simply turn your back and ignore it and it'll go away. Religious fanatics chalk up their sins to the temptations of the devil but that's a lie, being a protégé to a predator is stable ground. It provides unequivocal protection from absolutely everything, even those exaggerated Disney knights who can slay beasts with only their will.

Her lips were flames to my water. Destiny was too big a word for it. What could I call it then? Chance? Randomness? *Chaos?* Whichever label I chose, the choice was never a choice more than it was an illusion, because each and every one of these labels refers to the same thing: truth. And it was there, right in front of me.

\* \* \*

"That's romantic," she snickered for a second and then put her hand on my hand, stroking my fingers to the nail, "Tell me about your first date."

"I... uh... you're very curious Madame."

"I feel like I barely know you... *captain*."

She had a point, "Fair enough. She worked at the law library. She just walked into that lecture by chance and thought it was interesting. I saw her again the following week, checked out every book in her section and read them. When I brought them back I awkwardly struck conversation and we discussed the books for hours, *Rawls'* theory of *justice*, Dworkin's critique of legal positivism, *Dred Scott V. Sandford*. Anyway, the library closed and it was dark. Somebody I knew, Robin, ran the theatre and film club. He served on the board or something, and had access to the big screen. We had the place to ourselves, a Bogart double feature: *Casablanca* and *The Big Sleep*. Afterwards I took her out on my Ducati to this little hill nearby in the middle of the forest greens, the dewy air, and the misty hue... I propped her angelic body up on those handlebars and she sung *As Time Goes By*..." I noticed Elise hanging on every word but staring at me dumbfoundedly, "... The song from *Casablanca*. And that was it. I told my mom and she told me about her necklace," I rolled up my sleeve and drew attention to the bracelet I always wore.

"Wow," her pupils dilated with her gaze fixed on mine. I don't think I liked what was happening. "I have one too," she rolled up her sleeve and I saw a little bracelet with an embedded eagle on it. I ran my fingers through it, the embossed pieces of its wings pricked my fingertips. "It's Don's, he gave it to me when I was young. I never wore it though... not until he died, and sometimes I hate myself for it. I find myself thinking that I only wear it because he died and I don't want to forget him, even though I wanted to when he was alive," the carving of the wings were intricate enough to be custom-made.

"I understand Madame. It's human to want to feel. Natural to seek some sort of supernatural advice that helps you find out more about yourself. To find out that every decision and path you take will lead to new results even if those results aren't always good, and further, that results may never lie in success."

She meshed her fingertips with mine, "What happened? ... With Elsa I mean?"

"I was young and stupid."

"You're very cryptic... come on, be straight with me."

"She found a better man than me," I exhaled.

"That's hard to believe."

"Well... a more committed man," I got up with my plate and went for hers, standing in front of the sink. She watched me clear the table, almost as if she were daydreaming about a world different from this one.

"Leave that Vero. You're not a butler."

"Nonsense Madame. You cooked. I'd like to do my part."

"Still *'Madame'* huh?"

Always I thought, until I heard the Doppler effect of a roaring sports car outside the house sliding on the icy road. I stumbled to the front window with Elise's plate in my hand just in time to spot that enigmatic Aston Martin drift the corner. Only a clown would drive that car on this terrain in this weather, but you can't expect much from a guy who paid extra for a plate that says *Da King*.

"It's just the neighbors' kids Vero... they think country towns have no traffic laws. Don't worry. We're safe here."

She was right. Surprisingly enough, I did feel a sense of equanimity in this place, but it wasn't enough for me to be stupid, I'd seen that car in too many places to think it was coincidence. The probability didn't hold up.

She took the plate out of my hand, "We'll run the dishwasher," and disappeared into one of the rooms, "I'll be right back," her voice echoed through the hall.

I heard a hummingbird from outside the window and approached it. It guided me to Elise's black Grandmaster piano in the corner of the den facing the large window that looked into the woods. I imagined sometimes you could spot a deer, an elk, or even a bear.

The notes were as fluid as if Beethoven himself were guiding my fingers. I even improvised some notes that added an extra oomph, if that could even be said about a Beethoven piece. It was perfect. Every single note. And for those three minutes, I was at peace... finally.

I had barely noticed Elise having slipped in beside me, accompanying my improvisations as we went back-and-forth leading the piece to the point where both of us were out of sync and only serving to move our hands closer together until one of hers was over mine and one of mine was over hers. She turned my hand around and stroked one of the lines on my palm, "Let's go for a walk," she guided me up towards the door.

I made myself heavier and glanced outside, "Now? It's snowing Madame!"

"Don't be a baby," she tossed my hat like a frisbee and put on one of those toques with the braided strap things that ran along either side of her ears.

Snow danced in slow motion before landing on the ground. I told Elise to be careful while I wondered who I was and why I was there when it hit me square in the face... the snowball she'd thrown. It knocked my hat down and froze my face in a smile. I started chasing her before she threw another at me and disappeared. I stood still, listening for her footsteps in the snow. I knew exactly where she was: behind that third tree. I snuck over like a cartoon character, feeling a bit like Elmer Fudd. I saw her sneak around the tree and grabbed her suddenly, "Gotcha!" I whispered. I don't know why she pushed herself between my elbows and pressed herself onto my body.

"What brings you here Vero?" she pouted.

"The green fields."

She looked around at all the dead trees in the middle of her personal Winter Wonderland as far as the eye could see, "We have no green fields Vero…"

I chuckled, "I guess they lied."

She backed up and skipped a few steps, beckoning me over and dancing around the trees. It felt like I was in some sissy romantic comedy scene where the melancholic man sees redemption in the woman and falls in love. It was all too perfect. Too… good to be true. I looked down at my feet and saw a rose somehow still blooming in the heart of winter in the middle of a forest. One of its thorns pricked me when I tried tearing it up for Elise. I put it in my palm, examining its petals. A snowflake landed on one of the petals, it was the only thing she was comparable to, and it was perfect. It *was* Elise. A dancing rose blossoming during winter with snowflakes hovering on its petals. It was right there in my hand despite all odds, all averages, all facts, or scientific *truths*. Elise and the crimson rose were coterminous, and I couldn't shake the idea that somehow, I was exactly where I had to be.

I looked up from the flower and she was gone. I couldn't see her anywhere. Her footsteps were covered up with more snow so I couldn't track her. I stood still again to listen for her movements in the silence of the snowfall….

Nothing. A feeling of unwavering panic sledged in me.

"Madame?" I called out with only the howling wind hissing back, "Madame?" I looked around.

'Stupid! Stupid! *What are you doing Vero?*' This is a job, not some honey you can gobble up. Not a dame you can tiptoe around for cheap thrills. I reached over my belt. Great… my .38 was in the house.

"Madame!" I yelled out, shoving through the trees and

branches trying to imagine where she went and how I'd explain this to the judge, to deduce where the black Aston Martin was driftin—

## SKEPTICAL ENTRY

MY TEARS HAVE saturated this entry, and I am in a desperate panic to remain calm, having given into my emotions like Raskolnikov; even writing down what I have done is perhaps the dumbest thing I can do, but reading back what I've done may relax me in the future, and as soon as that happens, I will burn this particular entry. I bumped into, no, I saw Helen again by chance at the café, and this time, having practiced my smiling, could return her nod and flirtatious little smirk. We got to talking and to the credit of my stupidity and ignorance, she was *not* interested in me. Rather, she was only seeking out a platonic companion. She started telling me about this wonderful man she'd met and hoped I could offer her objective advice in assisting her close the distance gap between them. Apparently he is quite withdrawn and introverted, housing a deep sadness within himself. Although I'd suspected I'd loved her in the past, the feeling had never been this real, and the moment she told me she loved this other man my heart raced, stopped, and then raced again to the point of desperation, then fear, then despair, and finally agony. At last it landed on wrath, and I was filled with an ire I could only describe as hulk-like. I kept it bottled up until I got home and trashed my apartment.

I encountered her again in the thundering night air after I'd burned most of the unsent letters I'd written to her when we were younger. She had dropped by his place and he wasn't home. She was practically in tears hoping that he wasn't with another woman. It wasn't until she said 'Vi would never do that to me!' that my wrath returned and boiled. I had no plans of ever having a romantic relationship with her but felt that she was always mine nonetheless, and hearing that pompous prick had taken her from me trembled my fists.

I took pity on her until she started ranting about our feuding families and asked me why they've been fighting for over 40 years. I detected an ounce of hostility in her voice and it did not bode well with me. I thought she was purposely pushing me to try and get under my skin, and although I now realize I was wrong, at the time, for a reason unknown, I drew my .22 and shot her multiple times in the heart. Her expiring eyes watched me quizzically as she hobbled to the floor. Rainwater pattered her beautiful skin. Blood squirmed out of her mouth as she whimpered, "I thought you understood.... Don't let them use you," were the last words she whispered to me coupled with the sound of rain splashing on the pavement.

Although it will be easy to simply add Helen to the list of collateral damages that this particular mission has had (speaking of which, I had Hans plant the earring and the shoe in Vero's apartment. He is sure to take the fall for all of the killings... God I love this country), I can't help but wonder if I've failed my family. If I cannot manipulate the facts in such a way that the Calvanos are led to believe Helen's murder was not at the hand of a Torrino, they will surely seek retaliation. Not only that, but I have eliminated perhaps the one other person who'd understood me since Elsa's departure. Even now, I can't remember why I did it. A murder with no purpose or meaning is the worst kind, the other killings had a greater purpose.

I've become a murderer. A blackguard from some crime fiction novel. I can never call myself a good man again. I've lost my *giri*. The only chance I have at realizing my potential comes with capturing the targets as planned and reestablishing the Torrino name as kingly and ruling this cesspool of a city. Those who've read Nietzsche will understand my actions as necessary, and I will try to ascertain a way to fight the Kantians. Morality is limiting and useless. Politicians, bankers, lawyers, and governments figured this out long ago. I expect no opposition in brandishing these accepted ideals.

## Stile Antico

"BOO!" SHE POPPED out from behind a tree and poked me twice in the tricep.

I didn't flinch.

"What? You didn't even flinch!" the disappointed look in her eye was daunting.

I grabbed her shoulders, "DON'T EVER DO THAT AGAIN!" the tone of my voice ascended from fear to rage and eventually landed on fury with each syllable.

She flinched back and forth and blinked hysterically. I realized I'd overreacted, that I was scaring her and I let go, "Madame, I don't want—"

She pushed me back and slapped and punched me in the chest the way dames do and screamed, "WHY DO YOU NEVER SAY MY NAME?"

I calmed down and took a step closer to her. Our bodies pressed tightly against one another amongst the falling snowflakes, "What?" I asked in surprise.

"Why do... *you...*" she pointed to my nose "Never say my *name?*" she slowed her tempo, practically whispering each letter ominously.

I knew what I wanted to say and I knew what I *had* to say. Sometimes they aren't the same thing, one of life's many curveballs. You have to make a choice, to select what *you* think is best. Chances are, you'd be wrong.

"Every time I hear your name, it's like a whisper rejuvenating my essence. My heart stops, speeds up, stops again, and it goes back-and-forth like that. Your name has always been a part of me," and part of what I *wanted* to say was 'it wasn't about the money anymore. I'd give my life for you because you're a better person than me. You have a better shot at changing something, the world, lives, *a* life. You deserve to live longer than me, longer than any of us.'

She looked overwhelmed. Too much information in too little time. She stepped back and the snow flattened under her Italian leather boots, "Pffft. Is that what you tell all the women? You have *no feelings.*"

I tried remembering Virgil's rather quick response to this *you have no feelings* debacle but for the life of me I couldn't remember. Enough seconds elapsed in silence for me to realize it was too late to respond at all.

It takes courage and strength to be sensitive to things and even more strength and courage to own up to it or be vocal about it. Robots, the only things with a perfect lack of emotional capacity, are easily controlled, and I suddenly realized that's why the military often trains people to suppress their emotions. Unfortunately for them, humans aren't machines. We feel, we love, we cry, we despair, and we rejoice. Anyone who's ever tried to convince me not to feel is someone I shouldn't have trusted. The only reason you should *shut off* your emotions and emulate a robot is if you're doing horrible things. How fatal my decisions have been. How many people would be loving, rejoicing, and feeling right now rather than crying indefinitely in the depths of the afterlife? If only I'd figured this out sooner.

I thought about that chance encounter I had with my mom's friend—damn it what was his name? It had something to do with some superhero—and him telling me to follow my passions. To do whatever I loved. To be true to my nature. It was funny, because in those 10 seconds I thought I had a father, that a random guy with the unique timbre in his voice was more of a father to me for 10 seconds than my *real* father was for a lifetime.

She lifted her chin a little higher, "Hmmmmmm, or at least you pretend not to. I know how you feel," she rolled her ankle on a spot fixed in the snow.

"You *know* how I feel? Don't make me laugh angel…. How *I* feel. … Imagine a slither of hope in this world, something that makes you smile, some*one* that gives you a reason to live. Now imagine, if you can, that person abruptly gone…" I knew she could imagine it. I was being cruel and insensitive to her late brother, "Taken away because your *God* needed some Thursday night entertainment. A blinding rage tethers off your soul and anchors your body down. You try to fight it but no one can fight themselves or fight who they are. And this new *angel* circles around your heart like a hungry tiger waiting for its moment to devour what's left of you. Then suddenly, you meet someone who makes you feel as you did before, gives you that solace… but all you can think of is the previous moment when it was all taken away. You have no choice but to fight yourself and suppress that beating heart so the tiger can't pounce. That person's name is constantly whispered in the recesses of your mind and you start to realize if you say it out loud, it becomes real, and you might lose her again… not sure if you'd be able to put yourself back together. If your heart could withstand a duo of tigresses feasting on it like a politician at a charity benefit."

"Vero… I…"

I didn't want this to become a thing. Everyone around me has died and I didn't want her to fall to the same fate. "Madam—Elise, I'm being paid for sacrifice. Love *is* sacrifice, but ours is an illusion. I'm being *paid* to protect you, to sacrifice myself for you." It was simpler just to keep things simple.

"You might as well love me and make it official then!" she had a knack for being charmingly sexy when she wanted something, but that's what dames are good at.

Everyone I'd ever loved had been taken away. It was best not to get attached, not to have anything in my life I wasn't willing to walk away from in the blink of an eye. I brushed my fingertips on her shoulder, down her bicep and arm until I got to her palm. She took my hand and squeezed it tightly, straddling her leg over me and coming in for a kiss.

"Wait," I whispered.

She became self-conscious, looking down as if I'd broken a piece of her, "Am I not pretty enough? Virgil told me about the women you—"

"You're perfect. You don't have a single flaw, but I'm your bodyguard… I don't deserve you," the words 'I don't deserve you' echoed in my eardrum as if someone else had whispered them, someone I knew long ago but no longer.

She stroked her hands on my chest and rested her head there in the sort of hug you read about in those romantic fairy tales lost in the bestseller aisle of your department bookstore.

What had *I* done? What had my ancestors done that I should deserve this happiness, this redemption? Why had *I*, of all people been chosen as the recipient of this *luck* and gifted such an angel?

'You're an animal,' the old man's voice rung in my ears, foreground to the incoherent mumblings of the lipless little girl in the background of my psyche.

A snowflake landed on one of my knuckles and I felt it. The cold coursed through my body and through my veins before Elise shuddered a little in my arms.

I held her hand as we walked towards the house, wandering from the beaten path.

"Let's…" her teeth clattered together, "Go for ice cream!"

"Ice cream? Madame—I mean Elise," it reanimated my entire being just hearing myself say it, "You're freezing," her nose had turned the color of Rudolph's, "Maybe hot chocolate is a better idea."

"We didn't have dessert! Anything would be good! I know a great diner close to town. We'd have to drive though."

"It's not a problem," this rotten feeling in my gut let me know *that* imaginary boyfriend role Elise wanted me to play at the Harriet wasn't imaginary anymore. Not that I'd minded, Elise was the farthest thing from flawed.

It was an excellent day, living in seclusion away from the enslaving possessions we hold dear to ourselves in abundance. Away from the greed of dictators, emperors, presidents, or whatever the hell they're calling themselves nowadays with snowflakes idling in the cool breeze. The frozen lake in the centre rippled droplets of perfection around its circumference. It was more than an excellent day... so why this twinge in my stomach? This wincing augury of foreshadowed doom?

I watched heat steam up the air as it left my lips, listening to a crow sing on one of the dead tree branches as I neared the porch.

Elise went in and reappeared in less than a minute with a bigger jacket and a scarf, smiling ear-to-ear with her scarlet cheeks.

The crow was all I heard; it was so loud I couldn't quite hear what Elise said.

"Huh?" I asked again.

"Caw! Caw! Cacaw!"

She leaned in to kiss me over the sound of its annoying shrill but stopped just short of my cheek when an eagle squawked so loud it shut the crow right up. And again, I thought about how different it was from what the United States wants you to believe. It's a poetic, descending screech resembling a whistle, but the U.S of A does what they do best, deceive or distort, the real DOD. You'd think an ornithologist would tell them the audio-track they're actually using in every piece of media *ever* for their *national bird* is actually the red-tailed hawk.

I'd never heard one so close before but something told me it was an eagle, as if I could've understood its cries for hope. Its call boomed once more and I heard wings flap away from the trees near the branches of where I was hearing the devil's bird.

The eagle's lyrical song continued a third time before it slowly faded and morphed with Elise's voice: "Vero?"

"Yes my love? … I mean Elise… I mean Madame," these slips would be the death of me.

"Are we going to go?" there was no way she didn't hear it. I'm guessing she pretended not to and would certainly bring it up later.

"Of course."

She tapped her boots on the porch. The creaking of the wood miraculously lessened the churning I was repressing in my gut.

"Start the car. We'll go in when it's warm. That's why *I* got the remote starter."

I pointed the starter to the car from the stairs, turning back to Elise as I pushed the buttons, "We'll be well on our way before you know it."

Nothing. I pushed the buttons again, mashing them quickly, slowly, alternatively, doing whatever I could think of. The car sat dead.

"Must be the batteries… brrrrr," Elise quipped before she snatched the key out of my hand and made a beeline to the car.

The wincing in my stomach suddenly acted up again. Something was wrong. I'd learned at too young an age that *God* was a bully with a match burning our wings. At too young I learned that he gave you something too good to be true and just when you might hope again, just as you've balanced yourself on the edge of tranquility, happiness, or even faith, he'd take it away… laughing at your ignorance for his own comedic pleasure and scream, 'You thought that'd *actually* happen?' right before he showed you it *was* too good to be true.

I dove and tackled Elise to the ground from behind, jumping from the top of the stairs and rolling the two of us away from the car. "WAIT!" I think I screamed.

Nothing. She had a sense of humour about it when we stopped tumbling in the ice with me perfectly on top of her. "If you wanted to get on top of me Vero… all you had to do was ask."

Red-as-a-beet; bloody; Santa's suit; the passion in her hair, none of these would even begin to describe the colour of my face at that moment. At least that's how I felt.

I rolled off her instantly thinking of Helen for some peculiar reason, "Sorry Madame, I thought the car was unsafe."

The car finally shook to a start. She turned her head in the snow, "See? You're being paranoi—"

She hadn't gotten all the letters out when the car flew up in a scorching inferno and took my flask with it. The target seemed to be me: the driver, since its seat went up instantly in a particular kind of precision hellfire. I crowded Elise under me to protect her from the heat and any flying debris. The burning sound of bending steel and the smell of rotten metal overloaded my senses.

Elise was breathing heavily under me with a deer-caught-in-headlights *what-the-hell-is-going-on* kind of stare.

"You okay?"

She was in shock. It took a couple of tries, a couple of snaps of my fingers, a rub of the cheek, "Are you hurt Madame?" and a couple of minutes before she nodded… slower… than… a… tortoise.

She clutched my chest tighter when the fuselage marked the final explosion, and it was a big one. The car turned over and hissed so much hot air towards us it nearly melted my eyes.

So much for a kick-back-and-relax-with-a-babe-cuddling-your-chest-Sunday-afternoon-at-a-lake-house. It was *God's* day, and that always meant death and despair for the invisible sadist in the sky.

We couldn't stand too close to it but Elise was still frozen and my left shoulder blade caught something from the flying wreckage. It stung and hurt like hell, but I had a job to do. I carried Elise in, looking for my fruity phone and the .38 to call Virg. There was barely any service, no bars out here in the middle of nowhere. I used the landline above the kitchen sink.

"Virg?" I violently coughed up some blood while trying to rotate my left arm. My mobility and range were shot. The pain travelled to my neck. I could barely turn my head.

"Vi! How's country life treatin—"

"We have a situation. They're making a move," that's all I needed to say.

"Be there ASAP. Look after the girl!"

I heard the sound of footsteps flattening snow again. I spun the cylinder and cocked the gun. We were too far from town, too far from anyone to have heard what's going on here so quickly. Click.

I approached the door with caution. The explosion had disoriented me. I'd never been this close to one before. There's nothing quite like being in a 31 million dollar plane to detach you from the truth. It felt like hell, like I was burning alive. The movies lie. They lie big time. I tried holding my balance but it was hard. I saw double. I fell and crawled behind a table looking at the two doors... I mean door in front of me. I rubbed my forehead to try to focus and orient myself. I thought I was going to pass out.

I could barely lift the .38 I was holding. My muscles wanted to rest, to give up, telling me that the armour-piercing bullet in my pocket had won, that it came in many shapes and sizes.

A henchman walked through the front door. He wasn't even hiding who he was or what he believed. A straight-up mobster in a striped suit with gelled back hair and alligator shoes,

"Oh princessssss?" he sang in a high-pitched voice, the 'sss' sounding like a rattlesnake, "Come out come out wherever you are."

I was seeing two of him. Which one was real? I had to take down bad guys and save the girl. It sounded simple, but the hardest thing to do on this planet is live a simple life.

I stood up and fired at the one on the left, the bullet went right through him... he looked to his right, presumably wondering where the hell I was firing before raising an eyebrow at me... a real *Pulp*

*Fiction* moment.

He ducked his head, looked at me and fired, hitting me straight in the right shoulder just under the neck, "You're a horrible shot Vero!!"

Did he say my name? I penguin-walked two steps, feebly trying to close the gap between us so I could fistfight him with two destroyed shoulders... yeah... I'm that dumb, but I had to save her. I couldn't let anything happen to her. It wouldn't be right.

I sounded like a tragic anti-hero from some niche third-person-shooter video game, some fat kid with glasses reclined on a La-Z-Boy controlling me and letting the bad guys shoot me so he doesn't max out his first-aid inventory. Hell, if God exists, he probably *would* be some fat recluse without any practical understanding of anything other than diet sodas and the informative *articles* in Playboy magazine.

I slumped to one side holding my shoulder and feeling my hand wet with my blood. It was hard to stay awake. Nothing like the movies. I've been shot before but this was... different. My... eyelids met... it'd been a while. Was I... that weak? ... That fragile? That I couldn't even... protect... a....

# Canzonetta VIII

Entry No. 12, 223.

Time. 12:04 A.M.

Mood at time of entry: originally panicked. Battling a bout of nerves. Tense albeit marvellous at the potential for catharsis.

I visited mother at Golden Years Residence earlier today. The nurse or receptionist there is always very courteous and flirty; I can't pinpoint whether this is due to a schoolboy crush she has cultivated for me or if it is merely her beguiling personality. Perhaps she is just a coquette.

Mother was okay. Nagging and complaining about everything but that is nothing new. I humoured her and updated her on the family business, even the mess with Judge Phoenix. It was in fact mother's ruthless idea to target his children as a means to achieve our end. I thought this was quite cold and dishonourable, especially considering the fact that I know his daughter and she wants nothing to do with the life her family leads. A faint smile wrinkled mother's cheek when she heard that his son had been eliminated, and asked me for a status report on the daughter.

I told her that since his son's murder, the judge has retained 24/7 protection, to which she replied 'It changes nothing,' and pushed again for a status report. I showed her the surveillance photos Ahriman had procured, and to my surprise, mother seemed more interested in the target's bodyguard and asked if I knew who he was. She wanted to find out everything about him, even who his parents are, specifically inquiring about his inscrutable hat. This tidbit of information Sebastian had handy (he mentioned it to me in a previous conversation): the hat belonged to this father and was given to him as a gift by his mother.

Mother got this vicious look in her eye and said that the thin black strip was added later by hand. The hat is one of a kind... she'd only seen it once before, and it was in fact *my* father's hat.

This is impossible. Perhaps even my mother, 'the *great* Electra Torrino,' has grown senile in old age. She ordered me to focus my attention to *both* the target and her bodyguard (a task I had been contemplating for quite a while anyway), that it was of utter importance to *our* family. She was deliberately ambiguous. I couldn't tell if she meant *family* as in her and I, or if she meant *family* as a sort of Coppola's *Godfather* equivocation.

Even though I had a Kantian (for lack of a better word) problem when she ordered me to inflict pain on the target herself, I am bound by the infinite laws of familial rule and must obey my mother's word, especially in times when she at first seems wrong since that is when it matters most.

Ludicrously enough, I thought I heard them both in the retirement home out in the hallway when I first arrived. Later, even more unexpectedly, having followed the target*s* to some remote cabin in the woods, I received the unsettling news that Sebastian and Sofus had decided it was the opportune moment to nab them both like some scene from a bad horror movie. This was impulsive and stupid, as charging in without a plan is always sure to fail, and as expected, did in this particular circumstance. They could not find the female subject in the house despite a visual confirmation that she was in there! There must've been a hidden panic room. Sofus, in his flamboyant suit and overpriced gangster shoes, got lucky and shot the male target! Although it would've been easy to grab the male target, I hadn't yet relayed my mother's orders to them, and luckily so, since Sofus reported that the target was extremely cool under pressure and did not flinch at danger. I am the first to say Sofus is lucky to be alive, that a man like *that* doesn't miss too often... I know what kind of man he is and what he is capable of. I will however, believe these superhuman feats when I see them with my own eyes.

Naturally, we have tipped our hand to the targets and they are now on the run, and without his daughter, we cannot exert pressure on the judge.

~

The target is smart. He has left us no leverage, taking his only friend and his friend's girlfriend with him on the run. We won't be able to smoke them out; our only chance is to find them. This will not be an issue; I have placed all our people in a 5-city radius on alert at every hotel, motel, and hostel, only hoping that they do not leave the country by plane.

Meanwhile, the ease by which I acquired a 50 caliber sniper rifle was alarming and it was even more startling how much easier it was to hire a trained marksmen to use it when I require him or her (I do not know the gender of this particular employee, the codename given to me was merely 'Jaguar'). Make fun of their stupidity all you want, but Americans understand the depth of capitalism: for enough money anything is for sale, even souls.

I digress again, the sniper is to be used in the plan to retrieve the targets when they are travelling by car. This tactic has the greatest probability of success as the male target always drives and will therefore be caught by surprise. The sniper will rain bullets into the engine in order to kill it and when the target is distracted by the suppression fire, Sebastian and Ahriman (and perhaps even Hans) will trap them from behind with their Lexus and move ahead to take them both. I've instructed them not to touch Elise under any circumstances but had the unfortunate obligation to permit them to injure her bodyguard since I know he is not the type to go down without a fight. They can't kill him, but I'm sure Sebastian will find some excuse to shoot him somewhere non-fatal, or somehow cause him an excruciatingly amount of pain without killing him, which is sadly *his* morbid gift of understanding the human body *too well*.

Once I have them in my possession, I will acquire his best friend and his girlfriend, along with their third partner. This will be accomplished with ease. They're like the three stooges. I will tie them up and make him (the leader) think he is smarter than me by pretending to relinquish the upper hand. Pawns love thinking they're lions, kings, or eagles or any other predator. I will act like the quintessential villain in some corny book and will monologue and tell him of my plans to dominate the city's crime, masking my pursuit of my real motive for truth. Eventually I will make fun of his unsolidified identity and father; stupid men get attached to their non-existent fathers, even the withdrawn or distant ones. I will make fun of his honour. This plan will not fail, I know enough of Hobbesian human nature to manipulate a drunk, a degenerate womanizer, a quasi-philosopher, and two spoiled socialites. Should it come to a point where I *am* seemingly surrendering the upper hand, I will kill the womanizer. The world will be better without people like him anyway.

That's all for now.

# Melodeclamation

"You're an animal," the old man screamed, "You have no heart! No soul!" he tore my chest open and the little girl played with my intestines, pretending to suffocate herself with it, then biting into my guts and alleviating her hunger.

"What the..." Virg came over and knocked them back, "You're going to be okay Vi."

Beep. Beep. Blip.

"Vero? Oh my God..." a tearful Elise squeezed my hand.

A light approached me. It was so blinding I had to use my hand to block it from burning my eyes.

"Who are you?" it asked me, "Who is your father?"

"I don't know," I whispered.

"Who are you?" it asked again, "Who *was* your father?"

"I. Don't. Know," I repeated, feeling as if something was holding me back. I wasn't quite able to reach it.

"You're going to be okay. Stay with me buddy. You're not going anywhere, you're not going anywhere. You are not giving up," Virgil's voice made the light recede into a dark hole.

Beep. Beeeeeep. Bliiiippp. I was on some sort of bed. I could barely see, couldn't move. Virgil was talking to someone in a white coat in the background while Elise stood over me.

I could tell exactly when Virgil sat next to me. The smell of his cigar mixed with the residual aroma of women's perfume hung over the air around us. I felt paralyzed. I couldn't even open my eyes, the constant 'utter animal' or some variation by the old man rung in my ears.

"I never talk about my dad Vi, partly because of your dad, but mostly because I want you to know you're not missing anything. I mean, my dad was not without affection, but he was a clichéd old-school tough guy most of the time. He never cried. Never hugged me. Not once. He constantly called me a buttered-up Nancy mama's boy... but he did charming things for my mom: flowers, cards, jewelry, thought it made him a better man, a gentleman, his path to atonement I guess. Anyway..."

I couldn't breathe. There was a loud beeping noise to my right. Focusing on Virgil's voice was the only thing keeping me sane.

"... Every year on their anniversary, there'd be this bouquet of roses on the dinner table from my dad, and this bouquet grew with each passing year. My mom always said that it started with a single rose when they started dating. He always had a note with these bouquets, printer paper folded into a hand-made card with the words: *My love for you grows.* 39 bouquets and a lifetime of growing love were what he left my mom when he died. The first anniversary after his death I happened to be home..." his voice broken again, "And... uh... my mom was shocked to receive yet another perfect bouquet addressed to her from my dad. Heartbroken and in a rage, she called the florist to say there had been a mistake. The florist replied, 'There's no mistake ma'am, before he passed away your husband prepaid for many years and asked us to guarantee that you'd continue getting your flowers on every anniversary. My mom started sobbing and dropped the phone. She opened the card with trembling hands, '*My love for you is eternal.*' He wasn't much of a dad to me, but he loved my mom. I guess that's what I'm trying to say, you can't die Vi. You can't. It's selfish but I need you. I think I love Amelia," he looked behind him, lowering his voice to a whisper, "I want to be with her, and without you there by my side, without my brother-in-arms, I don't think I can do it. I can't. I want you there beside me when I marry her. I want you there as godfather to my son or daughter. I want you there at the barbecues we'll have with you and Elise, and I want you there when I depart from this world because I know you'd do me justice at my eulogy, you'd tell it how it is... wake up my friend, wake up... please," the desperation cracked his voice, I'd never seen this side of him before.

His prayers must've fallen on someone's ears because suddenly I heard my mom come into my room like I was 12 again, telling me and the guy whose name I couldn't remember "Enough banter boys," and I felt like Superman. My eyes opened in a hospital room over a deafening beep in the background while a tear-ridden Virg stared at me in the foreground; his shoulders pounced up at paradise and down at hell in quick successive jerks. A smile dashed across his cheeks.

"Elise! Is she okay? I've failed again," I tried to get up. My shoulders felt like they weighed more than the burned-up Land Rover.

"Easy buddy! Easy!" he slightly moved to the left and I saw Elise and Amelia hidden behind him. Elise's head rested uncomfortably on Amelia's shoulder and her legs went over the metal and impractical handrails. They were two sleeping beauties.

I was relieved. I thought she was dead; there was going to be no more pansy Russian roulette if she was hurt. I was going to load that armour-piercing shell right into the top cylinder, swallow the muzzle and squeeze the trigger after I killed every last one of them. But she wasn't hurt, she was okay, and I could rest.

"Thank…" I passed out again.

I dreamt about Elise and I dancing in the snow. She teased me, asking '*do you feel?*' But all I could think about was the systematic definition of the word. Trying to reject or accept an idea, a concept or belief requires an absolute understanding of it. What *are* emotions, feelings really? Merely the physical reactions of our minds. That's exactly what they are, bodies *reacting* to minds. *Reactive* things are useless, a lazy police force or a pre-emptive strike by an overzealous government with mythical proclamations to democracy. It's *proactive* behaviours that guide us, and if that's true, then doesn't that make those of us who are unreactive more reliable, more… human?

"How do you feel?" someone's fingertips ran up and down my forearm.

I opened my eyes to meet the gaze of an angel. Elise stood over my hospital bed looking like I did after days of no sleep and constant brooding.

"Vero?" she batted her eyelashes, brushing her hand on my cheek taking extra care not to lean too hard on top of me.

"Elise."

"I'm sorry Vero. If it weren't for me—"

"It's my job. Are *you* okay?"

"Yes! Thanks to you I got away. They caught the guy by the way. He was a Torrino thug."

"What's a Torrin-to?"

"The Torrinos? Donna Electra Torrino? They've been at war with the Calvanos ever since I was little."

"Why are they after you?"

"My dad's presiding over a case, one of their guys is being indicted for racketeering, one side wants him to send the guy to jail —"

"And the other to free him," I interrupted, "With you guys smack in the middle."

She nodded.

"I'm guessing your dad's doing the honourable thing and sending that goon to jail, which means the guy that shot me is from that same family, the... Torrinos?"

"Yes."

"I thought organized crime meant they're 'organized'... as in intelligent. They're bringing down heat on themselves by attacking a judge and his family. Where are the cops when you need them?"

"I never would've pegged you as an idealist. They used to co-exist: the cops and the mob. An eye for an eye. Then Don Torrino got caught. My dad was a DA then. Now it's... much worse."

"Their don was caught? How are they waging this war?"

"His daughter took over after his son was killed."

"By a Calvano?"

"No. By a contractor; an assassin they called the *Viking*."

I would've laughed if it didn't hurt, "*Justice.*"

"… When Electra took over things quickly deteriorated. She has no soul. She's ruthless. Cold. She doesn't care about anything or anyone except her son."

"Who is he?" Best-case scenario was I'd get to him and leverage him in exchange for Elise's safety.

"No one knows. He lives in Switzerland somewhere."

"We'll take care of them, they made it personal. Where are my clothes?" I looked around.

"Vero! You can't leave. You're hurt! You barely have mobility in your arm!"

I moved my arm a little, forming big circles with my shoulders as much as I could in that bed with that huge bandage/splint thing running across my chest and back, "But mobility nonetheless."

Virg walked in with an unlit cigar on his lip.

"Virgil, he wants to leave," Elise said to him as I pulled the sheet off of my legs, disconnecting all the nodes connected to my body and disrupting the rhythmic beating, "Tell him it's not possible."

"It's personal Virg, where are my clothes?"

"Sir!" a nurse walked in, "You can't just disconnect…"

"Don't tell me what to do. I'm checking out, bring me the form to sign. I'll waive your responsibility."

The nurse left to get the necessary information. They don't give a rat's ass whether their patients are healthy, they just don't want to be sued. If you sign that waiver, they could care less if you dropped dead on the floor right outside the hospital.

"Vero don't be stubborn," Elise handed me one of the medical nodes that was connected to my chest.

"I'm alright. Don't worry about me."

"Don't be ridiculous. You're not 100%. If you go out there you'll be exposed and vulnerable."

"She has a point Vi," Virg finally chimed in.

"A man earns respect in what he does when he is *most* vulnerable," that's what people don't seem to comprehend, these *bros, bankers, politicians*... complete nitwits for short. The idea that women might initially lust after the chest-puffing macho goon who won't think twice in breaking some idiot's jaw because he got out of line when he's out with a bunch of friends, but how many times would they endure that same man being bettered. How many times would they stitch, bandage, and set their bones? Bodies heal, and minds are not as pliable, and neither are dames.

The nurse came back in and handed me a clipboard, "Sir you understand that if you sign this..."

"Yeah yeah yeah," I signed it and handed it back to her, "My clothes?"

"Damn it Vero!" Elise exclaimed.

"I'll get them I guess," Virgil disappeared for a moment.

I took Elise's hand, "I'm going to end it Elise. Your dad, you, you won't have to worry anymore, don't you want vengeance for Don?" it was time to do what I was good at, and for something other than oil or water prices this time.

"Vengeance? Vero, those on the journey for vengeance must first dig two graves."

"Chinese philosophy? Besides, they know where we are. We're sitting ducks. We should leave here regardless. We'll go away if you want but we have to go away from *here*."

"But they got the guy! Maybe they just wanted to scare us."

"You're in the middle of a mob war Elise!" I slowly got out of bed, "If your dad lets the guy go to save you, me, or himself, the other family will just come after us! Maybe next time they'll get Virg, or Amelia. These people don't stop! They don't tire. They don't... care," my words trailed off.

Virgil popped in with a bag of clothes, "I heard my name."

"We're leaving."

I got dressed while Elise waited outside. Virgil stood behind the screen, "Hey man, listen, while you were out. I didn't know if you could hear me, but..."

"I could hear you. At first I thought I was dreaming."

I came out from behind the screen. My shirt was untucked and slobbish, but this was hardly the time for fashion statements.

"I want you to know... I meant what I sa—"

"I know."

"You know she didn't leave your side right? Right now's the only time she's left the room longer than a minute."

\* \* \*

We walked through the parking garage to the car the judge had given Virgil: the ML63 AMG. I heard footsteps behind us and stopped moving,

"Hear that? Get Elise out of here."

A car boop-beeped open, followed by a door opening and closing, and an ignition turning and tires moving away from us.

"It was just someone leaving Vero. You okay?"

I cradled my shoulder. A little blood leaked through the shirt but I covered it up with my jacket.

"It's hypervigilance," Virgil whispered to Elise thinking I couldn't hear him, "Happens after traumatic events."

"But he's always vigilant."

"Exactly! Imagine how he is now."

I got into the car, "Are we going to leave, or are you two going to stand there and talk all day?"

"We *should* go away. My dad can't leave but they can't get to him. They wouldn't risk it, the police wouldn't let them get away it. But *we* could go away, us three plus Amelia."

"Sounds like a plan," Virgil immediately responded.

I observed every car carefully, trying to remember whether or not I'd seen *any* of them before.

"Has to be a different country, a place where if they make a move, they'd have to send guys there, and they can only send so many guys. That way, if they do come, we'll have the advantage."

Elise looked at Virg and he looked back at her with both eyebrows raised and widened eyes. They probably thought I had PTSD or I was crazy but I'd lost sight of the job. My job was to protect Elise. It made no difference whether or not she liked me or if she agreed with what I said, I had to *just* keep her safe.

"Okay. We'll drop by my place and I'll pack," she said.

"Perfect," I responded while trying to remember if I'd seen a passing car before: a grey Altima with the plate '*Luvlif3*,' "Call Amelia. Tell her to be ready."

He was patronizing me but it didn't matter anymore; *nothing* was starting to matter again.

We'll pick her up on the way to Virg's. We'll stop at my place last."

"When do we get the tickets?" Virg rolled his eyes.

"At the airport is the safest best if we don't drive, cash only from now on. Leave no trail, tell Mack to stay here and keep an eye on the judge, they might make a move in desperation," things were getting serious. I hadn't seen Mack in quite a while but he was probably somewhere feeling alone and empty. Despite *nailing*—his words—so many *broads*—his word, he'd never embraced the warmth of intimacy, never truly grasped how to *feel* a woman. How to make a connection, and despite his apparent popularity, he was never known to anyone, least of all himself.

I started to sound like an over-analyzing fool, a character like

Sherlock waiting for someone to make a mistake or say something stupid so I could point out their contradictions; it wasn't a good place to be. I was losing touch with reality. I needed a drink to ground myself, and with that thought, the perpetual revulsion returned.

## APARTMENT
## 2 HOURS AGO

MY HEADACHE ONLY served to assist the old man's bellowing 'you're an animal' when I pressed G in the elevator. It whirred and hovered downwards, clanking the safety ropes as it descended. I wished, no, *hoped* from the bottom of my heart that it wouldn't stop anywhere. I wasn't in the mood to deal with some goon and make irrelevant small talk. In fact, I asked *Letus* not to stop at all save for hell. I wanted to crash full speed at the ground floor and lift the onus off my .38.

I was standing over a discarded copy of *Veritas Daily* open to the horoscopes: *'Danger is right around the corner. Be extra cautious.'* Thanks for the advice.

"Where is he? Vero Kóróna! Tell me!"

I heard someone screaming at the front desk as soon as the elevator slowed down. The incoherent mumblings now full of brevity as the doors dinged open. Was he talking about me? My last name isn't Kóróna... and there's no way on this planet there was another asshole named Vero living in the same building.

Bill Blake. The 30-something trusty concierge sonorously told the ogre with the members-only jacket and gelled hair that he couldn't give that info out even *if* someone with that name lived here.

He was stomping his feet and grunting like an eight-year-old as I turned the corner to the lobby.

"Tell me where he is," the archetypal antagonist screeched, wanting... I can only presume, to scare Blake. Little did he know, Blake was a Frømandskorpset stationed somewhere hostile—I never asked where. There hadn't been a horror or injustice he hadn't seen, nothing he feared other than Judgment Day, and despite that, he'd readily die because he believed in fate and predestination.

The *Michael Corleone* wannabe was a total stranger to me. I didn't like his hostility. I didn't like what I was forced to walk into, but like all significant events in life, what *choice* did I have?

"Sir, don't threaten me or the tenants. You can't intimidate me. I have no problem restraining you and calling security and the police."

I approached unnoticed with their eyes fixed on each other; Bill was standing up with his palms out attempting to calm this animal down while the guy flayed the guest sign-in sheet around, my apartment number and signature probably beside Helen's name under last-week's date.

"And, as if emerging through an ominous fog... Vero appeared with the whisperings of the supernatural," they both turned around to face me. Blake waited on my word to eject the *wiseguy*.

"Vero Króna-Bergljót?"

He *was* talking about me. What's a... Kókoona though? I was curious, wanted to see where he was going with this.

"That seems to be rumour."

He threw a manila envelope at me, "I had to hand-deliver this to you," he flipped off Blake and stormed out. How classy.

Blake and I watched him walk away from the building after rubbing his fingers on the glass windows and doors before slamming them to make himself seem bigger than he was.

I ripped open the envelope, reaching in for what felt like a single piece of paper, "Watch a little Scorsese and suddenly you're a goodfella."

"Don't I know it. He was screaming something about me *having* to give him the info..." Blake's friendly demeanour was always a pleasant start to the darkening sunrise.

A piece of paper with a stapled polaroid stopped my heart like an atom bomb. Red magazine letters cut out to say 'WE HAVE

HER' like the same psycho-killer from a bad horror movie that sent me the note at the hotel. A solemnly looking Elise stared at the camera.

"Hey... Vi... You okay?"

"His name..." I cleared my throat, "Did he tell you his name, or who sent him here?"

"No Mr. Bergljót," ..."Are you all right?"

"I need the phone Blake," I fell faint.

My hand shook when I dialled Virg's number. I hadn't pressed the last number when my pocket vibrated.

Virg. Slide to answer. "Virg, I need your—"

"VI!" he was breathless, in a panic, "I need your help," he wept, "They got her Vi. They have her. I need you. Please. I need you. God do I need you. Where are you?"

"Slow down Virg, what's wrong?"

"Amelia!" he screamed hysterically, "They have Amelia!"

I froze.

Silence.

"Vi? You there?"

"Yeah. They have Elise too. I'll come pick you up. Get Mack. I'm sure they're making a play for the judge."

"Why would they take Amelia then?"

"I don't know. None of it makes sense. We'll wait until they call. Let me think."

"They gave me an address. It doesn't say come alone, just 'NO COPS!'"

"All right. I'll pick you up. Calm down Virg, we'll get them back," what would the police do anyway? They couldn't find a pair of Cs at a strip club.

"I hope..."

"Hey! We'll get them back."

I peeled out with Don's LR4. The dash unlatched itself and my new copy of *Siddhartha* and *Principia Ethica* flew through the car.

I had little choice in wondering whether this was the inception in a fatal cascade of events that would lead me to the humid depths of a grave.

# Scherzo
## My Apartment

"DON'T WORRY, I'LL be quick," I looked to Virg as he pulled up in front of my building. "Don't worry Madame. We'll make it," I took a liking to reassuring her. The explicit albeit fleeting micro-smile that lasted on her lips made me forget about the bullet I'd vowed to my brain.

Blake saw me and buzzed me in. I hastened up the elevator and down to the corner unit, whooshed the door open and started packing the bare necessities. It took longer than I anticipated. The door was closing behind me—wait, what's that?

What's a shoe doing beside my kitchen counter? A woman's shoe, monogrammed 'HC.' Helen? One of her shoes? She was only over once, and she had both her shoes... right?

I re-entered the den and started searching for the matching—glance—left pair. What was going on? A sense of horror over-whelmed me as I looked under my bed and reached in between the two bedposts, pulling out Eloise's laced underwear. We went at it at *her* place. She'd never been here. What the hell was going on? A dead girl's underwear under my bed, a single shoe of another dame in my kitchen. I scraped myself for some equanimity, each step I took towards the door calmed me until I stepped on something that pricked my shoe. An earring, it had to be Helen's but didn't look like her style. I'd seen them somewhere before. But where? I searched my memory bank high and low trying to remember where I'd been and the dames I'd seen, but all I could recollect before 2 P.M. was an inevitable search for half-decent bourbon.

"Trish!" the old man's dolorous voice panged my ears, a hypo-statization of a lupine.

Trish's earring. According to *Vertias Daily*, Trish and Eloise were dead. Who was I to question the sage-like pursuit of *truth* by journalists and media outlets… if the news says they're dead, then they're dead. Perception is truth. How Theaetetian I'd become with no Socrates to guide me.

I should probably check on Helen. 'There's no time,' I told myself as I stuffed all of these planted items in a garbage bag and shoved it into my suitcase. I wasn't going to throw them away. They were evidence, they could have fingerprints, DNA, or whatever else forensic investigators conjure up in their pursuit of this disturbed murderer. *I* didn't kill them, and if I had, I deserved to be punished. They were just as innocent as the people in the village—I'd been to jail for that, even if the convoluted *justice* system really labelled it as something else.

I opened the fridge and stuck my head inside, freezing in solitude for a second before the hysterical sobbing of a little girl's mother at her funeral snarled through my mind. I shoved the bourbon in the bag. I might need it later….

"Bill," I blurted out as soon as I caught my breath in the lobby, "Check if anyone's been up to my apartment."

Some keystrokes on his trusty computer, "No Vi, no one's been up there since Helen."

"I think someone's broken in. Can you check it out?"

"Want me to call the cops?"

"No! Nothing was taken. I wouldn't want to waste their time. Just keep your eye out."

"Definitely."

I threw my bag into the back of the Land Rover and got in, hearing the liquid courage slosh around in the bottle, "We're driving. No airports. They probably have our names and pictures by now."

"Whatever you say *captain*," Virg condescended as he huffed some smoke out of his window and made a left turn.

## Affettuoso
### 64 Hours Later

EVERYTHING IS A blur when you're running away from something. All your contemplative stories to some fairy-tale horizon haze to an infinitude of cosmic nothingness. You always worry that the thing chasing you will find you... you fear its footsteps dragging behind you. But what makes you crazy, what drives you utterly insane is trying to outsmart your pursuer. Do you check into a grungy, rundown, remote motel miles from civilization? Or do you check into the Harriet's Presidential Suite? You're outside your comfort zone either way, anywhere you go could be deduced if the pursuer were clever enough.

It's hard enough when you're alone, even recluses and loners prefer to stay hidden from the demons chasing them but things change drastically when there are 4 of you being chased by two rivalling mob families. They'd find something to agree on, team up to come after you, and no matter how foresighted I could be, how... prepared, trained, or brilliant, we'd never be ready for them. We'd lose. We'd... die. I was sure of it. You can't run forever. Nothing lasts forever, not even time.

"We'll be all right," I whispered to Elise behind me in the backseat while she fidgeted with her freshly manicured nails.

Amelia rolled her eyes at me. I knew they all thought I was being paranoid, that they thought they were just *humouring* me. Only going along because it sounded fun to see a different country. The thrill of being a makeshift fugitive trying to find the one-armed man no believes exists. None of them pondered what it meant if the mob really *was* after us; the thought was too frightening and I never wanted to be proven right, to know the truth on whether my judgment was correct in this particular circumstance.

\* \* \*

My name had become just a four-letter reference to what people saw. There was no longer any meaning attached to it, no representation of *truth* as a means of what exuded outwards from me. I'd simply become 'Vero' rather than 'the guy who protects me,' or 'the guy who's always drinking and wondering if he'll ever work up the courage to completely load his revolver and blow his brains out,' or any number of relative statements I could think of.

The risk was our lives, and I had to consider if she was worth mine even if this consideration seemed absurd. I was after all, willing to throw my life away in vain if the fated bullet decided it was time to greet my brain. Would it however, not be more worthwhile to die so someone else could live? Or is dying in vain for no greater purpose the true outlaw way? To show the divine that you *won't* play its game. In this way, even if there were no God you win, for that would mean that everything was utterly meaningless.

More specifically, what was she *worth*? Sure I was being paid well but money has no relevance to worth. Was I getting paid *enough* to risk my life for my client? Every bodyguard has asked that question; wealth is useless when you're dead—the Egyptians learned this truth the hard way—so I knew it wasn't about the money. Her worth transcended some number on a check. It was never about the money anyway... or was it?

It *had* to be something more, something more valuable and respectable than a banker's best friend, at least that's what I told myself. I bounced back-and-forth whether she ascended cold, hard cash until I finally decided it wasn't up to me. It'd never been up to me.

\* \* \*

I watched the cars around us carefully, periodically having to remind Virg not to disobey the speed limit. There was no need to attract attention to ourselves. I finally noticed how tired he was after a couple of hours and offered to take over driving through what seemed like a black hole. There was no moon in sight, just a dark horizon with no illuminating streetlights. I had to rely on the car's headlights and my wits, and the latter was lacking.

Everyone was asleep. Virg caught a snooze with his head over the dash; Amelia and Elise had this sort of *on-each-other's-shoulders-BFFs-forever* thing going on and it was majestic. I wished things hadn't turned out this way.

I saw a car approaching rapidly in the rearview. I pulled to the side a little to let him pass. He overtook us like some school-boy poseur who'd never driven before. We drove like that for a couple of minutes before his speed stabilized and I finally saw his plate and bumper. It was a 2013 Lexus GS with all wheel drive, but the car itself was irrelevant to me, what caught my eye was the bumper sticker: *WWZD*. I'd never seen it before. It must've been some clever atheist joke, another pseudo-intellectual-hipster with more Kumquat products than brains. I let it go.

He was still ahead of us after about an hour or so and I was curious about the bumper sticker again. I couldn't let it go any longer and crept behind him on the solemn country road.

*WWZD*. I turned on the lower fog lights so I could make out the caption. "*What would Zeno do?*" I abruptly whispered. … I was too dumb to understand it. All for nothing. My curiosity meant nothing.

"*Who?*" Elise yawned, leaning forward enough for me to feel her right behind my ear.

"This guy's license plate says '*What would Zeno do?*' … I don't get it."

Elise snickered, "There's something *you*… don't get? Well isn't this grand?"

"Laugh it up Madame."

"Zeno was an ancient stoic philosopher. He's trying to be funny. Zeno would be indifferent in almost every circumstance. Such is the life of the stoic sage. I think it means never care. The

Stoics believed we should yield to nature and repress emotion. This is the only way to be free from worry."

"Hmmm… sounds much harder than it is."

"Of course. Myth has it one time Zeno was told that one of his *foes* had died. Suddenly he appeared to be quite moved—this is a big no-no for a stoic. 'Huh?' his disciple screamed, 'You weep at the death of an enemy?' 'It appears so,' the sage replied, 'But you should see me smile at the death of a friend.'"

"Smile? … At the death of someone you care for?" I had to give this claim much thought.

"Why not smile at death in general? It's inevitable. The only *real* truth in the universe," was she referring to my Theoretical Physics lecture?

"You're full of surprises. Ancient Greek philosophy?" she wasn't as air headed as she made herself seem in our first few encounters.

"Adorno's good too, some Camus, but he's really depressing and seemingly dense."

Seemingly. What a key word to use, I'm guessing she didn't appreciate him all that much.

"What's the story there?" she batted her curling eyelashes to my wrist holding her steering wheel.

You know when you wear something for so long you get so used to it that you forget it's even there? It was one of those moments. It was a thin gold necklace that belonged to my mom. I wrapped it around my wrist and used it as a makeshift bracelet.

It's a story for another time. The cops dropped it off with the rest of her stuff.

I pulled my sleeve over it, "You ask a lot of questions Madame!"

"I want to get to know you," she tickled my earlobe with her whispering lips.

Sadly there was nothing to know. I had no depth. No complex density like a character from classic literature. Others perceived me accurately. There was no big mystery, no sudden surprise or character trait that you'd failed to deduce if you'd spent more than 3 hours with me.

"So do I Madame," I sounded like a prick. All the poor dame was trying to do was make some connection with me, but I didn't want that. I had to push her away. I knew that our path would eventually come down to me risking my life so she could live. I didn't want her to feel anything for me. I *had* to push her away so she wouldn't get attached and hence wouldn't get upset when I'd no longer be. I wanted her to weep rather than smile at my death, for the former would only last a few seconds but the latter would last a lifetime.

## Darkness Always Prevails

"GIVE IT BACK you jerk! It's mine!"

"Never! It's mine now," he laughed, "Survival of the *strongest*."

"Donatello! Give... it... back!"

"Wow Lise, you're literally the only person on the *planet* who calls me that. Call me Don for Christ's sake."

"Christ was forsaken you dolt."

"What?"

"You said 'For Christ's sake' ... Never mind. GIVE IT BACK!"

"Nope! See? It's on my wrist now! MINE!"

"I'll get that back Donatello. Maybe not today, maybe not tomorrow but someday, I will have that back," she understood that the best kings are not necessarily the strongest physically; there will come a time when the strength of muscle will mean nothing. Rather, it will be strength of character that prevails. What are these no-neck goombas going to do when such a day comes?

"Over my dead body Lise."

\* \* \*

"Madame? We're here," I hated waking her.

"Huh?" she slowly opened her blazing irises looking for some clue as to our location.

"Found a Harriet and a Traven. Flipped a coin. We're going to the Harriet."

"Great," she yawned like a lioness, "A decision that could determine our survival is left to a mere coin toss."

"Chance is truth Madame. Universal, impartial, and balanced."

"Yeah…" she rubbed under her eyes with her index finger, "Maybe if you're a misunderstood comic-book villain or something."

Virg practically carried Amelia to the lobby, his hand all the way around her shoulder like some committed couple in a serious relationship. I approached the front desk and it only made sense to book two adjoining rooms. Luckily for us, the "Deluxe King" was vacant and met my standards: a king size bed for Elise, a balcony in case I mustered up the courage to jump, and an armchair which faced the door for the paranoid soldier in me.

I got our keycards after adamantly requesting that the minibar house no bourbon whatsoever. It was time to move on, to change, to let go of the past, and perhaps become a better man. Maybe I was just tired of blurring through life from the bottom of a glass. If there was nothing to tempt me, maybe I could beat this monster prowling inside me. Like all vital facts, my irretentiveness made my neglect the bourbon in my bag.

I was carrying our bags to the elevator behind Elise when she did a double take and looked at some fancy sign on an easel.

*'Indulge the artist in you. Join us for an exhibit of some exquisite paintings, ancient letters, and lyrical poems on loan from museums like the Louvre et al. tomorrow between 5 P.M. to 10 P.M.'*

Elise gave this pouting-puppy sort of gaze and rolled her eyeballs towards the sign. I looked at it closely, *'Paintings by Jacques-Louis David and LaTour. A letter by Chopin. Middle Eastern philosophy.*

*Refreshments will be provided. Networking with the other guests is strongly encouraged. Acclaimed international artist Otto Van Couperville will be in attendance.'*

I couldn't say no to her. I caved and nodded; her eyes lit up like Paris in a moonlit summer night. Besides, I think I vaguely remember something my mom once said about Chopin. Maybe if I laid off the sauce I could remember some of the things she taught me, told me, showed me, and gave me, even if they were things I never wanted to remember again. This pathetic ignorance of my past was only a trifling price I'd pay for my zealous sentimentality.

The room was fantastic. Home sweet home.

All hotel rooms look the same: generic minibar, moderately clean sheets and the smell of superficially fresh towels. The Persian Kashan spread over the living room made it look lavish, and it wasn't until I noticed the hand-crafted mirror frame above the bedroom's vanity table that I realized just how lavish this place really was with its rectilinear patterns on the wallpaper and antique-style round-tables. Elise's bed linens were anything but generic: Egyptian cotton with a thread count of over 1600. I have to admit, I was a little impressed, even if the place was just *a tad* overpriced.

The first thing I did was unlock the adjoining room door. Virg and I could go as we pleased, and I told him to keep it in his pants. I couldn't afford any distractions this far into the fourth quarter. I had this rotten feeling in the bottom of my gut that they'd make a move here. It sounded crazy but I thought that somehow, somewhere, I was connected to these vicious savages. They knew what I was thinking, knew my every move, and I'd lead them here, lead them to Elise. I touched the .38 holster under my jacket. I felt safer with it, even if I didn't know whether or not it was loaded. It was part of the thrill.

I sat on the chair facing the door and spun the muzzle of the .38, putting it on the glass table beside me. Elise was in the bedroom with the door open, changing and getting ready for bed, purposely sleeping only on one side of the bed "In case you change your mind." I had to focus, "We don't have to do anything Vero. You *can* just *sleep* beside me!" she said.

I didn't believe her. I couldn't afford a mistake. I couldn't afford to get attached. Nothing is free on this planet, not even pain. A deep sadness suddenly washed over me, I'd never been this sober for this long before, not since I got out of prison. My eyelids were too heavy, and the door slowly faded into darkness.

'The most obvious path is seldom the best.'

'What's your name?'

'… Has to be Latin for something.'

'Don't let anyone change what you want. Follow your passion. Always remember, the Dahaka only covers the most obvious route. Look for secret passages and shortcuts,'

'Nice haircut, like an Air Force pilot's; disciplined, maybe you'll soar through the skies as an eagle one day.'

'Elle, it's sexier!'

"Vero!"

'Sorry I called you old and stupid.' 'No one escapes the Dahaka.'

"Vero! Come on! Vero!"

'What's your name? … Whoa, you're named after—'

'No one escapes the Dahaka.'

"VERO! WAKE UP!"

My pupils constricted like an imploding planet. Elise's voice was a smooth transition to the land of the living, "You okay Madame?"

"I'm very much okay. Are *you* all right?" her white pyjamas rested on her alabaster skin like some spirit.

"Yeah…" I sat up in the chair, trying, and finding the .38 on the table beside me.

"You were talking in your sleep… who's Elle?"

"Who?"

"Elle. You said 'Elle, it's sexier,' who is she?"

"It was only a dream. I apologize for waking you," I shot a glance at the minibar but resisted the temptation. A drink would surely take the edge off. It'd warm my body and tingle my fingertips. It'd soar me to the sky, through the clouds and wind; it'd give me the courage to tell Elise how I truly feel about her. It'd make me smile about myself instead of my perpetual weeping for the watered souls I'd taken.

"It's fine. Seriously though… you can trust me Vero. Whoever she is, it's not too late."

She wasn't going to let it go, "Let it go Madame," but I thought I'd give it a try even though I knew her well enough to know there was no way she was just going to *let it go*.

"Vero… trust me, old girlfriend?" she put her hand on my hand, which I slowly retracted for fear of her feeling this little shake I'd repressed since my flask went up in smoke along with her car.

I shook my head to focus, "What? Not at all. It's my mom's boyfriend's nickname for her."

"What was her name?"

"Lyra," the whirring of the minibar motor called to me, whispering *one little drink won't hurt*.

"And he called her *Elle*? Did he love her? What happened?"

"I don't want to do this…"

"Sharing isn't pain Vero. Telling me actually make you feel better. You don't have to internalize these things, compartmentalize them and have them tear you apart from the inside slowly over time."

I chuckled, "It's a downer mio amore."

"Oh quit with the silent tragic hero *act* and just trust me!"

"If you insist…" I sighed, "Dead."

"I'm… sorry. What about him?"

A hysterical laughter overcame me, "Dead."

"I… don't know what to say," all it took was this little tidbit of information: everyone around me dies horrific and *ill-timed* deaths to render an angel speechless.

"Did she love him?" she looked straight into my eyes, moved her hand closer to mine again.

"It doesn't matter now does it?"

"No, I don't suppose it does… but their love was *real*. It was important."

"They're both dead now, how could it matter?" I felt like crying, wanted to walk out to that balcony, curse at the sky from the top of my lungs and then simply jump off. The easy way out never came. I didn't deserve *anything* the easy way. Not since the mission for *democracy* and *justice*.

"Don't be so cold Vero. I know that's not *you*," she rubbed her fingers against my chest, where my darkened heart was supposed to be.

'What is *me* then?' would've been the ideal question to pose but I wasn't in the mood, so instead I forced myself to gaze into her eyes.

She struggled to fit herself on the chair, part of her was on my lap and she laid her head on my shoulder, "Let me stay here with you for a while. I feel safer here anyway."

I listened to her breathing, realizing after an hour or so that she'd fallen asleep. Her musical breathing was a Bach Prelude, her perfect stomach contracted and expanded like some rhythmic dance connecting this world to the next.

Are our dreams real? They *feel* real when we're in them; we experience them, we sense them. Could Hume have been right? Is that all knowledge is? What we experience as a result of sense-perception? Even desire has to be in play, sure I want Elise. Who wouldn't want her? She's beautiful, smart, charming… she's perfect, but it wouldn't make sense if we were together, it wouldn't be reasonable. Someone like me could never merit someone of *her* degree.

The night was darker than a black hole. I felt around for a light switch but all the bulbs seemed to have blown out, the occasional switch I did come across did absolutely nothing. In fact, it was as if every time I heard the click of a flipping switch the place actually got darker. I felt around the walls but my hands fell on empty air. I felt as though I might fall into a bottomless abyss with each step I took in seemingly random directions; it would've been for the best, or maybe, the void had a bottom, and I was there at that moment, and *that*... would've been even better.

My mouth stung a little and there was this spicy taste on my tongue like I'd used wasabi as lip-balm after losing some schoolboy frat bet. I heard giggling in the distance, almost as if someone was whispering my name. LED lights lit up the ground like an airplane's emergency exit, you know the ones, from that stupid video you're forced to watch on *'What to do in case of emergencies,'* it always amused me. In an emergency, everyone is either going to die or survive; that's life I guess, but what really got me, what really cringed inside the pit of my stomach was how the idiots thinking up these videos or safety pamphlets expected others to behave in the event that the improbable happened and you survived a passenger airliner crash. When push comes to shove, when the *enemy* has these arbitrarily self-proclaimed *civilized* people in a checkmate, there will be no *'orderly fashion,'* no *'calmly follow the lights.'* These self-titled men and women of grandeur will eat those they deem forsaken or weak like Gods to their sons. They'd kill, plunder, rape, and pillage just to preserve their own half-witted ideals and *things,* especially their bodies.

I followed the emergency lights as the ground became like a plane's shabbily carpeted floor bit-by-bit. The irony was not lost on me.

I followed the carpet blindly listening for the giggles like some character in a mystery thriller about to come face-to-face with the antagonist that has also conveniently taken the form of the thing the *hero* fears most. I was constantly forced to make these abrupt 90-degree turns. I actually thought I was going in circles until the childish giggling stopped roaming the abyss, no longer echoing from all directions. The ground lights turned blood red, showing me the path I was to take... and like the fool that I was, I followed it like an eager beaver about to gnaw on a trail of logs that'd eventually be consumed by a river. I approached the giggling, which had since turned into a sort of innocent laughter. My lips tingled with a sparking pain. It was a girl in a little purple dress pointing and giggling at me. I had to go closer to see her face since it was so dark. She looked like the little girl from my nightmares but it couldn't have been her, this girl had lips. The instant I had this thought, the lights blinked and turned bright blue and my lips burned off as if someone surgically poured acid on them. I knew what I looked like, I knew *who* I looked like. I could only make this *mmmmm* sound in this disquieting pain I suddenly felt. She reached out to feel where my mouth lain, and her touch somehow seemed to ease the pain as if she were healing me, but as time progressed, I noticed that with each speck of healing skin on my face, hers was disintegrating until I assumed she'd look like she always did in my dreams. I wasn't going to cause her any more pain. I pulled her hands down and stood there staring at her. She looked confused; I had to save her, well... what would pass off as *saving* someone in this abysmal realm. Surprisingly enough, I got used to the pain and she began smiling, I imagine I would have too if I had lips.

Awake.

Elise was sitting at the breakfast table eating grapes from the room service tray with her chin in her palm and her elbow on the glass table just... staring at me with her liquid-clear eyes.

"Were you dreaming again?" her voice facilely carried across the room, easing my ears into the realm of *reality,* but who knew which was which.

"I always do," better to be honest sometimes than deceitful most of the time.

"What about?"

Who? What? When? Where? Why? She had a lot of questions, and like God, hipsters, politicians, lawyers, or bankers, I had no answers. I thought I'd make something up. It works for them... "I'm sitting on a roof smoking a cigar with this guy in a black suit holding a scythe."

"You're lying."

How in the hell did she know that? "Why do you think that?"

"You were smiling."

I... was smiling? "I was... smiling?"

"Yeah!" she giggled like the reborn schoolgirl I wanted to convince myself I'd saved, "Don't take offence! It was nice."

"How'd you sleep beautifu—Madame?" my neck was stiff. My mouth had this bitter craving of cheap bourbon and cheaper women. My arms were sore and my legs were asleep from being in an awkward position all night. It was a fantastic start to the day.

"That's twice now Vero."

"Twice what?"

"Slip-ups. Once at the cottage, you almost said *my love*, and now, *beautiful*," she giggled again and I thought about Nozick's *experience machine*; could this all be a dream? Some sort of simulated reality like the blue-pills in *the Matrix*?

"Oh... I don't remember. How'd *you* sleep?" I repeated.

"Perfectly," she quipped as she walked over with a plate of fruit: sliced strawberries, raspberries, apples, and mini tangerines. "I slept on your shoulder most of the night."

What a divine comedy, the shoulder she slept on was the only part of my body *not* craving the bourbon I implored the hotel not to have in our minibar. My other shoulder burned. It felt like the bullet was still in there, the cold piece of metal travelling through my veins as an inferior attempt at verisimilitude.

I smiled, "I hope you don't think this means anything."

"I know where we stand Vero. Stop shoving it down my throat," I couldn't tell if she was making some innuendo. I expected nothing less from her than complete confusion and mind games; she was like every other dame I'd ever met only more than you can imagine.

I took the plate and put it beside the .38 on the table. I wasn't going to eat it, a drunk can hardly keep food down when he's drinking and can never keep it down on the rare occasion he's sober. I barely kept that breathtaking meal she cooked for me at her father's cottage, and I got shot for my efforts on that particular occasion.

"How long was I out... what time is it?"

She opened the minibar, and I smelled the familiar smell I wish I hadn't.

"Couple hours max. ... For an internationally acclaimed hotel, there's no bourbon in the minibar! It's your drink right?" she called with her head submerged in the fridge.

"Am I that obvious?" a gentleman's true character is revealed only when chance calls upon him to resist temptation.

"Don't worry Vero, you're a closed book! It's what you said you wanted when I first met you."

"Good memory," who'd remember such a detail? It's so trivial and mundane, and yet, here she was, looking at me with her doe eyes, no doubt coveting some semblance of what passed for affection these days.

She fidgeted with a gold bracelet she was wearing on her left wrist; I'd just noticed it. Had she always had it, or had she seen mine and mirrored this menial accessory that only symbolized another loss, reminding me of the constant powerlessness pledged upon our world? There was an engraved eagle on it in a full wingspan pose. I couldn't remember seeing it before. It appeared my idiocy knew no bounds.

Hot shower. As I lathered my hair with the conditioner and opened my eyes, I noticed blood streamlining down my chest, and it wasn't the body wash; it felt like I tore the stitches on my shoulder and it only got worse before it got better. The pain relaxed me somewhat and made me feel alive, which didn't relax me as much as it should have.

I hopped out of the shower still bleeding a little bit and Elise bit a grape seductively before she noticed and ran over to help. She bandaged and cleaned the wound again, quipping about Aristotle's passive and active soul, assuming a second actualization of the human kind and making some assertion about me and the *ideal* way of life. I pretended like all of it flew over my head.

I stayed away from the minibar for fear of giving in to the temptation. A man must know his own weakness and I knew mine was the drink. The wind gusted my back forward.

It wasn't worth it anymore. I walked out to the balcony and looked down at the people beneath my feet and then at the sun glowing in the distance. I climbed the railing, standing over the cubed edge. I couldn't do it anymore. I couldn't take her to the art exhibit. I couldn't even protect her. I couldn't live with myself, couldn't deal with the sycophantic phonies or the pathetic know-it-alls who do nothing for the world but show off their extraneous possessions as if they were something worthwhile or covetous. If I couldn't protect her anymore, if I couldn't deal with *people* anymore, then nothing had any purpose; there was no point in living.

I inhaled and moved my left toe off the edge. The wind hovered on my chest, blowing through Elise's bandage and chilling my wound to the point of numbness along with the rest of my body.

'Fear is useless,' my mother's voice whistled in my ear. It was just my mind playing tricks on me, trying to preserve itself because it knew just how serious I was. I was no longer playing the odds with a cheap 1 in 6 mathematical trick.

I counted down from lucky 7, really having expected that damn eagle to be red, or even red*dish* at the least.

6. The wind tried pushing me back into the balcony.

5. I could hear Elise going through the dresser in her room, looking for the outfit she wanted to wear to the exhibit.

4. I pushed past the cutting wind and moved closer to the edge.

3. My heart beat a little faster. I couldn't wait for 2.

2. My body vibrated as if I were in an F-15 again.

1. My existence had no meaning.

An eagle's screech jarred me back, freezing the wind and I in some tranquil ambiance. Time slowed to a halt, Elise's racket from the bedroom was no longer audible. Virgil's, and perhaps others' footsteps receding and approaching rhythmically in the hallway ceased to inform me of their presence. I couldn't even hear the wind chill that enigmatic *'whooooooooo'* in my ear, serving to illustrate my lack of being.

Had I already jumped and flattened my brain? There was only the eagle's call in its adagio tempo. It soared to the railing in slow motion with an unhurried wing beat, whooshing its sharp talons around the cubed railing and graciously fixing this temporal lapse with a short squeak, as if to say *"Hey there, what in the hell are you doing?"*

I stood on the railing beside a goddamn eagle in a country *seemingly* devoid of any like we were in its aerie, tilting my head and watching it while it did the same thing to me, curiously craning its neck to the right and left. It gave me this yearning impression of comprehension for my actions or motivations. It opened its wings for a second beside me and its massive span cast a shadow over the entire balcony. I hopped down from the edge and walked towards it. I was right in front of it but before I could get closer it opened its wings again and cast a shadow over me, squawked something and flew away with two wing beats towards the sun. It was idyllic.

I went back inside, looking first towards the minibar then at the .38. Elise's clangoring jewelry box in the master bedroom made me think twice at what I wanted to think about. There was a copy of *Vertias Daily* on the room service tray. The front-page bolding the letters *'Police Chase Shadows; question suspects in slyly appropriated serial murders.'* Trish, Eloise, perhaps even Helen. I guess I should've expected it, there's no way an act such as levelling an entire city would be rectified with something as banal as jail time. Justice lies in perfect balance, something even *civilized* Americans seem to have forgotten.

When your diet consists entirely of booze and you live inside the arms of easy women, nothing surprises you, not even the death of those same women... even when you consider the possibility that you might be framed for their murders. The planted evidence in the back of Elise's new Land Rover tied a constrictor knot in my stomach and immediately tightened itself.

I slid the paper away from me and the pages propped open to the horoscopes; I couldn't resist. '*Everything is going well for you: love, money, and career. Still you seek other goals, and today you might be thinking of educational, intellectual, and spiritual matters that you've always wanted to pursue. Don't be surprised if you're preoccupied in sorting it all out. Don't feel you have to rush to make a decision. Be patient.*' Fringe advice wanting me to adopt the Count of Monte Cristo mentality, how informative.

The sound of nothing for a couple of seconds popped my ears before I was brought down to the harsh realities of present circumstances; Elise opening and closing the drawers on her dresser in the master bedroom.

"Amelia and I want to check out that art thing," she called from the room before the door slightly opened and she stuck her head out a little bit, apparently undressed. I nodded.

"I got you a suit. It's by the closet."

I stumbled over to the closet as the door joining our room to Virgil's creaked open, "Je m'en vais chercher un grand peut-être."

"Speak English," I said with my back to him.

"Pfffftttt. All right, 'I am off in search of the great perhaps.'"

"Hmmmm," I opened the closet and saw the suit: a made to measure Ralph Lauren Purple Label tuxedo, "Sounds spiritual."

"It's François Rabelais," he replied, "I'd never heard of him before this."

"Where do you get these from? Is there some morbid database

of people's last words?"

"Normally I search them up on my phone, but Amelia got me this cool *Last Words* book, so yeah, it is like a database.

"How... useful."

"Amelia and Elise are going to the art exhibit downstairs. Some famous artist will be in attendance too!"

I wanted to ask what happened to him. Had I been away *that* long? I knew the answer anyway. It was Amelia. He didn't care anymore. Everything excited him, made him want to smile and he couldn't hold it back. Stay focused and reserved. Temptation is impossible to resist.

"Yeah..." I took the tux out and set it down near the sofa, "I guess I'm going too. I'll see you there."

He looked at the suit cover before retreating into his room, "Nice. Very sharp," he chuckled and closed the door.

I looked at the suit: black with light grey stripes and a matching bow tie that I knew I'd struggle tying sober. I looked back inside the closet and saw its matching Hermès belt and the Tod's black leather lace-ups she wanted me to wear. Elise really went all out, but I guess she didn't want to be guilty by association. She always looked dashing; I had to look deserving if she was going to enter a gala on my arm, even if it was all for show. Perception is reality. People can never understand past what they see ahead of them.

Looking at the belt again I could swear I'd seen one before in my younger days but I couldn't quite put my finger on it. It was like the faint outline of a misty and forgotten dream. With all other fading memories, no matter how hard I thought, my remembrance of things past failed like I did the second my thumb pushed that button. It was some sort of repression defence mechanism: if I couldn't remember anything, I couldn't remember the bleak horrors I'd committed. But of course this meant I could scarcely remember who *I* was.

The immediate smell of bourbon suddenly emanated from the

minibar as if I was one side of a magnet and the fridge was the other. It called to me. I was hallucinating the smell. There *was* no bourbon in that minibar. Why was the smell so prevalent like I'd just cracked open a bottle right in front of me?

It'd been so long since I had a sip my body made me feel every second. My hand started to shake and tremble my mask of addiction away. I grabbed my wrist and squeezed it, trying to keep it still lest Elise saw me or came into the main room without notice. I started sweating and panicked for a second, wanting a bottle of bourbon so bad I raced to the minibar and stubbed my toe on the corner of the armchair I'd slept on, distracting me long enough to scrap such thoughts. Exhale. A barely-functioning alcoholic with a damsel to protect? I hoped if some foolish idealist ever chose to write about me that he wouldn't highlight this flawed-hero-with-an-obvious-addiction-saving-some-pretty-angel-on-earth-and-redeeming-himself as a tired literary device to sell more books. It'd be blasé. I'd rather blow my brains out than read someone's misunderstood ramblings vainly attempting to ascertain my grim psyche... ha ha... perhaps some dark humour would be advised in describing such a life.

Elise appeared behind me adjusting her earrings wearing a light-pink dress hanging slightly under her thigh, accentuating her marvellous legs. I turned to face her and stood with my hands behind me, clutching my shaking right wrist and also happening to squeeze my bracelet into the skin just to keep my mind off the drink.

She bent down at the table and drank some water before noticing me. Her eyes glittered as she walked towards me. I squeezed my hand tighter behind my back but it'd already stopped shaking.

"Can you help me put this on? I can't quite *get it in*," she fidgeted with the earring. My hand was still but I was afraid it'd start shaking at any momen... and it started shaking again. I couldn't risk pricking her ear.

"I have a headache Madame," I shook my head.

She roared with laughter, "That's the wrong excuse for *this* particular circumstance Vero," she rubbed her index and middle finger under my eye, "You should really get some sleep."

She was right. I was fatigued, thirsty, hungry, and in pain. I closed my eyes for a second to her smooth touch and practically fell asleep right there. "Perhaps later Madame."

My eyes were closed but I could feel her moving closer to me. I could smell her presence and I wished at that exact moment I'd read more classic literature so I could describe the elation she stirred in me. Words don't even cut it. Nothing existed. I never drank. I never joined the Air Force. My mom was alive and I knew who my dad was. I... existed but I didn't at the same time, not in the traditional way. I was independent of external forces around me. I was a serene planet floating in space and she was a shooting star, granting me all the wishes I'd wished I'd made.

"I've figured you out," she whispered in my ear.

"That makes one of us," I think I chuckled a little.

"Oh yes I have! You're only proving my point further!"

I opened my eyes and was met with hers: *two* shooting stars idling in an ocean of tanzanite.

"Your deflecting statements, the silent hero with a not-so-obvious weakness, the unrewarded intelligence..." she was nuzzling me in a kind of Eskimo kiss. "You push everyone away. This I don't know why. You avoid any real feelings or attachments, but this I know why. You're sensitive deep down. You've buried the *real* you behind this façade of... practiced insouciance. You're pushing me away because—"

'I don't want you to get hurt. Everything around me dies or comes to some acute misfortune after having crossed paths with me.' Is what I should've said.

My hand shook again. This time more viciously, throbbing even my wounded shoulder; she reached around and grabbed it, putting her palm into mine and rubbing her fingertips on it in seductive circles.

"Why are you so afraid?"

"Vulnerability."

# Transcendental Cassation

## An Hour and a Half Ago

I HAVE NO idea how I got to Virgil so quickly, driving through the congested roads of this garbage-infested metropolis I'd grown tired of. He was wailing uncontrollably near a storage locker Mack had rented.

Our weapons cache: rifles, pistols, and explosives from the *good ol' days*. They'd all come in handy. Mack calmed him down as I opened the locker and we filled some bags with the gear... I couldn't find the bulletproof vests.

"Mack! Where are the vests?"

"Vests?" he raised one of his eyebrows like that wrestler turned movie star turned TV actor.

"You've got to be kidding me..." I shuffled some more stuff around. Maybe he thought his abs of steel would stop bullets.

"Vi," Virgil hiccupped teary-eyed, "This is suicide."

"They're *not* going in your stupid book. Maybe if I said or thought it enough times some*thing* would hear me."

"He's right," Mack thought I cared about his opinion, "The risk is too grea—"

"Hey!" I slapped him lightly and his mirrored aviators flew off his face. He wouldn't even look me straight in the eye, "We're not going down without a fight. If we die, we've died trying to save two people we care about. And *that's* worth dying for. Forget living! What do you want to do? Wither away in some retirement home like a useless old gasbag? ... Or you want to die for something? You won't know who you are or what you're capable of until you're forced to make a decision like this. People haze through life never having such an opportunity. We should *be* so grateful..." and for a few seconds, I felt the bitter taste of our civilization's most dangerous illusion: hope. I wanted to live… at least long enough to save Elise.

Virgil had calmed down, checking the weapons in his bag and walking to the car. Mack forgot about his sunglasses until he stepped on them and shattered the lens, pretending not to care. I turned the ignition on the car,

"Virg. The address," maybe it *was* suicide … just another Tuesday afternoon, except I was sober.

## ARTFUL RIVALRIES

I READ SOME pseudo-intellectual-feminist propaganda once, it said in this male controlled patriarchal society, males are sexual and feel lust or desire whereas women are sexy and hence the object of lust or desire, and *this* mentality is the foundational problem of our society. I was lying to myself *and* to her if I said I didn't want her, if I didn't find her sexy. So what? That makes me sexist? Prejudiced against women if I admit I desire a female? I'm supposed to deny these feelings? Shut her out? Reject the truth that I want her like a man in the desert wanting *water*? I'd be damned if I listened to those money-grubbing whores who sell their ideals and principles for their fifteen minutes of fame; the ignorant buffoons that live in a one-dimensional 140-character world. Tweet tweet, roar roar, caw caw, more like baa baa.

Depth is no longer a requirement for *character*, no longer the norm for respect. Mediocrity is the status quo and instead of high-lighting *this* essential feature as the erroneous ascription of our problematic society, the best they can come up with is that men desire women?

\* \* \*

A man achieves nothing through fear except failure.

She moved closer, "And you think a man's strength is defined by his *invulnerability*?"

My hand trembled for a second and then was as still as a surgeon's. I lost control of my body and wanted to kiss her, the temptation was greater than the yearning for bourbon. I wanted to give into impulse, to ravish her like a famished predator, and I would have, had she not stroked my chest with her fingertips.

In a swift and gentle motion I used my thumb and index finger to hold her chin and gently pulled it towards me to close the little gap between our lips. I tilted my head slightly and only barely touched her lips, patiently waiting a few seconds before I pulled her chin a little closer, and I opened and closed my lips ever so slightly, getting a glimpse of that dangerous illusion. She *was* aqua pura.

After about 20 seconds or so, I got control my body again and backed away to gauge her reaction; she wasn't reserved but looked rather embarrassed. Even though I was in complete control I felt this sense of belonging; I'd never felt this way before and I must admit I liked it. I put my hands around her waist this time and pulled her towards me while I leaned back. Our tongues danced around in circles like two teenagers playing footsie under a restaurant table. I slid my hand up to her chin then to her jawbone under her ear and trailed it across while my other hand slid up her Olympian obliques. I pulled away a couple of inches again to catch my breath but that was only an excuse. I really wanted to *just* look at her. I leaned back in but didn't kiss her. I was teasing her a little, leaning in and out and forcing her to practically get on top of me while we were standing. She pounced forward and I couldn't react fast enough, biting her lower lip and pulling it a little. It was euphoric. No matter how much I massaged her body I couldn't get enough. I inched my fingers up her shirt and stroked her skin briefly and then I pulled my hand back out, hovering my thumb close enough just under her waist so she could feel it. I pulled her on top of me with my bad shoulder and she practically straddled me. I kissed her neck, moving further down each time my lips grazed against her body. I slipped her dress down gradually and kissed her where it caressed her soft skin, then kissed my way back up to her lips. I felt alive but hated myself for giving in to this temptation.

She kept pushing me back towards the sofa. Each step locked our lips further until she was completely on top of me over the couch—

Tip, knock, tap... *perfect timing.*

"Vi, you ready?" Virgil called from his room before barging in with Elise in my arms on top of me, blushing like an eighth grader.

"Oh! Sorry guys!" a smug smile took over his face.

I looked at him. He took a step back and hid in the doorway. I let her go and she hopped down.

"Come in Virg," she fanned herself with her hand as she walked over to the minibar for a bottle of water.

So he's Virg, but I'm *Ve-ro*? What was I thinking? A man trying to understand a woman is like a fish trying to climb a tree.

"I wanted to see if you were ready... it's almost nightfall."

Nightfall: wolves howling, people dying, and men drinking over the stench of overachieving goombas or underachieving bimbos, and all *I* had to do was watch some pretty girl without getting attached... so much for *that* plan. Still, we were in a strange country I'd never been to, a bar I'd never heard of with bourbon I couldn't wait to see—it was the only remaining temptation I couldn't give into.

"I have to admit I wanna check out this exhibit thing too. You ladies want to hit up the hotel bar after right?" Virg continued as Amelia came into our room wearing this killer navy dress. The two dames traded compliments and sat down on the sofa while I went into the master to change.

Elise hopping on top of me opened up one of my stitches and I'd started bleeding a little. I tripled checked my .38 to make sure it was loaded in case of trouble. I hadn't forgotten why we were here. Maybe I *was* being paranoid. I expected trouble everywhere I went but that's what kept us alive on the missions. That's what kept *me* alive, and I had to do whatever I could to keep *her* alive.

I left my untied bowtie wrapped around my collar and was the last out the door, but not before putting a small piece of tape above the frame so I could determine whether someone had been entering our room. I stepped into the elevator and Elise immediately offered to tie my bowtie. Much to my distaste Virgil laughed. I said I preferred it my way; she rolled her eyes and shrugged it off.

The elevator doors steadily opened to the second floor lounge already crawling with post-modern critics and homeless-looking artists. A hotel employee in a decently looking tuxedo offered us champagne. I never thought I'd say it but I wouldn't be drinking. I found some water on a table near the snacks and stood in the corner watching the people roam the posh ballroom.

I saw this fantastic-looking dame in a blood-red dress admiring one of the paintings for about 15 minutes. She impressed me, taking in every detail, every brushstroke; it was a breath of fresh air until a guy walked over with a glass of scotch, wrapped his arms around her neck and pecked her on the cheek. He looked eerily familiar but there was no way I was going to remember.

"They're like us!" I heard Amelia's voice behind me.

"Ugh... can you imagine?" Elise responded.

I turned around and approached them, catching a glimpse of the painting that'd mesmerized them: a woman holding an umbrella and another a letter, looking at the viewer at something like a three-quarter profile. The one with the letter donned an ever so subtle smile on her lips. I looked at the information plaque: *Francisco Goya. Woman with a letter. 1812. Romanticism. Oil on canvas. On loan from the Palais des Beaux Arts, Lille, France.*

"You like it Vero?" Elise asked while I was reading the plaque, "You've been looking longer at the info plaque than you did at the painting!"

"I'm curious to see what details they're focusing on."

"Bee! Check out this one," someone called from across the exhibit. A couple in their 50s or 60s understandably captivated by a Picasso.

"What about it Nicky? I don't see what you see," she said to him.

"The chair is bigger than the woman! She's lost in the chair. Consumed by this possession."

I liked this guy. I approached the painting to feed my curiosity, studying the plaque before I looked up at the painting lest my eyes biased me.

*Pablo Picasso. Woman Sitting in Armchair. 1948. Surrealism from the neoclassicist and surrealist period. Oil on canvas. On loan from private collection.*

This 'Nicky' knew what he was talking about. I strained myself in trying to understand a Picasso. The chair took up the entirety of the canvas and the woman was small and fragile in comparison, almost as if to demonstrate how frail we are as a species yet how everlasting our possessions are, which was really comedic when I considered how attached we are to inanimate objects. A cell phone with the chorus of a third-rate hip-hop song rang across the room.

"Yeah…" she scoffed, "It's Cindy," the voice called. "No I'm *at* the gallery," her heels screeched in circles. "Put me on the list too! … How many times do I have to tell you? … It's es-eye-en-dee-ee-ee. *Ugh… fine*, I'll be there!"

I moved on to the next easel; a much simpler painting of a woman standing in a garden wearing a multi-colored sundress. A vastly different theme and style than the morbid painting I'd previously seen. *Henri Matisse. Woman. Fauvism.* was all the information provided. They didn't know much about this one but I guess they didn't need to, a clever use of color showed the luminous sun in full swing. I liked Matisse. I'd studied some of his other paintings, "I wonder if this is the one," I thought out loud.

"Which one?" Elise appeared beside me looking at the painting, "That's… I like its simplicity."

"Matisse had his own gallery. They say one time a customer came into his gallery and studied one of his paintings for quite a while. He just stood still and gazed at a single painting. Matisse was daunted at this customer's perception and eventually went over and they both looked at the painting. Finally, after about an hour or two, the customer snared 'The woman's arm is too long.' A disappointed Matisse quipped, 'It's not a woman. It's a painting.'"

"Deep," was the only thing she said. "How do you know that?"

"Read it somewhere I guess. I studied art for a while," a *useless* anecdote I remember… life is nothing but a closed curtain of pain.

Elise looked over to the guy with the scotch and the stunner in the red dress, "That guy looks *so* familiar."

"I was actually thinking the same thing."

"Is he a celebrity?" she asked, "I've seen him somewhere before. I'm sure of it."

We approached one painting closer to them. I glanced over the plaque: *Francisco Goya. Picard Caught by the Bull. 1793. Romanticism. Oil on canvas. On loan from a private collection.* I wanted to eavesdrop on their conversation. They looked content, happy. I *had* to know his secret.

"Do you know the trinity of master painters of the high renaissance? *I*… don't think soooooo," he demeaned to the beauty in red.

Clearly his date wasn't *stupid,* not the person I saw studying every detail of that painting earlier. She'd know it's Da Vinci, Michelangelo, and Raphael.

"Obviously Da Vinci is one," she turned around to face him with the poise of a queen, "You never shut up about him! Then probably Raphael, because you're constantly talking about that paintings of the philosophers," *The School of Athens* from the early 1500s. "And I guess the last one would have to be… Michelangelo?" she read him like a book. She didn't know the answer straight away but delved so far into his character and psyche that she deduced the answer. Her attention to detail was indubitably immaculate.

"Damn it!" the man returned, "Fine, that's 3-1 for you." They probably had a fun little competition going.

"What on God's green earth is *this*?" Elise asked 3 paintings away. *God's* green earth? What earth was *she* living on? Our earth is muddied by unsolidified identities, greedy politicians, and misandric feminists.

I noticed Virgil studying a framed piece of paper, probably a letter, and it looked like he'd been standing there for hours.

I walked towards Elise. "What is it?" I asked and she pointed to the painting with her chin.

*Vincent Van Gogh. Owl Viewed from Front. 1887. Post impressionism. Pencil on paper. On loan from a private collection.*

"What's wrong with it?"

"It has no eyes! It's so creepy!" she shuttered.

"It's supposed to be creepy, most owls are solitary. *Wise*, which is just another word for outcast, misfit. They're the rebels of the bird kingdom."

"Why?"

"Because all they say is *'who,' 'who,'* and that's enough."

"How does that make them... what does that even mean?"

"That no one knows who they really are, not even the owl. It stays up all night trying to ascertain the answer to the question it constantly asks under the foggy moonlight of a pattering drizzle."

"... I thought eagles were the *rebels*," and she looked at me up and down. I imagined the eagle from the balcony giving me wings.

"Eagles are regal. They do whatever they want—they're like the American government, they can be shoddy, fascist, ... whatever they please and hold others to a higher standard they themselves don't follow. They have the power. Owls defy the status-quo."

"According to *you*."

I moved closer to the painting. It *was* spine-chilling, but I could only imagine how dark *true* justice or truth would have to be, and if that were the case, this painting was rainbows, treasures, and sunshine, "Yeah... they're probably smarter than most *people*."

Elise turned away from the painting to face me, "Why do you despise humanity... *us* so much?" a solemn look dwindled in her eye. She was taking notes from the beauty in red, trying to burrow her way into my mind.

"We're selfish, greedy, consuming hypocrites with no real identity."

"… Not always."

"*Always*." I stepped towards her, "… Remember the ridiculously foolish and short-lived *Occupy* movement? Young idealists protesting extravagant corporate honcho lifestyles while they were drowning in student debt?"

"Yeah… what's your point? How is that… that's not hypocritical."

"Those same idiots mourned Steve Jobs and all bought that stupid book about him!" that means some prolific member of this money-loving society profited from his death.

"So?"

"Jobs was the very thing they were protesting the week before! He was the CEO of a Fortune 500 messing with a political system that benefited it. A man who manipulated the economic realm to profit while others suffered, and they were all sad when he died because of clever advertising gimmicks and propaganda marketing devices. If that's not contradictory, then the definition of the word changed while I was—" inside, while I was inside, in jail, but I didn't want her to know that.

"Wow… you really believe that?" We slowly moved to another painting: Goya's *La Novillada. Fight with a Young Bull. 1780. Romanticism. Oil on canvas. From the Museo del Prado, Madrid, Spain.* The other bull painting was 1793; it took the bull 13 years to get even and acquire *real* balance, that's longer than a decade, it's practically a lifetime. Maybe time is just a fabrication, a unit by which we gauge relativity. It can't be truth since it's not constant for all beings or things in the universe. "That's… cynical," she continued without even looking at the paintings anymore. Now she just held my gaze and I can only guess felt my disdain for the luxurious purchases I'd watched her make, even if they were for charities or charity *cases* like me.

"It's all a joke Madame. Take for example, the CEO of Susan G. Komen for the Cure. She, I think her name is Nancy or Candy or

Mandy or something, makes nearly $700, 000 a year, which is roughly 25% more than other organizations of comparable size. Now lies the punch line: her organization only spends barely 21% of its yearly funds on research for curing whatever the hell they're saying they're fighting for. They're more worried about trademarking the phrase 'For the Cure' than *actually* curing a disease. They sue other charities for using the phrase in their events. That means they spend money on lawyers and court appeals to pursue, intimidate, and take money from other charities... isn't that amazing?" *This,* is our world.

"That can't be true," she was being naïve.

"Products. That's what we've become, iPhonies for what passes for personality nowadays. Watching dumbed-down TV shows and trying to become the fictional characters we see because they're doing what society has deemed desirable or cool. We fight only for causes we're told to fight for, none of which are really worthwhile. We willingly allow companies to sell our private information for profit. We give away what little *rights* we had to begin with to some absurd law of patriotism and nationality... we've become *things* to be used and thrown away when we can no longer consume like the system demands, when the bottom line doesn't meet anymore. We have no identity. None of us are anyone and no one is someone. We're *what*, not *who*."

"iPhony, That's clever... you're a brooding and cynical pain-in-the-ass but you're probably right. I never thought about it like that."

"I know," I wanted to end the conversation. I thought I heard the honey in the red dress beside us whisper to her date, "Wow... what was that? 5-0?"

"Four," her date whispered, "Becoming things, companies for profit, American fascism, and iPhony."

"Well... do *you* know the name of the *Mona Lisa*?" Elise asked.

"Lisa Gherardini," although the controversy that surrounds

that particular painting was too vast for me to engage in discourse about it.

"Okay now it's five," the man whispered to his date, "Plus he looks really familiar to me."

I guess they were as interested in us as much as we were interested in them.

Amelia walked over, "Lise, come look at this one!" and pulled Elise away from me. I noticed Virgil still looking at that letter in the corner of the room.

I roamed the place and eventually took my place beside him. A letter around some ancient frame.

*Hand carved early 19th century frame. Spain.*

Laughable. It was actually the stupid frame they were trying to show, but the letter inside was worth a thousand frames. I knew why Virgil was obsessing over it.

It was a letter by Frédéric Chopin to a friend, and I knew exactly which sentence Virgil was reading over and over again.

*'Because, perhaps to my misery, I already have my perfect one, whom I have without saying a word served faithfully for a year now, of whom I dream and in whose memory the adagio of my concerto has been written.'*

"This is my chef-d'oeuvre," I heard the homeless looking guy say to the 50 or 60 year old 'Nicky' as *Sindee* walked towards him.

"What the hell is it?" his sardonic disposition was more obvious than his age.

"Nicky! Be nice!" his wife, I can only assume, nudged him in the elbow.

"It's okay," the *artist* replied, "Not everyone *gets* it."

I walked over behind them to look at this *masterpiece. What the hell is it* was the right question, this 'Nicky' didn't disappoint when it came to recognizing hogwash.

*Otto Van Couperville. Life. 2013. Neo-postmodern classic impres-*

*sionism. Oil on canvas. For sale by painter.*

I wanted to buy this so no one else would ever have to look at it or in case Elise's cabin ever ran out of firewood. It was a black canvas with a single white line moving diagonally from top-left to bottom-right. The line progressively turned red as it neared the bottom and even ran around the corner of the canvas past the original setting. It was $2, 600.

"It symbolizes life, the light in darkness which then turns to blood when we die, but it doesn't stop there! No no no no!" Otto screeched, "It goes *around* the canvas because we don't know how far our decisions extend," the pattering of his shoes on the floor was only slightly less grating than the pattering of his querulous voice.

"I need a Cohiba," Nicky exclaimed before walking away, "I'll be back Bee."

It seemed impossible, but beside this masterpiece was another *work of art. Otto Van Couperville. Death. 2020. Neo-surrealism and postmodern-classicalism. Oil on canvas. Finalist for Best Original Piece in the 'Expression' competition.*

This second masterpiece was a white canvas with a gradual blue line that turned black and ran around the canvas. *Very* original. This one was painted seven years after *Life*. How could it be nominated for originality when it is practically the exact same painting as the other one? Bureaucracy gave me worse migraines than trying to sober up after a 5-day binge. This piece? $3, 850.

"Vero!" Elise came up behind me, "Amelia and I want to go to the bar now. Are you done here?"

Nicky turned around suddenly to see who Elise was talking to: me, and looked at me with a mysterious recognition even though I *still* had no idea who *he* was. He smiled and nodded, and I returned the gesture.

"Yes Madame. Let's go," and we left to my second, no, first home, leaving behind the mystery man and his woman in red.

The bar wasn't that busy. We stood near the front counter as

Elise and Amelia ordered weird sounding drinks with odd garnishes. Virgil ordered a gin and tonic and I had a club soda.

I saw the familiar couple dancing by the bar when Elise's craning neck alluded me to their presence. What game were we playing? Why did it matter who they were or what they were doing?

He came up to the bar next to me to order a round of drinks for his date like the gentleman he was pretending to be. I couldn't shake the feeling that I knew him from somewhere and finally got a good look at his face. I'd gone to school with him, but was it Harvard or Yale? It could've even been Oxford.

He turned to scan the bar and I saw his face close-up. His features were peculiar at best, a highlighted aquiline nose that curved like an eagle's—and I died a little inside when I noticed—a full set of lips that never seemed to shut up unless he was kissing some 'fit honey,' his words. A set of big dumbo ears that resembled Stoker's Dracula. Long, thick eyelashes that extended over a set of mischievous and still dark brown, borderline full black irises above chiseled cheekbones near a well-defined jaw and an octagonal chin that looked like a superhero's from those old comic books. A tailored designer jacket and shirt hung over a designer belt. His suit wasn't flashy but it was. I somewhat liked his style. He wasn't a poseur but stood out, turned women's heads despite not being *traditionally* attractive. I wondered if Elise found him charming or eloquent. From what I remembered, he was a master manipulator and well versed in almost everything like a know-it-all. I never liked him. A cunning intellect with no conscience. He did more to wreck things than fix things, which earned him the nicknames "Leo Cunning," or "Cunning Leo," a clever mispronounced pun of his last name. He was arrogant, entitled, and cocky… and now he was a hack writing abstract stories few could understand, God help us all.

"Don't I know you from somewhere?" he asked as I sipped my club soda.

"Upstairs. I was just at the exhibit."

"No no no. You look familiar. I've seen you before… I never forget a… *Vi?*" he suddenly remembered with furrowed brows.

"Yes. And you're Leonardo."

"At your service," oh and he was polite. I hated that about him. He thought he was some medieval king or something.

He squeezed my hand tightly and said something, I don't know what. I was thinking about Hele—Elise but I looked over and noticed his perfect posture: shoulders rolled back, chest out but not puffed like the hipster bros in this place, arms firmly resting on his side, holding his 21 year-old scotch near his thigh.

The old rivalries came flooding back. For a split second I was afraid Elise would like him before the stunner in the red dress came over and kissed him. She looked like some Icelandic or Finnish supermodel, even prettier up close than from afar. Was she his girlfriend? He was never the type. He whispered something in her ear and she grinned before shifting her gaze back to me.

"Lina, this is Vero… Vero, Lina."

"Pleasure," she said in a soft European accent.

She extended her palm facing down, I slipped my hand under hers and kissed it.

"Oh wow, your friend is like a knight of yore… or a *Viking*."

I guess that makes us 1-0 old friend.

Something flashed in his eyes. That feeling of fear and envy that he might possibly steal Elise from me? He was thinking the same thing about Lina. This was beyond awkward. I'd finally understood why male lions or tigers don't get along, but *sometimes* eagles do, even lions, *sometimes* is the operative word. This was *not* one of those times.

Elise finally spotted us amidst her conversation with Virg and Amelia and came over, "You… made… friends?" she spoke very slowly.

"Well well well, the plot thins," Leo just grabbed a strand of

Elise's hair without warning and brushed it to the side. She chuckled.

Tied at 1.

"This is an... old friend. We went to school together."

"Perfect! It'll give me chance to get to know Vero a little better. There aren't many people that—wait, you're..." I think she —"Leonardo Köning, aren't you?"—recognized him.

Great, now I'm down 2-1.

"That's the rumour!" he quipped with ease. I started to hate him again.

"I *loved* your first book. All the time lapses. Although the friend in it was kind of a prick wasn't he? Not really a friend. I liked the little kid though."

He looked at me, "So did I."

## Bacchanale II, From the Divertimento

THE FULL MOON hid behind the clouds in the night sky blinking its enigmatic pulses to the very essence of human nature. I didn't like what I was, but maybe, just maybe, I could change what I would become. How often can we change ourselves? How quickly? It is even possible to change your nature?

"You probably get this a lot, but mind if I ask you something? … About your stories, books, theories, or whatever you consider them?" Elise leaned closer to his broad shoulders.

"Sure," he sipped the scotch.

"Most of your characters, except the foils or philosophically rooted ones, are suicidal, they're always depressed… why?"

My ears perked up. I admit I hadn't read any of his books; they weren't really my style with all the ridiculous external analepses and internal prolepses and his usage of antiquated classic philosophy. I had enough trouble understanding who I was and what the hell I was brought here to do, let alone some fool's ideologies on temporal movements or humanity's abundant hamartias.

His slight smirk brought out the dimples on his cheeks but I could see right through it. I'd seen that smile anytime someone made a conceited comment about our *advancement* as a race or our *intelligence* as a species: fake as a Hollywood starlet's breasts. "You mustn't discriminate when you question everything," his blink rate went down and his eyes lasered in on Elise's designer dress.

"Don't be cryptic. What do you mean?" Elise's direct approach would surely catch him off guard.

"You have to question your own existence… your own purpose," he was starting to make sense, pretty girls tend to do that.

"… And how does that translate to suicide?"

He chuckled a little, "Sometimes, when we don't get an answer... *any* answer that makes sense, we equate it with meaninglessness, and if your life is meaningless, your actions... random, chaotic, and contingent not by free will, but by something along the lines of luck, ... or fate. Then all we are as a race and as each individual *thing* is a perverse aberration. Nothing more."

"Well," Elise twirled her finger in her strawberry hair, "I hope they're—you're... wrong," she matched his slow-tempo and pronounced each word carefully.

"So do I," he took another gulp of his drink, "... Because if I'm right, I wouldn't be here."

Lina handed me a drink that smelled like bourbon—how did she know, I'd been drinking soda all night—and walked over to Elise and Leo and handed them their drinks.

Amelia and Virg finally came over from wherever they were and Amelia whispered something in Lina's ear. Dames: how fast they make friends and how faster they abandon them. Lina nodded and said something to Elise. I couldn't hear what they were saying but Elise made it clear when she frolicked up to me and said, "We want to go dancing Vero!"

I nodded. I didn't want to say no. Besides, it was the first time in years I didn't want to off myself.

They all looked at each other, nodded and seemed to agree on "BODY. Should be a 10 minute cab ride."

We arrived at this absurd looking piece of infrastructure where half of a man's torso met with a woman's chest and the words *BODY* glimmered over it like a casino on the Vegas strip. A bunch of imbeciles idled in line so they could get into this *exclusive* club in order to feel good about themselves. We too stood at the back of the line for a while until a no-neck-semi-professional-has-been boxer or MMA 'fighter' opened the velvet rope to the club. One by one, we marched into the slaughter and the narrow hallway opened to a counter, a quaint place where we paid for something they called 'cover,' which was really just a sophistical word for this amusement park ticket where I assumed we'd soon make our entrance as the night's cabaret act. The whole thing was some sort of tragic comedy. A girl stamped the heel of my palm with the devil's trident; she had the right idea. The place was nothing short of hell. It was perfect. I was finally where I deserved to be.

Inside, the music was so loud it was practically the same thing as torture. I couldn't understand why people would subject themselves to such malicious surroundings but then again, I never understood other people well enough to pass judgment upon them. Virgil, Amelia, Elise, Lina, and Leo immediately made beelines to the centre of the dance floor where all the fake smoke and drunk animals slobbered all over the place like stray dogs fighting for scraps. I looked around the entire place for life before I spotted a print of Dalí's *Metamorphosis of Narcissus* on one of the walls by the bar. A painting of Narcissus with a bunch of narcissists making fools of themselves... how clever of the decorator.

It took another moment of me watching these dimwits thirst for the bartender's attention when I suddenly realized why the drink was preferred to sobriety. It became obvious why I'd always crawled inside a bottle like the intricate yet squeezed and make-shifted ship built by a bored old man. Booze deafened my failures as a human, as a person who once aspired to right wrongs, to care, and to love. Without realizing it, I'd become this cold, ruthless machine that calculated danger, survival odds, and other primitive factions of a mind that ceased to process like a man's, forced to take orders from fools and clowns. It was as clear as the Mediterranean Sea why all it really did was scream at me to greet the bullet with a smile, which, given my current surroundings wasn't something I was determinately opposed to at that particular moment.

The music shook my midriff and vibrated the poorly installed wooden floors. It was various 'top' charts *trash* remixed to sound like some stupid fool saying dumb things that the boneheads in here had deemed lyrical. *My* amusement was simple; I eyed Elise fend off advances from all the shirtless or weird fashion sensed schoolboys who thought they were lady-killers.

I stood against a wooden pole of some sort and watched these savages dance, all the while trying, and failing to ascribe any elegance or rationality to such reckless behavior. I looked over the dance floor where neon lights and red smoke filled this room the most, finally fixing my gaze on the exit sign, counting the seconds until I got out of there.

Lina walked over to the bar and like all pretty women, seduced the bartender's immediate attention and it only took her a few seconds to get drinks despite the congested line. She handed me a cold—sip—water, and said something inaudible. The music was so loud I couldn't hear her. I pointed to the ceiling and motioned with my hands; she wrapped her florid arm around my ear, "Are you ever going to dance?"

"Perhaps later," I whispered in her ear.

"You look so… out of place."

There's hardly a place on this planet where I *don't* look out of place. The only way to have fun in that wonderland is to be a brain dead zombie who never has any thoughts or beliefs of their own. Sadly enough, I actually wished I were *that* dumb so I could enjoy myself just a little bit.

"It's the people that blend in perfectly we should be worried about," I whispered in her ear with my arm around her slender shoulder.

She laughed too hard. I thought she was drunk and her stroking my chest before she leaned in again didn't help her case, "I should watch out for you!"

Elise caught my eye from the middle of the dance floor and tried to get out and move towards me but she was so deep in enemy territory that she had to force her shoulder through the *how to pick up 10 girls at once at the club* crowd. She looked sexy, but not in the attention whoring 'look at me' way the bimbos here fawned. Rather, she carried herself like a fair maiden from a bad fairy tale trapped to rule a kingdom she wanted no part of. She lacked the makings of a choice. If she could even step down and let *freedom* reign, there'd be anarchy. Despite what clever philosophers with witty wordplay want you to believe, complete anarchy would be detrimental. Imagine these same animals who barely pass as human *with* all these rules and laws we've set in place, now imagine those same people only without rules. These *civilized* citizens would ravage each other, enjoy it, justify it, and actually believe they've done the right thing.

Lina slowly moved back towards Leo, who had also isolated himself on the opposite side of the dance floor, standing in the corner and watching everyone like a hawk.

A couple of *gentlemen* made a clearing for Elise to pass through but it was only to cop a feel of her ass, and she slapped both of them hard enough to ruin their night. She smiled at me through the smoke. 'Thy sensuous lips, emerald eyes, ivory skin, and perfectly toned thighs. Thy blood-red hair lays my heart bare. Even thy seductive voice renders moot all choice,' were the sad thoughts that ran through the abyss that'd become my mind, it was borderline Shakespearean, tragedy and all. I threw up in my mouth and had to take my eyes off her and my abyss followed, asking about the bullet in my pocket. I got a headache thinking of her and *actually* had to throw up. I hobbled to the restroom, tearing up for an unknown reason. The door opened and closed behind me, drowning out the annoying itz-itz-itz beats in the club. My ears hummed in the quiet; in fact... they were playing Bach: *Air on G String*. Cello.

Really? Bach in the washroom? And... *that* drivel out *there* on the main floor? *This* is society? I felt for the bullet in my pocket. It was there, hibernating, waiting.

A guy beside me wiped something off the faucet counter and sniffed and wiped his nose, giving me a questionable wink when our eyes met in the mirror and he brushed past me to reenter the Inferno.

The place was empty, like I expected. Who'd use the restroom in a place like this? They could piss themselves in excitement out there and no one would notice. I walked up to the dispenser to buy some aspirin and had a riot. The condom sticker was a landscape of a mountain. It was nothing sexual. They use sex to sell absolutely everything in this society, everything except condoms that is.

I took the stall at the end and heaved, cried, and threw up the fruit pieces Elise offered me back at the hotel. You're not a real drunk until you can't keep food down. I'd earned yet another label. It'd be much easier now for the mainstream *intellectuals* to analyze me over their martinis, rum and cokes, and platitudinous remarks. *'Well, what do you expect Andrew?'* with the obligatory raised eyebrow, warming the brandy in their palms, *'He's an orphaned insubordinate alcoholic!'*

I felt like crap and stumbled out of the stall to wash my hands. I splashed water on my face and closed my eyes, weeping as I pressed the bullet against my temple with my palm, and like a horror movie, opened them to see an old man staring at me through the mirror from behind my back. I turned around immediately and hid the bullet.

Something about his eyes made me doubt he was the bathroom attendant. He was wearing this thin brimmed leather vest and a dotted red bowtie with matching dress pants. He was easily in his 70s or 80s. Before I could say anything, he just started chuckling.

"Why are you here?" he finally said with a stern voice after he had his fill of laughter.

"I'm just looking for a good time," who the hell was this guy?

He grinned again, "You almost sounded convincing there, 'looking for a good time,' HA!"

"Who are you?" I asked him as I took a step back with one eye on the door.

"Who are *you*?" his mischievous smile said it all. I had to assume this enigmatic old man didn't ask any question he didn't know the answer to.

"I asked first!" first-come, first-serve? What did I think this was? European Colonialism? Screw the natives. Kill the ones that talk back. This is *our* land, *we* discovered it. Home of the brave, land of the *free*, except when you disagree.

"This isn't colonialism son!" did he just read my mind?

I reached for the .38. Damn, I left it on the glass table beside the armchair back at the hotel.

"Looking for the bullet you were hiding from me? Or perhaps the gun you left back in your hotel room?" his entire demeanour gave me chills.

I grabbed his collar and pulled him towards me, "Who the hell are you?"

"I am merely an unknown," the peculiar grin on his face made me think I was supposed to know what the hell he was talking about.

"Make sense!" he was agitating me.

"I knew your father, and I must say, he was much more respectful than you."

"My father's dead to me."

"Do not blasphemize, your father cannot die."

"Who... are you?" I repeated.

He chuckled lightly again, "How's your brother?"

Brother? What the hell kind of new drug was this guy on? "Brother?"

"Oh the modern world. Things are so... complicated. The copy of the *Daily* tomorrow will answer your questions," he made his way to the door and walked out, whistling something; I could wager my life it was Für Elise.

I wanted to know what the hell was going on. Had I already pulled the trigger before I even took the job and had that fateful conversation with Virgil behind the Plexiglas? Was this a transfusion of all of the temporal elements of my life? Leo: the ghost of mysteries past, Virgil: the soldier of meaningless deaths present, and Elise: the beaut of love future, of hope? It was all too good to be true. There was no way I could hope for a better future, it was just the gods teasing me, baiting me to move forward before I was plunged into one of Dante's circles. I knew better, and Cicero was nowhere to be found.

I moved quickly, throwing the door open and looking for the—

"Whoa! Vi!" Leo bumped into me from the other side of the door.

"Which way did the guy go?"

"What guy?"

"The guy! The old guy that just left!"

"Lay off the sauce brother. I'm the only one here. No one *left* before you opened the door."

Great. Was I hallucinating again? It seemed too real, too—whatever.

The DJ on the platform above the dance floor shrieked "Ready to set the house on fireeeeeeeee?" and the sheep slammed their hooves on the wooden floor as the music blared louder than before.

Leo rubbed his temple and pushed in his forehead before looking at me and putting his index and middle finger to his mouth; he wanted to go out for a smoke. We made our way outside to a little fenced-in area they called the *patio*, which looked strangely like the yard in prison. He whipped out this huge Cohíba torpedo and handed it to me.

"Thanks."

"For old times' sake," and he had one for himself too. We lit them with his wooden matches and just basked in the silence for a couple of seconds. It was a lungful of fresh air.

"How's life?" he finally asked.

"It's life," I puffed some of the fine cigar, "Good, bad, etcetera etcetera."

"There is no good or bad," he looked through the fence at a closed storefront across the street, "*We* give things meaning; good and bad are manmade. The universe doesn't recognize inconsequential things like degrees of morality or righteousness."

"That's pretty funny to me."

"Why?" he looked at me quizzically.

"At school… I mean we went to a top *educational* institute, *hoping*, even *aspiring* to become what? The complete personification of equity investors' or lawyers' malversation in who we look up to as leaders?"

"And bankers," he continued for me.

"CEOS," there were enough examples, he got the gist.

"Those were *their* aspirations, not ours. Nothing more than clever societal gimmicks to resonate control. You can control people if you know what they want. If they get out of hand, you give it to them and they'll shut up. What better way to cultivate sheep than to make them want for material things that you can provide?" There is no pettier man than the man whose loyalties and beliefs can be bought with mere cash.

"So the things we've become, did we choose them? Are they the extent of our… capacity?"

"We are what we do, aren't we?" Virtues of Aristotelian philosophy.

I laughed a little, "You're asking the wrong guy."

"Might as well talk it through now. What makes a man, a man? What separates say, you, from a little boy; a little child from an overgrown one? If an alien landed right here, right now, and asked 'What is the difference between *you* and that boy, save for the size?' what would you say?"

What governs our identity was what he was really asking. I wish I knew. Was it nobility? And not the bullshit Disney nobility or the old *rich man's* nobility like the olden days of France and England.

Honour? Was it honour? No, it couldn't be. A child and some-times even animals fight with honour. Greed perhaps, that's the best answer for our society. Most people are certainly guided by greed. Even aggression would work. Predators are aggressive, they take what they want. So do we, we spread to an area, populate it, reap and harvest all of its natural resources until it's sucked dry, and then we're forced to move to a new area: consumption. We are a virus.

I couldn't even discern how we differed from other animals or plants. It couldn't be *rationality* like Aristotle claims. The fact is, we don't know whether other animals and plants are irrational, we only assume so. They could have their own language and means of com-munication. Just because we are too dumb or ignorant to discover it doesn't mean it doesn't exist.

"I don't know. Are we more than the choices we've made? More than the sum of our past mistakes? Than the problems we've created? Can we be remade?" was the best answer I could come up with on such short notice.

"Maybe, if you're right then we are more than the sum of what we've done in the past, more than the collection of memories we've chosen to cherish arbitrarily. But... if you're wrong, then all we are is the solidified identity of the past we've created, which implies that our decisions shape us, regardless of their precision or *correctness*."

"Sounds like a catch-22," I played with my bracelet, tugging it so it dug into my skin a little.

"Yep. We're screwed either way. I got to tell you Vi, after all these years, I'm beginning to think truth is an asshole."

"Of course it is, otherwise it wouldn't be so elusive and hard to get."

"Must be a woman," he smiled.

"You have Lina!" I laughed.

"Penso che sono innamorata di lei."

"What?" I didn't understand a single word he just said.

"Nothing. Besides... you have Beethoven's Sonata," he said

with his cigar on his lip and smoke huffing out in small bits as each word left his mouth.

"Then what are you complaining about?" I don't think he realized Elise wasn't my girlfriend.

"Evolution. Are we evolving, or devolving?" I wondered what Lina saw in him. She must like sad men; he was one depressing son of a bitch.

I had to contemplate my answer, reminiscing my Theoretical Physics seminar, "Neither. We simply... exist. There is no time."

"No, there certainly isn't, not for the things I've got in mind," he picked up his cup from the cement railing and cackled the ice in it before drinking it dry.

"You know I had the weirdest dream last night."

I turned to him, "How weird?"

"I'm in this old apartment I used to live in, this 3 feet walkup in the Netherlands from my younger days. I don't know how but there's a class in there. I don't know for what or how they even fit but it is what it is," he puffed his cigar and looked at his empty cup. "Anyway it's a group project of some sort. The teacher yells out 'teams of four!' and I'm teamed up with these dreadful personalities from high school. Everyone is assigned a question. I'm meant to go last. Everyone copies their question down but the third guy eats the paper... yes *chews* the paper up—"

"He *eats* the paper?"

"Yeah, just fully gulps it down, and now I don't have my question. How can I have the answer if I don't have the question? ... So I walk up to the teacher and ask for another assignment sheet. She laughs and says everyone had a particular question, of which one was printed and no one else knows only on *one* piece of paper. I'm out of luck."

"That *is* weird."

"I wish that was the end of it."

"There's more?"

"Unfortunately.... So I shrug my shoulders and sit down on my chair. I put on my headphones and start listening to Górecki's Symphony of Sorrowful Songs. Suddenly another teacher, a male this time, grabs my hand from behind and my headphones fall off... and screams 'THIS IS WHAT FAILURE LOOKS LIKE!' I feel like I have something to prove and I stand up and scream 'FAIL-URE?' and as I'm yelling at him I start flying. I whoosh around the room and break through the window outside in the dead of night. Everyone gasps. I slowly hover back in, and say 'Failure?' and laugh like a villain. 'Titans walk the earth you fools. Do not conflate my apathy and indifference with hatred or weakness.' And just when I feel like I'm about to wake up I hear a voice, the familiar voice of the only woman I ever loved—"

"Lina."

He let out this growling, dissonant snarl of sorrow and shook his head.

"She was screaming a painful yelp and I hovered above everyone to find her, to try to save her but can't. In a rage I fly back outside in the darkness and try to fly to space. It starts raining before I get there though. The first raindrop wakens me."

"What does it mean?" I queried.

"What am I? A sophist?"

I laughed, "I have one where an old man with a cane tears me apart after calling me a monster."

"What does it mean?" his sincerity was a breath of fresh air among the pollutants destroying the cityscape.

"That maybe I am."

He flicked his cigar over the fence, "We're all monsters... it doesn't matter anyway. Dream segments are pointless. A good writer never uses them."

* * *

I was bound to a huge rock in some misty mountain with my hands tied behind my back. The hailing pieces of ice cut my face up and it stung my eyes worse than a cheating girlfriend. I couldn't break free, my legs were asleep, and my chest was vibrating with this elusive pain bordering on just wanting to... let go. I could hear some hawks and eagles circling above me. My hat was on the icy-stone in front of me, tumbling through the snowstorm for two or three seconds before the wind threw it off the cliff. Great... probably the only thing I ever cared about other than hooch and it just... flew off the edge of some lustrous mountain. The eagle caws drew nearer as the pain in my chest worsened like it was being torn apart. I creaked my neck and looked down much slower than I thought—the cold lagged me—my chest was bare, open to the world. I could practically see my ribs and heart pumping blood. The barely flaying skin hanging off my abdomen was covered in blood only it didn't hurt as much as it looked but that was probably the cold numbing me to the pain. Deep down I knew I was a dead man. There was no way I could get free and climb down this mountain with an open torso. The wind cut my face some more as I tried to calm my breathing. The moment had finally come and I wasn't really satisfied with this death.

I could hear the eagles above me, they sounded so close... I looked up through the snow and flickered my eyes as two eagles swooped down in front of me. Before I knew it, a convocation of them were feeding on me, eating my organs and the cold no longer numbed the pain; their beaks punctured my intestines and veins, scalping their way to my heart. No matter how weak I seemed or how much blood I could see merging with the snow at my feet, somehow I was still alive and feeling every second. One of the eagles tilted its head at me and cawed in my face before shoving itself into my heart and biting a piece of it right off.

Awake. My sweat-drenched palm grasped my chest with panicked breaths drowning out the sound of Virgil and Amelia's clattering plates and muffled conversation in the adjacent room. My heart beat faster than the club *song* last night and even though I didn't have a drop of liquor, I couldn't remember how we got back nor how I ended belly up on the Persian rug staring at a cheap-knockoff of Ingres' *The Betrothal of Raphael and the Niece of Cardinal Bibbiena*: of a man of God elucidating some measure of divine love between two gifted souls in the living room of our suite. That particular painting did possess a somewhat irksome air. I stumbled to my feet feeling dizzy, light-headed, and barely made it over to the room service tray. The front page of *Veritas Daily* housed three Army portraits of young men who'd reportedly been gunned down overseas protecting our national interests, and even though I despised the premise that old men in expensive suits give orders so young men die for oil, I couldn't help but shed a few tears for my comrades. I knew better than most that you have no choice in a democracy but to follow orders, no matter how atrocious they are. It's the Western way, the tolerant and open way to deal with those who don't agree with our way of life. But it was the bottom fold of the day's paper that made me nearly faint from an anxiety attack. *Another Slain in Vicious Murder* was the headline, a picture of Helen lying dead on the concrete with bullet holes in her sublime body; I wrinkled the paper harder and tried to read the article. *Helen Calvano, a socialite known almost primarily for her philanthropy around the city, along with being connected to the notorious Calvano family, was victim to a robbery-homicide last night near the palisades. The Calvanos have been rumored to be an organized crime family operating in racketeering, gambling houses, and drug-running in the city, pitting them in direct competition with the ruthless Torrino family, who has since the incarceration of their Don, Vitaly Torrino, relinquished most of their power over the city.*

*The Organized Crime Task Force (OCTF) is searching for leads and urges any witnesses with pertinent information to come forward.* I skimmed the rest, looking for any other information on Helen, I had no idea she was—*although no comment was given by the detectives handling the case, this murder bears a striking resemblance to the other serial murders that have occurred in the city in the preceding weeks and we are wondering whether we are home to a brutal serial killer who preys on young women.*

I threw the paper to the side and went to the balcony for some air. I looked to the horizon and noticed a high school in the distance flying its flag at half-mast, no doubt for the fallen soldiers in Afghanistan, Iraq, or somewhere in Africa. I thought about my own flag, the flag of Vero, flying half-mast for Helen, Trish, Eloise, and all the other women I'd failed to save. The Stripes, the Union Jack, the Maple Leaf, all red with the blood of those we've spilled—both foreign and domestic—in the name of it. Long live freedom, love live *democracy*, long live *true* justice. How many innocents have died in this war? How many children? How many children have *we* killed, how many women... raped? How many kids have we made orphans, how many... widows have we created? It's all a bad joke.

I looked back inside the room, the minibar winked at me around the same time my heartbeat lowered to its *normal* range. I breathed in the morning air and looked towards the sun. There is a fear to the universe, of the unknown. This isn't anything new, of course we're afraid of what we don't know. I wondered though, if it's newly 'thought' about. 'We fear the unknown,' or is it 'We fear what we don't know,' are these different questions? We say, ask, and contemplate these ancient proverbs in vain hopes of sounding more intelligent than we actually are, but if we *really* thought about them, what would they mean? And *why* are we afraid? It's *this* world we ought to be afraid of, not any other.

The sun had risen and was staring back at me, and still, it was like looking into the moonless sky at 2 A.M. and wondering whether darkness would enter you and devour you from the inside. I couldn't get over the question '*why* do we fear the universe?' What is it about it that makes it so enigmatic? Is it because it's dark, cold, and unforgiving? Or could it be, perhaps, that despite our unrelenting pride, we actually know nothing about it... and if we gave it any real thought, we'd come to the realization that we really know nothing about anything at all.

I slid the balcony door open and stepped back inside. It was so quiet I could hear Elise shuffling under the sheets in her bedroom. I looked back down at the paper at my feet fallen to the horoscope and crossword section.

*62 across: ancient harp, 4 letters,* was the only clue that caught my eye but I didn't bother with it. *52 down* was *Transcendental Etude composer...* I was in no mood to solve a crossword.

I had a vague recollection of something I was supposed to find in the paper although I couldn't remember what I was looking for, like forgetting what you were going to say or walking into a room and forgetting why.

A whooshing sound outside the door caught my ear and I noticed an envelope being slipped under it. I looked under *Leo* before venturing to the door: *You are in control. Resist temptation. Get some work done. It's okay to fall in love.* Who the hell writes these? They were quite vexing. I walked over to the door. It was a basic white envelope marked '*Für Elise's Bodyguard.*'

Hmmm. I examined it in the light and tried to measure its weight with my hands. It only looked to hold paper, no explosives or anything, unless someone was... cowardly enough to mail me anthrax.

I used the breakfast knife to tear the envelope. It was a single piece of paper with magazine letters cut out like a note from a horror movie. A surveillance picture of Elise and I near her car from a week or so back. I unfolded the note: an off-white piece of paper with the words '*We know who you are...* ' glued to the center of the page. *We know who you are?* How original. Who am I? Who is anyone? Who are *we?* Or better yet, *what* are we and *what* is our purpose? To chase some vague piece of paper with some arbitrary number denomination on it? Whoever has the most zeroes at the end of theirs wins? No, it can't be. We aren't that hopeless... that ignorant... are we? Are we just pieces of meat after another piece of meat to connect, to share, to believe, or reject? *How* can we comprehend Aristotle's crucial definitions and descriptions in the Metaphysics? Plato's focused, albeit confusing references to 'The One' as the only outflow of truth and existence? How can we even begin to understand Hesse's tranquility of mind or Adorno's misunderstood and conflated aberration of the historical perspective without first understanding ourselves? Without first admitting defeat as weaker beings to others? How can we do all this without confessing our misguided and perverse attempts to deliver some brand of truth or justice that also happens to coincide with the hoarding and theft of others' natural resources? How can we grow as a people without first recognizing our flaws as human? Without first knowing *who* we are before diving head first in pursuit of *what* we've simply conflated as representations of our humanity viz. democracy? Human is too honored a word, too pure an expression to describe what we've become, devolved to more of a *what* rather than a *who*, *why*, or even a *how*, and all it took for us to fall were some fruity gizmos, some golden arches, bad coffee, and propaganda conflated with advertising selling us a definition of *justice*.

With all this, someone *else* has figured out who *I* am? I'll take that bet. I instantly opened the door and looked around the hallway to see if I could spot anyone leaving. Not a soul in sight except a guy in an opposing room down the hall traipsing towards the elevator after a casual "Good morning." The music playing in the hall was a somewhat ambient variation of Beethoven's *Dreaming of Elise.* ... I wish.

I peered my head back into our room and wondered if Virgil was playing some kind of sick joke on me as my eye caught yet another thrift-store painting of a raven flying into the sunset above the minibar. I walked over to the glass table to pick up the .38 when another piece of paper slipped through the gap. I picked up the gun and immediately opened the door to the sound of the stairway door closing at the end of the hall. These bozos were good. The message was different this time: a threat to Elise. So much for keeping a low profile and going about our days undetected. The *'You can't protect her 24/7,*' sent a chill up my spine solely because they—whomever they might be—were absolutely right. I couldn't protect her all the time, even if I was with her at all times; all it takes is a single second of miscommunication or a moment of bad judgment for her to lose her life. To lose her *life*…. What the hell had I gotten her into? Who was *I*, to try to protect her 24/7?

I felt like a schmuck from a grody Matt Damon action film. I galloped over and opened the bedroom door. She got startled and backed away, caught in the distance between her bed and the door, presumably on her way to the living area. I'd only beaten her to the punch.

I was cursed. She was so beautiful: twirling her right index finger in her red hair like autumn leaves idling in the wind while her left hand was rubbing the right side of her breast. She wore white from head to toe, a short shirt and unbelievably sexy pyjama pants. She looked like an angel, and for a second, the sun hit the window in such a way that the light reflected perfectly off her jaw and I thought, just for that second, that she really *was*. For a second I believed that there was a God and perhaps a heaven with people like her in charge. The second didn't last long enough and she pecked me on the cheek rather vigorously,

"Morning…"

"Morning ang—I mean Madame," they say slips of the tongue reveal your true nature, your subconscious. *They're* probably right.

She walked to the room service tray, opening the metal lid on the plate and slumping back at me as if to imply *this is still untouched, when do you eat?* She put a couple of cherries in her mouth and went to the kitchen for a glass of milk or orange juice.

"I can't believe you went to school with Leonardo Köning! What was he like?" she stretched her arm out and I walked up to the kitchen counter and grabbed the glass of—sip—orange juice she handed me.

"He's like anyone else… a cynical man who believes in nothing other than himself."

She chuckled, "That's the feeling I get from his writing."

"You *actually* read his books?" Great, my morning was about to be wasted talking about some politically incorrect clown.

"Well… yes. I enjoy his take on things."

"Elaborate," I was curious. Maybe I was wrong. Maybe, just maybe he *was* a good writer and had something to say. There *might* be some veneer of truth for the chosen ones who dare embark on the fictional journeys he sets forth.

"Hmmm," she ate a couple of grapes off the plate and craned her neck into the minibar, coming out with a bottle of Perrier, "Most of his novels are convoluted and complex but his short stories are pretty straightforward."

"Go on."

"Well," she pouted her lips and blinked those uranic galaxies of hers, "One of the short thrillers he wrote in his youth was about an average man who was kept prisoner in some French château."

"Okay…"

"After watching his captor leave the estate through a crack on the boarded windows, he wandered through the mansion with nothing but nameless dread, an eerie chill hanging over the curls on his hair, and an old flickering flashlight he'd found. It was gritty and intense. I'm sure you know his style by now.

"He did always have a flair for the dramatic." Nice to see some things never change.

"Anyway, the *protagonist*, Joe, chanced upon a locked room and exerted himself in forcing it open; finding a beautiful woman chained, not unlike himself in his cell, on an inclined surgical table: cut, bruised, and beaten. Some classic form of compassion forced the humanity into him, and he spent many nights sneaking in and out of his cell to aid his fellow-prisoner. She was less fed, less clothed, and less average than he was.

After much time had passed and he knew this woman well enough to have Cartesian conversations with her, he decided he'd save this damsel-in-distress and formulates a perfect plan to help her escape. Unfortunately, Joe was more of a Don Quixote and less of a fictional Hollywood action-star lost in the jostle of his own gratification. He flexed all the muscles except the one that counted, seeking to understand human nature ideally rather than pragmatically. He feared more the monster within himself than the monsters around him.

And during all this, what Köning demonstrated as 'time passing' was anything but: time never progresses linearly in his stories, characters live through flashbacks after death, or die never having lived, or things happen which cause other things that have already happened. In this instance, Joe's anger and impatience grew as a captive. He knew he had to conquer himself before he could understand the human psyche. His journey had to begin inward. He knew that even the greatest of men could be bought out, especially in this age of moral bankruptcy. He understood that men could be lost, destroyed, or ignored in this era of prostituting ideals. His erroneous view represented undying by an undying belief that he could become something more than a man to this woman, and hence become eternal and as immortal as *Fosca*. His idea was to rescue the female prisoner and live on the Amalfi coast with her, but most of all, deep within the most critical understanding of himself, he wanted to die fatefully as he rescued her. He'd never get a chance to have a meaningful death again, and Köning toys with the idea whether such a thing even exists.

Joe was caught within seconds of putting his plan into motion — Köning finds despair humorous. Joe was hung upside down by the bare of his ankles in front of the castle walls as a warning to others. The interesting thing about the character development in the story was that the woman didn't care. She simply waited for the next 'prisoner' to chance upon her, wondering if the eighth time would be the charm—and of course, this is revealed at the very end—the ideal that all men are prisoners in themselves with no hope of escape.

I think he was too harshly criticized for this little anecdote. He didn't really explore the depth of this average Joe. It's always been obvious from his work that normalcy and average sheep–his words– bored him to the point of suicide. He leaves it to the reader to think of the most common, 'quasi-intellectual sheeple' and apply those traits to Joe. Nor does he tell us much about this unknown Jane. Who was she? Why was she captive? How long had she been there? He didn't consider it a suitable literary device to inform the reader that Joe had a wife at one point, his one and only love… and she was taken from him by mere chance, by simply being on a sidewalk as a drunk driver pinned her to a '*Lost Soul? We can help*' religious pole along some quiet suburban street. He didn't feel it an eloquent writing style to tell the reader that Jane looked almost exactly like his wife — Lida… I think was her name. He didn't highlight these facts and instead left it to the reader to infer that it was not some knight-hood code of chivalry or some pursuit of higher abstract ideals that attracted Joe to Jane; rather simply, it was because she looked like Lida. Had it been anyone else, Joe wouldn't have flinched and instead would've withered away as a captive if he couldn't muster up the courage to end his own life or escape by pure chance."

"How are you commenting on what he *didn't* say?"

"Oh this stuff was in the epilogue. It was hilarious. He knew what people would say before they said it. It was dark and comical, 'I will be criticized for this story for not exploring'… and etcetera." So the story kept going. It didn't end with the ending. How fortuitous it would be of the dead if there really *was* a soul and it was immortal.

"That's funny," I didn't smile, "Go on… and people *still* criticized him?"

"A little more back-story was given on Jane on his blog, but anyway…. Where was I? … Oh right. That's what Köning excels at: illustrating meaninglessness, pointlessness. The general futility of living and breathing. In my opinion, he's the kind of person irked if the reader expects anything other than the dour truth hovering amongst our toxic planet like the mingling radioactive waste and cigar smoke above our heads, hoping for a light bulb to shake us out of our apathy."

"That's intense."

"Coming from a man who reads Plato, Hesse, O'Hara, and Foucault, I'm sure he'd appreciate the compliment."

I remembered the threat, "We have to go Madame. It's not safe here."

"Lighten up Vero. Nothing's going to happen here," she walked over and opened the connecting door to Vigil and Amelia's room, "Besides, I have you to protect me," she delicately bit into a slice of an apple she'd cut up.

I rolled my eyes and sighed. I couldn't argue with her.

"Who left a message?" her galaxies opened and seemed to point to the phone behind me, the red 'Message' light flashing. I was so out of it with the paper and the notes that I hadn't even noticed. I pushed 'Play' to the sound of Elise chewing another slice of her apple.

The long beep tired me enough to sit in the chair and just stare at the stupid red light on the panel. "New... message... playback. Yesterday... three... twenty... seven... P.M." I hope the actual message was this slow so we wouldn't have to leave the room and I could keep Elise safe for at least one more day. "Hi, my name is Detective Oliver Matthews. I'm trying to track down a... Vero Bergljót. I'd like to ask him a few questions." The plot thickens, *Detective* Matthews must consider me a suspect in these slayings. I guess it was a matter of time before someone found out I was one of the last people *every single* victim had seen.

"Call him back Vero!" Elise panicked, "Is dad okay?" she made a run for the phone in a hurry. I grabbed and hugged her, "He's fine Madame... he's fine."

She sniffled, "I don't know what I'd do if..."

"He's fine. Trust me, this is an entirely different matter. I'll address it eventually."

She nodded her head in my chest and backed away. Her galaxies showed me what red supernovas looked like, bloodshot with a kind of literary description that made me squirm.

# Accarezzévole

## Moments Ago

My LANGUID REACH for Trish's earring on the ground forced me out of the prone position, grasping it so tight the sharp end cut me. I could barely move from the pain, the cold floor sent this gnawing feel up the right side of my jaw and I couldn't help but wonder how I was going to get Elise, Virg, and Amelia out of this; Mack talks a big game so I assumed he'd take care of himself.

"Get up," one of the token-henchmen blurted out before kicking me again in the ribs.

"Give me a moment," I replied, trying my best to stall while at the same time bait him into coming closer so I could take him down. I should've been able to knock him out or least knock him back before his partner got close enough to hit me... I couldn't think about what I'd do even *if* I got by these two goombahs, I couldn't think about what might've lain behind the door in front of me. "It's getting harder and harder to find a quiet place to *bleed*."

"I said... get... up!" and another kick, to the chest this time, it nearly winded me.

He was a laconic man and this feeling of presage wouldn't be going away anytime soon. Things could hardly get any worse. "You're really getting a kick out of this aren't you?" I spitted out some blood and slowly rose to my feet.

He was faster than I gave him credit for. The guy behind me immediately jumped forward and held me while the guy in front of me got a few solid hooks to my face and chest. I spurted out more blood. He let go of me and pushed me into the door, then held me back again, opened the door, and shoved me out.

Another guy who looked like he was a dishonourably discharged military man with perfect posture greeted me on the other side of the doorway with his arms crossed.

"He's all yours Ahriman," the kicker scowled.

Ahriman... what an interesting name. He guided me down a minor hallway without saying a word. He had a sort of enigmatic air about him. He looked half West Asian, half Scandinavian. Unfortunately for him he looked more like an innocent man on America's terror watch-list rather than a gallant Viking possessing all the benefits of modernity. More like a villain in a Western fairy tale with his slicked-bouffant obsidian hair rather than the long sun-like curls that all great saviours of the poor have been obliged to possess. I squinted to the side towards him for a second and he caught my gaze almost immediately; his inky irises were comfortable enough to hold my stare indefinitely, his pupils seemed entirely ravenous as opposed to the feminist preferred oceanic turquoise, which for them is a *physical* demarcation of emotional sensitivity. He seemed like an uncanny *bad guy* any which way I looked at him, except of course, by his actions thus far, as he'd done absolutely nothing for me to make such radical judgments... but we're Western, who gives a hoot about *trivial* things like the truth? We're interested more in questions that answer: 'What does he look like?' or 'How can we antagonize him into a negative reaction?' rather than 'What does he believe?' or 'Does his character and identity merit my support?' and most importantly, 'Does his country have any resources we can take?'

He opened a door for me and I walked inside to the sound of what I presumed were Elise's muffled screams. A resolute terror consumed me at the thought of not being able to get her out of this and I asked myself how this happened, what in me had lapsed enough attention that I'd get caught in such a tactically disadvantageous scenario... twice?

My steps in the room were drowned out by Elise's hidden gargling behind the shroud they'd shoved on her face. The villain pushed me to my knees and I was so weak I slipped face first onto a newspaper. After a while I shook my head enough to dislodge it and looked at the paper, the same copy of *Vertias* with the picture of

Helen lying dead on the ground, only this time, the paper was soaked red with the blood from my face. It was symbolic enough to make me think that every time we as a species come close to what passes for progress, these damn 'free-thinkers' or quasi-inverted civil movement extremists send us back to the Stone Age. The first generation was told: 'you're unique,' so they age deluding themselves that they're God's gift to the universe and wish to bestow this gift onto mankind, more specifically, their children. 'But Dad, if we're... or if everyone is unique, doesn't that mean none of us are?' and so these gifts to humanity were left scratching their empty scalps.

The next generation got a little bit wiser with their bullshit: 'you're unique... in your own way,' giving carte blanche to all the psychologists, psychiatrists, and all other *experts* to print money. If everyone is *particularly* unique, that means no one can be deemed 'normal' or 'average' unless those same experts can label them as perfect sheep. Sophistry at its best.

Fatigued, we wise up a little and evolve our intellects by creating marvelous things in the name of science like bigger guns and the atomic bomb. We reject uniqueness and focus on birth: we are born *equal*. And again, this twists society into permitting idiots behind the podium to *reason* that countries not our own cannot have *weapons of mass destruction*—the phrase 'mass destruction' is also never conveniently defined by this crowd. A legislator's pen is more a weapon of mass destruction than a terrorist's AK-47 on any day of the week. We, as a nation, become the only nation *civilized* enough to bear arms which can annihilate another country at the press of a button, despite actually *being* the *only* country ever in history to use such a weapon. But others are never allowed since they are not of equal birth.

Years pass, and once more, slowly but deliberately, we evolve and gradually begin to heal from the wounds inflicted on us from the previous generation's lies by murderous politicians committing acts of false *justice* from oval, square, or rhombus shaped offices. This time however, the *free-thinkers* have reached the pinnacle of their intellect and tolerance: they demand that we force our tolerance onto other nations. They demand that we *police* the world. 'Everyone of equal birth deserves *Justice.*' Naturally, no self-respecting politician looking to stuff his pockets with blood money could say no to such an offer, and thus *democracy* is spread onto poorer nations with useful natural resources at the cost of their citizens' rape, murder, torture, and theft. We're so tolerant that other countries better do it our way. If we *wise* up again—should the world last that long—the next generations will be manipulated by some other clever word-games or ideals; *corporate* justice perhaps. Other countries *must* be informed enough to adopt our degenerate spending habits. 'Africa isn't spending enough on useless gadgets.' Those *poor* children need our help. They *need* Cosmicloots cafés and Kumquat phones to be considered *civilized*. Enter benevolent politician who will then selflessly shove that steaming cup of watered-down coffee down the throat of a homeless African child.

Ideally, the free-thinkers will realize their mistake and protest, argue, and break windows in the name of ridding the world of countries not observant to our consumerist habits. "They have a right to crappy coffee just like us," can be their mantra. And I began to wonder: is that a world I'd want to be a part of? To participate in? A great Orwellian future where every country is like the United States minus the thieving CEOS and nuclear bombs?

The following generation will no doubt study military history a little better than we did, "But Daddy, we're the only country to ever use an atom bomb over a civilian city," and I know I'll be the one forced to scratch *my* head… if I stay alive long enough and can cope with myself bringing life onto this undead planet.

My heart stopped. I tried getting up suddenly and freeing my arms but something hit me from behind and—.

## ADAGIO FROM THE SCOPE OF THINGS

VIRGIL AND AMELIA came in making jokes to each other, arguing about who said what as their last words. Elise wrapped around my arms like a Disney princess. Her hair was a waterfall of the autumn rain that unnervingly made me think about an oncoming cold winter. Could I keep warm... with her?

"You guys okay?" Amelia was so consumed by her conversation with Virg that her question came off as facetious.

"Fine," Elise sniffled, rubbed under her eyes and walked towards her. It tore me apart, a reminder, not that I needed one, that a bad day *could* get worse, in fact with my luck, it was a lock.

"We're going to brunch. Would you two like to join us?" Virg asked with a little more enthusiasm than was required, perhaps their relationship was taking strides in the right direction.

"No," Elise answered as she made her way back to the room service tray for a piece of sliced peach, "I got a bowl of fruit and Vero doesn't eat."

"Aaah, good point," Virg nodded and sat down on the stool at the kitchen counter, Amelia followed and took her place beside him.

Small talk ensued between the trio at the counter about the exhibit and the circus we attended last night. They swapped stories, talked about the music. I couldn't really figure into detail at all since I wasn't really listening... I gazed out the window towards the balcony wondering about the flags flying at half-mast that for me, weren't for lost soldiers but the women who were murdered. What kind of dark, twisted mind preys on young women? I think it was Poe that said the death of a beautiful woman is the most poetical thing in the universe, and if that was true... I was John Milton.

Before I knew it, I found myself on the balcony again looking down at the ground with the guys talking in the kitchen. I wasn't standing over the railing but I could just slip over it if I wanted to, and I kind of did. The old feelings I'd been repressing were tearing out of me, wanting their fifteen minutes in the darkening sun.

In my younger, more cultivated days as an abiding youth I played video games on a console *Santa* brought for me one year... and I could never get over how easy life was in a video game—no matter the difficulty—a single blunder and you could 'restart from checkpoint' or 'restart level' altogether. Even then, that wasn't where the magic laid, oh no, the true magic of a game was its 'quit' option. How, I always wondered, could you quit a game, and what does that mean in life? If a game ever frustrated you, enraged you, or you flat out gave up, you could simply... quit. The million dollar question was: What is the equivalent to 'Quit Game' in *real* life? The .38 lying on the round table? I was damned if I was going to disappoint some poor kid, or *God*, controlling me with such malice as never to restart any checkpoints or levels, leaving me with all my past errors of judgment. I wanted to 'Quit Game,' and hopefully the balcony or the .38 would abide.

I closed my eyes to consider this thought before Elise's whisper shook me out of the daze. "Vero? You okay?"

"I'm fine."

"I've been calling you for like... three minutes. Couldn't you hear me out here?"

"No." ... "You okay?"

"Of course. I'm fine," she smirked, "Virg and Amelia left. Listen... I was wondering if you wanted to go check out the old Air Force military museum with me."

How expected. The .38 would have to wait, "You decide Madame."

"Oh quit it with the employee employer relationship! Do you want to go with me or not?"

"Yes," it sounded interesting.

"Great, I'll get ready," she walked back into the room with that seductive gait that I had to assume was only one of the many things about her that beguiled men to be at her beckon, "See... told ya it's safe. No one would *ever* look for us here!"

"You were right," I thought about the notes I'd gotten. They *had* found out, so what were they waiting for?

The concierge winked at me as we passed through the lobby and I'd forgotten how we got into the room last night, leaving the tape I put up between the frame a moot point.

I reached up to flick my hat but only felt my hair.

"The car's a block and a half up," Elise sashayed northward, twirling back in my direction.

"Didn't we valet it?" the lobby played the Beethoven Consort's rendition of *Beethoven's Despair (Elise is Married)*, and the thought *was* despairing.

"We did. I asked them to move it. I want to walk."

You left the car on the street vulnerable to attack to anyone while there's people after us, "Oh... okay," I sifted through my pockets looking for the key.

"Looking for this?" Elise handed it to me.

The car was parked beside this empty wall graffitied with numbers that I scolded and ignored, but the numbers grew interesting as I neared the car until I found myself staring up at the wall. It was titled: *Soldiers*, which then split up into columns: Killed in Action, Suicide, and Civilians Murdered during *The War on Terror*, and it was petrifying to see. There was a tally of 203 soldiers killed in action for this year, each spray-painted black line representing a fallen man for oil prices. The quote under *Civilians Murdered* was hysterical, "The street isn't big enough for me to illustrate how many we've killed, plus I'm too tired." But what made it art, what made it a critical point against our dismissive society was the figure under *Suicides*: 412. I nearly didn't believe it, 412 men or women committed suicide after serving their tour out in the middle of nowhere and less than half that number had been *killed* by *terror*. It was the waning truth on any veteran that war is pointless, the under-standing that what you're really fighting for is to enrich the bank statement of an already rich old man. It was *art* in its finest form. *This* was the modern Sistine Chapel, I'd pay thousands for someone to illustrate this truth somewhere, to yell it from a mountaintop for all the world to hear… much better than a line drawn on a canvas by Odder Van Crapsville.

A whisper through the wind… 'Animal.' I ignored it.

I started the ignition on the car with the new remote starter and made my way to her door.

"Jesus that's morbid," Elise quipped as I opened her door, "Things like this just seem to… follow you around."

I adjusted myself on the driver's seat, "It sure feels that way Madame."

She tapped the on-screen navigation system a couple of times until that annoying voice returned: "You are on cou-rse. Arri-val time. Tw-elve min-utes. Des-ti-nation will be on the left."

"So we don't get lost," her voice was like fine bourbon calming me to the point of tranquility.

"We're all lost," and the thought of booze made me crave some as a flash of sudden fear jolted through me. Something was wrong.

"Vero… Can I ask you something?"

"Of course."

I felt her feel out this inaudible howl before she inhaled deeply, "Tell me what… tell me what I can do. To bring you out of this deep sadness. I want…" she exhaled, "I want to help you."

No one can help me. That much was clear. *That* much, was truth, "I wish I could tell you Elise. I wish I could just say the words and everything would be okay. I've wished I could stop noticing the things I see or think the things that bring me only misery. I wish I could pray and ask *Cristo* for some measure of elevated help in knowing that there's something more than *this*… to show me a sign that He's out there. To show me purpose, a *reason* for this pain. I'm rambling on. My mind won't let me believe such things for too long. A cyclical joke of cosmic proportions I guess."

I watched the road but I could feel her staring in my peripherals trying to absorb all I'd said.

"You're always in pain, always lonely. At least tell me why you never show—"

I stopped listening the second my gaze met with the spinning red and blue lights in the rearview. They could've been bought off by the mob; Virgil's "Don't trust *anyone*... even cops" echoed in my ear.

Elise guided my ears to the screeching siren behind us. I couldn't even risk bribing this fool, there's always that lottery-winning odd that he's some procedural pansy or a misguided idealist who thinks honesty is the best policy. Above all else, even if this was a routine traffic stop, running our names and the plate would tip the *bad guys* to our location so I couldn't risk it.

I was about to floor it when fate smiled on Elise, a wife-beater wearing degenerate on a motorcycle who thought he was a MotoGP racer pulled a wheelie past us and immediately got the cop's attention. The taxpayers' *slave* passed us in service to the law as I slowed down to a right turn away from this scene.

"You are... off cou-rse," the car condescended.

I looked behind us and noticed a midnight blue Lexus that I could swear I'd seen before screech around the corner with novelty looking saps holding weapons inside veering three cars behind us. I caught glimpse of their plate: *H0M0MRTU5*, which removed all doubt that I *had* seen this car before.

I reached for the .38 in the glove box and thumbed back the hammer. The click *hopefully* slid the bullet into place and Elise flinched.

"Madame, get down. Lie as flat as you can and fasten your seat belt!"

"Vero? What's happening?"

I practically felt her heart race and her pupils dilate in sheer terror of what was coming. I slammed the accelerator to the floor and started weaving in and out of traffic. A wave of nostalgia for the F-15's speed washed over me as I tried to outrun the Lexus. I turned left onto the route and swerved to the side, "You are off course— Reduce speed now!" the car screamed as I peered down to the speedometer blinking near 180 km/h. Suddenly that rotten feeling in my gut came running back like a clingy ex-girlfriend. A cold breeze froze my jaw. I glanced to the side and felt Elise's back and neck, *praying* that I wouldn't feel any blood.

A hole steamed up the hood of Don's LR4. Then another, and another, bullets were killing the engine. Everything fell silent. I heard the first four notes of Für Elise as my ears rang louder than a trumpet fanfare at an army rally. 21 gun salute… not for me. The faint voice of the placating GPS now only said "You are off cou-rse," and whistled in my ears while the hood was popped full of more holes and finally exploded off its hinges.

"Madame, get down!" I screamed in desperation as I tried to turn the car out of the area. The sounds didn't match. I tried looking around but couldn't see muzzle flashes nor anyone in the immediate vicinity. Bastard probably had a silencer in his sniper's nest. Coward was hiding somewhere safe and sound putting holes in as many places as he could. He was sloppy—another bullet pierced the hood —not a single one hit the windshield. As far as snipers go he was mediocr—oh… I realized he wasn't aiming for us. I wanted to get to another street but the GPS had this rotating circle with the words '*calculating new route*' etched onto it and I couldn't see the map. More bullets tore the hood off and the engine started dying. The Lexus was still gaining. I thought I'd outran it but this was clearly planned. And finally, the gas pedal stopped responding around the same time the engine started dying and the car progressively came to a full stop along with my thoughts of hope. The sniper was trying to pin us down, the same way we'd do it if we were ambushing someone. Professional, and if I had it right, the Lexus should veer up behind us to cut off our foot escape.

"I'm..." she heaved, "Okay!"

"All right love. On my count, get out of the car, stay as low as you can, and hide behind the door okay?"

"Okay," she nodded.

I snuck a peek through the back window and didn't see the Lexus. They had *half* the plan down pat. "3... 2... 1... GO Elise, GO!" *I know I'm not your favourite but please don't let anything happen to her.* I came out holding the .38 from my side and met Elise at the trunk of the car, "You okay?" I brushed her hair to the side and she flicked her eyes at me, "You hit?"

"No, no! I'm okay. Now what?"

"Okay, see that pole right there around the corner?"

"Yeah..."

"When I tell you to you're going to run behind the pole and then turn that corner."

"Okay... wait, what about you?"

I gripped the .38 tighter. My stomach was right. "You're not gonna stop running. You're not gonna slow down. You are not gonna look back! Got it?" I was hoping she wasn't a descendent of Lot's wife.

"What about yo—"

"Elise!" I screamed over the round of the sniper's suppression bullets tearing into the car, "Don't argue with me!"

*H0M0MRTU5* arrived a little late to the party but they were still early enough to catch us with our pants down.

Screw it. This would be a good death. I walked up to the Lexus before these party-poopers could get out with their automatic weapons in time to ambush us. I aimed at the driver first, squeezing the trigger as delicately as I could with a simple, deliberate exhale. Click.

*Really?* Oh right... silly me... it's Sunday.

Squeeze.

Click.

Come on!

"Vero! Get down!" Elise yelped.

I looked back and noticed I was no longer behind the car which meant I was in full view of the sniper. I opened my arms in his embrace holding the single-loaded .38. He didn't take the shot. The passenger of the Lexus calmly got out of his car. I pointed the gun at him, third time's a charm.

Click.

Luck *really* hates me.

"Just drop it Vi," he scoffed.

I guess I expected them to know my name. They've been watching us. How many times had I seen this car around Elise or myself suspiciously idling in our immediate proximity? There was another car too... a sports car with a ridiculous novelty plate like this one, but I couldn't remember what it was.

I threw the gun at him and used this distraction to lunge and make quick work of his face with a jab and uppercut. I heard a couple of his bones break and his groans of pain followed by his gargling of blood only affirmed my belief.

It'd only been a couple of seconds before the sound of a .45 being cocked froze my entire body sitting on top of this beaten soul.

"Hey," the driver whistled, "Stop that!" he shoved his gun into Elise's face, holding her forearm so tight she could hardly move. Clichéd, but effective.

I punched the guy once more and got up with my hands in the air.

"Good," the driver said as he forced Elise to move around to the side of their car.

The passenger could barely get up, broken bones and a broken ego will do that to a man, "I can't believe the boss likes this prick!"

and all I saw was red, the back of my head having met with the butt of his MAC-10.

"Do…" I could hear a faint conversation as I dozed in and out. They were dragging me somewhere. I didn't know where I was, "Dreams…" like a nightmare after a week-long bender, "… from?"

Why *did* I take this job? It wasn't Virgil that convinced me, it wasn't some internal attempt to do good in the cruel world. There isn't enough good on this planet for me to use to balance out the bad anyway. I couldn't see but I was semi-conscious, feeling and hearing my achilles drag on the ground as I heard my *other* achilles ask where they were taking me—it seemed simple enough but why take any job? Was I that tired of drinking? Of contemplating what I could've done differently? Of trivial sex and empty *relationships*?

## In Vino Veritas

"THE COPY OF the *Daily* tomorrow will hopefully answer some of your questions."

Awake. I inhaled as much air as I could and put my arms up ready to break more egos... I'm... in my apartment? A half empty bottle of *Double Black* with 2 glasses filled a quarter of the way rested on my nightstand. Was I drunk? I don't remember drinking nor do I feel drunk, but then again after a while it doesn't really affect you in the way you want, akin to drinking muddy water.

I had this blistering headache and didn't really want to move at all but I knew I had to find out just what the hell was going on. I slipped off the bed and took a shower. I noticed all the stuff I had in that garbage bag in Elise's trunk scattered all over my apartment again; the evidence in those grisly murders. There was no doubt in my mind I was being framed. Everything was real. I wasn't *that* drunk. I figured I should go to the judge, see what plays he was making while we were away to bring this pressure on us. My headache only worsened when the *ding* of the elevator started its descent to the ground floor. It was the first time in a long array of weeks that I didn't test the Grim Reaper with an exciting game of Russian roulette, and with this thought, wondered where my .38 had gone.

I knew, I damn well *knew* I wanted her, but what I thought I knew could fit on a baby's palm with plenty of space left. Theaetetus would be proud.

I heard murmurs of an argument behind the elevator doors as it slowed down, opening just around the corner from the main lobby.

"Where is he? Vero Króna! Tell me!"

# RHAPSODY

TICK. ... TICK. ... TICK. ... Tock.

...

"Maybe it's broken," some wiseguy with a half-cocked accent says.

Tick. Tick. Tititit. "This is a vintage Breitling you buffoon. It doesn't break."

I'm regaining consciousness. The ticking sound of this clown's watch wakes me enough to know what's going on.

"Uhhhh," I groan.

"Doooooooo... *you* know... where *dreams* come from?" he sounds creepier as the sentence goes on.

Elise's perfume glides me to focus. I take a pretty hard hit to the face and I'm pretty sure my nose is already broken. I can feel the dried blood on it. I can hardly breathe and the duct tape on my mouth and hands don't help either.

"Why did she love you? ... I mean I could settle for someone else, but *you*? An alcoholic psycho-killer?" he tosses my military jacket onto my lap and I look down. A satellite map of the city I'd levelled which was now nothing but a big black circle. "*How* could she *love* you?" and he rips the duct tape off my mouth.

I look at Elise, "I protect her..."

He tilts his head and raises one eyebrow, "And a fancy job you're doing at that!"

My brevity irks him a little so I embrace the silence to completely piss him off. He looks at me then at Elise, points to both of us alternatively, "You think I'm talking about *her*?" he laughs, loudly, grabbing her chin and shaking it from right-to-left.

I stare at Elise's lips pressed against the duct tape, she's trying to steer my gaze to the guy's face but I still can't see properly, almost everything is blurred. I have a concussion.

"I didn't want to kill her you know. I didn't want to kill *any* of them. But alas, 'the good of the many must outweigh the good of the one.' Don't ya' agree?"

"I take it this means you're not a Platonist, or a Kantian, or anyone worth reading or knowing, anyone interesting really."

He comes close enough for me to finally see his face. Henrik. "People usually converse with me with much more respect! Keep in mind I'm the only thing holding these two back," he points behind him where I see two blurry blobs behind him, wounded and hurt, courtesy of me.

"I don't even get what he just said. How was that an insult?" one of them says to the other.

"Shut up Sebastian. You're an idiot. Just stand there and flex!" Henrik yells.

Virg snickers beside me and it's the first time I notice him. The other goon leans in closer to his partner, "It's because Plato and Kant have objective accounts of autonomy and knowledge, they're not quite as utilitarian as the boss is making the world seem. Killing for them is wrong no matter what the circumstance."

"How can *he* say that?" he points to me with his MAC-10, "He's killed too!"

"I didn't kill the girl he's talking about. I haven't killed anyone *here*," I don't why I thought I needed to defend myself to these idiots, but they were standing behind Elise and I wanted their attention focused on me.

"Up close and personal you mean right coward? Because if we're talking *objectively*, in an adored Kantian sense, then you've killed more people than all of us put together," he points to everywhere in the room, including Virgil and Mack, who is just coming to. "What am I saying?" he rants on, "You're not even the philosopher! *He* is," he walks towards Virg and rips the tape off.

"Your monkey shot me in my favourite Springbank holder, I owe you for that," Virgil stares down one of the guys standing behind Elise and the guy just fumbles with his belt buckle. I think Virgil passes out again from the blood loss.

Henrik walks up to Elise and sniffs her hair, then touches it, "Just look at her. She's so beautiful," he starts twirling a finger in one of her ringlets, "I like your hair," he rips the tape off her mouth just slow enough for it to hurt.

"He's going to kill you you know," are the first words out of her pouty lips.

\* \* \*

Virgil breaks free eventually and runs to aid Mack. I can get up since my feet aren't tied but his magnum stops me dead in my tracks. Virgil tries, but can't save Mack.

"There! One less degenerate in the world," Henrik looks at his gun with a certain calm that I assume frightens Elise in his arms, and then lets her go towards me, "Ew. I have grime under my fingernails Ahriman."

Elise rushes up and grabs my face, examining it like a doctor, "Are you okay?"

"MMMMMMM," take the duct tape off!

Rip. "Get behind me Elise."

"No! Don't," Henrik points the gun at her and orders her back to her chair. How was I going to get her out of this?

I have to change gears, be the comedic buffoon, make him think he's smarter than me, and just when he thinks he has the edge. I'll attack. It should work. ... It *should* work. I hope it isn't Sunday anymore.

"Takes a big man to shoot an unarmed helpless tied up soldier!" Virgil sniffles and I can see the rage building up in his eyes, but my eyes tell him not to give in. I'm hoping he doesn't charge at them, because no matter how fast he is, that guy's MAC-10 is faster.

This was a perfect opportunity for me to take the lead, "He *is* a big man," I looked straight at Virg, pretending like Henrik isn't even there; he liked to be the centre of attention. I'm going to take that away, "Catching a helpless young socialite when she's shopping! He's a real leader!"

"HEY!" he screams as he spins the magnum's cylinder for effect, "I caught *you* didn't I?"

I turn to him as patronizingly as I can and scoff, "You couldn't catch herpes from a $7 Thai hooker!"

Virgil snorts with laughter and one of the bozos—Sebastian? —was repressing his own raunchy snicker. I was getting somewhere.

The shark smile on Henrik's lips showed me his perfect, pearly-white teeth, "It's either the sharp wit or the Zen-like silence. Both two extremes. A simple defence mechanism," maybe this was *his* plan, "You don't even know who you are! You're a complete failure," he shrugged his shoulder.

Maybe he was right, but I couldn't let him get under my skin. Not here. Not now. "I take it from that Jason Bourne note you left me back at the hotel, *you're* going to tell me who I am."

"Only if you want to know," he tapped his watch.

I'm satisfied as long as the attention is off Elise, "Okay. I'll humour you!" I sit back down on the chair. My hands are still bound.

One of his guys nods slightly as if they're waiting for my obedience. This was *Phase II* or something. The monkey brings over a chair and Henrik sits on it backwards with the magnum in his hands. Even if I somehow get free I can't make any moves, the back of the chair protects him... he's smarter than he lets on.

# FUGUE

HE COMES A little closer and studies my face, "I can see the resemblance."

"Make sense," I take a page out of Elise's adages. I have to admit he's getting under my skin.

"Enough with this horseshit!" Virgil screams and stands up. Henrik's ponderous gaze towards Ahriman widens my eyes, hoping he doesn't give the order to kill him. A little nod.

In the blink of an eye Ahriman is in front of Virgil, binding him to the chair and putting the duct tape back on his mouth. He walks over to the end of the room and opens what looks like a coal burning thing and comes out with a metal pole, red at its tip from the flames. He shoves it on Virgil's thigh and I try to get up but I see the gun. His screams are horrifying, a deafening 'mmmmm' behind the tape and the smell of burning flesh runs up my nose. Elise weeps a little behind Henrik.

"*Keep them in check.*"

I start paying attention, "What?"

"Your goons," he punches me on the nose again. This time I'm sure he—yep—broke it but he's the kind of gentleman to right his wrongs, and he pops it back in. I black out.

* * *

I don't know how long it's been but Virgil's groans of pain waken me to be facing Henrik once again.

"I like to converse in quiet," he presses his watch to his ear. "*Is* it broken?" he mumbles.

"Great... back with the Brady Bunch. Look," I spit some blood, "I have a prior engagement so do what you have to do, and do it quick will you!"

"Okay. I'm just going to come out and say it!"

For some reason I got a little excited. All the hype over this bit of information I was about to get, the *truth* that was about to land on my ears. Of course this is before I realize I can't trust a single word out of this guy's mouth.

"We're brothers…" the calm and poignant look in his eye somehow pierces through to my soul, remembering that strange old man at BODY inquiring to my brother's well-being… but he could've been hired. This could all be some elaborate hoax.

"I don't have a brother."

"You do… ME! And I have to admit it took some doing to figure it all out what with all the old-school traditions. … But we have the same father!"

I know he's in my head when I wonder if he's telling the truth. It was possible, what if my father—God I hate that word—was in fact some greasy wiseguy and my mom was his mistress, and *that's* why he was never around. Because I'm a bastard.

"I'll let this information sink in."

Elise's mouth gapes open in awe, speechless at the rate of the shrinking planet. I'm livid until my vexed eyes catch her gentle orbs.

Stay calm.

"Yep! And to make things better, he was a killer! An expendable goon my grandpa and uncle used to eliminate the competition before *judges*," he squats down to Elise's eye line, "Had the power to play God!" he got more and more unstable as he went on, ranting and raging like a lost soul at the sky on a moonless night, "… And boy was he good! He *always* got the job done. But what I really like about this story, what I *really* enjoy about this *family* reunion that I worked so hard to put together, is the sort of comedic irony linked to it. … I embraced my lineage, my… heritage, and you didn't, you ran away to … well anywhere you could as fast as you could, and here we both are… killers. Practically the same person! I guess it is nature over nurture isn't it?"

What's the plan again? How am I going to get Elise out of here? I look to Virgil, who's still dozing in and out of consciousness, and Elise, frozen in shock.

"Why'd you kill the women? Helen? Trish? Eloise?" stay calm, stay focused, stay conscious. Get Elise out, save Virg and Amelia. Get that magnum from him and kill him with it.

"To get your attention! I knew if I did something horrible enough you'd stay. I had to anchor you to catastrophe. Otherwise you'd just disappear. See people like you seek tragedy. It doesn't follow you around like you tell yourself when you're playing," he lifts his magnum, "Russian roulette," and here, a look of depressed disappointment covers Elise's angelic face, "*You* seek it out, follow it. Pain is how you tell yourself *you're* real, how you attach yourself to the things around you. Without that, you would've just gone somewhere else in search of yourself when yourself is really any- where *you* are," he walks around and stops behind Elise's chair and puts his hands on her shoulders. She flinches when he spins the cylinder.

"Even that hat you always wear... well, wore until you met this broad, was our father's. Like this watch," and the ticking of the Breitling gets louder when he says this. I can hear each second tick away. "He was destined for greatness, even if it wasn't in his own life, even if... he knocked up *your* mom off a one-night stand. He lives in *me*. It was *my* mom he loved. You... are nothing but a bastard that carries a posture, a resemblance, and an apathy that you reject. You're not worthy of any of it."

Focus Vero. You have to get out of here. You'll process this later, but you have him, you got him here. He thinks he's smarter than everyone. His strength is his intellect. Show him it's his weak- ness. "Wait..." I smirk a little, "If we're the same person, doesn't that imply *you're* a bastard too?" and Virgil wakes up snickering a little while Elise flashes me that smile she does when things are going the way she wants them to.

He takes a deep breath and his eyes constrict immediately, seeming to focus on something in the corner of the room, "I'm bored," he cocks the hammer again, "I'm just gonna kill *her*," he lifts Elise off the chair and puts the gun to her temple.

"No brother! Don't do it," I blurt out. I shouldn't have though, the best way to ensure her survival is to pretend like I don't care about her. He can't leverage her if I'm detached, but that's assuming he's not a psychopathic sadist, which judging by this elaborate plan and where we are, might not work out too well, so I really don't know what to do and would rather opt for the truth even if it costs me my life, or hers, as much as it pains me to think.

"She's *only* a woman," he says with a chilling glare.

"But…" I finally realize who I am and what I'm meant to do; it took her coming into my life for this realization, for this truth, "I love her," I look at Elise in the eye and her surprise only lasts for a second before she radiates with delight.

Unfortunately this enrages Henrik and he laughs with an unmistakable look of disdain, the laugh where you're so angry with everything around you and how things are going that you just laugh, chalk up fate as an asshole. "Love?" he scowled, "How… insipid. A four letter word ascertaining a fleeting moment of affection preceding years of pain. Love matters not but perhaps the *connotation* of that moment itself which the word really infers when we bring it up to our lips from the depths of our hearts is what we pursue. But *this*?" he points to Elise, "*This?* A spoiled socialite living on Daddy's money? You love *this*… woman? This… *thing* with more money than soul? More looks… than essence?"

"To say she is only a woman is to say a violin is a piece of wood with strings, and Dante is mere ink printed on paper," I have to look Elise right in the eye as I say it. I can't let anything happen to her but can't ignore the feeling in my gut. Maybe it's about that time *God* showed me a piece of hope before snatching it away, and hopefully, I could rescue her in between.

He slaps her towards me and then immediately retracts her into his arms.

My heart pounces. This moment, now, the second his hand touches Elise's chiseled face I realize it's not my job to save her. No, it's not my job, it's my purpose. I don't want to do it for a paycheck but for a life, to live, to grasp that next moment tighter than the last.

People think love is just a word for affection but it's not and what's even more tragic is that something like love is indescribable. I mean, I can say what I'm feeling or what I *think* it means. I could say Elise is like a raindrop on a rose petal, a warm shower after a trek through Finnish mountains. I could say her lips are a cold breeze during desert summers, but none of those would even come close to the truth, and here, I realize I don't give a damn about truth; it's nothing but fabricated doctrines by people we've deemed *intelligent*, but how can we know? How can we *really* know? We can't, and it's the not knowing we fear, the unknown. We seek to know, to aspire to better ourselves—well, par for politicians and bureaucrats—but as we age and *know* more things, we begin to realize how little we really know. In the end, we're left with one thing, to *feel*, and the best of all feelings... is love. How trite, I'll have to come to this thought later, . 38 in hand.

"Perhaps then, you have recognized this abstract ideal which you spew the same way science attempts to uncloak the truth... without it, we'd be lost."

I start laughing hysterically and practically stand up, trying to lure him away from Elise and it works. He comes closer to me and I look over to Virgil; our hands are tied but I need him conscious, I need him to fight. He notices. "You're joking right? Intellectuals are a disease on the 21st century. They rave about quasi-intelligent studies wasting thousands of dollars on useless information. They mock the faithful even though they fail to see they're dumber than someone who's chosen to believe in something more than this life, in God, in something more than an arbitrary method of denoting a façade of truth."

"Did I hit a nerve there… brotha?" he leaps towards me.

I take a step towards him. At worst I can still head-butt or kick him, the real issue is the guy with the MAC-10, "Einstein, Galileo… all the people we consider masterminds and geniuses; the forefathers of *scientific* advancement, they all had one thing in common: they challenged the *scientific* methods used in their societies, in their time. You can't get to truth by doing the same thing you've been doing for years. Only now, unless you accept this erroneous method of uncloaking what this idiotic community has labeled *truth*, no one will even take you seriously, you won't get published. Truth, isn't accepted anymore, everything has become relative. And everyday some prick 'scientist' claims to have unlocked the mysteries of the universe."

"Mmmmhm," Virgil acquiesces with the tape on his mouth.

Henrik watches me like a hawk, I'm guessing, to gauge whether or not this is some ploy. It is, but that doesn't make it untrue. "Despite being… enlightened and 'open-eyed' or 'open-minded' or whatever the hell they call themselves, they can't even see that they've replaced God with their method, which makes them even more dogmatic than religious extremists! Worshipping their method… with the audacity to reject a believer's position based on a sufficient lack of evidence? Give me a break… at least the religious dogmatists have something to believe in, *scientists* believe the words on a page *they've* put there as *truth*."

"What do the believers have that scientists don't?" his curiosity got the better of him. He lowers his gun and moves even closer.

"Boss, don't trust this guy!" the goombah in front of Virgil yells.

I ignore him, "Self-awareness. They know who they are, what they want and act accordingly. A *scientist* can't take a piss without the prior approval of his method. They'll never admit that all they've done for society is replace one God with another, and like all greedy humans plotting for more power, it *just so* happens that *their God* benefits *them* the most... control the flow of *knowledge* and you control the world—just ask the Mayans, the Aztecs, and the Natives —control the *method* to acquire knowledge though, and you control the universe."

"Hmmmm," I have him contemplating this, "I'm bored," he nods to the guy in front of Virgil and he walks behind me. A switch lights up the corner of the room. Amelia's tied up silently under a shroud. I look to Virgil and he starts shaking and trying to break free, making angry gestures from under the tape while the prick standing beside her just laughs. He lightly runs his hand up her thigh and sticks his tongue out. Virgil calms down and growls, thinking how he's going to torture him as soon as we get out of this, *if* we get out of this. I know the look in his eye. I have the same look when I play that 1 in 6 game. He doesn't care if he lives or dies.

"Stop that!" Henrik shudders as if Amelia is beneath him and drags Amelia's chair with her on it beside Elise.

It might've been *God*, science or their method, Plato, or just blind stupid luck, but the duct tape loosened its grip on my wrists behind the chair. It could've been the line of blood streaming down my shoulder and face that moistened it enough. I broke free stealthily, taking extra care to give the subtlest nod to Virgil. He smirks, now all we have to do is wait for the opportune moment.

"What's the plan?" Henrik points the gun at me again, spinning the cylinder, "How do you 3... well," he chuckles lightheartedly, "2 now... plan to save these plights upon the human race?"

I look at Virg, who is dozing in-and-out from the burn pain, and when I try to stand, I realize just how hurt I really am. My shoulder seems dead, my legs are giving out, but the eagle's call from the balcony throws me centre stage, "We don't plan..."

He approaches me with the magnum, "We improvise!" I butt the gun to the side with my forehead—not the brightest idea to have come from there but it was the best I had at the time—I free my hands and punch Henrik in the abdomen and push him back. Virgil at the same time kicks his captor into Elise who thinks fast and bites his arm as he reaches for a knife and trips him. The last guy points his MAC-10 at me and I grab the knife and lunge at him as his bullets spray upwards. This would be a good death.

"*Stupenda… è stupenda*," are the words he whispers before I slice his neck open. Blood gushes onto my face and shirt. It fills his whole body, his eyes turn bloody and he spits some out at me and it lands on my cheek. There's something eerily familiar about his last words, I'll ask Virg later. I escort him to the ground and look back at everyone.

"Any last words?" Virgil yells but doesn't wait or hesitate and ends the miserable goon's life with a bullet to the temple.

I reach for the .45 on the floor and point it at Henrik who's backing out of the door pointing his magnum at my chest.

"DO IT!" Virgil yells at the top of his lungs.

My finger shakes on the trigger. I start to squeeze—

"Vero!" Elise yells as Henrik raises his hand and shoots me again before backing out of the room. I fall on my back, huffing and exhaling as slow as I can before I look ahead of me and see Henrik make a phone call, no doubt to "Bring more guys! I need help! Yes at the Traven. The new location. The one being renovated you dolt! COME TO THE BASEMENT… idiots."

Virgil howls like a wolf and makes a weak beeline toward me and looks in the direction of the door, "Your very existence is an annoyance to us," and he spits towards where Henrik is running. I've never seen him this angry, "Swallow that gun and pull the trigger."

Weak. Can barely move. Blood everywhere. Under me. Over me. On me. My arm hurts and for a second I can't breathe. My mental pursuit to stay awake is only ripened by my ardour to save her. He could've killed us, killed *me*. Why didn't he? I didn't understand him. I guess because he was outnumbered, shoot me and Virgil kills him, shoot Virgil and I kill him, shoot any of the angels and we both kill him after years of keeping him in a dungeon and torturing him medieval style. I guess he was maxi... mizing his... odds—I'm passing out again—for sur... vival.

I can hear Henrik's receding footsteps until they've completely disappeared, or maybe he's still there and I've died. I know *that's* not true because Elise lifts up my head and hugs me. She gives me a kiss I *would* die for. She probably tastes my blood; I am... happy. This... is a great death.

"You're shot! ... Again," she screams, which electrifies my heart like a defibrillator. They weren't out yet, and I had to get them out. His backup was on its way.

I crawl to my feet, blood drips everywhere and Elise's look of panic makes me feel much worse than I actually feel, "It's just a sissy wound love," I bend down and pick up the .45. Check the magazine, it's loaded. I grab Elise's hand, motioning to Virg and Amelia that we're moving.

A bleeding and dying drunk, an enraged philosopher, and two traumatized European socialites; we weren't the first choice in a search and rescue op. What I'd do for some oil so America could come liberate us.

"Hey Vero?" Virgil moans behind me. He never calls me Vero. Amelia's "HELP HIM VERO!" rattles me as I turn around and see Virgil slumping to the ground.

I slide towards him on my knees and grab him before he falls, both Elise and Amelia stand far behind me in shock. "Hey old buddy. Tell me Da Vinci's last words again."

He throws up blood, "I think..." exhale, "We've moved off Da Vinci old friend..." and he coughs up a chunk of something bloody, "I think I might have to tell you... my own."

"Don't say that," what do I do?

"Tell Amelia my love for her is eternal."

"Tell her yourself tomorrow."

He bats his eyes, blood pools out of his shirt in quarts. He's drenched in it. How did I not notice before?

'He's not going to die' was the fleeting thought blaring in my head like a bad techno song.

He leans his head to the side and spits out a *gallon* of the viscous crimson ooze that keeps us alive. "All... the... time," he gargles and spits out some more blood. There's so much.

"Shhhh, Virg. I'll get you out. I promise. Just keep your eyes open. Think of Amelia. You can't leave her alone."

An almost audible hiccup flicks his eyes to the back of his head, he struggles to focus them, "I spent..." exhale, "Thinking what I'd say," he's putting all his effort into these words, "And I come up with 'Tell Amelia my love for her is eternal?'"

I smile. I start to doubt whether he'll make it out of here.

"How cliché," blood seeps out of his mouth and I try to lift up his head a little more so he doesn't choke on it. "It means something..." and he blinks far too slowly to give me any confidence that he'll make it through this. He lets out this exhale that unfocused my vision as if the winter air was running away from him, leaving him for Grim, "I guess," he looks at his fingertips covered in blood just before his hand goes limp and more of his blood leaves him, sinking his body like a fallen eagle.

Stillness. His eyes freeze in place; I put my hand over them and close them. He's 21 grams lighter. I don't weep. ... No, I don't weep. I smile.

The moment only lasts so long before I reach for the .45 with the hand covered in my friend's dying blood and take off after Henrik.

"Where are you going Vero?" Elise's shoulders shake like a black sky under a lightless sun.

"Samarra," I cock the gun, "I have an appointment there."

"Vero!" Elise raises her hand and my spine seems to vibrate out of place. The blood that ran down my face when she stood over me had stained her hands; there was no way I was going to think it was anything more than the literal attempts of an angel saving a forlorn man. I couldn't sift through the detritus of my feelings for her.

I had to finish this. I had to assume she was my redemption, even if the physical symbol I'd attributed to this manifestation of the Good had escaped me or more likely didn't even exist.

I run in Henrik's direction. The damn place is like a maze. I can't feel the pain in my shoulders or legs anymore and that means one of two things: either I'm dying and I've lost all feeling or there's so much adrenaline in me for me to feel anything, and I'm far too much a pessimist to believe the latter. Eventually I can hear whispering around the corner, presumably Henrik still on the phone trying to get his goombahs to come finish us off.

"Hey!" I make a bad tactical move and roar before I've turned the corner.

He immediately turns the corner towards me and starts shooting. So do I. Bullets fly everywhere and we both slide to the ground, sitting across each other, dying in a grungy unfinished hotel basement.

"Doesn't make sense. The hero *must* win. How'd we get each other?"

"We must not be heroes," it hurts to talk, hurts to think. It hurts to be alive.

"Was saving this for a special occasion," he says when he drops his gun and pulls out a cigar, "It's a Cristo. I guess this counts... perspective is everything."

I inhale slowly and exhale harshly. More blood fills near my chest where he'd shot me, and each puff he takes of his cigar stains his shirt with more blood.

"What is this? We're going to bleed here and exchange nihilistic last words? Our words will disappear sooner than we do," chaos was truth. There was no way I was going to abandon this ideal... especially not *now*.

"Screw you! I can't stand people like you!"

"That makes both of us," it's getting harder to breathe.

"Here, we hear they're bringing democracy. Over there, they're killing everyone: women, kids, old people.... Damn it!" he flicks but his lighter doesn't work and he exerts a lot of energy to relight it and freshen up his cigar. "If I'm not a hero, I guess that means I'm a villain, and that means my depth will never be explored. My past will be left as an enigma because all the analyses, the inner monologues would be from the 'perspective of the protagonist,' as a sort of pseudo-morality tale."

"Depth? We're killers," my eyelids get heavier and heavier, my breaths, shallower. "We don't get the girl. We don't redeem ourselves and ride off into the sunset to live on the Amalfi coast with her."

"He. He. He. Amalfi Coa... ow. You're assuming it's a traditional story... that it's a morality—" he tries laughing but it hurts too much.

"What," now *I* have to exhale between words, my mouth fills with what tastes like blood and I just drool it onto my neck and shirt, "Was his name?" a deep breath, ..."Our father?"

"K... Kl..." he heaves and stutters until he takes a big puff of his cigar. "His name was Clark, and he was—" he seems to forget what he's saying, "I'll hold Elsa in the next life since I could not have her in this one."

He really did do his research. He even knew about... Elsa. God it hurts to think, "Henrik... I—"

His eyes glaze over, slowly but surely becoming a referent shade of grey, and his last breath spurts thick, almost brownish blood from his lips down to his neck, which eventually stream to his fingertips. He tries to rub them together but doesn't have the strength.

## The First Entry

MY MASTERED APATHY, my predictable indifference has only been one dimension of the complex island others simply call "Henrik Clark Torrino."

'There is no spoon,' is the instant thought before one of the worst migraines I've ever had makes the room spin; it was the line from *The Matrix* and I didn't know why, I couldn't trace the genus of this thought. I was dizzy when the scotch slid down my throat, more tasteless than the water I hadn't tasted in about 60 hours; Scotland's best became my water so it was damn near poetic. I looked around, down the bar, staring at the lonely faces slumped as low as I was and as begrudgingly sober as I was. Was *this* where I should be? Are these... chronic degenerates my friends? My kind? My equals? Are they my *only* friends, or is *she*? Could I consider her my friend, or more importantly, would she consider *me*, *her* friend? All the tears and misery I've caused, might as well let the stool memorize my ass print.

I was considering whether I should go and see her; whether I deserved to see her and whether it was best if I just... stayed put like a good *stoic* should. It was a demon, a monster, maybe it was the monster in me, but I stared him down either way... trying to act cool and reserved when I quip 'Do your worst, I've already been to hell... you, and all others like you, bore me to death.' 'There's many ways to kill a man,' it smiles mischievously, 'There's infinite ways to die. Some dead already lives in you, this emptiness, this... isolation is eternal,' it laughs like some second-rate-movie-villain. I shouldn't have underestimated him.

The cigarette burnt my lips as I gazed fixedly on the blaze, I tasted blood; pain is simply a truth we choose to deny.

The automatic doors opened to the smell of latex gloves, hand sanitizer, and cold leather. The guy next to me in the elevator was nothing short of a clinical hipster cliché: bouquet of white roses with a big teddy bear with 'Get well' on its stomach in the shape of a heart. *My* stomach churned some acid up, sizzling my heart to the point of boiling it like some egg rich on Omega-3. The flickering lights in the hallway did very little to ease the migraine squeezing my temple vein up and down in between my skull and my skin. Here I was, 'It's better this way,' I thought, 'It's better this way... shut up, you're repeating yourself you buffoon, why don't you' —— room 416M. My choices diminished to destiny as I pushed the door open to still my heartbeat to the point of death—no such luck.

The elusive fading sound of the morphine drip synced itself to my heartbeat, my migraine got worse (men aren't supposed to cry, it simply isn't in our nature) for an unknown reason, my practiced stoicism couldn't stop the two depressed howling yelps that escaped my throat as I exhaled. A dying angel... how many times would God, science, or whatever the hell the idiots call it nowadays, bestow this truth, this... knowledge of inevitability upon me in his 'infinite' wisdom; if I ever got my hands on your God, on your science....

All the things I've done with a still heartbeat, a stoic soul, yet for some reason, at that moment, I shivered with the sickening foreboding to the sound of the beeping equipment designed to echo a beating heart. I saw this place in a magazine once: National Geographic: 100 Most Beautiful Places to See, one of them: The Lau Archipelago, Fiji, was described, 'Most people judge a place by its sunsets, but in these islands, it's the sunrises as well,' this ravenous thought gnawed at my heart: knowing that the number of her sunrises was so finite, so... evasive, and in that moment, I wanted to take whatever was paining her and put it inside me...

With no prior warning and for the first time in my life, this feeling of faith washed over me: in God, the *D*evil, just something with *real* power, not like M.D.'s, politicians, or lawyers. I just hoped *something* existed (and I hated myself for hoping) so I could make this trade: my life for hers, and my sudden urge to question absolutely everything to its root dissipated. A single tear from her once volcanic irises aged me 10 years, fading me into nonexistence. My will to live diminished every second I gazed upon her in this state and I couldn't find a single reason to go on. No matter how many times others called me talented, brilliant, genius, or whatever other abstruse label denoting some comparative quotient deemed 'positive;' I simply… ceased to be.

I walked back into the flickering hallway to regain what I'd mastered decades ago. Some M.D. with a clipboard looked down at me through his nose even though I had about an inch on him, "There's no saving her you know…"

Is idiocy a requirement for these schools nowadays? "Talk like that again and there'll be no saving you."

"Don't threaten me, in light of your circumstance I won't call security, I'm just…. Are you even on her visitor's list?"

"Where's your 'modern-medicine' now? Your science? Your God? Get out of here. Get into your overpriced beamer, go home, kiss your trophy wife, and hug your brat kids. Don't tell me what I shouldn't be doing."

So much for stoicism. The morphine dripped out of tune with my heart when I reentered.

"What'd…" she coughed violently, reminding me of the third act of a decent opera we attended on one of our first dates, "The doctor," her throat choked up… big inhale, her chest contracted and expanded, "Say?"

Kant was a poseur and an asshole: universal rules? What a joke… misunderstood proclamations to what he deemed truth*ful* like a wannabe-dictator.

"You're going to be fine babe," the hours I spent practicing this smile others see all the time had finally paid off.

"You're a terrible liar," unfortunately she could always see right through them.

I wished I were a politician or a lawyer or any of the infinite professions that values deception. I wished my *choice* in my vocation had been different just so I could've lied to this woman this one time in this one moment.

My ribs crunched outwards, my heart tore out of my chest and beat on the scuffed floor of the hospital room, meshing the squirting blood with the grim air.

I was awake, it was only another nightmar... beep... beep... beep... no, still here, must've fallen asleep beside her bed, clutching her palm in mine. Well, as hard as she can grasp something here.

"Hen," exhale, "Rik. You..." inhale, "Awake?"

"Of course gorgeous, what would you like?"

"I want..." the machine's beeping sped up for a second, "You to go..." and it slowed down again, "Home... *vai a casa mio amore.*"

"*Never neshama.*" This *is* my home, I wanted to say, but felt this charismatic fear that it would upset her, "There's nothing for me there," I couldn't satiate her pain no matter how much I wanted to.

"Hmmm," she smiled as she dozed in and out of sleep, and I could see how much it hurt her, the agony. The sapphire in her once blazing pupils seemed like nothing more than an already erupted mountain; a will that'd ashed and burned for too long. I was schooled in pain, practically had a PhD in teardrops and misery, so why wasn't this like that? Why wasn't I the one connected to these robotic machines coupled with this horrendous rhythmic beeping, and why wasn't she out there, living, loving, doing what young women are meant to do.... In the darkness of that room, to the sound of the morphine drip and her harsh breathing, I felt a familiar feeling crawling through my subconscious. There was no way in hell I'd anticipated this... weakness; this... sudden urge to cry, not until I realized how much pain had become a part of me in the last fortnight and how much I despised everything, most of all....

Night turned to day in the blink of an eye; the serene mist suddenly initiated this vicious downpour like something out of an apocalyptic novel.

"There…" she inhaled, coughing some blood, and I loathed myself for just standing there, "Is no…" she wheezed and cleared her throat, "Ahem, spoon."

"What?" I looked around, searching for some sign to affirm this deal with pseudo-science: my life for hers.

She tried to move the tray up and down, left and right, barely being able to lift it, "The spoon," exhale, "I need it… for the jello," I had to wipe the drained colour from her once-crimson lips, "What was that…" she sat up a little, "Look in your eye?"

"Oh… a *spoon*. I'll get you one beautiful," there are things you can't stop thinking about, those you can't stop caring for no matter how practiced your apathy or indifference may be. It's a mask that progressively slips until there's nothing except a bare face staring at an unrecognizable reflection of someone who only looks like you. She faded from my very eyes with the scythe carrier lingering over her patiently, waiting for the moment when he could inflict maximum damage on her.

My being diminished with every step I took outside her room and into the cafeteria to find the nonexistent spoon, until I simply… ceased to be, just as she would be soon.

# MOTET

THE CIGAR LAYS dormant on his lip, all his movements cease. I have to accept that he really *was* my brother. Well... half-brother, but I wasn't going to accept my mom was a mistress to some hired goombah.

Despite all that, I hold my newest wound—bleeding to death —and regard Henrik *as* a messenger of truth. Here, slipping into the great perhaps I try remembering the last things I've done; saving Elise, with the potential to be mine, and Virgil, my *real* brother. I have to accept that this is it, death *is* inevitable with this never-ending crusting and drying blood on my shirt. All the wrong things I've done and the darkness in my sullen essence will soon be un-knowable to me, and none of the mistakes I've made or the things that I am will taint Elise... I will come with you Grim... and finally wash the world of myself. "Good bye... brother," I whisper across the hall and close my eyes to the sound of Für Elise.

\* \* \*

I could imagine Elise walking down this hallway and seeing Henrik and I lying here, her once radiating pink cheeks becoming nothing but anemic; the sort of undying *truth* that the universe would force upon her life, and giving her no choice but to submit to its demands.

Love appears kind but like all things, appearances are decep-tive, and the faithless few recognize love as tragic and punishing. Henrik was right, it is but a fleeting wave of elation in that first moment which then slips from our fingertips to a sort of chronic despair, and this torturous cruelty bears a toll on your soul... and you start to wonder whether you can take it. Eventually you calculate just how much you can take and then wait for the day you break. Luckily for me, here, on this alien planet, I'd die first. He *was* right, neither of us really had a father, sure I had my grandfather as a strong male figure and I'm sure he had people on his *family* that acted as his father, but that doesn't explain the fury that built itself in our bones because we didn't have someone to teach us to shave or talk to girls like Elise. We had to adapt and learn ourselves. We were born clichés and only an optimist with no real understanding of the world could compare my grandfather or his *family*, with a real father.

Clark. I remember now. I remember it all. He *was* my father, that's why my mom was—

I can't help but laugh like a suicidal comedian. I'm only another gloomy man with a morbid past and no foreseeable hope for a bright future with yet another obstacle to overcome with seemingly impossible odds. All our hands have blood on them. Am I some literary proverb? Some remnant of a man or woman whose life had met the standards for the radio buttons on some publisher's computer? Did I even exist? Did this world even exist? Did my actions have any meaning? Did anything matter? I squeeze my eyes closed and open them again... I'm still here, so is everything else, but it's the haze of Henrik's cigar smoke that lets me know the truth, its smell, slowly dying away in my weakening nostrils. It has to be real... it has to be.

I sit up a little, resting my perpetually tired backbone on the overused plaid and off-tone wallpaper of this hotel looking down towards where I have to assume the lobby is. It was peculiar, strange even, that I lay my eternal rest somewhere where others have lain. Hotels are enigmatic comforts far from home anyway. Who knows how many people have died in this place? How long had they been here up to the point of their demise? Were many of them worse souls than I? A being pretty much without a soul who knows nothing of his father and whose mother was taken from him? Who am I kidding? Elise couldn't redeem me. She is after all... only human. My soul has no angel to redeem it, no sweetheart to worry whether he is alive or dead; a soul pale, like mine, a body... cold, just as I am to others and everything. I have... I had to be indifferent to everything, I couldn't accept that I was responsible for the loss of so many lives, for the death of an entire city. My soul had already become a corpse long before I fell here. I am a *thing* that's ceased to live, and I too, the physical manifestation of Vero have had enough of life. Why should I, or anyone, live through this cursed life that only serves to turn us into paling souls that wither away? — I can hear a church ring for the 2:00 P.M. mass. What a fairy tale *that* story is. How many souls have perished at this moment? How many mothers have been torn from their children? How many lovers scorned and torn apart? How many plans have wilted to the realm of non-existence? How much sorrow and tears have flown from the world of dreams in this melancholic marble?

Death will be a relief and it seems that it took this moment, here, now, for me to realize that justice, wickedness, good, or evil have come to be the same thing. Death is the greatest truth, so what would be the biggest lie? Life, since that is the exact opposite of the great truth. I must be, then, justified in my apathy since I was brought into this planet without any choice. A planet that stripped me of everything I ever valued, and even if I valued them *because* they were stripped, why was I forced to roam a world where not only I was useless but caused nothing except havoc and destruction for the price of some oil drops? What good would my continued existence bring to anyone? What good would *any* existence bring to anything? We are less than a dot compared to the morass of the universe. And hence, no action I've ever done or will ever do would amount to any meaning that would have any bearing on the only truth, no action except this action now.

I start to close my eyes and battle my body's survival instincts. It tries to force bigger and bigger breaths from me... but I take smaller and smaller ones.

As my pains worsen and my heart stalls to a halt. I feel numb, weightless, and alone... and I know that's exactly what I deserve, even if some other *being* doesn't think so.

## LACRIMOSA

"VERO?" ELISE CALLS into the hallway through the faint sound of distant church bells. "Vero?" her escalating panic lands nowhere but empty air.

"Vero?" she screams as she lifts his head up with her wrists. His eyes barely illuminate any life.

"They..." his breaths become shallower and fade as time passes, "Told me you were the prettiest girl in Sweden," he smiles with the cloud of death hanging over him.

She nods slowly and puts her hands on his chin, cupping his face in her palm. Her tears dilute the blood he spits out that stream down her wrist and fill her bracelet.

"They lied," he exhales as blood fills his lungs. It's only a matter of time now. She squeezes his chin harder, trying to get him to stop talking and to conserve his energy. "You are the prettiest woman in the world..." and his eyes freeze in place, no longer the darting piercing blue orbs trying to locate the nearest bar. His thoughts bleed further and further away from him.

She presses her palms to his face, soaking her seraphic hands with more of his blood until enough of it drips down her wrist and fills the eagle on her bracelet. And even though she knows he's already dead, she would swear to this day that he smiled the second the eagle turned crimson with his blood. Free at last.

END